CALL OF THE TREE

Other Titles in The Faithwalker Series by Darryl S. Markowitz

The Sacrificial Wood: Book Two

The Dead Forest: Book Three

Succession: Book Four

Unnatural Disaster: Book Five

Call Of The Tree

BOOK ONE IN THE FAITHWALKER SERIES

Darryl Markowitz

FaithWalker Publishing

The Faithwalker Series
Book I: Call of the Tree

Third Edition 2021

Published by:
Faithwalker Publishing
An imprint of Darryl Markowitz

Cover Painting © 2008 Steve Pinkerton
Cover Design by Daniel Middleton www.scribefreelance.com
Interior Design: Creative Publishing Book Design

ISBN Paperback: 978-0-9818469-6-5
ISBN eBook: 978-0-9818469-7-2

Printed in the United States of America

Acknowledgements

My deep appreciation for my artist, Steve Pinkerton. I do not know of another artist who could have captured so perfectly my heroine, Stephanie.

My deep appreciation for my cover designer, Daniel Middleton.

My deepest thanks to Scott Gelotti and Nathaniel Markowitz for our grueling hours of discussion, and the many drafts they read and reread for me as first readers.

My deep thanks also to some dear young friends, whom I met through this first novel, Call of the Tree: James, John, and Stephanie. The story continues. . . .

And special thanks to unrecognized faithwalkers. Their hearts and minds aren't afraid to ask the toughest questions because they know they'll get answers.

I won my wife Lana's heart with this book!

To all of you who have gone to www.TheFaithwalkerSeries.com and posted reviews, I cannot express deeply enough my appreciation for your invaluable feedback and generous promotion of this Series whose meaning and value has potential to inspire so many into the feelings and understanding which makes being a human being so precious.

About the author

Since fourteen-years-old responsibility came to this author's understanding that to understand WHAT is Life, Love, Wisdom, Understanding, Justice, Truth, and Peace is more than a calling, it is the reason for our Being. It needs to be pursued with all one's heart, mind, soul, and strength. Darryl Markowitz's books fulfill that purpose. Nothing else is more relevant than the sincere search.

The characters and events in The Faithwalker Series books are fictitious. Any similarities to real persons, living or dead, are coincidental and not intended by the author.

CHAPTER 1
The Party

"Where do thoughts come from, Father?"

King Mafferan looked deeply into his twelve-year-old eyes. "While I may not be sure all thoughts are my own, I am sure when I own them."

It didn't matter that she moved amongst hundreds of other children down the long, white hallway in a predetermined fashion; Stephanie was alone in her thoughts. *What's the big deal about one-hundred years? I* hate *all these ugly banners. If we really used to be the United States, then we wouldn't be celebrating the Second Civil War. Is everything just a big lie?*

The warning bell sounded, everyone sped up, but Stephanie seemed to slow. *But what about me? I'm more important than a stupid country.* Her biology teacher's question absorbed her mind. *I think it's an important question, but why should I have waited for a teacher to ask it? Actually, it should be the most important question of my life: 'What makes me what I am?' Am I really just a bunch of experiences all subtly piled upon each other . . .like a snowfall in the darkest night? Nothing more?* She got sarcastic with herself. *Life dumps all this* crap *into me, a few good experiences, I think . . . and the rest bad, then says 'Lookie, lookie, you're a person!'* It felt terribly wrong, but she didn't know why. The words shouted in her mind: *I'm more than that!*

She abruptly stopped in mid-traffic, but no one *ever* stopped – the *rules.* Several students crashed into her from behind and they sneered and jeered as they squeezed around her on their way to their next class. There was enough to be irritated about without such odd behavior. She didn't notice the pinches and grabs as all the others pressed on by because her previous teacher's lesson, for some reason, irked her in ways she couldn't begin to describe. *But even the snow has something to rest on. The teacher didn't mention* that. *I just figured* that *out myself. The shape of the ground . . . whether it's a hill, or a dip, a big rock, or a deep hole . . .* that *determines how the snow rests! So, why isn't the shape of the ground also me? For that matter, not just the shape . . . but whatever the ground is made of! The teacher didn't ask about that. What made me ask it? Not my experience, I don't think. It feels like this question is coming from . . . where? My ground itself? What am I talking about?*

Three boys squeezed against Stephanie just as she went through the classroom doorway, bringing her back to reality. She tried twisting away as they groped her but they prolonged their contact making it difficult to pass. Working her arm free, she shot it sharply into a boy's side.

Surprised, the boy grumbled, "Hey, how'd you know if it was me?"

Another boy laughed. "She never objected before. It must be you!"

She realized he was right. But right now, such disgusting actions from *anyone* no longer flattered her. The boy rubbed his side as everyone took their seats.

Bulldog. Stephanie thought as she pulled her fiery long red hair behind her and inspected Mr. Hardcord's boxy face for the last time. From the first day of class to this last, she expected her teacher to slobber. Everyone sat silently with their hands folded on their desks, their feet flat on the floor, and their faces forward.

The teacher's gruff voice filled the emptiness. "After today you'll be in tenth grade. Therefore, this last lesson shall be particularly special."

Internal groans were held in check and the teacher saw no sign of it as his hawkish stare raked over his students. "You're old enough now to understand about sacrifice."

Sacrifice. No one thought *that* sounded good. Heads didn't turn, but eyes darted around. The teacher's large presence loomed larger when he stepped closer to the front row where Stephanie sat. She swallowed once as he stared at her.

"You know it's been a whole hundred and fifteen years since the Great Religious War, when most people in the major cities were killed by plague and poisoned water. Stephanie, what happened afterwards?"

Stephanie tried to swallow again, but her mouth was dry. She cleared her throat before answering. "We used to be called the United States, but we weren't *united* at all. Afterwards, we separated from the South, because they wanted the government run by their fanatical religion, but we were more sensible."

"Right! And what did all the former religions lead to, Jason?"

"We know all the former religions lead to destruction. They're *all* at fault."

The teacher returned his stare to Stephanie, but this time he narrowed his eyes at her. "Why, Stephanie?"

Why! Why! Why did he ask me why like that? The silence seemed like eternity. *Oh, I've got to give an answer right away.* "That is a good question, Sir, but when something doesn't make sense, like the old religions, whatever they were, it's hard to answer a single, particular *why* as to destruction or fault."

"Excellently put! Very good! It is precisely because none of them made sense that they were destructive. And because they demanded people to blindly follow their fanaticism, they acted irrationally, therefore becoming guilty, but as you said, we of the North were sensible." Hardcord stood up taller, proclaiming, "Science and reason rule the day. That's why our new religion stresses support of the government, and not the other way around. What was the economic result of the Second Civil War, Karen?"

Glancing across to Stephanie, Karen smiled, whisked a strand of long blond hair from her eyes and sat up straighter, holding her head high. She answered smoothly, and offered much more than the teacher asked for: "The glorious Second Civil War, which we are now happily celebrating, finished some fifteen years after the Great Religious World War, drained all of our resources, and allowed us to be free of all old, foolish religions."

"Very good, Karen!"

But she wasn't missing this opportunity. "Excuse me Sir, I'm not done yet."

With a hint of sarcasm, Hardcord restrained himself and acquiesced. "Oh, ahh, please continue."

"In reaction against the religious terrorists of the Great War, to their destroying all of our cities, and to their different God, the South determined that everyone needed to worship only the South's God. They blamed our own lack of faith for the enemy's victories."

"Very good Karen, Thank . . ."

Karen interrupted, again, while smiling sweetly. "I'm still not done."

Hardcord frowned as Karen kept smiling at him. "Finish up. We have an assignment to do!"

"Many from the South were forced to move north to escape oppression. The fanatics up north were allowed to move south, thus, in a way, the South became just as destructive and threatening as the terrorists. We had to defend ourselves against our own countrymen, lest we be forced into their religion. The economic strain to defend such a long border across North America is, even now, tremendous and destructive."

Smiling sweetly, Karen checked to see if Stephanie had been bothered by her impressive answer. Stephanie ignored her.

Mr. Hardcord cleared his throat, signaling an end to the interplay. "Lengthy, but you are correct also, Karen. You've all learned this. It's taken a while for people to overcome their fears about the major cities, but now our government has undertaken a glorious restoration project to reclaim them. But to do so, requires us to *sacrifice.*"

There it was again. That word seemed to boom much louder than its actual sound, enslaving all who heard it. "The government needs more resources to build the cities of the future. Every one of you has some money the government allows you to earn at summer jobs. Your assignment, to be handed in on the first day of your tenth grade year, is to write a ten-page paper on how and why you have uniquely devised ways to sacrifice for the good of our country to rebuild our great cities. With your paper, you should hand-in the sacrifice you are making!"

Everyone's face turned red, but no one moved. "Take out your notebooks and create an outline of how and why you intend to *sacrifice*. I will be coming around to check each one in ten minutes."

Bulldog sat behind his desk watching the class. *Is that the hint of a smirk on his face? Sacrifice! Bahh! The school officials will probably pocket our money,* most everyone thought. *Future? Everyone knows there is none.* Immediately they embarked on their task.

Education had reached a new low. Everyone knew he could be kicked out of school for disobeying the teacher. As bad as it was here, being kicked out would be worse. Stephanie raised her hand without thinking. "Why do you think it's right to rebuild those cities and ignore all the small towns where we've all lived for so long?" When they heard her, small gasps resounded throughout the room.

Stephanie felt her face redden. *What am I doing?* Her stomach turned over. She squirmed under the teacher's silent glare, its message pounding in her head: 'Are you having YOUR OWN THOUGHTS?' Even though she quickly apologized, she was sure he knew she was thinking. That was *exactly* the kind of thing that got kids sent to the State Work Farm, she was sure of that. Everyone sat stone silent, barely breathing, but the teacher went back to his deskwork. Stephanie could still hear her words as if echoing in the room.

Fearing reprisal, Stephanie thought extra hard on her English assignment. *I'll get a summer job somewhere and give* half *the money to the government . . . maybe that'll keep me from being sent away.* A page later, she finally relaxed, noticing the cramp in her writing hand. She was done before anyone else.

Her eyes glanced up from her work. Hardcord sat staring at the class, rubbing his chin. She didn't mean to, but her glances became more frequent and lengthened, and every time she looked up, she looked deeper into his face. His concentration seemed magnetic, drawing her into it. When he turned his eyes upon her, she still stared for a second before realizing she was caught. *What am I doing?* Her heart skipped again. The teacher slammed his hands down on his desk; everyone jumped and Stephanie more so. Hardcord looked determined, as if he'd made some kind of decision. Stephanie knew it was about her and hung her head.

Folding his big arms across his chest, he stood up, and addressed the class. "What do you think about this Jargon fellow who's been on the news lately?"

There was silence. No one knew what to do. *What do we think?* That was the common thought. Stephanie would have none of it. *I've used up* my *quota of thinking for the whole next year.*

"I asked a question, and I expect answers."

How could he trap us like this? Why?

Jason folded his arms like his teacher and leaned back in his chair. He was angry and let it show. "I don't know how the hell the government lets him get away with it! Why do they even let him on TV? Anyone else would have disappeared a long time ago! And I hear he's developing a *following!*"

Karen responded with her aristocratic air, "But if you *listen* to what he says, he's not contradicting the government at all. In fact, he's for everything they're for." She folded her arms in same fashion and tripled her smugness. "Only he says it ten times better."

"Oh God, he's so handsome." Tracy let slip as reaffirming sighs resounded in the room.

"Jason, you asked a good question. Why do you think the government lets him?"

Stephanie heard herself blurt out sarcastically, "It's obvious . . . he wants to be our *King.*" She really couldn't believe she opened her mouth and with such sarcasm for someone so popular.

Karen sprang like a tiger on its prey. "Well, I wouldn't mind being his queen. Why shouldn't we have him instead of the government?" As soon as she heard herself say it, she knew she committed fatal error, her eyes widening in fright.

But Hardcord went with it. "Do you think that's what he's about, Karen?"

Karen was angry at herself. She *never* let herself be put into foolish positions before.

Jason rescued her. "There's got to be a lot going on here we don't know about. Even if he was the best government spokesman in the world, there's *no way* our government would let anyone but themselves be respected as *authority*."

"He's right," Gary chimed in. Gary was an anomaly because at fifteen, he should have been a grade higher but was repeating instead. That was unheard of. He should have been sent away but when he showed up for the same grade level on the first day of school, the teachers said nothing. Everyone knew not to ask questions. Everyone understood rules only applied to those who had to keep them. Gary was connected somehow to the government through family.

Stephanie watched her boyfriend as he continued, as did everyone else. If anyone knew what was behind this Jargon thing, Gary did. "This *Jargon* character," everyone including Hardcord was riveted on his words, "has a lot more going for him than we know!"

Then there was silence. Gary looked very important. He headed a particularly nasty gang of kids that was sort of like a mini-government, and most everyone steered clear. Hardcord flattened his mouth. Gary was challenging him in his own classroom by remaining silent and making him ask for more information.

"What would that be, Gary? Enlighten us with your wisdom." Hardcord's sarcasm was biting.

Insulting, Gary thought, but now the tables were turned. Gary knew he couldn't outwardly disrespect a teacher, no matter how connected he was. *But how much should I tell him?* "If the government allows him to continue, let's just assume it's in their best interest."

What does that mean? Everyone including Hardcord wondered. But the way Gary spoke left no room to question further, at least if one didn't want to be seen as begging. Hardcord just nodded and began walking around, checking everyone's work until the bell rang.

Upon finally hearing it, muffled sighs of relief unified the class in another rare, common expression. There had been no teacherly goodbyes, nor 'have a nice summer'. The point was even when you're on break, you're still in school. Hardcord's summer assignment made sure of that. But no one wanted to think about it now, as they got up from their desks and began to leave.

Just before Stephanie went out the door, she whirled on the boys behind her. Their smirks suddenly disappeared. Each boy looked at the other as if to ask 'Did you see what I just saw?' For an instant, did they see actual fire flare in her eyes? After she glared a moment longer, she turned her back, and for the first time, passed through the door alone. The common groping-doorway-ritual had come to an end. Stephanie wished it would end for the rest of the girls, too.

Advanced history was Vaughn's favorite subject but wished he could find some other sources for it. Vaughn mused that every year at this same time, it was the same rehash. *It's infuriating and insulting to say the least. For one thing, to call the South fanatical, and dismiss any credibility for their secession based upon that accusation alone seems disingenuous. It's not like our government is any less fanatical. I mean, good grief, they keep everyone in fear all the time. How does it make them any less fanatical just because they hate the old religions?* Vaughn ran his fingers through his wavy dark hair, trying not to ask the question, but then attempting to frame it with just the right words.

Mr. Coleman called on him. "Do you have something to contribute to our discourse?"

Discourse? Is that what you call it? Yes, let's have one. "Sir, if you would help me understand something . . . or perhaps you might not know. I'm sorry."

Coleman studied him. *I always wondered about this kid, what's below the surface. His question could be taken in so many ways.* "I'm here to teach you. Speak."

"I don't understand how the United States held together for over two hundred years and then split apart so abruptly due to religious fanaticism. We're told that those major religions had been around even before the United States. I understand what the terrorist attacks did, how they inflamed everyone's feelings! I understand how one side blamed religion, all religion, and the other side blamed our *lack* of religion, but why should all that lead to Civil War?

Coleman narrowed his eyes at Vaughn, but the boy's stare wasn't competitive or challenging so he answered seriously. "Sometimes things snowball. If you look at how World War One began, one small thing led to another, then an assassination! People kept feeling compelled to go the next step almost as if everyone were egged on by some external force that would only allow escalation instead of withdrawal. But before I tell you about the very point in time where our last Civil War began, I want you to understand something about how our population changed due to the plague. The United States was mostly left with a bunch of small towns and for the south, that meant a far stricter religious population than ever before. However, up north, due to its mega cities, there were a lot of highly educated people living on their outskirts who survived and they tended to be anti-religious. Not only that, but most of the high-powered, very experienced congressmen and senators died in Washington DC. Most of the representatives who survived weren't . . . ahh, well . . hmmm, well, they just weren't your . . . Anyway, at the United States last congressional meeting . . ." Coleman paused.

All the students had suddenly come awake and sat up straighter. This was something they'd never heard before. Many were suddenly thinking that Coleman actually knows something other than the government's textbooks.

". . . a certain very religious congressman from the South stood up berating his opponents, and began waving his Bible in one of their faces like this." Coleman came over, grabbed Vaughn's notebook from his desk and shook it vehemently at him pronouncing, "We need GOD! We need CHRIST in the government."

The teacher was actually a pretty good actor. It stunned his students to see his gestures, not realizing how much of a character their instructor really was, and then the notebook accidently hit Vaughn on the nose! A little blood came out as he flinched away. All the kids' eyes widened. Coleman smiled and turned to the class. "Now consider whether I hit Mr. Vaughn on purpose for asking that question . . ." He paused, suddenly appearing very mischievous, and everyone broke out in loud laughter! That was the first time ever in classroom history when they actually experienced joy. Coleman politely hushed them. "Shh, you want the principal to come in here and summarily execute me?" He was still being humorous but everyone took on a more serious tone. They were starting to really like this teacher.

Coleman finished up his challenge. "Did I hit Vaughn on purpose or not? Does it matter? Because when that Bible hit another congressman in the face, he retaliated by knocking the guy out! The whole last Congress broke into a huge brawl! It was downhill from there, each calling in loyal troops for defense, and then as tensions kept mounting, one armed side lined up against the other . . .

Ralph raised his hand, though he really didn't care one way or the other. But the irony of his thought caught him appreciating how funny his idea would be, so he decided to share. Coleman nodded to him. "Let me guess, someone lit off a firecracker and they all started killing each other."

"Bingo!"

Vaughn exclaimed in exasperation. "You're kidding!" But Coleman shook his head and the bell rang.

The halls were silent as everyone left the school for the year. Stephanie sneered at the blindingly white walls and the stupid banners that were the same throughout the whole building. But no one dared put a mark on them.

As soon as she got outside, a boy shouted, "What an *IDIOT*!" And he pulled at strands of her windblown hair.

Some of the other boys pointed, jeered, and mocked at her, repeating her class question, "*What makes the government right?* They're gonna lock you up and throw away the key." Several of them enacted what they thought that would be like, grabbing her and forcing her to the ground. "Lock up time . . . you're ours now!"

Humiliated, Stephanie knew they wouldn't treat Karen this way. *Why not? Why me?* she cried inside. Another taunted as he pinched her buttocks while she fought to stand and smack his hands away. "They'll do more than grab your butt at the Farm. Being Gary's whore won't save you then."

Even before Vaughn heard their cruel taunting, a particular feeling had swept over him. So when he emerged outside and spotted the gang of boys hovering over some girl he couldn't see, that same feeling jumped in intensity, but someone grabbed his arm and turned him away from the fracas.

"Hey! Vaughn, I really need to talk to you!"

After staring a moment into a thin face with sandy brown hair not particularly combed, Vaughn finally recognized the lad. "Ralph, right? Ahh, just a minute."

But Ralph wouldn't let Vaughn's arm go and leaned close. "It's business and could mean your life!" He led him around the building corner and maintained an uncomfortable closeness as he spoke further. "Look, I really respect you. Everyone's still talkin' how you knocked Gary's butt out last year. I can use a guy like you! Besides, you need my protection. Gary's not gonna let what you did just go, ya know?"

Vaughn flattened his mouth then said, "Well, he hasn't done anything so far. Like you said, it's been a whole year. But what *business?*"

"C'mon, Vaughn! Private enterprise. Why should the government take away our ability to make money on our own? And I'm giving Gary a hard time now. Sides are now being drawn. Do you want freedom or oppression? We can't help you if you don't join."

"And what *exactly* do you want me to do?"

Ralph smiled. "Tell you what. You don't even have to know what we sell. That's between me and my customers. But I need you to watch our back. If any of Gary's gang tries to interfere, you just step in their way, OK?"

Vaughn nodded, but it wasn't in agreement, but merely

because he understood. "I'll think about it." And he shook off Ralph's hand from his arm.

"Hey, man! I don't beg anyone, ya know?"

"I *said,* I'll *think* about it." By the time Vaughn got back to the scuffle, everyone was gone but the pressing feeling still remained.

Ralph sneered at Vaughn's back as he strode away. *I need them to fight again. I'll just have to throw some reminders Gary's way. Yea, start making bets on how long it would take Vaughn to knock him out again.* Ralph chuckled. The more his plan worked its way into his imagination, the more its pleasure increased, as if fate itself was congratulating him. He really liked this feeling of reassurance.

The pack of dogs followed her. Stephanie wasn't sure being Gary's anything did much good for her. *And where* is *Gary, anyway? Maybe he's scared of his rivals. Why did he even choose me if he's not going to at least* protect *me?* She let her long, thick red hair fall around her face. She headed for the other end of the decaying schoolyard, careful not to trip in the holes. Somewhere she remembered that when a defenseless animal trips, the predator pounces upon its victim. *Victim,* she cursed inside herself, still feeling humiliated, knowing she never again wanted to be forced down like that, but not knowing how to avoid it. Halfway there, the boys turned off in another direction, but not before yelling their final insults.

Seeing they were going different ways, Stephanie sighed in relief, then peering ahead, tried to decide where to sit though she always picked the same place. Stephanie carefully adjusted herself over the warped, uneven boards trying not to get a splinter. Many of the old bolts that held the wood to the bench frame were missing, so they shifted as she moved. It wouldn't be the first time she got pinched. *It really might be better to just sit on the ground.* But finding a smooth spot would prove to be difficult.

Stephanie stretched with a long, straining moan, finishing it off with a disgusted groan. She still shook from the teacher's hard stare, and couldn't believe how all the girls gushed over this Jargon character. *True, he* is *very handsome . . . but loathsome, somehow . . . but familiar somehow? What does he really want? Does it matter? Nothing's going to change this hell.*

Stephanie put it all from her mind, deciding to relish in the sun beating down upon her this hot, summer afternoon. It was the one thing in her life she counted on to remain bright. Her cares began to melt away as she basked in the sunshine. Her long, wavy, red hair looked like a deeply glowing coal of fire. Oddly, her complexion always turned golden instead of burning. She wondered if this might in some way have a greater meaning. She had learned about the advantages of genetic variation.

Delightful sounds of little children's laughter and frolic came from a pick-up soccer game unfolding not far in front of her. Around ten children, ranging in ages from about six to eight, were competing for a scarred, yellow-stained ball that had lost a lot of its bounce. *This last year, in particular, seems a lot like that ball.* The blond, brown, and black-haired girls were all clothed in colorful dresses or skirts. Typical boys all looked alike in dingy tee shirts and blue jeans.

Stephanie chuckled to herself. The girls were irritated by the silly antics and displays the boys put on, jumping over each other, even daring to tumble on the broken-up, worn-out concrete surface. More girls than boys were in the game, and they competed fiercely, more interested in serious play than in clowning around. Stephanie shook her head and rubbed her eyes and refocused again. *It's* still *there.*

She rubbed her eyes *again*, but there still seemed to be about a two foot, transparent, shimmering gray arm-like thing extended down over the head of a brown-haired girl, following her wherever she went. It looked like the cross between a human arm and an octopus tentacle. *What is* wrong *with me?* Odd kinds of things seemed to be happening to her more frequently, although she never remembered being without them. Dread mounted in her as she continued to stare at the girl. The ball went past the brown-haired girl twice, and a blond girl passed it both times to the same boy. The brown-haired girl stopped and put her hands on her hips, staring at the blond. The gray arm vanished.

Breathing a sigh of relief, Stephanie decided to take her mind off the game. *I have to think about my life.* But she found herself checking and rechecking. No sign of anything strange.

Bored after watching the game for a while, Stephanie turned her thoughts to her recent change of attitude. *No. Something does have to change. I can't go on like I've been living . . . no, dying. I think I'm right about what I've figured out.* But not too far into her thoughts, the hairs on the back of her neck stood up. Her head snapped up as she heard a word trailing from her mouth. "No!"

And then she saw the brown-haired girl stick her foot out and trip the blond girl who went down hard on her left knee and right cheek. Grabbing her small black purse from the bench, Stephanie rushed over to the crying six year old and whirled in anger at the older brown-haired girl. "What is wrong with you?"

The brown-haired girl glared back, as if to ask the same question! Then mockingly, she repeated the words back at her. "What is wrong with you? What is wrong with you?" She then ran off laughing to rejoin the game which had moved out of their way.

Stephanie couldn't help looking at that brat in disbelief then turned to the crying child. The sight of her bloodied knee caught her breath. Dark streaks ran down her little face as the dirt from the ground mixed with her tears. Stephanie knelt down, and took the girl in her arms. The little girl's sweetness made her heart ache even more.

"It's OK. It's OK. I'll help you." Hugging and rocking her, tears overtook Stephanie as well. They were a tiny island isolated from the rest of the world. More and more she felt convinced that was her fate. Everything around them seemed to disappear but Stephanie shook her head at herself. *I'm overreacting.* She brought her emotions under control. When the girl's crying began to lessen, the child's eyes began to widen as she gazed intently at her helper. Slightly unsettled by the look in her little blue eyes, Stephanie tore away from the child's stare to retrieve some tissues from her purse.

"This is going to hurt a bit," Stephanie told her as she began to wipe the dirt from her face. But the child just kept staring and smiling. Three tissues later, Stephanie was glad to see it was unharmed, not a scratch, not even a bruise. She cradled the child's cheek in her hand, thankful her sweet face would not be scarred. Her knee took all of the fall and her face just got dirty.

"OK. Now, for the hard part." Stephanie wondered why the girl was staring at her so much but focused on tending to the child's bloodied knee. Wiping around the edges, she was glad to see the girl wasn't flinching in pain, so she wiped a little more . . . a little more . . . and a little more until . . . there was no injury!

Stephanie gently touched the area and was surprised to see no sign of pain. She probed a little harder, as she stared into the little girl's sweet eyes. The girl abruptly threw her arms around Stephanie, gave her a hug and a kiss, then ran to rejoin the game!

Stephanie sat there on the playground shaking her head, looking at the bloodied tissues as the gentle breeze blew them away. When the game began to move closer, she got up and carefully took her seat back on the bench again, still shaking her head. *How could there be blood without an injury?*

But interrupting Stephanie's thoughts and pushing the incident from her mind, a thin girl, same age with long, straight, dark-brown hair sat down beside her. She wore clothing similar to Stephanie's, except instead of tight, black pants, hers were red, and instead of a pink tank top, hers was white. When Stephanie saw her, she decided it was a good time to try out her new ideas.

"Hey, Stephanie, do you ever go home?"

Stephanie twisted her mouth in disgust. "What for, Tracy? So I can hear my mother complain about how I ruined her life? Or to have her boyfriend make eyes at me? I'm fourteen for heaven's sake. FOURTEEN. Does he really think I would want his moldy body next to mine?"

Tracy twisted her mouth in the same fashion. "You'd better stay away from there." Then she grabbed Stephanie's arm in excitement. "Hey, come over and stay the night with me, we can pillow fight!" The gleam in Tracy's eye was unmistakable, but Stephanie gave her a serious look.

"I won't let you get me in your smother hold again."

Tracy's shoulders drooped, but she quickly followed up by begging. "OK, I won't do that to you. Promise. Please? I have some good stuff we can do."

Stephanie's eyebrows went up as she looked for the right way to begin. "Really? How good?"

"Oh, it makes you sail." Tracy outstretched her arms for emphasis.

Stephanie looked away and said sadly through a sigh, "I don't know. Lately I've been doing a lot of that . . . I don't know! I don't know if I feel like doing that tonight. I guess because I actually would like to *feel* something for a change."

Tracy leaned back for a bit, taking in her new attitude, reflecting upon it. *Wow, this* is *a change for her. I can't believe it. Her, of all people!* "You know, I think I've been feeling that way too, but I just haven't been able to express it like that."

Stephanie met her eyes, opening the door to her soul. "I've been thinking. You know when you really, I mean *really* feel pain, inside . . . inside your heart, your gut, you know, feelings *so deep* that it even hurts your body?"

Tracy's hidden patronizing transformed as she peered into Stephanie's expression that drew her into her friend's torment. In mere seconds, an unknown familiarity focused Tracy, causing her to worry with even the thought of such pain. She trembled, shaking her head. "Gee, Stephanie, I don't know, I never really thought about it like that."

Before Tracy could look away, Stephanie's solemnity held her attention. "Well, I've been thinking. For me, getting high, it's so I don't feel pain, and also to feel good. But for me, the good . . . it isn't really that good anymore, it's out of touch with reality." Stephanie looked away and hunched over, adding, "I've been thinking. I don't believe the choice I make is not to feel the pain, not really. There's so much more involved."

Seeing Stephanie turn away caused something to pull inside Tracy. She took Stephanie by the arms, straightened her up and turned her back to face her. "Well, what choice is it then, if not to feel pain? Myself, I think that's a pretty *good* choice."

Stephanie had a look of discovery. "It's . . . it's not to feel at all . . . at least . . . *nothing real!* Those *supposed* great feelings or thoughts we get from the drugs, I can never access them when I'm not high! Why do we even feel they're that great when we can't have these same kinds of experiences when we're sober? And, if we *should* have them, then don't you think we need to know how to be that way naturally? I mean, come to it naturally? And, if we don't come naturally, then how can it really be the real us? Which is the real us? Because each side of us isn't real to the other! When I'm high, I can't feel like I do when I'm sober. Why should I hate the consciousness I was naturally born with, by making myself unreal to it? Why should I *hate* myself? It's . . . *scary!*" Both their eyes widened together, as they reflected upon their common feelings, and a mutual understanding ignited between them, as they compared experiences.

Tracy spoke, looking into the distance of her internal self. "I guess that is sort of what happens . . . 'cause after a while, I just want to feel like a person again, and then . . . I feel like I've missed so much time being high."

Impassioned, Stephanie leaned forward. "Right! Initially, we think we're just choosing not to feel pain, and we think that being high is real happiness. But that high is not from our *hearts.*" She pressed her hands to her heart. "It's not from our *minds.*" She pressed her hands to her head. Then she held her hands out. "It's not from our *understanding.*" Feeling distraught, Stephanie dropped her hands onto her lap. "It's . . . not real."

She hung her head again, reflecting on herself. "It's kinda like that monster movie, ya know, where the monster stings its victim but the victim isn't paralyzed or killed or anything by the venom, but instead it makes him feel so good, that he doesn't run away, or feel afraid or feel pain . . . then the monster eats him from the feet up."

Her friend shuddered at the image, looking down at her feet. She knew that this applied to her also, so she sought to understand it more deeply. "You're saying, if we get high . . . we're really choosing not to feel at all . . . because . . ."

"Right. Not to feel anything real."

With that confirmation, Tracy sat back, and looked across the broken, crumbling schoolyard that had only the remnants of a concrete surface baking in the sun like a forsaken desert. She tried to imagine herself being happy lying in that schoolyard while being eaten alive from the feet up. Then, Tracy compared that to what she'd just said, 'I just want to feel like a person again.' *Oh God, it's true!* Shivering, she held back a sob as she desperately tried to drive that image away. Sounding as if she was in some distant place, Tracy's thoughts pushed themselves out through her lips. "Stephanie, you know, now that I think about it, I'd consider . . . well, I'm willing to try to quit if you are."

Stephanie picked up her head trying to gain her friend's full focus. "We can do this, Tracy."

Feeling herself being drawn to look deeply into her friend's eyes, Tracy turned back to Stephanie. "Hey, maybe I could sell my stuff to someone else and get my money back. Hey, then I could treat you to something, a monster movie, or maybe some special food!"

"Ehh . . . besides, I don't think we're supposed to sell *anything* without government approval. Gary's actually pretty proud of that." Stephanie shook her head slowly.

"I guess you're right."

Stephanie took Tracy's hands in both of hers. "But, I would like to help you earn some of your money back, *after* we get rid of the stuff." Warmth radiated from Stephanie.

Tracy couldn't believe her kindness, as no one *ever* offered money to another. "Oh, would you, Stephie? Oh, that's so sweet of you." Hugging each other, they felt a new bond grow between them, but suddenly Stephanie shivered, feeling cold inside. She broke off the embrace, quickly looking around. Startled, Tracy searched her friend's expression. "Stephanie, what's the matter? You look like the monster just got hold of you."

"Didn't you hear that?" Stephanie's eyes bore into her friend's.

Tracy backed her head away more, concerned at her friend's fright. "Hear what?"

"That terrible growl!"

For a moment, Tracy just stared at her. "Stephanie, maybe your decision to stop is going to prove a bit more difficult than you thought."

While searching their surroundings again, Stephanie thought, *It's got nothing to do with stopping the drugs.* She never felt so clear-minded before. "All my childhood I thought there were monsters hiding under my bed, in the closet . . ." then she spread her arms out wide and made a monster face, "... *everywhere.*" Tracy laughed, and Stephanie forced a laugh as they got up to go to Tracy's house. All the way there, Stephanie couldn't help hearing that terrible growling resounding in her ears. *Am I just remembering it, or am I really hearing it. Oh God!*

Carefully picking their way across the deteriorated rubble of what had once been Tracy's sidewalk, they held hands, trying not to twist an ankle. Stephanie noticed another red brick had fallen out of the wall of Tracy's house since the last time she visited. She grumbled inside, *And this is the best side of town!* Yet, compared to her small, flimsy, wooden house, Tracy's was a royal palace. Stephanie turned red with anger, as she remembered what her grandmother told her years ago. *It wasn't always like this; it was war and strife between people that bled all the countries dry.* She had also said, 'People used to get to keep most of the money they made'. Stephanie cursed under her breath. "*Sacrifice!*"

There wasn't anybody home. There was never anybody home anywhere in any house because each had to work in the little factories. Over-and-over she heard that saying in school until she was sick of it echoing in her mind: '*We're working for one another*'. What if she wanted to just work one day for herself? Besides, "one another" wasn't one another at all; it was working to support the government. Her grandmother told her the people actually used to *vote* for who was in the government, but admitted that was even a little before her time.

Entering Tracy's house brought Stephanie out of her deep thoughts, and she followed as Tracy retrieved her whole drug supply from several hiding places. They took turns ceremoniously dumping them into the toilet then both pushed the flush-lever together, watching as the cloudy water whirled them all away. Stephanie ritualistically brushed her hands together, signifying finality. "They're all gone. From now on, we're sober!"

Tracy followed by nodding her head in confirmation, saying the magic word, too. *"Sober!"* Then she eyed Stephanie. "So how are you and Gary getting along? Is he still a hunk to you?"

Stephanie was still staring into the toilet, lost in thought as she mumbled her reply. "He rushes too much."

"What do you mean?" *I can't believe she doesn't want the only man any sane girl would die for!*

"You know, when he does it, he rushes too much. I don't enjoy it anymore. He's invited me to a party tomorrow night. Wanna come?" Stephanie's invitation was unenthusiastic.

Tracy sensed Stephanie cooling toward Gary. "I don't know. I'm not supposed to stay out late, as my parents want me home when they return from work. So you and Gary aren't . . . serious?" She waited on baited breath for the response.

"I don't know, I guess I've been with him too long. I think I need to move on . . . maybe find someone different at the party."

Tracy knew Gary, how charmingly protective he was. She knew he'd be hurt. "Stephanie, he won't like that! He'll be mad!"

Stephanie shrugged her shoulders at Tracy. "I'm used to mad men, my Father *is* one. I don't care about his mad. Besides, I know I'm not his only one."

After their ceremony, the girls got supper and sat down to play checkers. It was one of the few games that seemed to survive from the 'old times.' However, they didn't know much about those times since it was about a hundred years before they were born, and the government did not encourage learning about them. In fact, that was an understatement. Yet, there were rumors that someone, somewhere in the government, had knowledge of the past and was for the past ten years slowly introducing past ideas as new ones, everything from clothing styles to music, but one just didn't know.

Stephanie's mind was wandering a lot so it wasn't surprising that Tracy beat her at quite a few games. More than once though, Stephanie could have sworn she had more checkers on the board than were there. Later in the bathroom, Tracy teased her about winning as they cleaned up before going to sleep.

Tracy had a large bed, and the last time, months ago, when Stephanie last slept over, they had shared it. That's where they'd fought the previous pillow fight. Now they both climbed in after washing and sank into its softness. Stephanie luxuriated in it, thinking she didn't know how she slept on her own bed. Now, the fluffiness of it melded with her thoughts to make her feel like she was floating on a cloud. In the distance, she heard Tracy shout, "Sneak Attack." Those were the rules because it wasn't fair to just *sneak attack.* But the warning and the fierce blow that knocked her from her cloud and popped her ears seemed to happen simultaneously.

After battling for a whole hour, they finally exhausted themselves and crumpled into uncontrolled laughter. Tracy broke her promise, though. Stephanie *hated* the smother hold. Yet, that conflict forgotten, their joy gave way to their exhaustion, and both girls drifted off into blissful sleep, until something dark seemed to enfold itself around Stephanie. A horror of great darkness descended upon her, but she was frozen and couldn't wake up from what seemed to be more than a dream . . .

"Alright, Scraback! I've had enough from these impudent kids."

Scraback acted like an earth child wild with excitement. "Master GrrraGagag, are you going to interfere? Lower your Great Eye upon her?"

"No, but I'm going to make sure our trollop doesn't THINK her way out of anything else. I'm tired of all this thinking. What do they think they are, anyway?"

"Master, how will you intervene?"

"Well, our little idiots down there could possibly fail all by themselves, but if not, I'll show you how to place thoughts and feelings into them subtly, so no one is alarmed. Actually, Gary seems to like it when I'm more direct with him."

Scraback winked his Eye, letting his Master know he was surprised. "So, you've done this to him before?"

"I've been training him, because I never know when I might need someone to just immediately follow a thought I give them. He is so in tune to reality that he sees no difference between his thoughts and feelings and mine."

"That's wonderful, Master! I can't wait to learn."

"Watch, as I extend my Eye over Gary's tree . . ."

Out of the deep darkness, a large, hideous snake floated in front of a smaller one. Their indescribable sickly gray, was accompanied by a profuse, choking stench. They floated before a glowing blue light that showed trees . . .trees that turned into people! Stephanie looked at one of those trees and it was hers! As the snakes floated, quivering, and shimmering . . . they approached Stephanie. The larger one wrapped her up in his powerful coil! *Pain!* Its huge mouth opened into endless blackness that began to suck her in. Stephanie felt her very self disintegrating . . .

She felt shaken but heard her name from far away. "Stephanie, wake up! You're dreaming! Wake up!" Her fearful moans sent chills through Tracy, making her attempts to rouse Stephanie even more urgent.

"Oh, *God!*" Stephanie whimpered, soaked in sweat and trembling. When Tracy saw her twisted face, she took her in her arms and trembled too.

"Stephie, what was it?"

She whispered her answer, "*Monsters!*"

Eventually, they both managed to go back to sleep.

CHAPTER 2

Kinds of Feelings

King Mafferan watched his thirteen-year-old daughter frown at the row of corn. "Why, Father, are some plants sickly and others not? I planted the seed from the same ear."

"Without the ear, would you have had any seed at all to plant?"

Staring intently into his rich brown eyes, she asked, "Is that an answer to my question, Father?"

"Indeed, that is a good question."

The President drummed his fingers on the old, worn, round table and the five other government administrators resisted the impulse to copy him. What looked to be a teenager nonchalantly leaned back his folding chair against the wall behind presumably his father. With unhidden disdain, the dignitaries eyed their uninvited guest, but he was sitting with them at the table and kept smiling though not quite warmly at them. This man stared at each of them, but lingered longest on the President before he finally spoke. "I'm here to help you fulfill our destiny. You can call me Jargon."

The govs all peered at their president and he voiced their common thought. "Who the hell are you? How did you even get in here? And what makes you think we'd even consider your help if we needed it?"

They looked at this Jargon's odd clothes, some kind of native dress obviously, consisting of a dull brown tunic with some faint embroidery, black shirt underneath with plain brown pants, but his neatly cut black hair and his young golden complexion all seemed to shine mysteriously. And there was that smile again.

To one man he said, "I wouldn't advise you following me or investigating me. I might get mad!"

To another he warned. "That gun you're holding under the table is useless."

Jargon ignored the only woman there but surprisingly addressed another man by name. "Fred. I like you. Don't you think women have far too much influence nowadays?"

Surprised, Fred nodded. Jargon turned to the woman. "You're dismissed. Don't come back!" Her mouth dropped open, but Fred couldn't help smiling.

Jargon then confirmed another official's thoughts. "Yes, indeed. I *am* the one who's been appearing on TV, speaking to the nation on the government's behalf!"

And to the President of the 'country with no name' Jargon said, "For now, the rest of you may remain in power until you make me officially your King. These things have to be presented properly to the country, for the good of the country. After my coronation, I'll still let you carry on business as usual subject to my approval!"

One man raised his gun but immediately dropped it as if it was on fire then grabbed his head as if in mortal pain. Suddenly, right before their eyes, Jargon vanished. The man was left screaming in agony. The president jumped up hollering, "Get our top agents in here! I want . . ."

Jargon reappeared. "I told you not to anger me." He lifted his hand and one of the seated men floated up with his chair still under him. With a swoosh of Jargon's fingers, the man and chair hurled into the wall. The chair splintered to pieces as the man slid down the wall more than dazed. Jargon smiled with warmth then said, "I'll be in touch. You never know when I'll just pop in. I think we'll work together just fine. And Oh, I know your favorite book is Orwell's 1984, but quite frankly, I found it a touch boring, too predictable. You know what I mean?" And then he vanished again.

Gary was fortunate. Unlike most people who couldn't afford to talk on the telephone, he had unlimited use because Glen was his cousin. Glen's father ranked high in the government, although no one knew what the ranks really were, except those who held them. That made it wise to avoid anyone at all with connections. Gary smiled at the genius of effective rule. One day he and his cousin planned to rule together, which made this Jargon thing troubling. They didn't need competition, but if the stories were really true . . . How could they be? Anyway, he was on the other side of the country.

"Hey, Glen! How's my cousin doin'?"

"Same old, same old. I've decided to finish schooling at your school next year."

"That's great, but how come? Aren't you going to miss your family and the west coast? I can't wait."

"Your school has the best political education, and my dad wants me there. I'll be staying with you. Besides, you have to pass this year. Your mother's been complaining to my dad."

Gary knew all about his mother's constant complaining. "Yeah, yeah, I know. It's just that with all that I have to take care of . . . I don't really care about school."

"Well, my dad said you have to pass this year."

"OK, OK, I understand."

"So what's up, Gary? Profits are down quite a bit. If you can't prove yourself . . ."

"There are a few people I'm having trouble with. Maybe you can help me."

"I'm listening."

"Oh, you know, some fools think they can have their way in the town without checking with me, so they've started a rivalry, and their numbers are growing, too."

Glen was shaking his head. "That's not good. Are they connected?"

"No, I really don't believe so."

"The nerve! Still, we have to be careful. You know how we like to take care of things, nothing overt if we can avoid it. Having people disappear is far more effective than open brutality. You know, we don't want people seeking vengeance. We want them afraid of their shadow . . . that's better."

Gary always enjoyed the way his cousin relished in describing these things, as he sounded just like his father, Gary's uncle, brother to his mother. "I know. There is just one other problem that's been nagging at me."

Glen's eyebrow shot up as he pressed the phone tighter to his ear. "Shoot."

"About a year ago, this raunchy kid, Vaughn, made me look like a fool. I hate to say it, but he sucker punched me and knocked me out."

"Mmm, hmm, I heard."

Damn it! How's he finding out everything? "I figured you would, eventually."

Glen gripped the phone tightly. "Look, you can't let that kid live! Who will fear you or *won't* challenge you if you don't fix this? It may not have seemed like much back then, but see how it's progressed and undermined you in just one year? Is he the leader of your rivals?"

Gary was embarrassed. "No, actually he's just a nobody with only one friend . . . and he's another nobody, too."

Glen was incredulous. "That's *worse.* What the hell are you doing?"

"But it's been a whole year since he did it. It's just that every time I look at him . . . Actually, I was playing around with the little jerk and never expected him to pop me."

"Well, what have you been doing with all the drugs we sent you? I see profits started dropping this year, because they're buying from someone else because you now appear vulnerable. So now you're challenged, and he's not even connected. You know how bad that is? Private business? Why the hell would you even take a chance on appearing weak?"

Gary hung his head. "I don't know. Vaughn just disgusts me and I decided to have some fun with him."

"Well, you see what your fun gets you? You have to be smarter than this. You have to send a message so you'll be feared."

"Sorry Cuz, I will. Hey, what's with this Jargon thing? Even my teacher was pumping me for info!"

"You're kidding?" *Damned Jargon!*

"Nope, Hardcord even asked us our *opinion!* Asked *me* to explain."

"Look, everyone has weaknesses, but we just don't know what his are yet. You wouldn't believe what this guy can do. But, he can't do everything himself, as he still needs the government. He just wants to be at the top. Actually, it might not matter that much. Think of it as everything remaining the same, but just adding a sort of figurehead. We'd still have all our power, but we'd just have to bow ultimately to him. So we'll bow, so what."

"But why?" *Glen's hiding a lot, and he's never done that before.*

"Can't tell ya that Cuz, as Jargon made it clear he'll let everyone know when he says so. Anyone crossing him pays dearly. Believe me, I've seen it!"

"But . . ."

"No buts, Cuz. Focus on what *you* have to do. Hey, how's the women?"

Gary brightened. "Same old, same old, women are the *stupidest* things on earth. All you gotta do is figure out where their little hurt feelings are, or if they don't have any, create some, and then make 'em believe sex is the greatest thing they got goin'. Oh Cuz, it's so great, they'll do anything after that. And *I mean anything* just to feel like they matter. The stubborn ones fall the best after you give 'em some drugs, because they've been holdin' back for so long. The best thing to do is get a virgin, set her up like that, then draw back until she comes beggin' for it. Then after you get her, throw her away. They get the funniest look on their faces. God, I can't believe how *stupid* they are. They just hate to admit the truth. They're worse than dogs."

Glen challenged him. "How many you up to now?"

"Twenty-three, and I woulda had more but this red-haired puppy took too much of my time. Somethin' about her just had me comin' back for more to see how much further I could push her."

"No excuses, Cuz. I got you beat. Thirty-three for me! You ever try trappin' any?"

"What you mean?"

Glen lowered his voice just a bit, perhaps out of reflex. "Get 'em somewhere they can't escape. Since they got no excuse for willingly being there, no one would believe 'em if they told, then you force 'em to do whatever you want."

"Nah, why do that when you can get 'em to do anything anyway."

"Like you said, Cuz, the look on their faces, like when you break a virgin and then dump her."

"How'd you ever come up with that?"

"Imagination, my friend, it's the door into a whole other world. Gotta go!"

"*Hey*, one more thing . . ." Gary just had to tell him. "You just made me think that's one more reason why I should kill that kid that popped me."

"What?"

Gary had a fit of laughter that lasted so long Glen had to remind him he was on the other end. "Well, you won't believe this, but after I set this kid Vaughn up good to thinkin' he was a fag,' he rushes out to get him a woman to prove otherwise, right?"

"Yeah?"

"Well, the other day I heard, keep in mind he screwed this girl almost a year ago, well, the other day I heard he apologized to her for screwin' her! Told her she was a *person* and he didn't treat her like she was."

Glen was incredulous. "Oh, God. You're kidding?"

"No. So I've decided she's gonna to be my next whore, just so I can prove to her how much of a *person* she really is."

Laughter overcame them both until Glen finally broke it. "Any man that stupid deserves to die."

"You got a point there, Cuz. Isn't it great to be government? Bye!"

In the morning, Tracy let Stephanie take a shower as she could see her friend desperately needed it. Stephanie relaxed as the warm water washed the night away. Tracy even fed her breakfast before they hugged and said their goodbyes, and they promised to see more of each other.

Even before she walked out Tracy's back door, Stephanie knew where she was going. It rushed upon her in the shower. It had always called to her like that. Not a calling to the mind, and something more powerful than mere feelings. She concluded that, *It must be some genetic thing like whatever gives birds the drive to migrate.* That was the call of the countryside for her to walk in its midst.

Old invigorating memories flooded her as she headed out the door, and she felt a tear in her eye from the exhilaration. The power of these burgeoning feelings of life had a double effect, her reborn emotions made her realize how much they'd been missing from her for the last year, and then she wondered why they had left. It had been almost a year to the day since she had last visited nature in all its undisturbed beauty.

The walk down the back road seemed to vanish from time. Stephanie looked up from her deep meditations, but didn't remember getting this far. She only remembered examining her reborn life feelings and comparing them to her previous dead feelings. It seemed that being that deep in thought was like being in a whole different world. She now found herself upon the wooded path that encircled the whole town.

Just a quarter turn up and she automatically took the left into the mixed hardwood and pine trees. She used to come here often when running away from home, as it felt safe, and nature seemed to comfort her. *What am I running from now? Or am I?* While heading into the deeper woods, she abruptly stopped. *What changed me from coming here?* She paused to search for an answer. *I've just been running away to different places, but they don't have the same kind of wonderful feeling. What* are *all these different feelings?*

Smells of the early morning forest instantly charged her with satisfaction. Feelings of life and peace from nature flooded into her as she inhaled deeply then brushed tears from her eyes, taking in the full glory of all the life surrounding her. *Is this normal to have such strong feelings like this?* Then she saw it.

Amazingly, her shelter, though fallen down, still had all its parts. After studying it a while, Stephanie pulled out the heaviest branches and piled them up, then in another pile she placed the cross branches, and in another the thinnest. She then gathered up all the old pieces of raincoats she had painstakingly collected for two years. They never seemed to stay where she put them. She laughed as she remembered how her acquaintances couldn't understand what she wanted them for and she never told them. Remembering her shelter had collapsed several times before, she was determined to build it to last this time.

She began rebuilding, this time by wedging the bottoms of the heaviest branches between various tree roots that bulged from the ground then she leaned the branch tops into each other, hooking them together where they forked. The cross branches she wove side-ways, and the thinnest went vertically woven between those. Instead of just laying the raincoat pieces on top, she began weaving them between the vertical branches. Then she paused. *If I begin at the bottom and put the bottom of the next higher piece over the top of the one below, it won't* leak *like before.* She shook her head with a broad smile and wondered why she hadn't realized that sooner.

She wiped the sweat from her forehead. Raincoat pieces were strewn all around so she could choose the best fit. *Piece on top of piece, begin from the bottom and work your way up.* There was something special about the exhilaration of serious work uniting mind and body into a singular, meaningful purpose. Every carefully judged move, each expenditure of energy seemed to draw something in her together from the inside-out, although her mind preoccupied itself with matters at hand.

Finally, she finished positioning the last coat piece at the very top, and as she did, something changed inside her. She sat down on a log to stare at it then began to quiver and then weep. She felt as if a part of her had just been put back into place, and it was that part which was crying. *Why am I crying so hard? Where is this coming from?* She looked into a tangle of emotions that she realized had been there a long time, and began trying to sort them out, to trace their origin so she could understand them. *Pain, lots of pain . . . but my shelter and nature are like love. I feel life all around . . . calling to me. This is meaningful to me. I can feel again . . . Oh God, I can feel again . . .* Tears dripped off the end of her nose and it began to itch even more than before. It became so bothersome it took her mind off her heart.

The gold ring in her nose had been itching ever since she entered the countryside, so she finally took it out and put it in her pocket, and laughing to herself she mused, *My nose ring must be allergic to nature.*

Feeling drained, she yawned then crawled inside the one place in the whole world that was truly hers. The pine needles she had gathered over a year ago lay inside. Pine needles have a very long life so they don't decay easily at all, so she just fluffed them back up. The old blanket she snuck out of the house last year with the last raincoat was also surprisingly preserved. Stephanie curled up inside her shelter listening to animals skittering and birds flittering as she began to fall asleep to tears she didn't understand.

So many wounds were like so many feelings churning in a tempest sea. The drug-induced haze of the last year was gone. What is the silent conversation in a heart where so many currents swirl together? The mind is tossed upon the surface, yet deep down there is a stillness that says I am. The heart yearns, the heart explores, and the mind seeks understanding. Sometimes, mysteriously, the depths answer plea; a sense of still being spreads where once the sea frothed. When faced with overwhelming conditions, sometimes, instead of fearing, a profoundness of *Being* draws one's full attention, causing torments to grudgingly give way.

Around noon Stephanie stirred from the calls of nature. She had eaten well at Tracy's house. She stretched, not remembering when she had ever had such a peaceful sleep. In the stillness after her stretch, a new feeling glowed in her heart, "*Thankfulness. That's thankfulness,*" she said to herself out loud. But necessity called more urgently, so she exited her shelter, pushing some branches up to hide the little doorway. She was now a lot stronger physically than a year ago, and was able to make the shelter much sturdier. As she departed, she glanced back at it thinking. *This time it will last a long time without falling over.*

Because the calls of nature were increasingly more urgent, Stephanie took the main road into town. As she hit the town's edge, she replaced her nose ring, remembering how Gary had taken such a liking to it. It was then that she realized why she hadn't visited the countryside in so long. The call to walk in its beauty had been supplanted by the call for . . . *What?* Stephanie stopped in her tracks and searched the mental picture she had. *What? What's the call? No. Sex didn't take me away from the country. Anyway, sex is* part *of nature. It should make me feel good like being in the country makes me feel good. We never even did it in the country. But I don't even think that would make it feel right, although I think it should be beautiful to make love in the country. Love? That's the difference. What took me away from the country? It's not really companionship, either, because Gary and I don't really have companionship. Parties, drugs, and hanging out. That changed all my feelings. But I belong somewhere now, I guess. Our group is like brothers and sisters. But that's a different belonging than what I feel in the country. But I became* somebody *with them. Then what was I this morning? I never felt so beautiful, even when I was crying.*

Stephanie fingered her nose ring, then pulled it out again as she looked inside herself. The peace of the country morning sang to her. She then put it back in again, and looked inside herself, but then her bladder made spasms and her gut cramped so she hurried on. Though deeply engaged, she had to end her investigation because physical urgency forced her to enter the nearest place at hand.

The government church had two huge, gray stone columns on either side of the door. The word 'God' was carved into the right pillar and the word 'Country' into the left. The word 'And' was on the top beam connecting the two. Stephanie entered through the large wooden front doors and instantly felt swallowed up. Her mind searched for memories to help her cope, but she realized her flash backs were all through the eyes of a small child. *It's been that long . . . and I still feel out of place.*

She was there because of urgency, that's all. *Get in and get out . . .* that was the plan. Seeing the signs for rest rooms, she turned right and rushed into the women's bathroom.

As Stephanie sat in the stall, she mused. *It feels so* good *to take care of basic necessities, but how different in quality these feelings are compared to the deep thoughts and feelings I've been pondering; each is intense in a different way.*

Before leaving the bathroom, she checked herself in the mirror, turning from side to side. She nodded at her physical fitness, rubbing her hands across her flat, tight tummy and pressing a bit. *Those sit-ups really do the job.* She laughed as she readjusted her breasts and made the honest opinion to herself that, *I'm hot! It drives the boys crazy.*

Coming back down the hallway, intending to leave straightway, Stephanie suddenly let another new feeling stop her. To her left was the way out, but to the right led into the church. Part of her couldn't believe she turned right, but it was another one of those calling feelings that she seemed to have to follow.

There was a main aisle down the center and long rows of very old wooden benches to either side. Something about the place had a wonderful feel about it. Stephanie thought it came from all the old wood of the benches and the trimming around the room. She loved wood. But there was also a terrible feeling in this place. Adding to the incongruity, something compelled her to explore. Her stomach would have to wait on food.

Following her feelings, she walked down the aisle, not really knowing what she was doing. A fat, balding man in some special black attire came up to her, his eyes first fell on her nose ring, then, seemingly evasive, roamed the rest of her body, all of which Stephanie was keenly aware.

In too prissy a voice for any man, he spoke to her. "What can I do for you? Ahhh, Missssss!" His 'miss' sounded more like a hiss, and Stephanie realized she had involuntarily backed up a step.

"Ahhh, I just . . . came to pray!" She was shocked at her own words, but hoped they would cause this very uncomfortable encounter to end.

With a half sneer, half leer he said, "You may follow me."

She didn't want to follow him *anywhere*. Staring above his head, refocusing, she saw what she expected, except there were two gray arms reaching inside *his* head!

He took her past several old ladies whose glances bore into Stephanie. *If these are Godly glances, I don't want to meet the God they serve.* She was glad when he directed her to sit in a far away corner, but Stephanie could only muster a nod for a thank you.

Seeing a thin little book on the shelf built into the pew in front of her, she reached for it, opened it, but almost feeling guilty for doing so. The page read as follows:

GOD REVEALED HIMSELF TO US AFTER THE GREAT RELIGIOUS WAR EXPOSED ALL OF THE PAST RELIGIONS OF THE WORLD AS FRAUDS. HAIL AND GLORY BE TO OUR UNNAMED GOD, TO OUR UNNAMED COUNTRY.

WE CANNOT NAME HIM BECAUSE WE CANNOT KNOW WHAT HE REALLY IS. WE CANNOT NAME HER BECAUSE NO SINGLE NAME WOULD SUFFICE.

GOD HAS GIVEN US OUR GREAT COUNTRY THROUGH WHICH WE SERVE GOD.

SINNER'S PRAYER:

WE PRAY FOR EVERYONE TOGETHER TO WORK HARDER TO PROSPER OUR COUNTRY THAT WE MAY GAIN HIS GLORIOUS FAVOR.

AMEN.

1. HONOR TO COUNTRY
2. RESPECT TO THE GOVERNMENT
3. PAY YOUR TAXES
4. Give to the church

Suddenly, a booming voice came over the loud speaker. Stephanie yelped, almost dropping the prayer book. The old ladies all turned their scorn upon her, as Stephanie, red-faced, turned and nodded her pardon. The voice was the prissy voice of the man who had not really greeted her. "We shall now do our duty and pray together. Young . . . ahh, Missssss, please lead us in our devotional!"

Stephanie's mouth dropped open. She was sure all the old lady's veins were popping in their necks. The room seemed to close in on her. She was taught in school that whatever you were told in church, you *had to obey*, or it was a crime against the government. She scolded herself. *Oh no, why did I come here in the first place?* She stood and held the sacred writings in front of her so as to hide her breasts from the man's stare. Stephanie began to recite. "We pray for everyone together . . ."

After he made her recite most of the book, he proclaimed mealtime and any who wanted to join were welcome. Stephanie's stomach was in major revolt and it seemed to drag her, against her will, down the stairs where that prissy priest went. But all the old ladies followed, too, so she felt safe.

Once everyone had picked up their meal, sure enough that prissy man with the weasel eyes walked right up to Stephanie who was standing not too far from the tables of food. "Well, Misssss, did you learn anything from our prayers today?"

Good grief, she thought, *this isn't school. What the hell is this about?*

"Oh yes, of course . . . ahhh, Sir."

He stepped up closer with his protruding stomach only inches away from her, and Stephanie shrunk inside. "And what did you learn?" She had to look up because of his towering stature, as the only other choice was to stare into his gut.

All the old ladies watched with the eyes of hunting birds and listened with the ears of foxes. To avert answering, Stephanie pointed to her mouth to show that it was full, making excuse me signs. Her main objective now was to eat, that's all, so she blocked everything else out.

The roast chicken was ambrosial as Stephanie wolfed it down from underneath the giant. It gave her time to think, but as he stood there waiting for her reply, he was peering straight down her hot-pink tank top. There was nothing she could do about it because she didn't have the prayer book with her to block his view, not that it would be an easy task to hold both it and her food.

Finally, she swallowed and answered, "I've learned, Sir, to ask questions!" She didn't know where *that* answer came from. Stephanie was as much a spectator of herself as everyone else was of her.

The priest showed surprise at her response by straightening his back, causing his stomach to stick out even further. Stephanie instinctively backed up another step to protect her plate of food. Not wanting to say more, she shoved a roll into her mouth. The bread was freshly baked, and was sweet tasting like she loved it.

He finally brought himself to another question. "And how did our devotional do that for you?"

She found herself quickly swallowing, despite wanting to savor the taste, and take her time. The answer seemed to be pushing itself out of its own accord. "Because, Sir, devotionals are *supposed* to be inspirational, and inspiration is such a powerful force that can't help but provoke a person to question how to live better!" Stephanie noticed she was looking the man dead in his eyes.

He looked away, muttering as he left to go talk to the old ladies. "Yesss, Yessss . . . very good!" The old ladies surrounded him, but they could not help from glancing over to Stephanie.

She decided to stay and eat her fill. *What did I just say? I was inspired, alright, but not the way* you *think.* When she finally left, no one acknowledged her; it was as if she had never been there.

Once again she was about to leave, but found herself turning back into the now empty worship room. She sighed at herself. *OK. What am I doing now?*

As she walked all the way down the central isle, past row upon row of old wooden benches, the huge picture that hung behind the altar became clear. Her memories of the church, from when she was little, were merely of the back of the bench in front of her. Because the odious priest had initially guided her in today, she hadn't paid the picture any mind earlier. As

Stephanie's focus grew sharper and sharper the closer she got, her thoughts were shouting inside her. *What the hell is that?* It was a huge picture, as seen from outer space, of the world that had a huge gray foot resting on top of it. Inside the foot in gold letters were the same words as on the outside of the church: 'COUNTRY AND GOD'. Underneath the world, in more beautiful gold letters surrounded by red, was some kind of wise saying . . . well, perhaps wise: 'AS WE FIRST LEARN LOVE FROM OUR PARENTS, WE LEARN GOD FROM OUR COUNTRY. THE EARTH IS OUR FOOTSTOOL.' She heard herself say "*What crap!*"

As Stephanie reached the sacred stage, she climbed up the stairs without hesitation and headed straight to the back. She stood only inches away from the picture so that she could see the very texture of it, a woven tapestry. She craned her head back, her mouth opening wide, taking in the enormity of it. Shaking her head, she tentatively reached out her right index finger and briefly touched it. It seemed safe so she touched it again, watching the slight give in the material. Then she gently pushed her finger into it, pushing it several inches. After considering, she briskly poked at it, watching as a ripple spread through the whole tapestry. It was as if she was testing the very validity of the idea it expressed. She shook her head, as she thought aloud, *"I don't believe this."* It wasn't meant as a mere statement of dogmatic disbelief. "This isn't about God, but our government wanting to rule the world." Quickly she looked back toward the doors to see if anyone heard. She knew the disgust in her words was far more dangerous than the words themselves, remembering how stupid she was for opening her mouth in class yesterday. She turned away and went to the wooden podium, where on top rested the same sacred book distributed throughout the church.

Something didn't feel right. Stephanie walked around the wooden stage searching for the out of place feeling. Even though the wood had a wonderful feeling, there was an empty feeling there as well. *That's it. The feeling that called me in here and is supposed to be in here to meet me* is not. *It feels empty here!* Stephanie shook her head at everything and at herself as she asked, *What am I talking about?* But as she went to jump off the podium, she heard two words.

"Find me."

Startled, she turned to her left, even though the voice, on second thought, didn't actually have a voice, but the words were there anyway and seemed to call from that direction. She focused intently on a plaque of a carved wooden tree on the wall. It drew her concentration deeper into it. "*It's . . . glowing,*" she heard herself say. But then the more she analyzed it, there was no glow for her eyes to see. Grabbing her head in her hands, she shook it fiercely, growling at herself. "Find what?" *Idiot! Why don't you call the whole world in here!* She growled again and left the worship room and this time took the exit.

Stephanie had enough of indulging her mysterious feelings. She had enough of asking herself what she was doing. She needed some routine now and so decided to head for her regular haunts to pass the rest of the day until she could crash that night at Gary's house. She hoped his party wouldn't last that long. Her nap was superb, but she still felt drained from last night's nightmare though she had pushed the scary dream away in favor of reality. *There are no such things as monsters, after all.* She was smarter than that, having gotten an A-plus in Biological Evolution just this year. *If they were genetically viable, they would still be around. Huh, if they ever were around. Besides, there are no monsters in the government's religion either. So, if there was any truth to them, you'd think they would show up somewhere in their scriptures. Come to think of it, God isn't there much either. Why does the government even bother to sponsor a religion, seeing as how it's perfectly clear they're making God up?* But if there was a God, Stephanie was sure of one thing, God had nothing to do with this government or its religion.

Although Stephanie slept over at Tracy's house the night before and still hadn't been home, she pushed thoughts of home still further to the back of her mind. Yet in spite of everything, yesterday's accomplishment sung in her heart because flushing the last of that poison down Tracy's toilet had wonderful finality. All day, thankfulness had been welling up inside of her.

For the first time in a whole year, Stephanie felt clearheaded. Now, at fourteen, Stephanie reveled in the development of thinking, amazed at how smart she had become. She felt healthy now, in both mind and body. That strength finally enabled her to go to the party.

Still wearing yesterday's clothes, and being very late, she strolled toward the house party, although for some unknown reason she had delayed going earlier. *If there was some other place I could go . . .* Realizing that the same poison still controlled the rest of her close friends, she felt compelled to figure out a way to help them, too. After all, they were all she had. Stephanie deliberated the situation as she walked. *I don't think I can approach them like I did Tracy. Oh God, I know I can't approach them as a group, so I'll have to do it one at a time...maybe even slowly. Hmmm, I can't let them know I've quit, not yet anyway. They couldn't deal...*

While pondering, she peered into the shadows of the houses she passed. A cold feeling drove through her as her hair fluttered in the warm, gentle night breeze. She refocused her line of sight past the large houses and spreading lawns to a distant house, hoping to arrive sooner than her feet could carry her.

The town block was made up of old two and three-story red and yellow brick houses in disrepair. In the daylight, one could see how honeycombed the bricks were, mortar was missing everywhere. But at night, there was still a sense of how beautiful this very old neighborhood must have been a hundred years ago, just before the Great Religious War depleted everything. Stephanie thought to herself: *This had to have once been a wealthy neighborhood, because the houses are spaced so far apart. Too bad everyone is so poor. That's what people get for fighting over their stupid religions.*

At last, Stephanie crossed the huge lawn and made it to the front door of Gary's house. Loud, jeering laughter drifted away into the black nothingness as the stars twinkled on this quiet, stifling summer's night. Stephanie knew she would be welcome, as they saw more of her than of any of the other girls. All the boys' eyes popped when she strode in like a queen through the old, cracked and creaking heavy wooden door.

The feeling of the room instantly reminded Stephanie of the bounceless soccer ball. *It never struck me that way before! Why?* A long, chipped table stood in front of a worn out orangish couch where Tracy propped her feet at one end. Her long brown hair cascaded over her white top, which was half tucked into a short, powder blue skirt. Stephanie was immediately surprised to see her, but said nothing.

Reclining at the other end of the couch, Karen's very long blond hair shined like the sun against her long, tight black dress. Squeezed between Karen's lanky form and Tracy were three skinny boys in short-sleeves and blue jeans. They had the same color hair as the mean girl from the soccer game. Suddenly, Stephanie remembered the gray arm and scolded herself. *Now is not the time to think about such things!*

The filthy tan carpet was threadbare, and assorted throw rugs were distributed to cover up the holes. Faded tapestries hung on the walls at odd locations, probably covering holes there as well. For some reason, Stephanie thought it gave the room a wholly dishonest character. There was a dusty bookcase stretching across the back wall that looked like it had been untouched for years. Strewn on the floor were several cushions of various faded colors and patterns. Dingy tee-shirted adolescent boys in cut-off pants sprawled over them in various positions of relaxation, looking very much like lazy house cats.

The floor had plenty of room to dance and carouse. Two matching sofa chairs in the same condition as the couch were in the two right corners. Gary, a large, looming black-haired boy, occupied the one next to the front door. Stephanie shook her head. *It's amazing what I can see now that I'm not high.* The decrepitude of the room seemed to meld with the common personality of the teenagers to produce a grayish gloom. It wasn't a vision like the gray arm, but it was just as uncomfortable.

Gary cheered. "Hey, everyone, it's Stephanie!"

One lusty looking boy on the floor patronized him. "Gary, the life of the party has arrived."

Another boy from the couch hollered, "Woohoo! Shake it, Fanie, shake it!" Stephanie twirled around and shook her bottom. Her hips flared out nicely from her thin waist, and her hind parts formed tightly but fully into an upside-down heart shape. They could see how her flesh jiggled through her tight black pants. All the boys' eyes narrowed.

Another hungry boy from the floor shouted, "GARY, it's not fair, you've been keeping too much woman for yourself!"

But Gary sneered and then laughed. "All you guys, you just keep your eyes on, but your hands off my woman!"

But another protested. "Hey Gary, C'mon, you're keepin' 'em all for yourself."

But Stephanie chimed in with a not so sexy voice with an edge to it. "Hey boys, don't you think I have a say in it?"

They all just shared a knowing laugh that felt like sandpaper on her skin. This night was the same as every other.

Stephanie was accustomed to their innuendos, but this evening she felt less tolerant. Something seemed to be in the room with them just out of her sight and hearing.

She shrugged it all off and changed the subject. "Hi, Karen!

Tracy! Where are the other girls?"

Tracy was obviously high. Her head leaned back on the couch and her legs splayed over the table, but she managed to speak to the ceiling. "Oh, they decided to stay home tonight."

"Yeah, they didn't want to stay out late," Karen said in her sickeningly sweet voice.

Stephanie felt a wave of nausea spread through her as she looked at Tracy, and a pain streaked across her heart as sadness fell like a weight upon her. She turned away, leaned over hugging Gary, her boyfriend of a year now, and gave him a kiss on the mouth before turning back to the couch. "That's a laugh, as I've never known them to be early birds before!" Stephanie pushed her long red hair behind her shoulders to reveal the shape of her breasts in her tight, pink tank top. The firmness of her naked tummy accentuated their prominence.

One of the boys on the floor near her peered up and howled as the others quickly cheered their agreement. "Hey Gary, you know Fanie's got the best body out of all these girls. She's tight."

Gary gave his official approval to the line of conversation, this was *his* woman and *his* gang. He added his expert opinion. "Yeah, I *know*, I like her top, the way they move even under her shirt, and they have *perfect* shape. Hey, Fanie! Do like Camille did on stage last week!"

Stephanie grabbed herself and squeezed, then squinting her eyes, she began flaunting her bosom by shaking her shoulders. "Well, some girls got it, and some don't. That's why I wear everything *tight*, so everyone *knows I got it.*" She smiled seductively. Those were Camille's words.

The cheering was intense.

"Yeah, make 'em bounce some more!" They all urged her, so she shook her shoulders again.

Another boy yelled out, "I like her ass. She's only fourteen, but she's *all* woman, tight but full, full but not dumpy. I could just put my hands around her skinny little waist and lift her right . . ."

Another boy cackled with leering eyes, "Hey, where else you got piercings?" His imagination created images from what Gary had told him.

Stephanie poured it on. "Hey, wouldn't you like to know? Maybe I'll show you some time." Her thoughts seemed so clear. *These poor, pitiful, horny boys. It's so much fun to tease them and leave them. At least a woman has* some power *over a man.*

Gary spoke sternly, "I think I have a say in that." It was a matter of control and for the first time, he sensed something in her that wasn't in his control. Karen had warned him that Stephanie would dump him.

Stephanie spoke to her boyfriend, the *leader* of the gang, as if he were a little child, "Oh Gary, are you planning on marrying me? There *are* girls that even marry at fourteen. And I *am* mature for my age. But *I* decide when and what I do."

Gary mysteriously backed down. "Sure, sure, Fanie! Of course you do. Hey, c'mon, we got some *great* stuff!"

Stephanie raised an eyebrow at his meekness but then brushed it aside 'cause it was so out of character.

"Yeah, Stephanie, it's making me soooar!" Tracy rolled her head around.

Stephanie tried not to be obvious in her disapproval. She worried Tracy might tell them she quit so she stared at Tracy, saying, "Maybe later, I . . ."

Karen broke in with her sweet voice, "Oh, what's this? The queen of the whores has become too good to sail with us?" The sugariness of her tone conflicted with the meanness of her words.

Stephanie began to ponder it. *Why would she call me that?* She began to ask her, "Karen…" But Gary broke her concentration when he pressed the cold glass with the drug in it on the back of her neck and Stephanie jumped.

After she took the glass, he explained Karen's remark away as he turned and sat back down, "Oh don't mind Karen, she's just jealous of you. Go ahead, drink up, and make us all feel better."

All eyes were glued to her every move, everywhere. Stephanie looked down into the cloudy mixture in the glass.

One instant her hand struggled not to drop it, and in the next moment not to raise it to her mouth. *Oh no, it's so difficult. No wonder Tracy broke her word.* She looked at Tracy sprawled on the couch, then down into the glass again. *She looks cloudy, just like the glass. Doesn't she remember the monster eating from the feet up?* Stephanie's hand felt heavy in holding it. *If I drink this then Tracy will know I've broken my word, too! All I've worked on . . . it'll all be for nothing. I'd be nothing but a big lie . . . then how could I help anyone?* Stephanie took some ice out of the glass and rubbed it on her bare tummy. "Thank you Gary, you're a true gentleman. Oh, the ice feels so good, it's *hot* outside . . . mmmmm."

Gary growled as he studied her. "You're supposed to drink it, not rub it on your body."

But she looked alluringly at him to subdue him, "Come 'ere, so I can whisper in your ear." Stephanie drew him with her seductive eyes.

The mob of boys went crazy with lust as Gary stood up and stretched to show off and then went over to her.

She whispered, "It's so you can lick it off later. I'll drink after I'm cooled down."

Gary shouted out his orders, "Hey, you guys! Shut the drapes, we don't want anyone sneaking a peek."

"Sure, Gary!"

Stephanie headed over to a large palm houseplant in front of the bay windows in the right wall. "Oh, what a beautiful plant, what kind is it?" She raptly inspected it, delicately touching the leaves and walking around behind it.

Gary was annoyed, spitting out his reply, "How should I know? It's the same dumb old plant my folk's been having for years. You've never noticed it before?"

"Look, I can almost hide myself behind it."

"Yeah, yeah, great, c'mon out from there, we've all been waiting!" It was a command.

"Whooo, whacha put in this drink?" Stephanie seemed to swoon while behind her plant cover. She rustled the plant and it sounded as if a wind had blown through it, making a loud staticky noise.

"Ahhh, just Angel's Seed. The same old thing," a floor boy hollered as he stretched provocatively.

Stephanie thought to herself. *Oh well, thank God for plants, anyway. I wonder if this plant is going to get high. I'll have to tell Tracy later that I really didn't drink it. But how would she believe me? I know she can quit, I just know it.*

Karen sounded so very sweet, even sweeter than usual. She was relieved Stephanie had drunk the whole glass, "Hey Stephanie, we've been thinking."

Stephanie gurgled trying her best to act high. "Oh no, Karen, are you sure that's safe?"

"Oh yeah, real safe. I told the boys here that even though you're the hottest looking around, I'm the hottest action, but they don't believe me." The disappointment in her voice was clear.

The two girls were silent, challenging each other in their silence.

Karen broke it with enthusiasm. "Let's vote."

There was one unanimous, rousing acclamation from the crowd. "Yeah!"

But then Tracy cried out. "Oh no, I just remembered, I'm gonna get killed." *I can't deal with this!*

Stephanie hoped this would bring a change of atmosphere. "What, Tracy?"

"My folks told me they wanted to take me somewhere in twenty minutes."

Gary cursed. "Damn! Just skip out!"

"If I don't show up, they'll come here looking for me."

"OK then, we don't need your vote anyway." he said as he gestured his hand shooing her toward the door, a command for Tracy to leave.

Stephanie hurried out from behind the plant, set the empty glass down on an end table near Gary and started towards her. "You know what, Tracy? I'd better walk you home, it's late!"

"That's OK, Fanie, I'll be fine." Tracy briefly glanced up at her finding it difficult to make eye contact then rushed out the door hanging her head. *I can't interfere, I just can't!*

For a split second, that seemed much longer, Stephanie perceived something as if she were standing above it all, and seeing a much larger picture. *Eyes . . . eyes . . . eyes . . . there's something in Tracy's eyes that's making the hairs on the back of my neck stand up. I know she's ashamed of disappointing me, but there's something different in Karen's eyes too, although I know she hates me. Well, the boys always look that way. Still, something's not right!*

A boy on the couch yelled out. "Hey, Fanie! Ya lost in thought again? C'mon, let loose, you're not yourself tonight. Ya need another glass?" he asked while holding the one in his hand up.

Stephanie felt she needed to remove herself from their attention, and would have gone home except she didn't want to face her mother for being out for so long. *Besides, I just don't feel like having Mom's* boyfriend *make eyes at me tonight.* She was just going to crash here all night as she had so many times before.

"Oh, I can barely stand up now, so I'm just gonna go over to the chair and take a nap for a while."

Gary responded sweetly from his sofa chair. "Yeah, yeah, after we have the *contest.* You don't expect to just come here and then go to sleep do you? This isn't a hotel!"

Her make believe demeanor vanished, because there was no mistaking the meaning of his tone. Her vision was bringing her something she couldn't quite understand, but she spoke as sober as she ever was. "What are you talking about Gary?"

"You do me *first* and then the other guys and then we'll vote on whose better, you or Karen."

Stephanie froze and her mouth dropped open. She knew all of these guys and Karen and they knew her. How could they expect this? They were like family to her.

"See, I told you she's all talk." Karen chided.

Stephanie couldn't tell if she was kidding or serious, but something stern pushed words out of her mouth. "OK guys, that's not funny, just back off," she said as she reached out her arms as if to balance, staggering toward the empty sofa chair in the far right corner. *Maybe they'll leave me alone if I act too stoned to comply.*

Gary called out from his corner by the door, "Hey, what's the difference? It's not like you're a virgin or anything. In fact,

I know at *least* two other guys who've had you, and I hear you're looking for more!"

Stephanie was sober again. "*What?*"

But he jibed right back. "C'mon, you don't think guys talk just like girls?"

Her retort was even sharper. "Then ask *them* to vote," she snapped back as she sat down distancing herself from them on the other dingy orangish sofa chair, with all eyes intently on *her*. She was beginning to feel sick inside, her stomach was in a knot, and her heart began pounding. She felt a presence all around that was greater than her, than all of them, and it wasn't a good presence.

Karen again broke the silence with smugness and challenge. "I can't believe Gary even touched you after you went with *them*. Prove you're worth it!"

Stephanie made up her mind. Even home was better than *this*. "Forget it, I'm outta here." She bolted for the door as intense fear, fear like she had never known before seemed to swallow her from out of nowhere. But she didn't get more than three steps before she yelled like an escaping animal caught by a predator, when Gary's meaty hand grabbed her delicate neck by the throat. Meanness poured from his eyes into hers, as she looked for the very first time into their depths and then quickly looked away.

"You'll leave when I say you'll leave!"

"Can't . . . breathe! You're . . . cho . . cho . . . king me." As her bladder spasmed, she tried to press her shaking legs together but the loud ringing in her ears also scared her. Then she saw that same transparent gray arm shimmering over Gary's head, and her knees buckled as he held her up by the throat. She remembered the playground and knew something terrible was really going to happen to her.

Everyone just stared with a hunger that seemed otherworldly, waiting to see what would happen next. Thoughts, feelings, impressions instantly flooded her, but through that overwhelming sense of evil a single thought cried as she searched for a shred of humanity. *This can't be happening*! *They all know me . . . I* know *them. I don't have anybody else.*

Gary commanded her in a deathlike tone. "Take your hands off my hand and look into my eyes!"

She dropped her hands helplessly to her sides, his large body looming over hers. His steady commanding voice seemed possessed of a power and confidence Stephanie had never heard him use before. She suddenly knew the evil presence in the room was infusing him . . . infusing them all. For the first time she began to realize just how accurate her odd perceptions really were . . . but it was too late.

Gary's eyes opened wide as he stood eye-to-eye with Stephanie, and spoke slowly and commandingly, "You . . . Will . . . Do . . . Whatever . . . I . . . Say!" He shook her by the throat for each word to deepen the point. She felt abandoned, worse than when her father left years ago, making her feel even smaller than that now, smaller than she had ever been before.

"OK. Can I . . . go to the . . . bathroom first, *please?*" She didn't know if she would simply fall to the floor when he let her go, as she didn't feel like she had the strength to stand.

"Yeah, Gary! Let her go first," one of the hungry boys said as he began undoing himself.

"GO! But don't be too long!" he ordered as he yanked his hand away, leaving the impression of his fingers on her neck. She almost collapsed in front of him, but she was too scared to do so. She wanted to run to the bathroom, but didn't have the strength. As she slowly walked past everyone, she wanted to die. She tried to will her heart to stop beating. *Just stop! Please just stop beating!* She could feel them all watching her. Her insides desperately wanted to crawl out of her body and disappear, to never exist. *To never exist is better than this.*

The bathroom was down a hallway, off the left corner of the living room. She knew they watched her to make sure she went in. As she went down the hall, her hands went to her mouth and she heard herself whisper her thoughts, *Brothers and sisters...* Excitement began to tingle through the people in the room. Karen's smile was ear-to-ear as she followed Stephanie's every move, relishing in her perverted empathy.

Stephanie locked herself in the bathroom, but knew that it was no defense. Quickly she spun around-and-around, like a caged animal. Dizzied, she threw her hands to her head. There was no escape. She cowered, staring at the window. This part of the house was on the second floor, so the window would be no help. She spun around and around again, the window, the door, the window, the door . . . then she collapsed to her knees between the reeking toilet and the brown stained tub, and the smell of old urine stung her nose. Then she thought, prayed, and wept out loud, trying to keep herself from losing her mind. She looked up at the window, but knew it was too far down.

Help. I could call for help. *No, that wouldn't do any good. They'd be through the door in no time before anyone could help, and I doubt anyone could even hear me this far away. He'd* kill *me.* Then she got up and pushed the window open wide and swung her leg over the ledge, leaning herself halfway out, straining to see, but there was nothing but deep shadow below, so dark she couldn't see the ground at all, couldn't tell how far a drop it really was. She tried to force herself to jump into the blackness, but her stomach lurched. Then the window lost its hold and fell, hitting her in the back. She whimpered from the pain of everything and as she pulled herself back into the room, so too passed any glimmer of hope.

Falling back down on the filthy bathroom floor, caked in blackened, greasy dirt, she felt her life ending. A cry from her depths took her over as it poured itself out while she rocked back-and-forth. "Oh God, oh no, oh no, what have I done? What have I got myself into? If this happens to me I'll be nothing, nothing at all. Oh God help me. *Oh God!*"

She kept rocking herself back-and-forth, losing her mind to the repeated prayer. Her beautiful red hair spread across the obscene bathroom floor.

That same night, Vaughn and Waverly had talked for a long time until they finally laid down on the twin beds. Though Vaughn slept over often, now he couldn't seem to relax so he rolled onto his stomach to begin his unique form of meditation. He shoved a pillow under his belly for support, rested his forehead on the back of his hands and began to gently bump his head up and down. Up-and-down, up-and-down his head moved until the outside world vanished. . .

Blackness everywhere, an endless tunnel with a gray floor that shined a gray light is all that exists. No distinct sound. No distinct voice, but Vaughn knew he had to walk down that tunnel. Walking, walking, forever… Nothing changed. He cried out, "Why am I here?" The gray floor split under his feet, and he jumped back to avoid falling into the deep blackness. Swirls of black essence, blacker than his surroundings, rose from the crack in the floor; it fascinated him. A human heart as big as an elephant descended from up above. Beating, beating, beating. The black essence swirled around the heart. The heart twisted. It cried. It howled. It changed. It blew apart. The pieces fell into the crack in the floor. The floor closed up and Vaughn walked on.

Another human heart descended. Beating, beating . . . He lost count of how many hearts he saw just like the ones before, and then one descended that didn't die, but changed, becoming grotesque as the black essence melded with it. Its sound terrified. It roared like a lion. It floated toward Vaughn, and he knew it called to him. *Fear*. Vaughn cried out, "What do you want?" It wanted him. He shrieked, "What are you?"

"I'm you!" the heart spoke from within him. Vaughn fell backwards. "No!" he screamed as he back peddled with hands and feet in a crab walk. The grotesque heart slowly closed in.

There was no hope. Every beat seemed to suck in additional blackness.

Vaughn stopped. Shame filled him from fleeing from such abomination. It had no right to make him feel so small. *What's the point in running? Will this endless fear give me* life*? Will I run* forever*? There's no winning this way.* He felt the injustice of it. *Better to die fighting, being what you are, than lose the battle from within.* Rule one, *The Art of Fighting*.

Anger flooded him. He became blacker than the blackness in the heart. His level voice was menacing, "I won't be you." He stood up, and the heart stopped its advance. Vaughn's teeth clenched, and his muscles tightened, summoning all their strength. "DIE," he shouted as he lunged into the abomination. The heart vanished.

A light appeared in the distance. Though it was far away, he could see into it. "Help me. Help me," wailed a little girl no more than five years old. Her mother lay in bloody pieces on the forest floor. The blackness rose from the earth, and began to surround the little girl. "No. No!" Vaughn cried as he came out of his meditation.

Or was he out of it? A voice inside of him, but outside as well, "Save the child, save the world." And his inner ear strained to hear more, but he couldn't find where to listen. *Am I awake yet?*

It wasn't a dream. He often fell asleep meditating, but this wasn't a dream. *What is it?* He urgently wanted to climb back into the trance and save that little girl . . . *but from what?*

Stephanie had locked herself in the bathroom, but knew that was no defense, just a stall tactic to delay the inevitable. Quickly she spun around-and-around like a caged animal. She cowered and stared at the window. Again she spun around, her mind fretfully racing between . . . *The window, the door, the window, the door . . . there's NO ESCAPE!* All she could now see was how her own wanton lust had delivered her to . . . *But I wanted to help them, I didn't even take the drug. . . maybe I should have . . . Oh God!*

Help. I could call for help. No, they would be through the door in no time, if anyone could even hear me this far away. He'd kill *me!* Then she got up, pushed the window open wide, swung her leg over the ledge and leaned halfway out. It was so dark down below; she couldn't even see the ground. She strained her eyes, but dizziness overwhelmed her. Memory of her dream of being swallowed into the monster's deep, tormenting blackness tore mercilessly at her. Weeping, she ordered herself, *Jump . . . Jump, idiot! Oh God, I can't . . . I just can't!* The window lost its hold and fell, hitting her in the back, sending sharp pains through her shoulders. Jerking herself back in, she hit her head on the fallen window bringing more tears to her eyes. *That's what I get for being* a *coward.* And as she slumped to the floor, so too passed any glimmer of hope. *Was there ever any hope at all for me?*

Kneeling on the filthy bathroom floor; caked in blackened, greasy dirt, she began to rock herself back-and-forth. Her life was ending. *But why does it have to take so long? Oh*

God, what if they don't kill me? No, they have *to, I'll* make *them!* Her pronouncement stung her heart.

Gary was getting impatient, but everyone knew women always take a while in the bathroom. *Besides, if I let her wait a little longer, it'll just increase her torture.*

Rocking, rocking, rocking . . . she finally surrendered to her fate. Suddenly, she felt how *precious* her life was. Memories of her shelter, of being thankful...made everything hurt that much more. *If they don't kill me, would I be able survive such a thing?*

"Oh God, oh no, oh no, *what have I done*? What have I gotten myself into? If this happens to me I'll be nothing, nothing at all. OH, GOD! HELP ME, OH GOD!"

She rocked herself forward-and-back, forward and back, over-and-over again, losing her mind to the repeated prayer. Her beautiful red hair spread across the obscene bathroom floor. A strange scraping sound registered in her ears but not in her mind. Another sound grew more insistent. Finally, she looked up from where she knelt.

"Huh, what?" A sound from the window!

"Hey! *Hey*, get up off the floor and open the window some more. I can't hang like this forever!"

Dazed from her torments all she could muster was ask, "What? Who are you?" She called through the six inch gap in the window where a pair of hands had grabbed hold of the inside sill.

Annoyed at the ridiculous question, given the situation, the voice responded in an insistent whisper, "Someone who's going to fall if you don't let me stick my head in." Her prayer had stabbed him in his heart. Her pains had invaded him, giving him an extra sense of urgency.

It worked, she became meek to him. "OK" Realizing the speaker couldn't be someone from the other room, Stephanie lifted the window as quietly as possible. In popped muscular arms sticking out from a white undershirt. There was a presence about him, and she couldn't help but study his features. His head was full of somewhat short, wavy, charcoal-brown hair, almost but not really black, and piercing eyes that were so dark-brown they also could have been black. It was a handsome face for a boy with the beginnings of a fine-haired mustache that seemed more like a shadow above his lip. An intense face of balanced proportions stared at her, but she honestly couldn't remember ever seeing him and backed away a bit, questioning, "Do I know you?"

"I've seen you around." He had actually only glimpsed her once before, outside the school building acting whorish with some of the very people she was now with. It seemed now she was facing the consequences but . . . there was something different about her . . . and that *prayer!*

"What are you doing here?" she heard herself say.

"Well, I couldn't sleep, and from the looks of it, I guess I'm here to answer your prayer!"

Tears filled her eyes and a lump rose in her throat. "Huh? But how?"

He shook his head, opening his eyes wide in amazement. "I don't know myself. I just had this terrible feeling I had to come here. In the ice-cream shop, I overheard a couple guys snickering about the party, but I couldn't quite tell what they were talking about. *It just didn't feel right.* I just couldn't stay away, but knew I wouldn't be welcome. Then, just as I came up to the house, I saw you look like you wanted to jump out the window! *Oh God,* I said to myself. *Why would she want to do that?* Then, that same feeling I had that sent me here, sent me around the house, looking for something, anything, I didn't know exactly what. Then I saw an old ladder lying against the back of the house, so I started to climb up and heard you crying."

She rushed to squeeze beside him and looked out the window, but didn't see the ladder. He was just hanging from the window ledge.

"*What ladder?*"

"I'm standing on the very top rung. It's dark down here, so you can't see it. I grabbed hold of the spaces between the bricks to pull myself up the rest of the way."

She couldn't imagine how she could get to a ladder she couldn't even see. She was far too short and she couldn't see where to hold on. She pulled back out of the window to face him.

"But . . . but, what do you want me to do?" Terror and helplessness consumed her as she whined.

His tone aggressively challenged her, "What do *you* want to do?"

At first it drew a blank. But as she looked into his piercing eyes, eyes that seemed to reach into the depths of her soul and pull something up, all of a sudden she heard herself speak out, "I want to *get the hell out of here.*"

"Alright then, I'm going to climb part way down, and then you climb out and put your feet on my shoulders. I'll ease down and guide your feet to the ladder."

"WHAT?"

"*Shhh! Keep your voice down.*"

"Hey, what's going on in there?" Gary shouted.

She whirled toward the closed door and spoke loudly through it. "Spider, a spider was climbing up the wall!"

"You've got TWO minutes!"

She turned back to the young man, doubting whether he could support her weight. "You're . . . you're small."

He challenged her again. "Yeah? Well, if you think you can climb down by yourself . . ."

She was timid again. "No, I can't see where to climb to, besides, I know I'm not strong enough to hang for long."

"Yeah, well, I *am* strong." She pushed her head beside him again and looked down as he hung there on the ledge. "Look, I'll climb down a couple of rungs. My shoulders will still be higher than the top rung. You put your weight on my shoulders and I'll ease down until your feet are even with the top rung and I'll guide them onto it. All you have to do is find something to hold onto to keep balance. I can do this. I know I can. You can too!"

"ONE minute!"

She could see the rest of his stature past the window and thought to herself, again. *How could he support all my weight?* "But . . . but, you're small!"

He challenged her yet another time. "Yeah, and you've got a stupid ring in your nose. Compared to you, I'm not small.

Besides, I'm strong, *very strong,* and I've got strength people don't even believe!"

She pulled her head back in to face him, and like some little child, she stopped only about six inches from his face, which allowed her to feel his presence. With tears streaming down her cheeks and trembling, she whined, "I'm scared," then she pushed her white knuckles to her mouth, as her eyes riveted on the boy's eyes.

He reached out a hand and took her arm. "So am I," he retorted.

But she didn't take the answer for comfort and whined again. "You are? But you said you were strong."

But he countered with sharpness. "I'm strong, but I'm not an *idiot.* I can't beat all those guys. Will you *come on?"*

"Time's up!" Gary boomed as he strode down the hallway toward the bathroom. It had been way more than two minutes but he figured her prolonged anguish would make her exceptionally enjoyable.

The next thing the young knight knew, she was pushing him out the window. He grabbed a crevice for support and one foot after the other descended to the second rung. Keeping his back straight and belly pressed against the wall for balance, his feet descended another rung. Now, both hands tightly grabbed the jagged top of the ladder as he descended yet another rung. With the top of the ladder now even with his waist his balance was restored. "C'mon!" Her feet set down on his shoulders. *I'm really doing this. "Oh God,"* she whimpered, as she dreaded the next step. They could hear the bathroom door being pounded.

Vaughn knew. *One more rung and I'll guide her feet onto the ladder.* As his left foot descended to the next rung, her full weight fell on him and caused his fingers to hold on like vice grips to the ladder's rails. He began lowering his right foot, but then he started to shake. "*Oh GOD,*" she cried as she felt it, but he went slowly to ensure his foot made it safety to the next rung. Her fingers frantically clawed into crevices to hold her precarious balance as the banging on the door intensified.

"OK, I'm gonna lower my shoulder a bit so you can slide your right foot forward to the top rung." He began leaning forward, rounding his shoulders to help her and then she screamed, as her stomach cringed and her feet slipped off behind him. In that fraction of a second, she felt her fingers begin to slip off the loose bricks.

In that instant, time seemed to lengthen. Instinctively, instantly, his hands grabbed the rails with all his might as he leaned forward and stuck out his backside, just as her fingers lost their grip on the crevices between the bricks. As he felt how swift she fell, he braced for her full impact, gritting his teeth. Her chest smacked down onto his inclined back, and her arms instinctively wrapped around his neck in a death grip. But her momentum pulled the ladder backwards away from the wall, and sensing this, he tightened his grip even more, immediately pushing with his legs, and flattening himself against the moving ladder. His heart pounded as his mind fought the paralyzing fear of falling. The ladder went totally vertical. A sinking, helpless feeling consumed him, as the upright ladder seemed to hover there for an eternity. Then the ladder teetered a shade more backwards. "*OH GOD,*" she screamed, squeezing his neck so tightly, pains shot through his arms and legs. Unbelievably, in the next instant, as if in slow motion, the ladder shifted forward just a bit, then gathered speed, and then banged back against the wall, jarring their insides. She wasted no time wrapping her legs around his waist, still squeezing his neck for dear life. He ignored the pain of her grip. They were motionless, speechless, in disbelief as their hearts pounded. Vaughn could feel her beating heart against his back, and she could feel his heart through her arms.

Vaughn ultimately broke the silence. "Not so tight, I can't breathe." She loosened her hold around his neck, slightly. He was aware of his thoughts, *I can feel her breasts mashed against my back and her legs wrapped around my waist . . . she's not weak.* Vaughn descended the ladder with her still clinging to him for dear life. Once back on the ground, he rasped. "OK, ease off me now!" He bent his knees so her feet could touch down, but her hands wouldn't respond to her mental command to let go. He gently helped her loosen her grip and then promptly grabbed her hand and pulled her into a run.

"She's gone!" Gary wailed.

"What?" An angry, very frustrated boy yelled back.

Gary was peering out the window as a car's distant headlights passed by. "DOWN THERE WITH . . . I can't believe it!" Gary shouted orders. "Get them! Find them! Spread out!" They dispersed through the city block where Gary saw them run.

As Master GrrraGagag peered through the dirty blue orb at Stephanie fleeing his trap, he lost control of himself, something he never really did before. His roar terrified his underling. "If it wasn't for you, *underling*, I would have had the time to see this coming." He smashed his underling against one wall and then the other, and the other. But Scraback gladly took the punishment, as his plan was still intact!

"Masterrrrr, no! There's still plenty chance to make things better! I, I . . . have an idea!"

CHAPTER 3

Scraback's and Stephanie's Beginnings

Alpha Code of Ethics and Bylaws of Behavior *(Revised by advanced underling Scraback and duly approved by the* ***Father****)*

Rule One: *When the Earth's humans are purged of all glow, we shall be able to reclaim our Earth, since glow will no longer have any connection to reality, it will therefore become unreal, since ALL REALITY IS CONNECTED.*

First definition: HUMAN *— 1. A being that bridges the three parts of reality: The physical. Our ethereal. The glow; 2. A general resource – A means through which we can create all forms of real life for us to mingle with, to pleasure with, to consume; 3. Food.*

Yesterday, Master GrrraGagag had turned various shades of sickly, dark gray while peering into the dirty, blue orb. He couldn't let the *glow* free itself in her. Floating before the orb, his long, thick, serpentine body slowly coiled and uncoiled. His arm-like appendage, just below his sizable bulbous head, slowly reached out, drew in and reached out. His huge, central, glistening black Eye strained. He had not had this kind of trouble since he graduated to be Alpha, and that was a very, very long time ago. The last thing he wanted was interruption, but it seemed that now he had yet another assignment to teach. He didn't want any more underlings. His small mouth, used for communication only, flattened when his new student appeared in his ethereal doorway.

Master GrrraGagag considered how to treat this new pest. The underling was only half his size having only fed on the leftovers. But his head, with the all-important central Eye, was near to his same size. After consumption, the body grew much faster than the head.

The best description of Alpha relationships would be serious chickens. Not the cliché of cowardliness, but the all-important pecking order. Every Alpha had its current position in hierarchy because they couldn't force themselves any higher, but were able to keep the rest below. At the top, of course, was the mysterious Father whom everyone remembers as always being there.

Master GrrraGagag had long since decided to play the role of a temperamental spirit, an unpredictable Alpha given to outbursts. Not only did he find it fun to terrorize his students, it also kept all the other Alphas from understanding his cold, highly rational, and calculating nature. In fact, his hyperbolic act disgusted them and convinced them that he was nothing more than a cheesy human's demon stereotype, which was fine for the humans to believe, but insulting to see any Alpha really act that way. Yet, true enough, everything he did to humans or Alphas had a reason, including the way he did it. But unknown to him, his new student, pound for pound of ethereal essence, possessed just as much deviousness as he. The question Scraback asked himself was whether he could outsmart his Master. From birth, Scraback decided he would play the buffoon. In fact, he played it so well, his sire, High Councilor Premion, was ashamed of him. Having made himself less than unremarkable, no one paid him any mind when he was given the task of revising the old Alpha handbook.

Master GrrraGagag's student immediately rushed upon him and wanted to know what was going on. He rushed up so quickly that he knocked into his new Master and bounced off. Alpha had solid and ethereal properties within their realm. Master GrrraGagag, having developed over thousands of years, hardly flinched. If the High Councilor hadn't been still floating in the doorway, seeming to hide a snicker, GrrraGagag would have instantly responded to the clumsy insult. Instead, they faced off at each other inside the Alpha's personal, dark gray ethereal room. His student seemed to be dazed. For the sake of High Councilor Premion who brought him, Master GrrraGagag decided to put on a show. *Be polite and show him the Earth vision inside the orb,* he told himself.

"Alright, Scraback, I've had enough of all this from these impudent kids." Scraback acted like an earth child, wild with excitement. He could tell right away this would be most irksome to this tired *old* looking Alpha who was his new Master.

"Master GrrraGagag, are you going to interfere? Lower your awesome Eye and consume someone?" Scraback bounced up and down enthusiastically as he asked. But he had to scold himself severely to keep himself from laughing, knowing the effect his role-playing would eventually have on his Master.

His Master paid him no mind. "No, but I'm going to make sure this little trollop here," he pointed with his tail into the orb vision at one of two girls, a red haired girl, sitting on a playground bench talking, "doesn't *think* her way out of anything else. I'm tired of all this thinking. What do they think they are, anyway?"

"Master, how will you intervene?" He squeezed between his Master and the dirty blue orb.

"Well first, let's make sure that our little *idiots* down there aren't going to fail all on their own. But if not, I'll show you how to place thoughts and feelings into them, subtly, so no one is alarmed. Actually, Gary here," his tail pointed again as he continued, "likes it when I'm more direct."

Scraback winked his Eye, letting his Master think he was surprised though he already knew these things from study. "So, you've been doing this to him before?"

"I've been training him because I never know when I might need someone to just immediately follow a thought I give them. He's so in tune to reality that he sees no difference between his thoughts and feelings and mine."

"That's wonderful, Master. I can't wait to learn!"

"Watch, as I extend my Eye over Gary's tree."

When the High Councilor saw how absorbed they were in teaching and learning, he left. Master GrrraGagag knew he wouldn't be back for a very long time, if at all. He pushed the underling aside and turned angrily to face him. He wasted no time starting the lesson, and asked, "Do *we* have any direct connection to the *glow*?"

Master GrrraGagag had uncoiled a bit to hover menacingly above his trainee but Scraback's answer was quick and confident, he even straightened himself though just a bit, but not to appear challenging. "None."

"Very good." GrrraGagag lowered back to Eye level and his tone almost hinted at congeniality. "Now do you see the utter importance of rule one and why it is number one?"

"I understand it in theory, Master GrrraGagag." Scraback's Eye twitched nervously.

Master GrrraGagag squinted at him, sending him the signal that he noticed the twitch and did not approve but kept on with the lesson at the same time.

"The humans are connected through the ethereal to us. It is possible for them to see usssss. They connect us to the *glow*. But, if no *glow* in humans, then no connection to us, if no connection to us, then *glow* becomes unreal *since?*" GrrraGagag's Eye quickly closed the distance between them upon inflecting his last word.

But Scraback held his ground and suppressed his twitch, exuding confidence. "All reality is connected."

After hearing the correct answer, Master GrrraGagag eased away for a few seconds studying him, thinking of where to strike next. GrrraGagag's massive Eye quickly returned to just inches away from Scraback's, intending his threat to be felt in his every ethereal fiber. The Eye was used for seeing, *and consumption*. Master GrrraGagag had grown quite large from consuming more than but a few souls and Alphas! "Why is there no connection between the glow and us?"

Scraback's reply was quick and fearful. "Because the glow . . ." GrrraGagag's threat had worked. His snarl sent shock waves through Scraback's form and it rippled with fear. "What *inflection* are you supposed to use when saying that *word*?"

Inflections were instituted long ago. They were now considered a trivial matter born out of overreaction from worser times. Master GrrraGagag was the only Alpha known to enforce them still but he knew underlings were easily caught by them, even though he was sure they were forewarned. It's just too difficult to watch ones speech for such things. The threat had helped to distract Scraback further.

"Forgive me Master GrrraGagag, forgive me . . . *glow, glow, GLOW*." The Master folded his tail into his arm and tapped. The tapping always had an unnerving affect. And so, the proper terrorization of this underling had begun. It would make for a small diversion, in light of GrrraGagag's other pressing problem. But he already had plans for how to correct the girl.

"Better. Proceed."

"There is no connection between the *glow* and us because *glow* is an aberration, it is not understandable. It is a corruption of reality that disturbs our peace. It is an insult to our ever-present ethereal being. There is an ancient prophecy, of disreputable origin, that says one day *glow* will separate us from reality and make us unreal."

Tap, tap, tap went the Master's tail. "All these words you have learned in lessons, but you are here to learn from me by experience. Look here and tell me *exactly* what you see, from the smallest detail, don't leave anything out, do you hear me Scraback? I'm not peering into the deepness of your Eye for nothing. Leaving out a single detail could cost us gravely."

Scraback decided to be encouraged by his Master's effort and he showed his enthusiasm. He turned to where he was directed, as he was eager to learn. But it was also time for him to pay his Master back for the abuse. "Yes Sir, Master GrrraGagag. Ahhhhh, I have heard tell of this magnificent, ancient device."

GrrraGagag growled menacingly, because he hated excursions away from his exact directions. Scraback knew this however, as he had researched his new Master before he met him.

"Yes, Sir, Master, sorry! I see a three dimensional oval, like the shape of things I've studied from the earth called eggs, except both ends are equal. Its dirty blue in color, yet seems to be clear, and about as wide as my vision can see from side-to-side when I stare straight at it. It seems to be floating before us in the middle of your room, and seems to be only made out of that dirty blue light." Scraback paused at his Master's threat then shrank back as he added. "Sir, why are you lowering your Eye at me?"

His Master growled at him again. "Look deeper."

But like all students who have been intimidated too much, the affect was wearing off quickly. As Scraback bent toward the blue orb, he reminded himself to act a bit more scared than he really felt. The very fact that his Master delighted in terrorizing him could be used to his advantage against GrrraGagag, as it meant Scraback could do things, then later predict his Master's response. *Predictability is a weakness,* he thought. *But figuring out how to use it is another thing.* "Uhhhh, I see . . . an endless forest! It just appeared inside the ancient egg. Except for the left over blue coloration, I see endless trees. Is that funny, Master?" Scraback thought he was being mocked by his Master.

Master GrrraGagag did something actually for the first time. "I smile because you were able to see the first step, and because you will ask me your next question." Master GrrraGagag knew it was far more affective to mix in a little kindness. It lowered their guard, yet increased the terror. *This* student *will come to* hate *my kindness just as much as my terror.* He solaced himself with his prognosis.

Scraback shook himself when he realized his Master may truly be pleased with him. He couldn't shake the terrible fear of his unpredictability and scorn, but what good would it do to doubt his Master's new found pleasantness. "Well, why do I see a forest? I had heard that this device sees all of mankind, past, present and future . . ."

Scorn erupted once more followed by a severe growl. "Never say that word, *never!* Do you hear? This device sees the past because it existed already, and it sees the *present* because it exists now, but there is *no* beyond. The present is for us to steer so that the *present* will be pleasing to us."

Scraback quickly refocused. "Master GrrraGagag, how can we see the past?"

Upon hearing the question, almost like an automatic switch, his Master reentered his teaching mode. "Our Existence enfolds what man calls the physical. To its utmost reaches, we reach beyond. Long ago, our Great Father set a device wrapped around the edges of mankind's physical existence. All light, sound and sensation is recorded by it and fed into this device here that you see. The front line of trees is the present, and those further back are those lost to mortal time." He smiled at his last pronouncement.

"But where are the men?"

GrrraGagag smiled at that question, too, and anticipated his underling's reaction when he saw the answer. "Reach out with your arm and touch a tree, or wave your arm across an area."

As Scraback waved, he jumped back. "Aha! The trees become men, but . . ."

"Because it's easier to tell what's important about man if we see them as trees. Our Father's wisdom has proven itself always. Because it's not their body we're interested in, but what goes on in their thoughts and emotions, what they call their mind and heart, and as these are complex, they are better represented by a tree and its relationship of roots, trunk, and branches. Wave your arm again to turn them back to trees then I will show you."

Scraback was overcome by the new knowledge his Master had given him, but the question was would it be better to try to consume GrrraGagag sooner or later? Sooner would not be expected, but later gave him more knowledge to work with during the attempt.

"Will I ever be enshrouded with the thick gray that you have, Master?"

GrrraGagag felt uncomfortable with such adoration from this mere offspring of High Councilor Premion. Of the three Councilors, GrrraGagag hated him the most. He longed for the right to reproduce that the Councilors had, and because they knew it, they had viciously made him a teacher.

GrrraGagag growled again at his student and realized this growl was not part of his act. "I told you not to think of the beyond. If you want the privilege to train, you will never again speak of it. But I am glad you recognize my superiority to you. Now, look at those trees over there and tell me everything you see."

Hmm, it's not the beyond he doesn't want me to think of. . . just my *beyond.* "Hmmm, that one has broken branches in just the right spots, beautiful. Oh, all the ones behind are *perfect.*"

"That's right, they're past. They're no worry to us. They've realized we're real. There's no sign of *glow* in them. There's no ugly chaos of *living* leaves confusingly scattered all about. Nor are there branches chaotically spread out. Such aberrations result from the *glow life.* But every time we see chaos begin to form, we know exactly where to cut the branch to form beautiful order. It's far more difficult when we have to look at their ugly human form. That's why we invented make-up for their women, to try to make them look more like us. Some do manage to capture the essence."

Scraback seemed eager to do well and to impress, and he wanted everyone to know it. He watched his Master closely as he asked excitedly, "When will the Father come to visit us?"

Master GrrraGagag hated this underling's exuberance. He paused to study him. A plan was formulating as to how he might use this particular student to lure one of the High Councilors. This student seemed to be exceptionally stupid and therefore wouldn't be mistrusted nor expected to be a part of his plan. Consuming a High Councilor would give Master GrrraGagag the right to reproduce now. Yet, there still was an Alpha responsibility to train this underling, which Master GrrraGagag did take seriously.

"The Father leaves us alone to run things but if we . . . well, I'll just have to teach you." GrrraGagag leaned closer to his underling with an air of solemnity. "Scraback, remember this lesson: *It starts with the individual soul.* One soul, possessed by that cursed *glow,* can set us back thousands of years. We cannot risk that, now that we are so close to purging the whole world. Look over there and I'll teach you. The one over there with many broken roots and branches has suffered great injury to her thoughts and feelings. This can be very advantageous to us."

Scraback studied the young, mangled tree that he had seen before. The broken branches were perfect. "Advantageous?"

"Point your arm at her tree and concentrate on her past." Master GrrraGagag placed his arm on his underling to guide his mind in the effort.

"Yes, Master. I'm concentrating on her past. Ahhh, a baby."

Little hands and feet wriggled and wiggled in uncontrolled ecstasy as a little round head full of deep red curls stared intently with rich brown eyes. She only had one pink booty on, the other was in her mouth. Her Mother, with medium brown hair and natural red highlights, and dark brown eyes seemed to fill the whole space above the crib as she beamed over her only child.

The underling examined the baby's thoughts through the dirty blue orb at Master GrrraGagag's direction.

Oh what joy, hiccup, hiccup…it's in my sight, it's moving, it's, it's, it's…

"Red, Stephie, red, see? And this, yellow, and this pink . . ."

Oh what joy, what joy! That face, those eyes, THOSE EYES . . . smile, love, "hiccup" *Yes, red!* "Rrrrr"

"Yes, Stephanie, red!"

"Ma, ma, ma . . . eh, hiccup!"

Master GrrraGagag all of a sudden startled Scraback by shouting and pointing with his tail at the baby.

"There, *there*, did you see that?" Scraback didn't want to disappoint his Master, or incur more ire, but he had to ask.

"Yes Master, ahhh, I see, but why are you screaming? It's a baby."

His Master growled, "I told you, underling, to pay attention to details. We look at thoughts and feelings. What do you see?"

"Sir? I see a baby and its Mom teaching."

He growled even more sternly, "Look at the child, *closely,* as close as I'm now lowering my Great Eye on you!"

Scraback complied and leaned over closer to the orb. Its blueness shined on his grayness and stung a bit. "I'm sorry Sir, but I can't see what you want me to see. Why are you smiling?" Scraback had that odd sense of being mocked again.

"Turn her back into her tree for that point in time and tell me what you see."

Scraback did as directed and was startled and befuddled. "Uhh, I see a small tree and its trunk is glowing brightly, but why?"

With his big smirking Eye, GrrraGagag continued instruction. He liked this underling more than the others he had been forced to teach. "Ahhh, that's right. You couldn't see that before, could you? When you were looking just at the person, you couldn't see, but I could. I don't need to look at the trees so much anymore. I can see what the person is without it."

"Forgive me Master, but I still . . ."

"*Idiot,* that glow means there's the forbidden with *that* child, the *glow.*

"Oh, that glow."

Master GrrraGagag found himself yelling again at his student. Scraback's utter stupidity was getting to him. "Yes, of course! What other glow?" Master GrrraGagag's Eye began to bulge a bit, but then he calmed. "Because it's in the trunk, she was *born* with it from the beginning. She didn't happen upon it, was *born* with it, the worst kind. Look again at the person. Hurry up and change her back!"

"Master GrrraGagag, I see no *glow*."

GrrraGagag went back to tapping his tail in his arm; he looked impatient. He thought to himself: *I'm too old to be doing this anymore.* Then he explained, "*That* child just isn't learning like most other babies. She's not just happy because she's learning, growing, being spoiled, and appreciating the world she's in, even a stupid color... She's appreciating being alive! What an insult! What ignorance! What is there to her stupid little babbling infant life that she should do such a vile thing? *That* is where her *glow* comes from, from something that doesn't make sense! We are the greatest and she should pay attention to us. Look closely at her eyes as she watches her mother, you'll see all the other things there, for sure like learning, spoiling, but look deeper, *there*."

He practically shoved his whole tail inside the orb when he pointed with it. He had his arm around Scraback's neck and leaned over at the same time, and Scraback feared he might fall into the orb. "See that hidden, far away glow in her eyes? She loves life! Even though she was just a foolish little infant, she was obviously a top priority. I personally have helped correct her. It makes our existence worthwhile, meaningful, Scraback, to do such important work. It's our whole purpose, to make our lives pure by getting mankind to appreciate reality. Even when they can't see us, they can still appreciate us by living for us, and that purifies us because all reality is connected, and then we shall be able to reclaim our Earth."

Finally a darker grayness began to appear in his student's Eye. "Sir GrrraGagag, all the trees I saw didn't glow like that, why should this one little tree be such a concern?"

"*Idiot*, do you understand that *glow*, there? Reach out with your arm and lower your Eye on it and try to feel it, understand it, but concentrate on her present so you can make the connection. Do it!" GrrraGagag still had hold of his neck and he shoved him forward with his arm.

Scraback did as he was told. Pain! *Eye pain!* He tried to recoil from it but his Master held him a bit before allowing him to retreat. Scraback half growled, half howled from the experience.

GrrraGagag was elated, and howled with laughter. This made up for all the frustration this underling had caused him.

"Sir! Sir, what happened? Why did that cause me pain?" His words were sporadic as he noticed all his rippling was out of sync. His Eye was tearing, but this incident meant more to Scraback than suffering such humiliation. He saw a lot more than he let on. Now he had something to work with.

Smugly, and with not so hidden glee, GrrraGagag's Eye smiled at him. It was a lesson well taught. "The 'why' isn't important. The reality is that *glow* causes us pain, and that's all we need to know to seek its destruction. We cannot return until reality is purified."

Darker grayness spread even deeper into Scraback, but his Great Eye still teared from the *glow.* Master GrrraGagag still clutched his student closely to himself. He hadn't let him go since he shoved him into the orb. Scraback wanted desperately to redirect his Master back to teaching him the regular lesson so he would *let go*. "Are you going to reach out with your arm and touch her? Lower your Great Eye on her?"

GrrraGagag tossed him away and Scraback floated back a bit more, his bulbous head throbbing from not just the *glow* pain but more from all the knowledge.

When his Master yelled, it throbbed even more. "*No! You can't do that.* At least, long ago we tried to intervene directly, but trunks started to glow all over the place, so we quickly learned how to manipulate mankind to choose the things we want them to choose, of their own free will. That's what you saw me do earlier when I extended my arm over Gary. Look again at the child, but bring her up to just after her seventh birthday. Concentrate on that age and you'll see how we deal with such things.

Stephanie was in a long, pink frilly dress, with tears running down her cheeks. Her heart was breaking.

"Daddy, please don't go, *please*!" She grabbed her father by the arm and he jerked it back and scorned her.

"Stop your crying. If only you were a boy. If you *were* a boy, I wouldn't put up with it at all. Take your daughter. I can't have her hanging on me."

"No, Mommy, no! Don't lock me in here! Daddy!" Her mother grabbed her by the arm and dragged her to the bedroom and locked the door. But no sooner than the door was locked, Stephanie pulled the bobby pin from her hair, stuck it in the hole in the center of the doorknob and popped the lock. She quietly snuck back down the hall to listen, unseen, from around the corner. Her father's words came out like acid. Hearing the tone of it made her want to die. She felt so small inside.

"Can't you make her understand how to act?"

"I'm sorry, she can't help it. It's not my fault!" her mother begged.

"She learned how to do all that crying from *you. Pathetic!* I should have had a son. I'll send you money to care for her, and I expect you to raise her *right*—how to be a *real* woman." He slammed the door as his now former wife called through it.

"Fred. Please, don't leave me. I can make it better!"

In excitement, GrrraGagag grabbed Scraback and shook him, making his bulbous head bounce helplessly about.

"You see that Scraback, those last two lines were the key because the child heard them. She listens to her parents' private conversations by popping the lock and sneaking down the hall. I gave her the thought, although she probably would have thought it herself."

"But, but what about those lines?"

"*Idiot,* don't you understand? First, her father shows that he doesn't value his child being a girl by wishing for a son instead. He proves he doesn't value women by how he treats his wife. Then he tells her he expects his daughter to be raised right, to be the right kind of woman, but there is no right woman in his eyes, a*nd now in the child's eyes, also!* So, she'll grow up hating and rebelling against anything her mother tells her about how to be a woman. But this gets even more beautiful because of the mother. Instead of defending her daughter, she blamed the *child* for Fred's anger and disappointment. The wife was ready to do anything just to have her husband back. That will make the daughter hate her mother and being a woman even that much more. What's even better now, the daughter will be forever in the depths of her heart trying to gain the proper love from her father but that *love* will only continually disappoint her. She can't find value that way. And she shouldn't find value at all because of that *glow.*"

"I knew from the first time I saw her, I knew she thought too much of herself. But now, look at her trunk, no glow there now. And all it took was a very few well placed thoughts to help the man think how very important he was and how women's purpose is solely to please *him*. And then, some well-placed fear into the woman, making her willing to subject her daughter to what you saw. And that, my underling, is how we do our work."

GrrraGagag's Eye simply beamed with blackness. "I'll instruct you upon proper continued Forest maintenance, later. The beauty of all that I just showed you is that it's all driven into the child's heart and causes her to act upon it automatically. Her mind will never understand what's going on, or why she acts the way she does. That's why her tree's roots are so broken up. They're her heart. No connection between heart and mind. Ahhh, my new upstart, now flip ahead to when she was thirteen, and after that I'll show you a girl of *real* value."

Scraback was dubious as he looked at the tree at thirteen years old.

"Is that *her*?"

"Check the position of the tree. One life for one particular position . . . usually."

"But she's already lost most of the branches I saw gone in her present life."

"Good observation. Observation is important. I knew there was a reason you were sent to me for training. The best time to get humans, to make them see our reality, is the teen years. The earlier the better, because they are just starting to have the ability to think for themselves. Because this ability is so new and powerful, they can quickly be made to believe they know *everything*, when they really know less than when they were a child, because they lose their heart knowledge. Then we can get them to fall fast and hard with a few well placed thoughts and feelings that seem oh so right to them, that they think they thought of all by themselves. But *after*, as their ability to think independently and abstractly deepens, they begin to understand what terrible things they've done, but it's too late. They've already done them.

"So they're ashamed and can't bear it. So they push it to the back of their mind, lie to themselves, do all kinds of things to take away their feelings . . . It's great! Many never recover, even into old age. Some manage to act like that life never happened. They grow up, get married, carry out a role, but they're hollow inside...just as they should be, just like some of those earth oak trees that get hollow inside and crash to the ground during a wind storm. Some find religion, but I'll save that lesson for another time. Go ahead. Look at our beautiful work."

Scraback was in awe and troubled at the same time. He liked things to make sense. "But Master, you make it all sound so easy. If it is, then why are we so troubled?"

GrrraGagag took on his most serious Eye and whispered, "You just can't trust that *glow.* We're so close. Go ahead. Look at what she is at thirteen. Turn her tree into her person"

Scraback's Eye bulged in surprise. "What's she got in her nose?"

"A piece of metal, like some animal with a ring through its nose."

"*Why?*"

"*Idiot,* because she doesn't want to be what she was born to be, that's why she does everything to change herself. Mind you, that's not necessarily the reason *her* mind tells herself. But remember, it's her heart calling the shots. It's there that she has no feeling for the sacredness of her body."

"But Master, our form is sacred to *us*; we would never alter it so. Why don't they have the same sense?"

"Our form, our thoughts, our feelings are all one, but the humans split themselves all up into parts. Many of them don't see bodies as sacred but as an object much like a toy, or a billboard. Some don't care about their minds, to them feelings are all that count. And to others, all that counts is their minds."

Scraback shook his bulbous head. *How could such stupid creatures taste good?* "Isn't she a little young to be doing that with that young man? My previous instructor taught me . . ."

Master GrrraGagag frowned deeply at the mention of any previous rival. He scorned his underling, poking him repeatedly with his tail for emphasis. "Pay *close* attention and I'll *spell . . . it . . . out* for you . . . *real* . . . slowly, so even *you* can understand."

The Master paused, waiting for his underling's Eye to fully meet his. "In her mind she's a woman because she can have sex, but because of her father, she hates being a woman because it's not possible to be right being a woman. Since it's been driven into her heart that it's not possible to be right being a woman, that feeling takes away any reason not to have plenty of sex, regardless of the fact that the boys have no respect for her. The sex feels good; she loves it. But that makes her feel more like a woman, which makes her feel more worthless because she can't be right, which makes her have more sex. She can't escape. But the real beauty of all this is that it all happens in her heart, *women are feeling creatures,* and her mind can't stand all this so it lies to her, makes her think her sex gives her power. *She* actually *thinks she's exerting power over the boys that use her, or even that she has some value that way!* But even her mind's rebellion is actually living out her father's raising, confirming that she's worthless, all because she wasn't able to understand or face reality. It's perfect. She should be using her sex to control someone she's able to control, but all she does is just waste herself."

"But what if that *glow* comes back?"

His Master growled again, but Scraback hardly paid it mind. "Don't even think about it, it's impossible now, because it's buried under rings of black growth. Soon, her trunk may even split open and the *glow* fade completely."

Again, Scraback acted shocked. "You mean she still has it?" But that's what he hoped to hear. He thought as much because of what happened earlier in the orb. The tearing from his Eye was just beginning to ease, but his Master paid none of it any mind.

"*Idiot*, of course, she was *born* with it. Even those who weren't born with it, but find it later, keep it within. But every year the tree adds a ring, and the next year's life is based on that ring and so on. All we had to do was make it a black ring so that the *glow* couldn't shine through. In other words, humans' development of thoughts and feelings are based on what went before, and when those are degraded, then what follows will be degraded also, and as the degradations build upon themselves, it's as if a tree adds black rings upon black rings. If she keeps drinking that drug though, the tree will get hollow inside and then she *will* lose that *glow*. We can only hope. Now let me show you a girl who becomes a *real* value. She has a *right* to feel very valuable"

Karen, all dressed up in a short, frilly, white dress with long blond hair down to her waist, watched with eyes like daggers and a fake smile on her lips. Her thoughts burned inside her as everyone milled around in the little front yard: *She thinks she's so cute. That stupid look in her eyes. Why'd she invite me to her stupid birthday party anyway? She's only seven, but I'M EIGHT. Ugly long red hair. She should color it like the whores my dad goes to. She'd make a good whore. My hair is so much prettier, straight and blond. Hmmmm, I have the prettiest hair of anybody. She's got ugly, brown, doggy looking eyes with that stupid doggy look in them. Oh, damn, I have to wish her a happy birthday.*

"Oh! Hi, Stephie! Happy birthday! I got you a ribbon for your beautiful red hair." *I rubbed it on my butt first.*

Stephanie hugged her affectionately and kissed her cheek. "Oh, thank you, Karen! You're the bestest friend."

Oh God, she kissed my cheek! I'd rather be kissed by a dog. How come she gets such a beautiful birthday cake? That's not fair.

"Karen, look out!" The cry from Stephanie's mother startled Karen but she went ahead and banged into the rickety card table anyway to cause it to fall over.

"Oh, no! I, I . . . I'm so sorry, Ma'am. Stephie, I didn't mean to." She sobbed uncontrollably. It had taken many hours in front of a mirror to perfect her sobbing routine. It came in handy for all sorts of things.

"It's alright Karen, don't cry. There weren't enough people here for such a big cake anyway. I think I can salvage enough for you, Stephie, and Tracy. The rest of us grown-ups don't need anything."

Stephanie looked down at the beautiful, smashed cake on the ground. She had never ever had such a beautiful thing. She was planning on making a special ceremony of cutting it and handing out the pieces. She heard herself speak as if hearing an echo. "Mommy, you better give my piece to Daddy."

"Alright, Stephie!" Her mother said as she handed pieces to the other two girls. Karen smacked her lips loudly. "Mmmmm, this cake is so good! Isn't it, Tracy?"

"I'm glad you like it, Karen," Stephanie's mother said, "I baked it myself."

"Thank you so much, Ma'am," she said in very proper fashion.

Master GrrraGagag was truly excited. "*There.* Do you see that, Scraback? *Isn't she beautiful?* She'll make some man a good wife one day. In fact, when the time is right, I've got the perfect mate for her. There should be more born like her. *She knows she's better than all the rest.* Wait till you see how great she becomes. She's someone whose eye we can open."

"Master? What do you mean by *that?*"

GrrraGagag paused. *Should I show him? Why not.* The Master waved his arm and the orb came up for Karen's yesterday while she laid in her bed at night thinking.

"OK enough! Why are you in my head?" Karen spoke coolly.

The Master paused and peered at his underling who promptly asked, "Is she really speaking *directly* to you?"

Master GrrraGagag resumed the orb's recall.

Karen spoke sweetly. "Don't play coy with me. If you don't answer, from now on I'll block you! Wanna see? Go ahead, try now!"

After several minor attempts to invade her thoughts, the Master realized she had a bit of power so he waited on her.

"I want to speak *directly* to you. You obviously want something from me. What?

Above her bed, a very rare direct earthly portal opened but since she asked for it of her own volition, Master GrrraGagag knew he broke no rules. "Alright. I'm here. As to what I want, well, the possibilities could be endless!"

"That's what I thought, but it works both ways! What do you have to offer?"

The Master abruptly terminated the replay, did something Scraback couldn't see then stepped back waiting. When Scraback tried to retrieve the file and play it again to see the finish, it was nowhere to be found. Laughing, his Master informed him. "It's my secret, or, you might call it an experiment. Just like Jargono likes to experiment with ours, I enjoy experimenting with theirs. Don't bother to try and find the file, or do bother, either way, you won't find it."

Scraback coolly observed his Master while doing his best to conceal his contemplations. *After I consume you, I'll possess all your secrets anyway. Though I doubt you're better than me at orb technology. Hmm, what experiment? Why would Master hint at so much anyway?*

Maybe he wants me to investigate . . . or perhaps to keep me from what I really want. No, I won't be sidetracked. The redhead is far more interesting.

Later that day, Scraback opened a book he took out of his ethereal pouch under his arm that he had taken from the archives.

THE FOREST

Chapter One: Where Did It Come From?

From the time of humans, the Forest has always been. First there was one tree. Then there were two.

We hungered. We suffered the worst of times until finally the crop yielded its first harvest. We were able to correct humanity and begin fulfilling our great purpose.

The Forest is ours to tend. Our responsibility is to purify reality by purging all *glow* and all signs of *glow life.* Every human born into the world immediately has a tree in our forest. They are connected. This book explains the meaning of all tree manifestations. It is instructional on proper pruning and harvesting.

It is a common human misconception that only *life* causes growth. But in our Forest, our trees grow in death even as Earth trees grow in life. Thus, a 'dead' branch will actually thicken, lengthen and become more glorious in its order, thus proving it is not 'dead,' but just another form of life, our life, Alpha life, the true LIFE. Do not allow human definitions to corrupt your perfect understanding.

The Forest is real. The orb is a gateway into its realm . . .

. . . What the *glow* causes to grow wildly, we redirect through pruning.

Concerning the purported superiority of what humans call good over evil, I merely state the obvious. If their so-called good was stronger, would we have such a magnificent Forest? Would we possess such a great ethereal realm which we successfully purged of all *glow*? Would the Earth reap unto us such a bountiful harvest? Do not let human misconceptions prevent our full appreciation of our powers and destiny.

"Oh, my grayness!" Scraback heard himself say. "The Forest is real!"

CHAPTER 4

Vaughn's Beginnings

"Do we have to die, Father?"

The King rubbed his seven year-old son's head. "That answer is within you, my son. It also depends on what eye you look through."

His son closed one eye, then the other, and kept blinking each in turn. He saw his father's face move back and forth.

Once again the Master's tail pointed, this time without even looking, while the images seemed to move sideways across the blue orb. He knew his trees, and Scraback was impressed. "His name is Vaughn, another trouble maker, but I deal with him differently. There, that tree over there with the roots sticking out and the scars on the trunk."

Scraback was eager to impress. "I know what to do Master. Watch, I'll start with seven years old."

A skinny short boy lay twisting on the living room floor making inhuman noises. Scraback, notably irritated, asked his Master. "Why is he screeching like that?" But his Master just growled, indicating he should just watch.

The father, his short hair already graying at the sides, screeched back at his son as he walked into the room.

His younger wife, with her black hair always perfectly curled, reprimanded her husband. "Oh, Alex, don't imitate him."

"Virginia, maybe if he hears how stupid he sounds, he'll stop it."

With frustration mounting, she spoke what she knew would be lame. "I don't know what's wrong with him. Vaughn, why do you do that? *Stop it.*"

Vaughn stopped twisting for a second to whine. "I don't know! I can't! Eeeeeee!"

She ran over to him and grabbed his left hand. "Are you biting your fingers again? Stop it! What's wrong with you?"

"I dunno!" Jerking his hand away from his mother, he rolled away on the floor.

"Oh shit, Alex! Maybe we have to take him to a psychologist."

"Oh, stop with the crap! There's nothing wrong with him."

"Do you know how much a psychologist costs?"

Vaughn's screech pierced their ears causing them to cringe. "*STOP IT, Vaughn!*" His mother shouted.

"Now, who's yelling at him?"

She shot him a death look as she ran over, grabbed and shook her son. "What's wrong with you, Vaughn?"

"I don't know! Leave me alone!" He squirmed away, so she whirled on her husband. Vaughn's stomach somersaulted. He sighed as he'd heard it all before and before and before . . .

"Well? Aren't you going to do something about your son? You know, I work my fingers to the bone for everyone; I cook your dinner, wash your cloths, and you rush off to play cards. You don't know what I have to go through. I watch our money. I've done good budgeting. Without me you wouldn't be anywhere. I'm the one who got you your job, now. If it wasn't for me . . ."

Her husband grabbed the newspaper off the chair and sat on the couch. "Oh, you didn't get me that job, I got it myself!" he half-heartedly yelled from behind the paper.

"Oh yes, I *did* get you that job. Who found that ad? Who pushed you to go to the interview when you didn't want to? You would be *nothing* without me!" Her voice became more and more shrill. There was the usual slam of windows from neighbors trying to block out her unbearable sound.

Vaughn postured and screeched even louder than before. He tightened up his arm till it hurt, shook it out, retightened, twisted . . . got frustrated at himself more than his parents. *What am I doing?* He twisted in agony.

"Yeah, yeah, that's what you always say." He turned a page.

"I thought I was marrying somebody. You acted like a king. I didn't know I was going to have to live the next ten years with your *family*."

Her dig about his family always bothered him and he actually shouted back in defense, "We had our own apartment. It was a good arrangement. It enabled us to buy this house!"

"Yeah, Mister, you look here, I had to slave at that place. I had to clean the halls when your sisters wouldn't . . ."

"Oh, you didn't have to do anything."

He should have kept quiet like he did most other times, but this time he just couldn't.

Her voice grew even shriller. "What? And leave it dirty so they could talk behind my back? I was always the problem, always *me!*"

"You just didn't know how to stick up for yourself."

"Yeah, like you would have backed me up?" She took a few steps closer across the living room, the veins in her neck beginning to stand out.

Vaughn, lying on his stomach, began gently banging his head on the back of his hands that were resting on the living room floor.

"I sure would have," bellowed his father proudly.

"Well, how noble you are. That's why you were always running out to play cards with your father." She took another step closer to her husband.

"I wanted you to come too."

Her voice then hit a new high note. "*What*? I hate cards."

"You hate everything." He turned another page.

"Hey, if it wasn't for me, you'd be nothing. I've scrimped and saved, and I worked, too!"

Vaughn blurted out several shrill screeches in a row, and his mother turned to look at him.

"Oh shit, now how are we going to afford a psychologist?"

"Heck! Virginia, if we have to, we can afford it."

She whirled back to the attack. Her neck veins were definitely prominent now. "With what? You never know what might happen. You have to put away for a rainy day."

"He'll be fine, he'll grow out of it Virginia." His father decided that escape might be better. He turned another page.

Scraback thought he should be getting used to being amazed. He was a student and supposed to learn new things, but all this . . .

"Master, how did you get his parents to treat him that way?"

"I didn't. They're just like that!"

Scraback's Eye bulged in amazement. This wasn't part of his act. "Really? What did you do to them?"

"Nothing! That's the beauty of this lesson. Sometimes we don't have to do *anything*. These idiots are often their own worst enemies, even for their own children. Look ahead a couple years." Master GrrraGagag realized he had let his persona slip a bit. He should have scolded his underling for asking the second time. He would have to be more careful. But the fact was that he too was overcome by his own lesson.

Vaughn, nine years old, was crying, pleading with his parents to stop fighting as they always did. It was the same scene over and over, except sometimes his father read a book instead of the paper. But mostly, he preferred the paper for these times.

"Stop fighting. *Please* stop fighting."

His mother managed a few words in his direction, "This doesn't concern you," then whirled back to her husband, "Listen you son-of-dog, I worked my fingers to the bone, I slaved and scrimped and saved. I put up with your *father* and your *family* and their stinking *card* games. No one ever thought about *me*. Are you listening to *me*? Put that paper down. That's all you do is read your paper or your stupid books."

"Leave me ALONE," he yelled.

"Leave you alone? Leave you alone? I'd like to leave you alone, you stupid son-of-a-dog. But we don't have enough money. What would we do with the kids? All my life I've had to put up with you."

Scraback wrapped his tail around his ethereal ears trying to dull the pain, but it was of no use. *Is it the actual sound through the orb or just what she's saying that hurts so much?* Scraback wasn't even sure whether his tail wrapping was part of his act or his real response.

His Master burst out laughing at the sight. "Oh Scraback, oh, my Eye is tearing. She will only get worse. No, actually, she stays like that. She's always at her worst. She's one of those who believe she comes from rock. Nothing is of value to her but money. Money and her fear of not having it, and her desire that everyone know she has sacrificed everything *because* . . ." He had a fit of laughter. ". . . *because*, well, listen and watch!"

"Why are you always fighting? Why do you hate so much?"

Vaughn whined in tears.

"Hate? Hate? Are you crazy?" She had reached a new shrill high.

Vaughn blurted out a prolonged screech followed by twisting till it hurt.

"*I love you*. I work my fingers to the bone. Look at all I've sacrificed. I, I . . ."

"You see the beauty of this, Scraback?"

"Master?" Scraback was scratching his head with his tail.

"Oh, this is too good. She does everything out of *love!* That's her answer to her son's question as to why she fights. LOVE." GrrraGagag had another uncontrolled fit of laughter.

Scraback, however, wanted to understand and interrupted. "Why does the child act that way?"

"Screech? Bite himself? Kick and pick at himself? Isn't it obvious?"

Scraback sighed and hung his Eye. "Master?"

But *GrrraGagag* took a circuitous route to explain. "What did his tree look like at seven and nine?"

"Let me see." Scraback flipped the scenes back and forth. "Master, I knew it *glowed* at seven, but it *glows* brighter now at nine. I don't understand. And what does that have to do with the child's scree . . ."

Tap, tap, tap went the Master's tail in his arm. "Underling, I'm beginning to think you are not as smart as I thought. *He's* another born with the *glow*. As he grows older and his inner perception through that *glow* deepens, he feels everything more strongly. That's great."

Scraback's Eye twisted in confusion. His Master was positively delighted.

"Master, but I thought we didn't want the *glow* to grow?"

"Oh, spare me your *stupidity* Scraback. That's what makes the way I am handling this one so ingenious. The stronger the *glow* grows with him, the greater the chance it will kill him!"

His underling was speechless. He realized his Master was far more devious and cunning than he thought. He waited for the explanation.

"I can see by the dullness of your Eye that I'll need to spell it out to you. Those born with the *glow* have no choice about having it. It was there before they had a choice, just like the earth is there before the seed is planted. The seed is *made* out of earth. That *glow* has a course it must follow. But the beauty is that this child was born into completely blind surroundings. Not his parents nor anyone near and not so near even has the slightest feel for it. He has no way to understand *what's* in him. But it makes him feel things much more strongly, in a way, more clearly than anyone else!"

"And that's good, Master? Because he'll then know we're real?" Scraback totally misunderstood.

"No, you *idiot,* not that kind of clearness, but, *any* spiritual perception is always superior to the plain physical. Actually, he can sense us, too, but that's even more disturbing to him because this *glow* has a backward perception of its own. He perceives through it as it would feel and see. So, his parents seem terrible to him, and everyone else around him, and he's tormented by sensing us, too. But, and this is very important, our nature is there inside him, too, because we're very real to his parents. So, he feels our reality inside, too. You see? He has no way possible to resolve these two very intense conflicting ways of perceiving and feeling. If he would just give up the *glow* then he would be fine. No conflict. But he won't let go, so he screeches and all those things. He's expressing *exactly* what's going on inside himself and he feels terrible about it. But the more he expresses it, the more he feels like a freak, and the more he feels, then the more he expresses . . . it's just a matter of time as the *glow* grows stronger and the conflict increases that he'll kill himself or go crazy."

GrrraGagag started to talk more loudly. "As he should because he doesn't deserve our existence. I'm glad I don't have to directly place my presence in his wretched s*oul.* Flip ahead to thirteen!"

Vaughn was sitting in an office chair across from a thin, gray-haired man with a full salt-and-pepper beard who sat behind an office desk.

"My parents, I hate them. I can't stand them."

"Mmm hmmm."

"All they do is fight and criticize me. My mother never stops with her stinking worrying, her fears. I *HATE* her screaming."

The psychologist passively nodded. "Mmmmm. How does that make you feel?"

"Terrible. I can't stand them."

"Give me an example of something that troubled you specifically."

"Like when I wanted to leave my school books at home. I told her I didn't need them that day. She didn't believe me. I'm thirteen years old. I can think for myself."

"So, what did you do when she told you to take them?"

"I yelled back at her."

The psychologist was busy shuffling papers around, not looking at the boy, but he asked him more questions. "And you don't like it when your Mother yells?"

"No. I can't stand it. That's all she ever does."

"Why don't you like it?"

"Because it's wrong, you don't have to yell about everything. You should be . . ."

"I should be? Are you talking about me?" The man seemed to be hunting still for some paper.

"Ahhh, well, no, I guess. Ahhh, I should be . . . I should be!"

"If yelling is wrong a lot of the time, then if you yell, you're just like her, aren't you?" He stopped shuffling and waited for Vaughn to reply, and Vaughn waited for him but lost the battle.

"Oh, I hadn't thought about it that way. But I'm right when I yell."

"You think you're right when you yell?"

"Yes, because she doesn't treat me right."

"Does she think you treat her right?"

"Well no, I guess . . ." He waited again for Vaughn to think until Vaughn resumed answering. "OK. So you're saying . . ."

"I'm not saying anything." He accidently dropped his pen and bent behind his desk to pick it up, speaking from where Vaughn couldn't even see him. "It's up to you, what you want to say and think and do."

"OK, so maybe . . . maybe, I don't have to do the same thing. I guess if I really hate what they do, then the only way to be right would be to . . . act different?"

The man kept a straight face. This wasn't about what he thought the boy should do, this was all about what Vaughn thought he should do for himself. "What do you think?"

"I think that's right. Wow, I hadn't thought of this before." An incredible smile spread across Vaughn's face. A smile he had never savored before.

Master GrrraGagag growled and shoved his student out of the way so he could be directly centered in front of the blue orb. He was visibly upset and didn't have to put on an act.

Scraback had never seen him that way. It was quite unnerving.

"Master GrrraGagag, what's wrong?"

"How could they have let this happen?"

"Master?"

"*They were never supposed to let him think.* They let him get the wrong psychologist, they . . ."

"Master, who? I thought you were . . ."

GrrraGagag focused on the orb while he spoke through a low growl. "I knew the boy wouldn't be trouble, so I assigned his watch to some underlings who were to alert me if anything interesting happened. Obviously, they found something more *valuable* to watch than *him!* Granted, watching this kid would be boring at best, but now I'm going to have to review his life starting from that point." His arm pointed into the blue orb.

"Master? Why that point?"

"You *IDIOT*! Can't you see what just happened? Come look at his tree right before that encounter and then right after."

Scraback watched as his Master flipped through the stages. "Master GrrraGagag, there's an extra branch on the tree, and, and . . . it's *glowing!*"

"That's right, *fool*, and we never, EVER, want that to happen. To let the *glow* escape the trunk is terrible, painful . . . we have to remedy this."

"Yes, Master, let me help. What shall we do?"

"We have to get rid of that branch. The *glow* in the trunk must not have a way to escape."

"Why don't we just touch the branch and chop it off?" Scraback began to reach his arm out toward the branch, wanting to comfort his Master, but his Master's tail quickly yanked him back.

"*Idiot*, that's almost two years ago! We can't change the past. We have to examine his life from that point on to tell how bad the damage is. *And remember,* we can't take direct action, unless it's absolutely necessary. Hmmm, if it's limited to just one branch...ahhh, yes, we can stimulate other branches to grow much more quickly, crowd out the *glowing* branch, or, we can set a worm in the branch."

"A worm, Sir? But he's not really a tree."

GrrraGagag grabbed him and whirled him around Eye-to-Eye. "*Idiot!* He is more a tree than a tree is! A worm is a thought similar to something connected to that wretched *glow,* and so it's easy to slip it in undetected. But it's of our reality. Like the difference between just lusting after sex and their *love* with its natural desire to mate. But because the worm conflicts with his *glow*, then we'll have brought back the terrible frustration he had before. The infection will attack the branch along with the trunk, and it'll even be worse for him than before, because he tasted the outlet for the *glow* and lessening conflict, only to be thrown into deeper trouble. Hmm, maybe he could even be made to hate the *glow* for causing his new trouble. Yes, *even* kill himself because there's no escape. Quickly, let's examine the rest of his life!"

They had gone through many of the psychologist's sessions rather quickly, boringly, and then the Master halted cold on this one. His Great Eye seemed to tear.

"Another thing I hate is when my Dad says, 'Do as I say, not as I do,' I HATE that! He's a hypocrite. He yells at my mom but tells me not to, even though she's wrong. He tells me to go to religious school, but he doesn't care about God, nor even believe in Him. It's just the government's religion anyway, *and*, he still claims to be someone special because of Him! So I told him, I'm not going to that stinking religious school, 'cause I don't see anything special about our country's believing people compared to those who don't believe, 'cause they do the same evil things everyone else does who don't believe! So, how are they special? Besides, the government made it clear it doesn't care if you believe or not! Just don't believe in anything else."

The psychologist showed no emotional response, but was pleasant in his speech. "Do you feel good when you yell at your Mom or Dad?"

Vaughn snapped his answer. "No! I *hate* it, because yelling like that is wrong. There's no good in it. I don't want to be like the things I hate, I HAVE to change!"

"How will you do that?"

"Hmmmm, I don't know."

"What feelings do you have when you yell?

"I'm angry. Very angry, and that's why I yell."

"And you like being angry?"

"No. Just like I don't like yelling, but I'm right."

"Then keep yelling, you're right!"

"No, NO, that doesn't matter . . . Hmmmm!"

"What do you want to accomplish by yelling?"

"I want them to stop, to change."

The man raised his eyebrows at Vaughn. The gesture was the first indication at all of his insight. The man was silent.

"Oh! They never change when I yell. They can't! Because it's just the same thing! I do just the same thing! Ahhh, because it's just the SAME thing. I'm being like my parents whom I hate . . . so I screech and do things because I hate what I am inside, because I've got too much of *their* feelings, and the more I act like them, the more I . . . but I'm not that inside, but . . ."

"So, how can you be different?"

"Well, since I want to help them truly love . . . I have to act with love. I, I . . . I could be calm when my mom yells at me. I could . . . I could explain my understanding to her, YES, how it's not love to do those things, how much I care about her, how we can talk things through. And if she won't listen, I could say kindly, 'I know you don't agree with me, because you don't understand, but that's OK, but I'm still gonna do what I want.' Yes, that might be good."

"Well, why don't you try that and let me know how it works out."

Scraback went flying through the ethereal air when his Master's tail whipped him across the head.

"Masterrrrr!"

GrrraGagag laughed to himself. "Sorry, Scraback, I lost control. This problem is bigger than I expected. Look at his tree now." His Master gently drew him back with his ethereal power and reset him in front of the blue orb.

Scraback didn't know whether his head hurt more from the knocks or from the sight. "Oh no, another glowing branch! What does it mean?"

"The first branch was the beginning of an understanding of that wretched *glow* in him, so it gave the pressure an escape in his mind. The second branch is a branch of action, which is why it's opposite to the branch of understanding. It's a branch of action that balances his understanding, giving both an outlet and extra life. This is all turning out to be very serious, and we've still got another year of his past to work through before we can act."

"Oh, Master, what about that *root*? It's *glowing*, too. And, why do some of them stick out of the ground so?"

"They stick out of the ground because he's not connected to his family, nor are they connected to him. If they were connected to him, but he not to them, the soil would pile high around the raised roots. If he were connected to them but them not to him, they would sink deep, but the soil would be hollowed out into a hole, leaving the roots bare. As for that wretched root *glow*, that's part of his heart, the part connected to those *glowing* branches of his mind and the branch of action. These human beings are infernal creatures, so complicated, so much to be careful of. We have to watch all parts of the tree, all the time, because the *glow* could begin to escape at any part of the tree, and then . . ." He grabbed his underling tightly with tail and arm, *"And then*, whatever part escapes causes the other parts of the tree to grow and *glow* with it. Very terrible once this gets out of control because the heart, the mind, and the soul begin to work together, to understand one another in a wretched kind of way. Look at our Forest, Scraback."

His Master began to rave. "Look. *That* is reality, all those leafless, glowless trees, that's how it's supposed to be." He followed up with a roaring growl and then calmed as if he never lost control. "That's why there are only a few trouble-some trees around. They are an aberration. We *must* purify reality!"

Scraback distinctly detected Eye odor from his Master and was doing his best not to be repulsed. He needed to redirect him so he would *let go*. "Maybe we should skip ahead . . ."

But Master GrrraGagag had purposely not washed his Eye from the day before as soon as he had heard he would have another underling. He grabbed Scraback even tighter on hearing his suggestion. "NO, we dare not do that. We must understand exactly what has happened to be able to cure it. Details, Remember? Details."

They continued to study Vaughn's life through the blue orb, boringly wading through more stifling childhood. Then, the Master jerked to a stop again. *It's time to watch my other plan unfold.*

Images whirled by until arriving at Stephanie's and Gary's trees in the present. Smiling, Master GrrraGagag straightened and extended his arm through the blueness. He beckoned with his tail to his underling to come forward and watch. His tail pointed at Gary holding Stephanie by the throat. When Scraback saw it, his ripples almost stopped. His Master didn't notice his disappointment, and Scraback forced his ripples to move along. Scraback was watching a key piece of his plan being destroyed.

His Master thrust his gray arm further into the orb. "I taught Gary this, to have his prey look him in the eye. He then pulls their mind into his so they can experience the full helplessness they have by feeling the complete control and determination he has. Watch, my friend, and feel through your Eye as she is forever destroyed this night. She'll give us no future problems. She'll never get a chance to really use those powers of hers."

This was serious. *I thought Master didn't know of her power.*

Master GrrraGagag's tail pointed. "You see this, Scraback? She's totally captured. Notice how she speaks with no *glow* at all behind her voice. She looked into his eye and he captured her." Master GrrraGagag narrowed his Great Eye upon his underling. "Much as I *love* to do, when I *consume* delicacies."

Scraback quickly looked away from his Master. He kept trying to force himself to ripple, to act normally, to hide his disappointment at the girl's destruction, but then he realized his Master would just think he was responding to his threat. *All the better,* he thought, as he let himself go sickly. His Master laughed.

If I had known Master's plans, perhaps I could have engineered the girl's rescue. I need her. May his Great Eye rot. Scraback nudged closer, wanting to ask anyway though he told himself not to ask. It didn't make any difference now. *You should think before you speak.* But he just wanted to find out what his Master knew about her powers. *Which powers?* "Master, powers? What powers?"

Master GrrraGagag was preoccupied, watching the unfolding scene and didn't want to be bothered.

His underling made the mistake of continuously tapping him on the back with his arm. Tap, Tap, Tap. "Master, powers? What powers?"

Scraback's Master whirled on him. "You insolent idiot!

NEVER touch me like that again. Powers? What powers?"

He and his underling went back to raptly watching the unfolding scene. Scraback thought it best not to ask again.

Master GrrraGagag wondered whether his student was too stupid to even take the bait. *It should be obvious now that he should go behind my back to investigate her. If he does, it will be a valuable experiment for me.* GrrraGagag wasn't sure to what extent the redhead was gifted. *But the more gifted, the tastier she'll be for me.* The only worry he had was that Gary might kill her too soon. *It would be best just to abuse her. Then she'll be even easier to manipulate until the time is best to dine.* He pushed his arm further into the orb trying to ensure the best outcome.

As Master GrrraGagag continued to peer through the dirty blue orb he couldn't believe his Eye. "Who's *THAT?*" He growled.

In the next ethereal moment, Stephanie was fleeing his trap. Master GrrraGagag lost control of himself, something he never did before, though Scraback couldn't tell the difference between his Master's act and the real thing. His roar terrified his underling. "If it wasn't for you, underling, I would have had the time to see this coming." He smashed Scraback against one wall and then the other, and the other.

Though he was bounced around like a racket ball, Scraback gladly took the punishment. His plan was still intact! *Soon I will eat you!* Scraback solaced himself between bounces.

"Masterrrrrr, no! There's still plenty chance to make things better! I, I . . . have an idea!"

CHAPTER 5
The Party Continued

"Why does evil exist, Father?"

The King leveled his gaze into his fourteen-year-old son's eyes. "There is no good reason."

Relieved, his son answered, "Thank you, Father. I finally understand."

"Hey, Gary, who would have the *nerve* to come to your house like that?"

Gary, head of *the* gang, stared out the window just barely seeing them flee. "That *bastard*, Vaughn! I'm gonna *kill* him! No one will ever miss him . . . Everyone knows he's strange! He'll just disappear and no one will even bother to care! Find THEM!"

No one doubted he meant it. Meanwhile, Vaughn found a hiding place between some evergreen bushes on the side of another large house. He could hear them searching. Soft light escaped from a window above the trees.

"Here, behind these bushes, stop crying or they'll find us." Vaughn sat down and pulled her onto his lap. "Come 'ere. There, there, it's OK, I'll protect you." *I've got to quiet her.* "Hey, you know, you have really beautiful hair." He wrapped his strong arms around the trembling girl and began to smooth her red hair over and over to calm her. His feeling surrounded her, embraced her, sunk into her, but it was his words that unnerved her.

"What?" she whispered.

"Yeah, I love long, wavy red hair, and you have very special brown eyes. I've never seen that color brown before."

She looked confused and heard herself ask, "You do? No one's ever told me they like my hair or my eyes before." All of a sudden it was as if she was transported to a different world inside of herself. His stroking her hair and his strange words and . . . something different!

Vaughn thought to himself, *Thank God she stopped crying, but I do really love them.* "Yeah, well, eyes are everything," he said knowingly.

"I *hate* Gary's eyes. I never *really* looked deeply into them 'till tonight."

"There, there, it's alright!" He kept stroking her hair.

"When I looked into them, it was like I was falling down a dark hole," she said with the terror remembered.

"Peek-a-boo!" One of the boys startled them as he grabbed Stephanie by the back of her hair and yanked her out of Vaughn's arms.

Stephanie screamed with terror. Enraged, Vaughn leapt up, grabbed the hand holding her hair, and with one powerful twist felt bones snap.

"Aaahhh, you little bastard! Hey! Help! They're over HERE!" The boy screamed, holding his injured hand out.

Stephanie felt Vaughn pull her behind him with his left arm, and in a continuous motion he kicked the boy in the gut with a cross kick of his right foot. The boy doubled over and crumpled. Out of the corner of his eye he saw another approaching as his back was turning toward his new enemy. Vaughn sped up his circular motion and swung his left foot in a back kick and caught his attacker flat in the chest whose feet promptly went out from under him as the blow knocked his upper body backward. He slammed down hard to the ground.

But then someone grabbed Vaughn from behind, hitting him in the head with something hard. Vaughn's scream, half pain, half anger and frustration, mixed with his lost bearings as everything seemed to suddenly spin.

"I got him!" Another boy yelled as Vaughn found himself pressed to the ground on his stomach. While lying atop Vaughn's back, the stout boy twisted Vaughn's arms behind him.

Visions of the *Art of Fighting*'s loose pages strewn on his bedroom floor flashed before his eyes. *Twist your wrist. Break his hold. Grab the thumb. BREAK IT!*

The thumb popped out of joint and Vaughn was free. The boy rolled away in searing pain. Vaughn rolled to chase him and sharply swung his elbow into his enemy's face. The boy screamed in further pain. *Make sure you disable your enemy before you leave him,* his book had taught.

Vaughn sprang back up and whirled. His fist caught another boy square in the cheek and crushed it sending blood everywhere. He heard his thoughts. *Whirl, punch . . . cheek crushing, blood,* his *blood!*

But then he was tackled from behind again by yet another boy and he went down hard with a miserable grunt.

"I got him down, get his legs! Get his arms!"

"Leave him *alone*, you bastards!" Stephanie shrieked and jumped on the back of one of the boys clawing at him, trying to get to his eyes. Her hair was flying everywhere.

"Gary, get your woman off my back."

Stephanie screamed as Gary yanked her off by that beautiful hair and threw her like a rag-doll to the ground.

Vaughn squirmed onto his back and turned his attention to the boy lying over him. His thoughts were his actions. *Crush his throat!* Vaughn's hand encircled the boy's voice box and squeezed, feeling something pop inside. Gurgling sounds accompanied him falling off Vaughn.

Another boy fell onto his legs. *Can't move my legs, throw him aside . . . uhhg, pain, NO! Can't give up! She screamed! I scream!* With a tremendous scream and burst of strength, he twisted and his legs began to work free.

"He's getting loose, look out! Ahhh!" The boy yelled as Vaughn twisted his legs again and kicked him off.

"*Damn,* he's strong!" another said. But they began ferociously kicking him all over.

Kicking me . . . oh no, pain, can't breathe! No!

"I'm gonna kill you, you little faggot. Then I'm gonna dump your body where no can find it. Hers too! And when they ask about it, I'm gonna say Vaughn *who?*" Gary sneered fiercely as he kicked him as hard as he could to emphasize his last word. Then he drew his foot back for another kick.

NO! Catch the foot . . . Pain! . . . Keep hold of it! Pull!

Gary yelled and flew backwards, landing hard.

"Hey, what's goin' on down there? The keepers are on their way!" A voice from the window above the bush where they had first hidden warned them.

"Gary, get up, we'll finish this another day!" A boy yelled. "Bitch!" Gary called out.

"Pig!" Stephanie shouted back.

PAIN, Terrible pain, Darkness . . . Vaughn passed out.

Stephanie crawled over and fell onto Vaughn's chest, taking his broad shoulders in her arms with a massive hug. Her hip throbbed painfully where she had landed when Gary tossed her to the ground. She gently shook her savior. "Vaughn, VAUGHN!"

Guilt began to sear her. "We have to get out of here, the keepers are coming. They don't care who's right or wrong."

Vaughn was only half-conscious, helpless in her arms. He was heavy, bigger than her, though not nearly as large as Gary.

Something invisible seemed to wrap around Stephanie. There was no way she was going to let evil befall this young man who so bravely fought for her. Her heart pounded into her mind, but this wasn't helpless terror, this was determination. She knew what she had to do and there was no accepting failure. She didn't know from where her strength came, as it should have been impossible for her to lift him.

"C'MON, I'll take you home!" She squatted between his legs as he lay on his back. She leaned forward and grabbed his tee shirt in both hands, and pulled back with all her might, standing at the same time. Using all her weight, leg strength and determination, she stood him up and quickly pivoted under his arm, throwing it over her shoulder. She ignored her stabbing pain and made him shuffle while she supported his weight. They escaped across the huge grassy lawn into the darkness of a clump of tall pine trees just as sirens could be heard in the distance. The twinkling stars pierced the night, dotting the darkness . . . there was no moon.

Stephanie never expected to ever feel relief upon walking up to the remnants of her sidewalk, but her heavy sigh marked the end of a journey that seemed to have taken forever. Her whole body ached from supporting and half-dragging Vaughn all the way home. Even though Stephanie's house's wooden siding had long since lost all its paint, one could hardly tell in the dark. And for all her house's lackluster looks, her feeling of *home* for the first time became apparent to her.

It was a small split-level house with small rooms. Her neighborhood was much newer than many of the others, only fifty or so years old, but it was not built out of durable materials. Even students now refused to live in the area, as the University kept putting up cheap housing in new undeveloped areas, but they still reaped the rent from the old ones.

The wooden siding rattled when she pressed Vaughn against the wall beside the front door. After opening it, she slung his arm back in place and dragged him inside. Her mother's sharp voice made her heart skip a beat. Then their eyes met.

Her mother stood in a faded brown dress. The one she always threw on after coming home from working in the government shoe factory all day, and sometimes into the night. Her hair, once a luscious brown with red highlights had all the red turned to gray and then some. She was only in her mid-forties, but looked older. Her eyes darkened as she recognized the strange, embarrassing boy the whole town made fun of for years because of his screwy behavior. Recently, she heard he talked crazy to everyone. The only redeeming aspect of her job was gossip. "What are you dragging into my house?"

Stephanie's feet froze on the bare wooden floor. The carpeting had long since been ripped up. An old sofa and a sitting chair were neatly wrapped and tucked with dingy faded covers. Stephanie stopped cold just a few feet into the house with Vaughn draped over her. "He's hurt Mama, he's hurt bad."

Her mother continued the assault. "What do I care if he's hurt? Throw him out!"

Tears filled her eyes as she begged, all the while feeling let down and helpless. "Mama, *please*, he helped me."

Her mother's tone lost some of its intensity but none of its acridity. "He can't even help himself. Isn't he that strange kid whose parents don't know what to do with him? I'll not have him screeching in this house."

Stephanie realized she knew who he was now. She looked at him still leaning on her with his head down. *I don't care about any of that crap.* A strange fire lit in Stephanie's eyes as she found herself for the first time challenging her mother. "*What*? What are you talking about? He just saved me from getting *raped!*"

"Yeah right, as if it would make a difference to you! I know what you do."

Stephanie's mouth dropped open, her chest suddenly felt tight, and she felt like she was falling inside. If it wasn't for her holding onto Vaughn, she felt like dying. How could she be any more worthless than that . . . and from her own mother?

As Vaughn leaned heavily on Stephanie, he managed to pick his head up and speak softly. "*Woman*, how can you be so *cruel* to your daughter!" He coughed some blood, but quickly swallowed it to keep Stephanie from knowing his injury. He continued to hold her mother in his powerful gaze.

His deep, dark eyes pierced her and she could swear she felt smacked in the face. "Go ahead! Take him to your room if you want. I'm going out. He'd better be gone when I get back," Stephanie's mom cautioned then rushed out the door.

Stephanie led him down the hall to her bedroom. She was crying in fright for him. He fell off her onto the bed, and she picked up his legs and turned him to lie straight. Sniffing and sobbing, she said, "Vaughn, lie here on my bed. Let me take off your shirt. I don't know anything about medicine, but I think your ribs might be broken." Feelings she never had before swirled around inside her but predominant was her guilt for causing this brave, young man to be hurt for the likes of her.

"No, if they were broken, I'd be coughing up blood. I'm just bruised. I got the wind knocked out of me, that's all."

She stared at him. She could see blood in the corners of his mouth, but there were no injuries to his face. Something was different about him. He liked her eyes! Her heart pounded more because of his attempt to hide the seriousness of his wounds. "Oh Vaughn, they kicked you so hard," she gasped in memory.

"It's OK, you can stop crying. I'll be OK." He smiled weakly.

"Let me cover you up, bring you something to drink, to eat."

"No. I'm fine, really," he said softly.

Sitting on the bed beside him, she placed her hand gingerly on his bare chest. His eyes opened wide in surprise. He could feel her feelings through her hand! *Wow!*

Stephanie could barely look on him. "I don't know what to say. No one in my whole life has ever, *ever* stood up for me, let alone fought for me, almost *died* for me!"

He tried to play it down. "Oh, come on now, I wasn't going to die."

She knelt over him even closer to look straight at him in all seriousness. "Vaughn, look at me, in my eyes. Yes, you were going to die! I know because I looked into Gary's eyes." As soon as she said so, that memory flashed vividly. "Yes, he would have *killed* you!"

He reached up his hands and held her arms softly as she continued to lean over him. "I don't even know your name! How'd you know mine?"

"I heard *Gary* call you by your name. Mine's Stephanie," she said as she smiled slightly, pulling her hair back and hanging her head down.

He lifted her chin back up. "That's a beautiful name to go with a beautiful smile, beautiful hair and *really* beautiful eyes!"

She forced her head down again. "Vaughn, you don't know me, I was hardly worth the risk."

For some reason her words felt like they cut him in two and he seriously scolded her. "STOP that! Don't you *ever* say that!" He paused to make sure his words sunk in. "Stephanie, you're a person, first of all, and that alone is of infinite value."

She could feel his anger, but it wasn't anger that hurt her. It was anger to help her. Stephanie didn't understand it. "But . . ."

He softened and pleaded with her. "What but? What don't you understand about being a person, about being able to appreciate life?"

She stared at him with wide eyes hearing words that she knew the dictionary meanings of, but she also felt something that vaguely seemed familiar, and there was something so different in his eyes. "But..."

"You can't run from it, Stephanie. We're all people. *Persons*."

"Gary's not a person." She looked away remembering and shivered.

He squeezed her arms a bit. "Mmm, he is, Stephanie. I hate to say it, but he is. But he's chosen to throw away his personhood."

She shook her head. "Ha, uh, his what?"

"Personhood. My name for whatever it is that makes us a conscious living person. More than just a body, a person *lives* by ways of Life, that's with a capital L, by ways of conscious Life. But Gary doesn't have any of those living ways because he thinks they're foolish, worthless. All he has, all he *is*, is a conscious existing *death*! He's a person without personhood!"

Her eyes widened. She could feel the meaning of his words sink into the depths of her heart, and somehow she recognized their meaning, as if she had known these things before. It was like a memory, but she knew she had never thought about it before and became confused. "How do you know such things?"

"Because I think, Stephanie, I think. I look deep into myself and I'm honest about all I see."

She saw fire in his eyes and her heart pounded because of it. She recognized that fire, but how? She had never seen it before. Stephanie stared into his eyes for a very long, silent moment. It was as if she was learning through his eyes, feeling his thoughts. She heard herself speak softly, passionately, truly. "I thought I would never say this to anyone, Vaughn, but I look into your eyes and I see beauty there."

Vaughn was dumbstruck, having never heard such words, especially spoken to him. "You do? *Really*?" He was totally shocked, even a little afraid of what he heard, per chance it would be taken back.

She looked at him oddly, confused by his reaction. "Of course. Didn't you know it? How could you not know that with all you were just saying?" Stephanie was perplexed and her questions sent home the fact that she was, no doubt, sincere.

In her words, her eyes, and her touch, he could feel her appreciation, her understanding of him and her help by showing him something he had not known before and by making him *think*.

Vaughn felt an overwhelming presence surround him as her words and eyes seemed to carry a power far beyond their simple utility. "Ahh, I don't know! Ahh, I just didn't kn . . . know." Tears crept into the corners of his eyes.

"Vaughn, are you in pain? Why are you crying?"

"It's nothing. It'll pass." He sobbed once. Somehow, it seemed like his own prayer was being answered, as he felt a presence greater than himself all around him. Love. It had surrounded him when she had asked him how he could not know she saw beauty inside of him. As if it wasn't just her asking, but Love was asking him to realize what he had become and was becoming even more of, a beautiful *person*.

Stephanie hung her head down and said, "Vaughn, it's true what my mother said about me. I'm really not . . ."

Vaughn snapped out of his thoughts and found himself speaking before he even thought of the words. "Don't go there. How can she speak truth when she doesn't even know her own self? I can tell just by looking at her. No mother could treat her daughter the way I just saw and know much truth about *anything*."

"But Vaughn, I *am* nothing!"

Vaughn's tone grew angry again, "Yeah? Then what was the meaning of the prayer you prayed? I heard it! You said if that happened to you, you would be nothing. But it didn't happen! So, what something are you still, now?"

Confusion filled her face that mingled with growing tears. "I. . . don't know!"

"Stephanie, *I know!*" he said confidently.

She picked her head up wondering. "What? How? You don't even know me!" She wept with memories that were *all* shameful, all she could see, all she could feel. She felt like nothing, even more so as he held her arms. She felt she didn't deserve to be held by such a gallant man. She wanted to pull away, she was so acutely aware of her wretchedness.

"Stephanie, I know, because I can see it in *your* eyes, even through the tears and sobs."

That undid her, and as she wailed, she blurted out. "See *what*?"

"A light shining in your eyes. Behind all your pain is a *beautiful* light. Don't weep, *please* don't weep." He held her as she collapsed onto his chest, ignoring the pain. He hugged her tight, but she was embarrassed at crying.

"I, I . . . can't help it! *I'm just a woman* and I'm getting your chest all wet. I'm sorry!"

He picked her off his chest to look her in the eyes, but she hung her head. "Why are you talking like a foolish girl? What do you mean by such *foolish* statements?"

"I don't know what *you* mean." She sobbed.

"Why do you feel like you have to apologize for your true tears? It's an honor to me to be wetted by them."

She shook her head, "What? Huh?" She picked her head up, looking strangely at him. He was doing it again, transporting her to . . . somewhere. Her gaze went into the beyond.

"Why are you shaking your head at me?" Vaughn began to worry. It was too good to be true.

"You . . . you're so . . . different! How do you say such things?"

"I'm sorry, I know I'm weird." He looked away from her, knowing she saw him, now, like everyone else, how *different* he was.

All of a sudden Stephanie understood. She remembered the stories, the jokes, the teasing of him. *But that hasn't been done in a while.* She felt as if lightning struck her, as she saw him shrinking away before her very eyes. "Now *you* just wait a minute!" She scolded him with fire in *her* eyes, feeling where he was going, feeling as if *she* was stabbed in the heart. "I wasn't saying it was bad. Different doesn't mean bad. In fact, I think you are so . . . beautiful! What you say . . . it makes sense to me in ways I can't even understand."

They both looked at each other through tears. "You're kidding me. You're joking," he said.

"No. Why would I joke?" She raised then scrunched her eyebrows at him, confused that he would doubt it, yet deeply understanding.

"You're serious. You really feel like I make sense?"

She rolled her eyes at him. "Well, yeah, don't you make sense to yourself?"

Vaughn thought about what just happened to him inside. *There. She did it again to me. She asked me a powerful question that said so much more than any simple answer. I can feel the meaning but . . . it's all in a big picture! I'll have to remember to come back to this in my meditations to understand it all. I want to know it all. I think she just told me to have faith in myself and what an idiot I was for not having it!*

He laughed to himself at the way she rolled her eyes at him. "Yeah, I guess I do make sense to me. It's just that no one has ever believed me before or been helped by what I say. Do you have any idea how wonderful you have just made me feel? Let me tell you . . ."

The dam burst open. His mind summoned the last year's major experiences, and he began recounting his life to her:

His mother was scolding Vaughn at the dinner table.

"Why are you crying? You're too old for that. If you don't like it here, why don't you go back and live with the ancient natives since you have so much against our culture. Way out West I hear they just discovered the remnants of some ancient tribe still living in the hills." His mother said it with particular scorn.

"Mom, modern things don't make a happy life. All you do is worry . . . worry all the time about money. There's more to life than that."

"Of course, I love you. But someone has to worry about it. Your Father doesn't."

"Mom, all you do is yell, fight and worry. Fear, fear . . . fear is not life! Fear is death, because that's what you're really looking at. You're afraid of something terrible happening to you if you don't have *money*, eventually a tragic life, which you perceive as some kind of death. But you're dead already! Mom, if you loved life you would appreciate the things *of* life."

His mother reacted like a stirred up hornets' nest. She threw down her spoon onto her plate with a sharp clang and grabbed her husband's arm in a vice-like grip, "What? What is he talking about? Alex, what is he talking about, talk some sense into him."

"Leave me alone, he's crazy. We work hard to give him a good life."

Vaughn couldn't help asking. "A life of screaming and hypocrisy? That's what you call a good life?"

His father actually thought for a while then replied, "He's right!"

The instantaneous reaction was to be expected. "WHAT? *Are you crazy too*?" She decided to save her fight with her husband for later and refocus on her son. "OK. You need money. What are you going to do without money? WE work hard because we love you."

But Vaughn lost control, he couldn't help it. It was as if some greater presence had come into him. It wasn't anger that shouted. "LOVE! Love, you don't even know the first meaning of the word!"

His mother countered. "How you going to live then?"

Vaughn waited, felt something move in him and he heard himself say and agree with what he was saying. "Love, if you really follow it, by love!"

His mother was flummoxed. She returned her grip on her husband's arm, fixing her beady eyes on him. "Alex, did you hear that? He's going to live by love! Ha! Love didn't put food on your table. *We did.*"

"You don't understand! Love is life. It's a part of life because it's good. If you really live by love, Life will make a way for you because Life is Love. It wouldn't let you down. Can't you feel that?"

"Alex, have you ever heard of such craziness? Where does he get such craziness from?"

The flow of words began to pour from Vaughn and he was awed at the power of them as he felt them come out of his mouth. "Look at yourself, you're *dead* already. Don't you see? We can love, so that's a part of life, somehow. Not just a physical life, but a heart-life and because Life gives us love, it must have a way for us to live by it and not starve. I don't know how it would be done, only that it would be, because I've found out inside myself that this life is alive because of love, and I didn't create these ways, they created me! Life is more than just me, or you. Life has its own way to it . . . and . . . and we can only live by that way . . . and, and . . . that's why Love would help us!" Vaughn never spoke such words before. The understanding, the words, the actions all seemed to come together in the moment. Yet, they felt connected to him, like the words had grown from where he had been before.

"Alex, stop reading the paper. Would you listen to him? He's crazy. Talk some sense into him." She grabbed his paper away. She hated it when he read at the dinner table.

"Leave me alone. He'll grow out of it."

She refocused on Vaughn, "Where did you get such garbage? That *stupid* psychologist, I knew I didn't like him. You know, Alex, he told me I was hopeless! That's why he stopped our visits!"

"Well, you are hopeless!"

Her eyes almost popped out of her head. "Go ahead! Stick up for him! You're always siding against me."

The man raised his arms above his head and shouted. "You're hopeless, I'm hopeless, he's hopeless, we're ALL HOPELESS!"

She shook her head and looked away, almost laughed. Her tone softened. "You idiot, stop throwing your arms around like a crazy man. How can you joke about something like this?"

He spoke humorously and kindly to his wife, "Because it's funny. Let the kid alone. He'll grow out of it when he sees what the real world is like."

But Vaughn was incredulous. He took an instructional tone with his parents. "Mom, Dad, I'm fourteen, I see what the world is like. And, *no*, I did not get this from the psychologist. He doesn't really do anything but ask me questions. I…I just sit and think, and I do a lot of thinking at home . . . when I'm rocking or bumping my head on my hand, I'm thinking, feeling deeply, like meditating about life, to block out the world and see life. I came to this understanding on my own, from what I really see in myself and about life. You mention God, and you make me go to services and all that crap . . ."

Ooops! Vaughn shouldn't have lit that fire. His father had been a neutral party until then.

Alex lowered his glare upon his son. "Crap? *Crap*? We spent good money to send you there."

"Your money doesn't mean a crummy thing." Vaughn shot back in anger before he could help it.

Both parents responded as one with a prolonged, "*What*?"

Vaughn was rejoined by that presence inside him and he spoke boldly, "That's right. All they teach is pride in something that is *not* life. Country, religion, pay your taxes, give money to the church, and recite those *ridiculous, boring* prayers! Do you really think God would hear that *crap*? Bleh! If anything should be called God, it would be this Spirit of Life I am talking about. Not someone's psychological, political construction of traditions and junk like that, an excuse to feel special. Like the ways they have are not really death, just because they believe in some God. If they really believed in a true God, they wouldn't be dead like you!"

Both his parents' mouths dropped open. They had heard of teen rebellion, but this was more than a teen's ranting.

His father was silent and his mother could barely get out the words. "The Lord helps them who help themselves."

But Vaughn had meditated on his Mother's favorite saying. It was a true saying in one way, but she used it to mean the opposite of that. "You *hypocrite!* You only say that because you only have faith in your money, in your supposed power to *get it.* What you mean by this statement is that you can't count on God. You can only count on *yourself.* In fact, the way you speak it, you discount God all together! I, on the other hand, truly follow that saying. I search for truth and because God sees me search, He helps me!" As Vaughn said it, he realized it was true!

His Mother was stone quiet for a few moments. Really in shock, then she barely said, "Can't believe this kid. Where does he get all this *crap*?"

Master GrrraGagag's head was pounding. He spoke the sentence along with her, equally in disbelief.

". . . he get such crap? Who does he think he is? What does he think he is? It's all that stupid *thinking* he does. Scraback, we have to stop him from thinking. Give him something else to do."

Scraback felt more and more accepted by his Master. And his Master's order potentially gave him orb freedom. That was good for his plan. *Why not make it a double experiment?*

Master GrrraGagag thought, *There's something odd about the boy.*

Lying beside him in her bed, propped up by old pillows, her hand still upon his chest, Stephanie couldn't believe all Vaughn had just told him. "You really said all that to your parents?"

Nodding, he replied. "And there's much more I have to tell you!"

Stephanie heard herself say, "More." But she couldn't imagine much more.

Vaughn had decided to select the things from his past that he thought would also help Stephanie. *This is a good way to do it,* he thought. *Helping her without her knowing, that's my intent. I don't want her to think I'm preaching at her.*

He was about to go to the next major event when Stephanie asked him, "Vaughn, why does your mother act like that and why doesn't your father do anything?"

The last part brought a huge laugh from him. "My father is. . . like oatmeal!"

"Huh?"

"He just sits behind his newspaper like oatmeal sits in a bowl looking like mush! But truly, I don't think there's anything that can be done with my mom. I've tried. You see, my great grandmother, so I am told, lived through the terrible terrorist plague. She had ten kids at the time. *Ten!*"

"TEN! How could they afford it?"

"Well, I'm told she belonged to some very old fashioned group or something and they believed in big families."

"What group?"

"I don't know. I get the feeling the government forbade this kind of knowledge to be passed on so they just didn't! I think it was a former religious thing. It would have been too risky for parents to tell their children. What if a kid started talking about it in school, then the government would find out and take them all away, accusing them of trying to bring back the old destructive religions."

"But Vaughn, this government's religion *is* crap! Why do they even have it? It's obvious it's a lie."

"Stephanie, I think you just said the reason they have it! They created it so people would believe God is a lie and, therefore, leave all religion alone eventually!"

Stephanie stilled, digesting the extent of Vaughn's words. She whispered, "My God, Vaughn, that's terribly evil. Create a religion to destroy people from all belief in a Greater Good."

"Yeah, so all they'll believe in is science, reason, and the government. By reason I mean *only* the government's reason. You know, the war wasn't called the Great Religious War for nothing, and notice that our government blames the South and all former religions for that war. But we up north are the only good guys, because we were liberal enough not to be tricked by the old religions and hence, the War wasn't our fault. And then low and behold, lookie here, our leaders discovered the only true religion! How convenient. Stephanie, hardly anyone goes to church now."

"I know it, just a few old ladies, and the local *priest.*" Her last word sounded like she spit.

Vaughn noticed her extra disgust with the priest and made a note to himself to ask her later. "They make us go to church when we're young to make us afraid of the government more than fearing their God. And I think, so that we can realize we don't need religion!"

"God! Vaughn, that is too devious."

"Well, I don't have any proof of it, but it really seems that that's the result, and I have to believe they like the result, otherwise they would change things." Vaughn paused, realizing he'd been sidetracked. "Anyway, getting back to my mom, my great-grandmother apparently was in a terrible situation because after the plagues, when the North and South were still together as one country, other countries launched huge bombs they called nuclear missiles against the terrorist countries where a lot of the oil and gas came from. Anyway, from all that happened as I understand it, the economy collapsed and money was worth almost nothing. People had to work to be paid in food, and my great-grandmother kept threatening she was going to sell the children who didn't work hard enough!"

Stephanie gasped. "I think that's even worse than what I went through. Vaughn, that's *terrible*. But what does that have to do with your mom?"

"Well, my mom's mom was one of her kids, and she grew up terrified of not making enough money and was in constant fear."

Stephanie's hand went to her mouth. "Oh, my God! She passed that same *crap* down to your mom. But then when does it all stop?"

Vaughn leveled his eyes at Stephanie and they seemed to turn even darker for an instant. "With me, Stephanie. It stops with *me!* I won't live like that. It's death." Vaughn saw Stephanie's brows knit together.

Her eyes went distant with the look of deep thought. "My father, who left me when I was only seven, he *hates* women. But I think he does because I remember him saying his mother was very mean. She tried . . . no, I remember, he said she *did* rule over his father and everyone else with terrible meanness, and that his father was weak like yours." She paused and then looked deeply into Vaughn's eyes. "But I don't see any of that in *your* eyes. I mean, you have very similar conditions as my father did, but you don't hate women. You're *nothing* like him. You've been so careful with me to make me feel good and show me *I am a person* and that you're no better than me . . ." She left her statement hanging as if to also ask a question.

Vaughn nodded again. "Because I *think*, Stephanie. I *refuse* to let the *outside* dictate what I should be on the *inside,* not even if it's my *parents* doing the dictating! I have my own heart and mind, and I'm responsible to Life, capital L, to be a good person, to *understand* what that really means. Your father grew up hating women because a woman was mean to him. Well, what caused her to be so hateful, or my mom to be so wretched? Perhaps it was even worse men! But does it matter now? All that matters is that we be brave enough to put a stop to the whole miserable cycle and honor what Life would have us to truly be." He paused and searched her face. The look of wonder glowed in her eyes.

"Let me tell you some more about myself before you go thinking I'm so great."

Around noon Vaughn was standing in the middle of his spacious bedroom holding a book open, *The Art of Fighting*, when his mother walked in. He was just in the middle of working through a triple move: rotate, cross kick right, back kick left, backhand left, when she startled him. Her voice gathered intensity. "Vaughn, what's going on here?"

He didn't want his Mother to know, but now he had to tell the truth. He hung his head a bit. "I'm learning how to fight, Mom."

This was *not* what she wanted to hear. She had always taught him to run away from fights and not to get in trouble. You couldn't trust people these days. Besides, they were wealthier than most and above such guttural things as fighting. Her lips turned into thin lines and her eyes narrowed. "I taught you not to fight."

"Mom, *please*, I have to become a *man*. There are all kinds of bullies at school, and I can't run away from them. There's no place to run. I'm just learning how to defend myself . . . in case I can't run. "Vaughn realized he needed to change the direction of the conversation. In the *Art of Fighting*, it specifically said that when facing a losing battle, one must change directions to change the situation. His mother was always a losing battle. She put her hands on her hips trying to decide if he had complied with her demand. When he noticed a book in her hand, he decided to redirect further, and pointed, "What's that, Mom?" It worked; the battle was over as she focused on the new situation.

"I bought a book for you." She tossed it on the bed. Vaughn was touched by the surprise gift. He felt love.

"Thank you, Mom. What is it?"

"Well, since your Father doesn't want to tell you anything, and I don't want you to just pick it up on the street . . . well, you need to know about this. This book is highly recommended, so make sure you read it. Just remember, don't be getting some girl pregnant."

Vaughn hesitated and Stephanie thought he was done. *What a strange story,* she thought, *but actually kinda useful. Hmm, his learning how to fight saved me.*

"So that's how you learned how to fight? Like what you just did earlier?"

Vaughn nodded. He was still trying to decide whether to tell her the next part, as it was embarrassing, but he realized she was terribly ashamed of *her* immorality. Her seeing how he dealt with his might be a help to her. Also, in the back of his mind, he didn't want her to think he was too good for her.

Vaughn sighed. "I'm going to tell you some things that I'm not proud of, actually ashamed of. But I just feel like I want you to know them before you go looking at me like I'm some great hero person."

Stephanie started to protest that he didn't have to, but he touched her lips to silence her. She realized his mere touch was enough to accomplish it.

"The book my mother gave me was all about sex."

CHAPTER 6

Sex is . . .

Instructor Claynomore opined. "Our superiority to humans is evidenced by our differences in reproduction. For them to reproduce, they must start out with the tiniest parts of themselves, even single cells, and they have no say at all in what offspring they get. We, on the other hand, consume whatever we desire and consciously choose which of those meals we wish to mingle with what part of our own essence.

And, we don't waste anything. From that, we know exactly what offspring we get."

Underling Scraback pondered. "Is that why it's so rare for an offspring to consume his Sire?"

Instructor Claynomore Eyed the youngster. "Well, nothing is foolproof."

"I went through the pages of the book my mother gave me for the *third* time, studying the female pictures and reading the male functional descriptions. I told myself, 'Oh! Hmmm! I never knew that. Pleasure, *intense* pleasure . . .

hmmm, how could that be? You just, huh? Oooh, so that's why it does that! Oh, that's what the other kids were talking about, only with different words. Hmmm, gee, I've been such a jerk!' But I was a complete *idiot,* Stephanie! I didn't know what the hell I was doing, only that I could."

As Vaughn continued sharing his history with Stephanie, Master GrrraGagag mused aloud, "The *fool* didn't even realize what he'd done to himself. He was enamored with the pleasure, the fun. It's the teenage secret, you know. It's why so many of them fall so fast and hard. And we have his dear, loving mother to thank for this one. I could . . . kiss her, her and the great, wise child psychiatrist who wrote the book to help millions of children. Ha! I know him! Do you know what he fantasizes about, Scraback? Ha! Kids! He had such a guilty conscience, he had to produce a theory of sex and a publication to bring everyone onto his level so that once the norm changes, then that becomes what's right, and poof, no more guilt. A brilliant man! How great their society is to allow such people such a say over their children's lives. But his mother didn't have to go through that trouble, because next year I've got all the schools listing that very same book as required reading.

Stephanie didn't know what to say, but all of a sudden she had an urge to tell Vaughn about *her* life, about *her* shame. But before she could begin, Vaughn began another story:

"Days later after I got that *gift* from my mom, I sat beside a much larger boy who held a magazine of naked women that I eagerly wanted to see. 'Let me see. C'mon, let me see.' But the big fellow took his time showing me, so he could build the suspense. He knew *exactly* what he was doing, boasting, 'Oh yea, she looks really hot! Stop grabbing the mag!' I could hardly believe the excitement, the absolute awe. 'Wow, I never knew women looked like that, and . . . did *that!*'

"The kinda fat boy asked, 'Are you getting hard?' He placed his hand on my crotch and squeezed. I was busy with the magazine but I pushed him away, telling him to stop. The pages had *real* people in vivid sexual acts and there was this scintillating story we both read to ourselves. I had the magazine over my lap, hiding my excitement that by then flooded every fiber of my body. I kept repeating, 'Wow!' He asked me if I wanted to do it but I was oblivious. Some part of me just wanted release and didn't care how.

But his *trap* was sprung so this boy keeps moving on me while we sat right there on his back porch! A part of me just ignored his hand while I finished reading that *lurid* story and like an idiot I kept gasping, 'Wow! Wow!' Then suddenly he calls me 'faggot, faggot!' After grabbing me again, he jumped up and jerked the magazine away, saying to me, "Oh, this is great. What an absolute piece of garbage you are, and that look on your face, I'll always remember it!" I was bewildered and didn't know *why* I let him do that and I ran home.

Stephanie flashed with anger. "*Gary* did *that* to you?" Surprised she figured out it was Gary, Vaughn just nodded.

GrrraGagag pondered the incident, too. Scraback was in awe of how utterly twisted human minds and hearts could be.

"Oh, superb, marvelous Master, let me guess. Because the other boy touched him and called him that name, he should think he's not right for women?"

"Let's just keep watching," his Master said, demonstrating a bit of patience with his underling.

Vaughn resumed his narrative. "So I locked myself in the bathroom where I knew my Mom wouldn't disturb me and began to think . . . Faggot. Faggot! That's when two men . . . But how can people do that? Hmm, what if they're just born like that? Well, one thing is for sure, it's wrong to fault anyone for being born what he or she is. They didn't have a choice. But was *I* born like that? How did I let him do that to me? I can't believe he even got the chance to do that. How . . . this desire I have, it comes and goes. Hmm, what if someone had an intense desire and the first thing that came into focus for him was another person of the same sex?

"Hmmm, I suppose they could trick themselves into thinking they were in love with the same sex. Hmmm, no, not love, but desire all the same. Hmmm, for that matter, I guess they could fall for a tree, if it happened like that. Faggot. Could I? I'm a man, or at least I'm coming to be . . . and my nature, my nature is . . . What does it feel like? Hmmm, the words. The words . . . How to put it into words . . . it's different from a woman, I can just tell, even from pictures or my own imagination. Different, how? I can't see myself with another man.

"But why? Let's see, I imagine I'm with a woman. I feel this way, reaching out, giving . . . and, and . . . yes, treasuring her. Why? because . . . she is . . . delicate, soft, and receiving. My strength is accepted by her softness . . . my strength cherishes her softness, appreciates it, not just her body, her person . . . and . . . and, ahh, her softness of both body and person, *femininity*. Yes, that's right, her *femininity* sort of does the same thing to my strength, but in reverse. Her softness embraces my strength, appreciates it! Ahh, *we work together*, each appreciating in the other what each does not have in themselves so we need that from the other. We both give and receive but the giving and receiving is different for both.

Now, let me imagine, two men together . . . oh, both can't be what they are at the same time. One has to try to be like a woman, that kind of feeling inside the person. Hmmm, could I be like that? Hmmm, *no*, I know that would be a lie. I would be going against my own self, my own feelings. I'm not a faggot. I'm gonna get me a woman."

GrrraGagag nodded. Scraback was in awe at the boy's ability to think. He always admired thinking.

"Master GrrraGagag, I can't believe that boy's ability to think. How could he possibly do that? Think for himself like that."

But GrrraGagag remained smug and explained, "All is not lost. He *still* intends to *get* himself a woman. I can tell. He'll do harm to her like that, because to merely *get* a woman, is hardly better than what he does in the bathroom! Actually, it is better! Because he'll bring the reality of meaninglessness to her, as well as to himself, but maybe even more so, because *each* will have to devalue both themselves and each other when they use themselves just for meaningless pleasure. Oh, let me see that little vermin boy talk about love *then*."

Stephanie riveted her eyes upon him as she still expected him to tell her about the women he had been with. She had so many different, strange feelings tumbling through her but Vaughn didn't begin by telling her about women. He began with what he did to Gary just days after his embarrassment. And as he continued his story, she realized, *I have met Vaughn before!*

"I had planned out what to do to Gary, thought it out, reasoned it out, and imagined it through and through, just like the *Art of Fighting* instructed. Rule eight: When declaring formal war, plan, then think about your plan, then reason about it, then imagine it until you are sure you have fought the battle ten times. Then I asked myself, would the actual doing of it be as sweet as the imagination?

It was even better that my friend, Waverly, was along to see it. Waverly's a tall, broad shouldered, very mild fellow with odd, deep gray eyes. You've probably seen him around. Anyway, I called out, 'Hey Gary, come 'ere!' And he replies with his usual arrogance, 'What is it, fag . . .' But he *choked* on his final word because even though Gary was a whole head taller than me and broader all the way through, he still flew up and backwards when my *fist* slammed up under his chin. Well, Waverly just stood there gaping while some red-haired girl ran over to tend to the *poor* unconscious victim."

Stephanie burst into his story. "Vaughn, that was *me!* That was *me* . . . a whole year ago, right after I met Gary. I turned just in time to see Gary going down and I rushed to his side. You and I met . . . sort of. To think I actually felt *sorry* for that *bastard!*"

"Sorry, I really didn't know because your hair hid your face and frankly, I wasn't interested."

Vaughn then recounted the conversation after the punch. "Waverly was amazed. 'Wow, Vaughn! What ya do *that* for? You *knocked him out!*' I replied, 'Truth, Waverly, *truth!* Besides, even if I was born that way, *which I'm not,* it would still be wrong to be treated like that.'

"Waverly shook his head and his eyes sorta widened trying to see if I'd become crazy then told me 'Huh? My folks taught me that it's *always* wrong to fight.'

"So I put my arm up on his shoulder as we walked away and smiled this big reassuring smile at him, then explained, 'First, there was no fight. It takes two to fight, and he's in no condition. But more importantly, a punch doesn't make itself wrong because it's a punch, but the *reason* for the punch makes it right or wrong.' So Waverly asked, 'Well, what reason could possibly make *that* right?'

"My answer was the same: 'Truth, Waverly, truth.' But he tried to corner me, by clarifying, 'But you didn't *say* anything to *be* true.' Well, I had thought it all out beforehand and said, 'Oh yes I did. Actions speak too, Waverly. And some truth is best believed when put into action, only believed when put into action. He *won't* be calling me *that* anymore, and hopefully, *no one else, either.*' Waverly looked me straight in the eye and said, 'I believe you, Vaughn!' Then I begged him to stop shaking his head, it wasn't that big a deal, but I was quite glad to see I'd made a believer out of him."

Stephanie didn't say a word as she contemplated her own disapproval of violence, so Vaughn continued recalling that momentous day. "Waverly invited me to sleep over that night so we could play Cressen. I hadn't whopped him at that yet, and we usually stayed up all night talking, which I love to do. Anyway, I agreed, adding it was a great way to get away from my parents again.

"'All these stinking years, all they do is fight, but with no truth behind the blows. They won't listen to me. They think I'm crazy. Not because I do weird things, because I *don't* anymore. It's because of the things I *say!'* But Waverly said he thought I had a way with words so I pointed to his head and then his heart, and said 'Waverly, see where I'm pointing? It's up here, that's all, up here and here in the heart. All you gotta do is just *think*. Think and feel, and think about what you feel, and feel about what you think.'

"Waverly laughed, replying, 'Vaughn, you sound like you're discovering the lost treasures of that ancient King!' I asked him who and he told me, 'A little while ago they discovered this ancient tribe out West, all these years they hid themselves. Their story was actually on the news! They told an old tale about their ancient land and a boy who killed this all powerful wizard king.'

"I frowned 'cause there are no such things as wizards, they're just make-believe. But Waverly insisted, 'Yeah, well, this king had super powers like a wizard and the story goes that this boy outsmarted him. He was a thinker, just like you. But then he became king and is said to have written a book of wisdom.' Now I got interested in *that* and asked, 'Yeah? What's the name of it?' But Waverly said no one knows, because no one ever found it."

Stephanie uttered the same question Vaughn had asked Waverly, "How'd they know he wrote it, then?"

Vaughn replied with Waverly's explanation. "'Because people passed the stories about it down through the ages, and this strange looking native girl on the news told us about it.' I also told Waverly that I sure would've liked to read *that* book so I asked him, 'What stories did the people pass down? Did they get written down? Maybe his wisdom is recorded?' Waverly answered, 'Maybe. I don't know, the girl didn't say. Everyone's turning this story into sort of an old saying, though.' Want to know the saying, Stephanie?" His question definitely amused him and then her.

Nodding vigorously, she smiled so Vaughn recalled Waverly's answer. "'When someone thinks you're acting too smart, they'll say, So you think you're a king Metran . . . where's *your* book of wisdom?' I told him I *hate* that kind of attitude of arrogant sons-of-dogs but then I recanted, saying I shouldn't have called them that. So Waverly asked if I'd sworn off swearing so I explained that I don't believe in swearing except if the *meaning* is accurate. When I called them sons-of-dogs, I think I might have been insulting dogs, or the kingdom of dogdum! Waverly fell to the ground in laughter repeating, 'Kingdom of Dogdum, insult dogs?'"

Stephanie laughed, too. Vaughn liked her hand on his chest and fancied that she was somehow pouring strength into him, as he did feel a lot stronger, and the pain continued to lessen. He asked her, "Have you ever heard of such an ancient king? I'd really like to find out more."

She had never even heard the story before so she just shook her head.

Unfortunately, those eavesdropping did not share his sense of humor.

"Kingdom of Dogdum. I can't watch any more of this right now, Scraback. I have *other* business I must also attend to. Our lives don't revolve around this wretched boy and that trollop." *This should give Scraback the time he needs to meddle with the girl and boy, if the* idiot *takes the bait. Underlings should always be counted upon to do what we're not allowed.*

"But Master, I thought you said it *starts* with the individual soul." Scraback wished he could have called back his words even before he started them. He was going to have to do something about his habit of speaking before thinking.

Master GrrraGagag narrowed his Great Eye at him, and his forthcoming words gathered intensity as he spewed them. "Idiot, thoughtless spawn, they're *teenagers.* Even a year or two makes absolutely no difference to us in their miserable lost lives. They're so vulnerable we can interdict and correct them anywhere along their pitiful teenage life. What I'm planning is *perfect.* What I've got in mind for the boy, you'll see, his thinking won't do him a damned bit of good. One tiny little victory on his part has hardly made any difference to his tree.

His next move is probably going to be to have sex with the girl. As far as the girl is concerned, did you forget? Gary won't stop until they've destroyed her. It's just a matter of time." GrrraGagag vanished.

"Master? Master?" *Master is gone.*

Scraback pulled out his book, *The Forest.* He was a fast reader, consuming most of the book in a single ethereal night. Something had caught his Eye near the end:

> Orb Technical Difficulties:
>
> Problem 233: Orb vision blinks intermittently. Check Master Spyware to improve discrete orb self-monitoring.
>
> Index:
>
> Master Orders 1124… Master Record 2348…
>
> Master Spyware 3b Appendix… Master Switch…
>
> Appendix 3b…
>
> When Master Spyware is on, the orb may blink. See Master's Orb Handbook.
>
> *Master's handbook? I can't get a hold of that. Spyware? Hmmm…*
>
> Problem 491-Spyware didn't record proper time. Check timer located . . .

"OK Stephanie, all that was a whole year ago, but there's a lot of other spiritual stuff I want to tell you, but you need time to think about what I just told you first. But I want to tell you how I came to Gary's house tonight."

Stephanie nodded and for some reason goose bumps began to rise all over her arms. She sensed something greater than herself, but this time it wasn't evil, it was like Goodness surrounding her. She felt her heart opening up in some mysterious way.

Vaughn hadn't forgotten that he wanted to tell her about the woman he'd been with, but he knew he couldn't tell her about the details. It just wouldn't be right. But he could tell her this way, and that would serve all the best purposes.

"Last night I pushed the board game with my finishing move across Waverly's rickety old table. The little table's between the two twin beds upstairs. It almost fell over, and I sure didn't want that to happen because I finally won! But just listen how the rest of our conversation went.

"Vaughn, I can't believe you actually beat me."

"Ha, maybe there's a first time for everything, huh?"

"I don't know, you played very differently than I've ever seen you play before."

"I'm *fifteen* years old now, Waverly, and I'm able to do much more than when I was younger."

"Yeah, even if you're still *short*.' Waverly laughed."

Vaughn paused and looked wryly at Stephanie who remembered how she kept doubting him because he was small, so she blushed. "Sorry" she said, knowing exactly why he had emphasized that particular point in the story. *His size really didn't matter. He saved me, anyway.*

Vaughn continued recounting last night's events. "I said, 'Look. Waverly, last year I was two inches shorter, and you saw what I did to Gary even back then.' And he replied, 'Oh yeah, that was great. It's funny, he's even bigger now, but he avoids you like the plague. It's so funny, I think you scare him.' I said, '*I hate him.*' Waverly's a pacifist and looked *so* worried and said 'C'mon Vaughn, that's a bit strong.' I admitted that but I can't explain it . . . I have this intense hatred for Gary, and I don't know exactly why. Every time I look at him . . . I think it would be right to kill him! . . . that he should be dead . . . not allowed to walk the Earth."

Seeing Stephanie's reaction, he reassured her. "I would never do anything like that, though. That's what I told Waverly, that it's just a feeling, but I can't help thinking that somehow I'm seeing something about him that others don't see.

"Waverly did compliment me by admitting, 'Vaughn, I think you see a lot of things others don't see. That stuff you talk about, life and love, you know, it's pretty good. I mean, I don't know about that too much, but somehow it makes sense.'

"Then I tried something. I focused deeply into his eyes trying to sorta reach through them into his mind to inspire him. 'Waverly, to understand it, you have to feel it, you can't just think it. You've got to use your mind to bring love into clear focus in your heart, the essence of Love, itself. When you try to do this, all kind of crap will get in the way. I think it's mostly all the crap we absorbed from our parents and surroundings. We're too young, I think, to have manufactured all that ourselves. At least, I'd like to think so.

"And to that, Waverly just responded, 'OK, I'm listening. Continue . . . I'll try not to fall asleep.' Can you believe he said *that* after all I just explained?

"Anyway, I tried to get through to him, saying, 'Very funny, this is important, pay attention. After I fight through a lot of the crap by reasoning about what love cannot be, I get a sort of vision that will come to me, that is more than just thought, more than just feeling, but both together in one, and says in both thought and feeling and action, I AM LOVE.'

"But Waverly just yawned then, so I had to kinda scold him. '*Listen!* Because that's just the beginning of knowledge. After you get in contact with Love, you have to let it teach you, because our mind doesn't have the capacity to understand it right away, or even at first to stay in contact with it for very long. It may only start out as a quick glimpse. But it's so real, so beautiful and . . . powerful. It's Life, Waverly, it's Life!'

"Waverly yawned again. 'Yea, well, remember that when you feel like killing what's-his-face.'

'Waverly, that's the scary part, that's why I just told you all this, so you can understand what I'm now about to say. I've come to feel and understand a lot more about Love and Life, and I can tell where my thoughts are coming from now, but it's not like it sounds. The thoughts are my thoughts, too, because I agree with them. They're never forced upon me like different kinds of feelings and thoughts. Waverly, the scary thing is that wanting to kill Gary is coming from Life itself!'

Stephanie sat bolt upright now, the same as Waverly had done but she didn't say anything. Vaughn continued. "Waverly held firm to his convictions though, even got upset, and scolded me, saying, 'That doesn't make sense. I think you've thought so hard, my friend, that you messed yourself up. I don't think it's good to think that much. It's . . . scary!'

"Stephanie, I can see you think this is . . . well, a little far-out, but I answered him honestly, 'I don't know Waverly, I don't know! I never proceed in my thinking unless what I've gained has proven itself over and over to me, how and why it's right. I know Love, my friend, and Life, I just can't stand that no one else seems to. You have no idea how miserable I feel. You're the closest person I've gotten to understand.'

"Unfortunately, Waverly contested that last part, saying, 'I wouldn't go that far. I said you have some interesting ideas, but to hear you talk now, I think maybe not. We'd better go to sleep.' He wanted to end the conversation, because it had gone way too far but he couldn't help but make one more comment. 'Vaughn, just one more thing and then we're *done* talking about this. *I don't like it,* but I have to say, that if you would do something like that, Kill Gary, I just can't help but feel something terrible would happen to you, too, down the line.' At that point, we each climbed into the twin beds. I'd become a regular at Waverly's house and felt at home there but I couldn't help being disappointed in him then.

"Anyway, I tried to explain further so Waverly wouldn't feel so uncomfortable with me, telling him, 'OK, I know what you mean but I feel this strange something inside, I don't know, a push in me. But not really a push, but more like an urging. It's not like it controls me or anything.'

"And after I said *that,* you know what Waverly said? 'Sounds like the need for sex, my friend. Hey, speaking of which, have you even gotten your first woman yet? Hey, how far'd you get?'

But I looked away, Stephanie, in actual *pain,* but my friend didn't notice. I just said, 'It doesn't feel right. I'm ashamed. I went with this girl, all the way, not long after the truth landed on Gary.'

"Waverly then suddenly regained interest in talking. 'You sure have a way with words, but I think you're CRAZY. If you find any more girls willing and you don't want 'em, pass 'em to me, good friend?'

"I *further* explained to him, 'Look, after it was over and I looked into her eyes . . . well, that's just it, I couldn't look into her eyes, and I didn't want her to look into mine. I've always looked people in the eye. It was the most terrible feeling of my life besides growing up at home. I couldn't wait to leave her, and I still can't look at her.' But Waverly asked who she was, joking, 'Maybe I can get some.'

"I couldn't help sighing at him, Stephanie, and I shot him this menacing look, assuring him that 'No. I won't tell you *that,* it's not right, and . . . I wasn't right. What would you say if I told you I was going to apologize to her?' Well Waverly rolled back and forth on his bed, roaring in laughter. I'd figured as much and was glad I didn't tell him I already had apologized!

"Waverly tried to convince me that, 'She wanted it as bad as you *still do.*' But I replied, 'That doesn't change the way I feel. Doesn't make it right. Maybe she could see it right, too.' But he added that if I apologized to her, she'd be insulted, not grateful, *insulted!* 'She'll think she's a whore.' Waverly didn't know just how very accurate his explanation was.

"And well, I guess if you think about it, that is what she is. But I told Waverly that, 'I don't see that my apologizing would all the sudden turn her into the whore she wasn't! So why be insulted? Not that I'm any better, but I will be, and maybe she can, too.

"Well, Waverly was shocked and politely reasoned with me, saying, 'Do I have to teach you everything? *You're wrong*. Girls want to do it as bad as we do, maybe even worse. So, when they do it, even though somewhere in their little girl minds they know they probably shouldn't, they want to do it and not think about the other thoughts, otherwise they can't enjoy it. So, they're not thinking about being a whore during or even after, even though they *are* whores. They do this girl thing and just put it out of their minds and strut like they're queens, even though they've been around the block ten times. If you apologize, you'll destroy that from her, and not only will she be *insulted*, she'll be *angry*, angry at you! I wouldn't go there if I were you!' When I thought about it, I had to agree that what he said was true enough."

Vaughn smiled broadly at Stephanie. "After that, we said our goodnights, but I couldn't fall asleep. Not ten minutes after we said goodnight, I snuck out of Waverly's house and came to you. The pull I felt wasn't sex, it was the spirit of Life leading me to *you!*"

Stephanie hung her head and couldn't look into his eyes. Wanting to cry for sadness competed with wanting to cry for joy, and strangely, the clash kept her from crying. Vaughn's spirit of Life and Love reminded her of her country meditations and the beauty she rediscovered. But this clashed with her terrible ordeal brought on by her utter lewdness. She remembered pulling out her nose ring and putting it back in to compare her two very different sets of feelings, but she hadn't finished her investigation of it. Now, Vaughn's stories brought both sides into clear focus like a mountain falling on her head, and silent tears slowly began to run down her cheeks, as now her internal clash evolved into grief.

She spoke flatly, "Your friend was right . . . about women being whores." Vaughn remained silent and after a pause she went on. "At the party, Karen called me the Queen of the Whores, and I acted just like your friend described. I completely blocked the truth from my mind. It's unbelievably clear to me now, but up until this time I'm sure I would've acted *just* as he described."

Vaughn could tell her mixed feelings. "I feel so bad, Stephanie, for having acted the way I did with the girl and other things. I did apologize to her and she did act like Waverly said."

I don't want to be like her! I don't want to be like me! Stephanie replied sobbing, "I feel very badly now, too, for the way I have acted."

Vaughn smiled. He had helped her to where he knew she needed to be, but he could tell she was now wallowing in her guilt which wasn't good either. "Stephanie, I guess one of the reasons I told you about myself was to help you think about yourself, too."

"I know, Vaughn! I could tell. It's sweet of you to do it that way. You're so kind and sensitive." She hung her head again in shame. "But . . ."

He interrupted a thought that he knew needed to be interrupted. "I am so glad for you now because of what you said!"

She shook her head. "Huh?"

He smiled. "The key words you spoke."

"What words? Which words?"

He smiled even more broadly. "'It's unbelievably clear to me now, but 'up until this time' That's what you said, Stephanie, and that means understanding has now changed you from what you were!"

She sat dumbfounded. Not because what he said was true, for she saw it was, but for the way he managed to bring its meaning to her, and the *way* he said it implied so much more. She looked him in his eyes with more tears slowly dripping and a hotness burning in her heart. "I want to thank you for saving my life." And they lingered in each other's eyes after she spoke.

They talked even more. Stephanie told him about her life as they lay in each other's arms, and Vaughn studied her closely. *Save the child, save the world. She's not the girl from my vision. She can't be. I don't think. Maybe I should tell her about it. Maybe she could help me find her.* But on further consideration, he balked. *No, she'll think I'm crazy.*

Vaughn finally concluded the conversation. "So, now you know why you've made me feel absolutely wonderful. You've asked me important questions, and I intend to meditate on them. I need the answers even more deeply because they're important to life, so you've made an important difference in my life already. No one has ever listened to me before *and understood* the things so important to me, but I can see you do, and that you really love what I say."

He didn't tell her how much he loved how she was caring for him, or how he loved to look into her eyes, or how he loved her touch because it was so gentle and caring, and that when she touched him, it seemed like he could feel her heart through her hand. His eyes told her though, without him even knowing they had. But it was her turn to doubt the goodness being delivered to her, as she felt oh so small.

"I have? Really? I made you feel good, *inside*?" she asked with all the innocence of a three-year old child. At that instant, her eyes looked three, her tone sounded three, and her touch felt like a three-year-old child.

He reached out his hand and held her cheek. "Of course, why wouldn't you make me feel wonderful? I don't understand *your* thoughts. I just explained some of why you do."

Stephanie shook her head. "I think I'm confused, or something. It just doesn't seem possible that a woman can make a man feel good *inside*."

His hand gently guided her eyes to his. "Stephanie, look into *my* eyes." Both hands were now cradling her face and she purred.

"Your hands feel so good on my cheeks." She squinted from the pleasure of truly being cherished.

"Look, please, don't squint."

She looked deeply for a while in silence. "What do you see?"

"I see, I see . . . so much . . . I see . . . the truth!" she said as if in another world.

"That's right. You're a woman, at least you will be when you grow up, and you make me feel wonderful *inside*, because you understand something about me that no one else does, and you *really* appreciate it. There is no greater honor from a woman than true appreciation like that, and you make me *think*. Now that I look inside myself . . .!" Vaughn was gently laughing. He noticed the pain in his side and gut no longer restrained him because it was almost gone!

"Silly, what are you laughing about?" She hit him lightly on the chest.

"A new feeling, dear! A new feeling. . . Stephanie, you make me feel like a man!"

She thought about *her* feelings. "Well, now that you mention it, you . . . you . . . make me feel like a . . . person . . . a woman person."

Just then her mother came into the bedroom and saw them holding each other. Vaughn's shirt was off.

"*What* are you two doing lying in bed together?" she quipped.

"Mama, we weren't doing anything. He's hurt and I was just holding him because he was cold."

"Get out of here before I call the keepers!"

"*Mama!*" She cried, truly hurt.

Vaughn smoothed back her hair from the side of her face. "It's OK, Stephie! It's OK. I'll be fine now. Remember what I told you about my parents and how to truly be free?"

She looked into his loving eyes with her own love. "Yes, Vaughn, I do, I'll listen . . . and do."

"What are you gibbering about?" Her mother's impatience was more than obvious.

Stephanie turned her gaze deeply into her mother's eyes for the first time, and locked her there! She paused to be sure her mother knew she couldn't get away. Something beyond her mother's will grabbed her, and they both knew it. "I love you Mama!" was all she said with the power of a unified truth in her heart and mind.

Decimated, her mother couldn't even get a whole word out. "Wha . . .?"

Her daughter pressed the assault with tenderness. "I love you, and I know you don't understand, but I've always loved you, even way back when you were teaching me colors!"

Her mother threw her fists up to her mouth to muffle her gasp. "You . . . you . . . remember way back then?"

"Yes, I do, Mama. In fact, it's a wonder now all of a sudden I remember. You were very happy for me as I was for you, *Mama.*" Stephanie's sniffs broke up her words. "I'm sorry . . . things . . . didn't . . . work out . . . for you!"

Tears were streaming down her Mother's face. "But, but . . . Oh GOD!" She collapsed to the floor, her heart breaking from all she had done and *didn't* do.

Stephanie rushed to her side, and Vaughn pulled himself up in bed. He had regained strength. "*Mama!* Are you alright? Vaughn, can you help me get Mama up? Mama, don't cry!"

"I'm, I'm . . . sorry . . . too! . . . Oh God!" Stephanie's mom wailed.

"Help me, Vaughn!" He pulled his tee shirt on, eyeing the weeping woman. The bitter taste of her cruel words when they first met still soured him, and more so now that he knew Stephanie. He could still feel the knife she had plunged into her daughter's heart, yet something was truly shaken in the woman.

For the last year he'd been trying to move even just a grain of sand within his own mother, but she'd somehow only gotten *worse.* But only knowing Stephanie a short time, and transferring to her just a tiny bit of Love's knowledge, she had quickly made it her own and produced this tremendous affect. *Is it just the fact that our two mothers are so different? Or, is it that Stephanie is somehow very special?* He had seen how strangely she had locked her mother in her stare, just watching, he could hardly pull himself away from it. *Or, is it* both *reasons?*

Vaughn went to her mother's other side and grabbed her around the waist, helping Stephanie lift her from the floor, but she hung limply. No venom to be found. Tears crept into his own eyes feeling how broken she was now. Stephanie had truly impacted her mother. His grip around her tightened, as he felt her suddenly to be precious, but at the same time, the gaping hole concerning his own mother widened. They put her in her own bedroom on her bed where she wept uncontrollably. Stephanie closed the door and led Vaughn to the front door.

They stood in the doorway and she didn't want to take her eyes from his. "Well, goodnight, then. I can't even put into words . . ."

He placed his finger on her lips. "I touch your lips, because you have done the same thing for me. This has been a night so full it seems we have lived a thousand years." He took her in his arms and for the first time hugged her passionately. But the way he cradled her was as if he were holding someone precious, important. And the straightness of his stance, into which he drew her, had dignity all through his posture. It was a passionate hug of the utmost respect, holding a woman of value, and she *knew* it.

She hugged him back with the same feeling. "Oh Vaughn, to hug you feels so . . . different."

"Same here, so alive, so meaningful, but . . ."

She sensed he was displeased with her and backed her head away to look at him. "What is it?"

"Could you *please* get rid of that stupid ring in your nose?" Her face tingled. "Ha, you're blushing!" He noted with a laugh.

She stepped back and paused. "I'd forgotten all about it. And now that I remember, I feel . . . *stupid* for even ever having it." She put both hands to the ring and undid it somehow, nudged Vaughn to the side of the door, and threw it as far as she could. Then, she put the back of her left hand to her forehead and tilted her head delicately to one side and with a sing-song-like voice said, "You know, Vaughn, I think I was temporarily insane."

"Ahhh, I love that sweet happy tone in your voice, you look so much better. You know, you don't need all that makeup either! It just hides your beautiful face. Besides, it doesn't mix well with tears. We'll meet tomorrow where we agreed upon so we can figure out what to do. We can't let those people continue on, or they'll surely do us in. You're right, I'm sure Gary wants to kill us. He has to be stopped. I think if we stop *him*, the others will have no heart to continue."

Stephanie's mind agreed with the decision. She very much wanted him *dead,* but as she listened to him say so, pain shot through her heart and he noticed it. "What is it Stephanie?"

She hesitated, and he gently squeezed her arms to urge her. "Vaughn, what about Waverly's warning? He said if you kill Gary he was sure something terrible would happen to you."

Vaughn stared at her. She could see the helplessness in his eyes. She grabbed his tee shirt, pulled him close and kissed his cheek. Her hands slid up his muscular chest to hold his face while she stared deeply into his eyes. "This is the face I saw in the window that saved my life."

He still felt life pouring into him through her. As she slid her hands up to his face his whole body energized with strength. When she held his face, her hands seemed to be love, itself. He took hold of her hands and kissed them and left. Stephanie went to talk with her mother. All of a sudden, she felt like a very new person – strong.

CHAPTER 7
Plans

"Do the devils really have power, Mother?" asked her son at sixteen.

"Does a hole have power if you fall in?" asked Queen Yinauqua.

"Father, every year I have answered your question the same. If the fate of the world depended upon someone and they didn't know it, I would tell them."

"Are you reconsidering your answer, my Son?"

"Yes. I believe in order to save the world they would have to keep from falling into holes. Telling them would not help, it might hurt!"

"Why?" asked the King.

"Because such a terrible responsibility can only be fulfilled through true love and understanding that comes naturally. Telling them would make them feel obligated. Obligation is not as strong as the other reasons. It might even interfere with what naturally comes through love. Obligation can be a loveless hole."

Both the King and Queen smiled. She answered, "If they are motivated by truth, then they will do right regardless of obligation. Our ways always seek the strongest life. That is why we do not believe in obligation. You are always free."

"I will always love you."

This was the most special thing she could think to share with Vaughn, she was so *very* proud of her shelter. Nothing in the world belonged to her, but *this* did. Nothing in the world said 'This is Stephanie', but her shelter did.

They walked hand in hand through the woods. As she turned, the familiar left reminded her of her country meditations before that terrible night. She wanted to go back to those thoughts right then and there, but didn't think she could if she wasn't alone.

As her hand went to her nose, she smiled. She remembered how profound her thoughts had been, but now, upon inspection, they seemed elementary. She had grown in knowledge without even realizing it! *How did that happen? I haven't thought on these things since last time. It wasn't that long ago.*

I never really belonged *to Gary or that group. They weren't really anything like brothers or sisters to me. It was all just inside my head because I wanted it to be that way. But then how do I determine what is truly real from what is in my head just because I want it to be real?*

The path through the woods narrowed, and Vaughn had to walk behind her. He smiled as she enthusiastically guided him which way to turn at each fork. At every turn she became more excited. He fancied himself a woodsman, having worked for the last two summers with farmers who taught him woodsmanship. But he was sure he would need Stephanie to guide him back out, because, frankly, he was lost. It truly was a secret.

He couldn't imagine what she'd built out here. Earlier, he tried to pry it out of her, but she demonstrated a stubbornness he didn't know she was capable of. He tried his best charms, his best psychology, but she rebuffed all of it like it was nothing. She wouldn't tell him a thing. 'You just have to see it for yourself,' she had said.

Vaughn grabbed Stephanie's arm and pulled her to a halt. The abruptness of it startled her. She turned around, but before she could say anything more he held his finger to his mouth, but it was the look on his face that kept her silent. She could tell he was listening for something. Deep blackness filled his eyes, scaring her. Not because she felt threatened by it, but because somehow she knew it was reaction to danger, and *that* scared her.

Then a low growl came from somewhere, nowhere, everywhere. Crashing of trees, something thrashing in the brush, and then it stopped somewhere to the right, but the vines, shrubs and trees hid it. *Was that a voice? No! . . . Another growl, an animal in terrible pain! No, a voice? . . . It was both!*

Vaughn was still holding her by the arm, and his grip began to hurt. She took his hand and tried to ease his fingers loose.

"Sorry," he said, as he let go. She grabbed his arm in both hands, pressing tightly.

Vaughn remembered the fifteenth rule from the *Art of Fighting:* Better to hunt the hunter than to be his rabbit. "This way," he whispered, heading back the way they came.

Stephanie wanted to ask questions, but knew she shouldn't talk. She watched him move like some hunting cat, swift but quiet, and tried to imitate his actions.

Then, he turned off left, then, another left. Stephanie made note of it, as she knew how easy it was to get lost in these woods. *Maybe that's all it was, a lost pet,* she thought. Then, they came upon a swath of crushed, broken brush and small trees. Something had definitely crossed the narrow path and cut its way through from right to left.

Vaughn stopped and stared right, then left. He pried Stephanie's hands loose and left her on the path as he went left a bit into the animal's trail. He touched where a small tree had been snapped. He stretched out his arms over some of the crushed bush. Stephanie's eyes grew larger. *He's measuring! He's trying to figure out how big it is!* He waved for her to come, but she wasn't sure she wanted to. But, on the other hand, she was sure she didn't want to be alone.

He knelt down and brushed dried leaves carefully aside. Underneath was some kind of print, partly the shape of a human foot, but longer and with claws. Stephanie could now see deep blackness swirling around Vaughn. She'd never seen such a sight. Ever since she was a little child, she had seen many strange things, but never this. She put her hand on his back as he crouched, feeling the track, measuring its depth with his finger. He shook his head and then stood up. Another growl, this time it was with words.

"Help me, kill me, *I'll kill you.*" Then words and growls

mixed unintelligibly. Then, "Death is life. This life is dead." More growls. "*Food!*" They crept slowly closer.

Why are we going towards *it? We should be running* from *it.* She grabbed Vaughn and pulled him to a halt, but he already had answer as he whispered, "You see how it moved through these woods? You can't run from something like this. So, we might as well go to it!" Her eyes told the story of how she felt about such a ridiculous idea, but then again, it made sense. Then, they rounded a bend in the newly forged trail and they saw it curled up, lying on the ground, panting.

It was a man dressed in ragged, brown clothing. Stephanie's heart immediately went out to him. She began to rush to his side, but Vaughn grabbed her and yanked her back hard. Again, the look on his face told her to listen. *He knows something! I can tell. He knows what this is!*

Images from the visions Vaughn had when he meditated swirled through his mind and heart. The feelings from the trance flooded him. He remembered the grotesque heart, half-human, half . . . pure evil. He put Stephanie behind him and motioned her further back. They walked closer. The thing sensed them and rolled over to see. They froze.

It had a face. A human face that appeared distorted as one of the fun mirrors in a circus twists one's image. Its ears were pointed. Its arms were long and powerful with clawed hands. It shimmered with a sickly gray light, reminding Stephanie of the shimmering of the gray arm-thing over people's heads.

It growled. Then it spoke to Vaughn! "I'm you." More low growls. "You'll be me. You all will."

Vaughn remembered the questions he asked while in his vision-trance. "What are you?"

More low, tormented growls emerged as the thing looked like it was trying to hold itself together. "A *man* no more!" And with a bitter cry it tore itself apart from the inside out!

Vaughn couldn't see it, but a sickly blackness left the creature that floated straight for him. Stephanie knew it wanted Vaughn, but all she knew was she loved him. Faster than thought, fire burst into her eyes as she tackled him from behind, pinning him to the ground, covering him with her body. *If he dies, I die.* He felt an invisible fire all around him. Stephanie didn't have to be looking at that blackness to know exactly what it was doing. She felt it hover over them, trying to find a way to him. She hugged him tighter. Tears fell from her eyes. "*Oh God*," she cried, as her love burst out in her like fire. The blackness fled. Somehow, she knew it went in search of someone else.

They lay like that for some time. Somehow Vaughn knew this was Stephanie's call and he had to listen to her now. He wanted to ask questions. Instead, he waited on her to explain, but she didn't know what to say. *What did I just do? What was that all about? There are no such things as monsters, not in science, not in the government's religion . . . they lied!*

She couldn't take him to her shelter now. That *thing* had spoiled it. It made her angry. *Should I tell him what I saw? No. I can't. I'd have to tell him everything else I see. He'll think I'm crazy. I'll not be called crazy anymore. Maybe he can see the same things. No. I don't think so. Should I tell him that blackness is looking for someone else? What's the point? How did he know what it was?* She decided not to press him, but would wait for him to tell her.

What was that fire I felt? I'm sure it came from Stephanie. Should I tell her about my trance? What would I say? Oh, by the way, I was in this trance and saw pure evil coming to destroy the world. No. That's ridiculous. Should I tell her I knew what that thing was? But what was it? They walked back in silence, holding each other tightly. Just before the edge of town, a question occurred to Stephanie. "Vaughn, do you think that thing is what all those strange rumors have been about?"

For the last year there were rumors about people disappearing, dead cattle ripped to shreds and grotesque remains just like what was left over after that *thing* exploded. It had finally been confirmed on TV when Jargon promised to help the government put a stop to it. He believed it was a vicious attempt by foreigners and outcasts, living near the border, to take over the country. Others thought it was the government experimenting with genetics. Still others thought it a new disease, or a plague left over from the old Religious War.

"I don't know Stephanie." *Why was I shown that vision?*

She stared at him, wanting him to say more, or wanting to speak herself. Instead, they were silent.

Vaughn lay in bed exhausted, desperately wanting sleep as his mind raced about. A voice startled him. Opening his eyes, something like a cloud hovered above his bed. It glowed.

"Vaughn." Its voice was that of a young man with lingering, echoing tones.

Vaughn pulled the covers up tighter, feeling himself shrink beneath the cloud. There was no place to go. How could one run from something like this? But this wasn't evil, or at least it wasn't the same evil that blew up the man. Or, was this something good? Or, is this God?

"*Vaughn.*" Its call was more insistent.

"I'm here."

"Don't you want to stop the evil from destroying more people? It will continue."

"I do. How can I stop it?"

"It seeks a home, like everyone else"

"I have no home for such a thing."

"But you do. The people blow up because they cannot contain the presence. You are able to contain it . . . but you must *willingly* accept it."

"I cannot accept such evil. How can you ask me to do so?"

"If it doesn't blow you up from the inside, would it still be evil?"

The question confused Vaughn. He felt his mind become fogged. Something didn't feel right. He rubbed his eyes and strained to look into the glowing cloud, but couldn't see into it. "I know it was evil."

"How do you know?"

"I just do. You must be evil if you ask me to do such a thing."

"Don't you love my people?"

"I love people."

"How much?"

"Very much."

"How much is very much? If you love them, you would sacrifice yourself to stop the evil from destroying anyone else."

He's right . . . or is he? Love requires sacrifice . . . but, but . . . how does Love think of me? Vaughn focused on the Love he knew. Thankfully, he could feel it this time. "You Sir, or whatever you are, are a liar! I am just as important to Love as anyone else. The true God wouldn't desire me to give myself to evil, no more than Love desires anyone one else to be destroyed. We are equally important."

"The presence would make you powerful beyond your imagination. You would be able to do *anything*."

Blackness began to swirl inside Vaughn, intense anger raged inside of him. *Who, or what is this?* He answered his own question. "Doing *anything* is not true power. If you're God, tell me what true power is! If you can, I'll listen to such power."

"True power can only come from true sacrifice." The cloud vanished.

Oh God, I think that's true . . .but it, the voice didn't tell me what true power is. Hmm, besides, true power doesn't come from true sacrifice. True power enables true sacrifice. Hmm, but . . . but . . . the sacrifice, being an act of love, then increases love's power . . . but . . . but . . .Love wouldn't require me to destroy myself! . . . Would I really be destroying myself through a true sacrifice?

It had been her favorite Sunday morning ritual, and although there seemed to be less zest in running to the mailbox to pick up, *Teen-14*, the featured article, *How to Be*

Hotter than the Rest, had long been anticipated. This was every teen's bible on how to be the best woman possible. This time, however, *I wonder what Vaughn would think about this.*

She quickly scanned the highlights: a) Which fashion gives him the best glimpse? b) How to really look naked with your clothes on. c) Eat fat for fuller breasts, exercise to leanness everywhere else. d) The Right Attitude: How to make the boys come to you.

Opening the magazine's centerfold, the featured teen fashion this time didn't strike her as hot. *Oh God!* Her reaction, so new, so different, froze her in self-analysis. *It doesn't look at all like it used to. Yuck! This isn't hot. It's . . .*

It didn't sound like Vaughn's knock, too sharp, almost cold. *But who else could it be?* With her other hand swinging the door open with expectancy, Stephanie's joyful greeting was truncated. "Hi . . ." Her stomach turned over. *Oh God! That black suit, a dead giveaway for the government.*

Black suit, black, short-cropped hair, and empty, young eyes with an icy voice asked, "Are you Stephanie from the ninth grade, Mr. Hardcord's?"

She stood staring, unable to speak. *Oh God, I've got to speak.*

"Yes, I mean, tenth grade, now."

Her promotional articulation bore no effect on the young man's unchanging visage. "I hear you're unhappy with the way we take care of you."

Stephanie's eyes widened, feeling a bit dizzy. *Oh God.* "Oh no! *No,* not at all!" *I've got to think fast.* She eyed the silver handcuffs dangling from his black belt. Softening her voice, looking shameful, embarrassed, she added. "Sir, I . . . it was my time of the month . . . I was having a bad day. I quickly apologized."

He stared at her, laughing inside, *Time of the month, how original.* "Girls always get to pull that one . . . *once.*" He rested a hand upon the handcuffs as Stephanie swallowed again, going even paler.

"What's this I hear about some kid, Vaughn? What's all this *stuff* about being a *person?*"

Oh, no! Stephanie was in shock and could only ask, "Person?"

"Don't be cute with me."

"He just likes to talk, that's all. I mean . . . about being . . . decent to everyone."

"What kind of *religion* is this being a *person* thing?"

"Religion?"

"Are you going to repeat *everything* I say?"

"No! No, no, ahhh, no religion. No. He just hasn't been treated well and he doesn't like girls treated badly." She didn't mean to, but power seemed to creep into her explanation. "He just wants us treated like persons."

He eyed her, then asked, "What's he say about love?"

"Love? Sorry, ahhh, you know, he says he loves me. What's wrong with love?"

He eyed her again more sharply, not at all being diverted. "Love is dangerous. People betray one another for love, betray their Country. He's been heard preaching *love.*"

Stephanie was shocked even more. "Preaching? Sorry. Oh no. He doesn't preach. He's just . . . passionate . . . about doing good! Vaughn *loves* this country, I do too. We're the greatest . . ."

His mouth flattened. "Skip it. Do you love him?"

Oh God! Shame overpowered her. *I can't say that.*

He read her face. "See? Love is dangerous! You should have immediately said, '*NO,* I *don't* love him'."

He paused then stared deeply into her, watching her shrink evermore under his stare. "We'll be watching."

He turned brusquely and left Stephanie standing motionless in the doorway, still holding *Teen-14.*

Her heart still pounding, tears creeping into the corners of her eyes, she heard the word 'Bastard' form in her mind and heart. And for some reason, a strong desire cried out within Stephanie. She wanted to be much older than she really was. *But what good would that be? The adults are even worse than kids!*

CHAPTER 8

Truth and the Eye of the Beholder

Knowing his youth would allow the transgression to be overlooked, Scraback earnestly asked, "Where did we come from? Why must we be held in abeyance by the glow?"

Instructor Claynomore studied the underling. He's different from all the rest. "If we have always been, then there is no place from where we came, since we are the essence of reality. As far as being held in abeyance, in one way, we must turn away from the glow. But in another way, the glow loses to us. Are you sure it is us, and not them who are being held? Who has more souls on Earth?"

Scraback looked troubled, and his Master gave him the ask-the-question Eye.

"Master, before, when I looked deeply into the girl and it caused me pain, it was almost as if she looked back at me! Can they *really* seeee usssss? How?"

"All reality is connected. Consciousness is an aspect of reality, a greater aspect than the physical, since consciousness is obviously greater than being non-conscious and inanimate, and can't possibly come from those things. Because man is both physical and conscious, he is living proof that all reality is connected."

Scraback assessed his Master's smugness and decided to risk a question. "Forgive your *stupid, slow* underling, but I just wanted to know how she could see me." He was treading on dangerous ground, his Master being unpredictable to say the least, but Scraback had important reasons for wanting to know *exactly* how.

GrrraGagag looked at Scraback's almost shimmerless form and was appeased by his fear. It was important for a Master to be difficult, and to be feared. Because this underling seemed particularly *stupid* to him, he decided to be even more difficult. *Perhaps if I'm really hard on him, it will spark some rebellion. I've never known an underling to be so docile, so obedient, so unwilling to plan something for himself. It's* disgusting*!*

"All reality is connected because human consciousness is able to touch the physical world through his will, first within his body, and then outward, do you see? All reality is connected *because* the physical is a manifestation of conscious will, otherwise consciousness would not be able to so finely control and interact with the physical, and the physical wouldn't be in the forms it's in that serves conscious will.

"Consider this, the human eye is so intricate that it reacts to photons. That means its nerve cells which are far larger than photons, these cells possess very tiny photon specific apparatus in which to detect light. When light photons strike their apparatus, it reacts creating an electrical signal and these signals are then sent to their brains. The signals themselves are just mere minute differences in electric potential. But all of this, someway, must be translated and detected by their conscious spirit. Their consciousness existing within a physical body requires mastery of the physical at its most minute levels. This demonstrates that consciousness has complete power over the physical world for nothing can escape its influence when even its most tiny aspects are controlled. In fact, full mastery over the physical is *required* for consciousness to exist successfully in a physical body.

"The key here is *relationship*. How can consciousness relate to the physical at such tiny levels? There must be a fundamental connection. Remember, consciousness cannot come from the physical, so even the tiniest aspects of their *interrelationship* must come from consciousness. This has all the requirements to prove the physical is manifested by conscious will. However, human consciousness is weak, and most are not able to directly extend their influence outside of their bodies. *But*, when all their *glow* is purged, then *we* will be able to combine that human ability to interact with the physical with our own ethereal abilities! We will be *Masters* of both worlds. Our great ethereal power will be able to manipulate the physical world.

But their *physical* eyes can't seeee ussss, that's backward, man is backward, but that wretched little infant didn't put her eyes first, that's why she could look back at you! Since all reality is connected!"

Scraback figured his Master thought he wouldn't understand, but indeed he did, as it wasn't difficult at all. But his Master's last statement confirmed an inkling he had, and that understanding hit Scraback like Alpha venom in the face, and he raged in disgust. "AAAHHGR, SHE HAS AN EYE!" Indeed, Scraback had suspected, but now he was sure. He was appalled that such stupid, physical creatures should also have the precious Eye.

Scraback noted the circuitous route his Master took to show him such a loathsome thing. All the technical explanations put him completely off guard for the revelation. *Now I understand what the girl did to me in the orb, she used her* eye. *But does Master know what she can do with it? What other powers does she have? He said she had powers. But does he know about that* particular *power?* Scraback had already erased from the orb any sign of that particular ability. There would be none forthcoming unless GrrraGagag saw it in real time.

Master GrrraGagag was amused at his underling's disgust. A strange feeling of Alpha kinship crept up on him but quickly withered when he thought of how *stupid* Scraback really was. Master GrrraGagag explained further, "They all have the eye, but she used hers, put it first. *We* can open her eye or the *glow* can open her eye. It all depends on what she appreciates. She looked through it first *then* through her eyes, and that's why the trunk glows so much. When the eye is completely closed there is no *glow.*

Things look *different* through the *eye.* When you made contact with her, she felt it and looked back at you! Your pain came from looking into her eye and seeing and touching the *glow* as I instructed you to do."

Scraback just nodded, satisfied his Master didn't understand. It was important now for him to change the subject, to hide from his Master the importance of the conversation. "But I don't understand. We are all reality, all consciousness, but we can't see what makes the trunk glow."

Tap, tap, tap went the Master's tail. He sensed this underling was getting dangerously close. "It is the humans that are the bridge. It doesn't matter that we can't see it. All we have to do is destroy man's connection to that mystery and it doesn't exist! Do you see? If we don't see it in mankind, then it doesn't exist for us. No connection! So the *glow* becomes unreal!"

His underling couldn't help asking. "But, since all reality is connected, and everything we know makes sense, what's the point of that *glow*?"

GrrraGagag suddenly writhed, his shimmering stopped and his gray turned sickly. That was the last straw, as humans say. With a roar, there was a loud thunderous crash as the grayness split and his lightning arm lashed out, sending Scraback hurling through the ether.

"Masterrrrrr!" Scraback slammed up against the very dark gray wall of GrrraGagag's room and his bulbous head bounced off like a basketball and then hit the very dark gray floor. He instinctively coiled into a ball and came rolling back to his Master. Looking up from the floor from between his coils, he heard his Master continue to berate him but Scraback was pleased. *Maybe I don't have to change subjects so drastically.*

"NEVER, *ever* speak a thought, think a thought like that again!"

But Scraback begged. "Please Master GrrraGagag, forgive me, please explain so that I never sin again."

As fast as Scraback was hurled away, his Master drew his arm inward and by ethereal force pulled him violently to him, Eye-to-Eye.

"*Just this once,* but if you sin again, my Eye will consume you *slowly.*" GrrraGagag stared deeply into him and paused to make the point. "Since all reality is connected, even though you would ask such a fowl question, *that question* can be heard through the ether by everyone! Even our Father heard that thought, and if I had *not* immediately punished you . . . well, you understand, it causes pain for all of us who know. Now that you know, it will cause you pain too, if you ever even think to ask it again."

"I'm sorry Master, forgive me. I did *not* mean to cause pain."

Then his Master strangely whispered as if he himself were afraid. "But worse than the pain, even mankind can hear such a question when asked, whether in the ether, or on earth."

Scraback was truly captivated, even though he was yet being held only inches away from his Master's great, stinking Eye. He very softly asked, "But what happens when they hear it?"

The answer came in a trembling return whisper. "It makes all the trunks glow brighter!"

That sent a terrible stillness through Scraback and both his rippling and shimmering almost stopped. "Thank you for being merciful upon my wretched existence, Master GrrraGagag."

His Master let him go so Scraback hurried to the blue orb. There was another question he had, but decided to find the answer himself, rather than risk asking. He began to concentrate upon it. He flipped through the forest this way and that, and the more he did the more frustrated he got until once again his Master gave him the *ask-the-question Eye.*

Scraback knew he was trapped, as he couldn't disobey his Master's Eye. He prepared himself to be slammed against the wall again. *This time I'll coil up* before *my head hits the wall.* Tap, tap, tap went the Master's tail. He had to ask.

"Why is the Forest so thick just back there, but up here it's much thinner?"

GrrraGagag's Eye widened in pleasure. "Ahhh, another important question. About a hundred Earth years ago, the humans went crazy with great religious wars …"

Scraback stopped rippling. Surprised, he blurted out without thinking. "But forgive me, Master!"

"It's alright, ask."

"But rule two says that we are not supposed to destroy all the humans. They're for our pleasure, to raise, *and to consume.* Why did we then . . .?"

Master GrrraGagag interrupted, waving his tail around for emphasis. "WE didn't!"

Scraback floated in amazement, his shimmering almost ceased as well. Master GrrraGagag's grays grew more vivid, his shimmering more lively as he saw how ignorant his underling was, and how much he reacted to even the tiniest bit of information. He continued to throw out tidbits.

"So much to learn. The humans still have a mind of their own, and we can't always control them. That's why it's so important to bring them to live by *our* reality. Oh, it was a terrible week back then, all those departed souls floating around. There were far too many for us to consume right at the moment." GrrraGagag's Eye looked almost mournful, then almost delighted. He reached out his arm and drew Scraback's head close, Eye-to-Eye, and with a tender voice said, "There is nothing more delicious than catching a freshly departed soul and *consuming* them in that instant. Ahhh, I can still feel them inside of me, Mmmmm, delicious! You know we grow best when we consume them in that instant."

Scraback's Eye quivered. No, he *didn't* know! All underlings only got the leftovers.

Then his Master's Eye grew very dull, and his words were flat. "But they become so tasteless after having floated around a while. It took us *weeks* to hunt them all down and consume them. I tell you Scraback, when the Father saw what happened, he consumed not a few of *ussss*, I tell you."

Scraback's Eye twitched, and both rippling and shimmering almost stopped still. "Master!"

"Oh yessss, and after that, all of us worked nonstop for weeks, putting thoughts to the humans, reorganizing, restructuring, so their society could never again hurt us so much. I tell you, Scraback, it's a very hard job, because humans are not all susceptible to the same suggestions. And you have to be careful on the whole what suggestions you make to all humankind so that when they start comparing ideas we don't end up with a bad combination. They'll end up fighting amongst themselves anyway, but we've learned through experience that certain combinations are worse than others."

Scraback bowed his Eye at being humbled by such great knowledge. "Master, explain, please."

"For instance, one of the old ideas we decided to retain for them is that they come from rock."

His Eye shot back up upon hearing the word. "ROCK?" Scraback was astonished.

"Yes, I know it sounds *stupid*, how could they be such *idiots* to believe such a stupid thing, you are probably thinking. But we've managed to get quite a few to really believe it!"

Scraback shook his bulbous head in dismay. "How, Master GrrraGagag? How could they possibly believe that when they're *conscious* and the rock is not?"

GrrraGagag threw his arm out and thrust his head back laughing. "For one thing, the belief is self-serving." Then he leveled Eye-to-Eye to impart understanding. "If all there is to all their reality is just their physical world, then, since they are the wisest, most powerful creature of the physical world, they figure they can rule it! *The belief* works for us because they want to believe it!"

Scraback's mouth flattened in disgust, his Eye disbelieving, "But Master, they are conscious. No matter how you mix atoms or molecules together with their energy, they're all still just a bunch of unconscious matter and energy. They have no will of their own, no self-awareness. How can they believe they get consciousness from *that*? I, *myself*, can't even conjure an explanation or even imagine how that could possibly be, even if the belief is self-serving!"

"We keep them busy discovering more and more about how their brains work so they just simply ignore the more fundamental question! It's really beautifully stupid, isn't it? It would be like trying to figure out how one of their cars drives to the grocery store by simply examining the car without considering the driver. Oh, Scraback, it gets even better than that. When the car breaks . . ." Laughter overtook him. "When the car breaks down . . . oh my! . . . that's the PROOF there is no driver . . . that's proof, HAH! They simply assume because the car went to the store all those years, it drove its self!" He burst into more uncontrolled laughter.

"But Master. The car isn't conscious!"

Master GrrraGagag leveled a serious Eye. "Precisely! Neither are their brains! But they're so enamored by their complexity, they ignore the fundamental question. I told the High Council they would. They didn't believe me." Master GrrraGagag's Eye twinkled. He was the one who set the original plan in motion but his fellow Alphas didn't believe it would work. When it did, he was appointed to the position he now held.

GrrraGagag went into a prolonged fit of laughter and Scraback was once again wondering how such stupid, physical creatures could even be tasty or pleasurable. There seemed to be a bond forming between his Master and him. He waited for his Master to continue. Finally, he leveled his Great Eye again.

"But there is even a greater reason why they choose to accept such foolishness. They believe it because, in part, they are like us! They don't want to be connected to the *glow.* When they sense *glow,* it unnerves them because it's a part of their reality that's beyond them. They can't *rule* it. So they push it away. See how well this belief works for us, Scraback? It's wonderful."

"But how then can we bring them fully into our reality if they believe only the physical part of them is real?"

"We don't have to have them believe in our ethereal part of reality for them to *be* in our reality. All we have to do is make them believe our ideas and separate them from the glow." Master GrrraGagag got completely carried away with the glory of his vision and Scraback sat and watched, listened, and learned as his Master waved arm and tail, twisted, untwisted, and emphasized.

GrrraGagag continued. "Also, such a belief is far safer for us than their religious beliefs. Religious beliefs are so dangerous because they kill far too many people too quickly, like what you saw in our Forest from the Great Religious Wars. We can't properly enjoy when so many die all at once, because their nutritional value becomes sub-par while they wait to be consumed, but then, later, there's not enough! *Heaven*, Scraback, those lunatics killed half of mankind in just weeks with the diseases and poisons they spread, and, they killed themselves at the same time!"

Scraback was motionless in astonishment, and his Eye was never wider. "Master, *please*, to hear such an abomination, *to kill your own self,* such foolishness, such stupidity, even if they're just human, well, well . . . I don't even . . ."

His Master put his tail across Scraback's neck to console him. "I know Scraback, but it's even worse than that because they think they go to what they call *heaven* for doing it! They think the *glow* will reward them!"

Scraback straightened out his coils and floated backward. "*Master, please,* I can't bear anymore. I know we have no connection to the *glow* and we don't understand it, but even *we* know enough about it to know that it's just the most insane idea. No one, not Alpha nor the *glow* would sanction such *abomination.* How could we even consume such perversions of reality?"

Master GrrraGagag shook his bulbous head in sympathy. "I know, Scraback, many of us didn't want to, but you know the Father, He hates waste, and He made us consume them. *Heaven*, Scraback, some of them *still* would destroy the whole world and themselves over their perverted religion, thinking they go to what they call *heaven*."

Then Master GrrraGagag got clearly irate. "These people must be hunted down and destroyed. Even the *glow* doesn't interfere when we hunt them. If those psychopaths succeed, both the *glow* and us would be isolated, FOREVER. We both would be locked out of the physical reality, and it would become unreal." Then he calmed back into his teaching tone.

"But, when the humans believe they're just a bunch of dumb chemicals, they believe their physical life is all they have.

They're less likely to do themselves in, in great numbers, because they think they have no after existence. We have worked extremely hard to reverse the damage of the Great Religious War."

"Master, how could they possibly have pulled off the atrocity? I know the humans guard against such things."

GrrraGagag nodded. "We were surprised, too. We had to do extensive orb research and make a full report to the Father. Apparently, the religious terrorists decided to prepare the attack very slowly, over twenty tears."

"Twenty years!"

"Mmmmm, Hmmm, they slowly put people near all critical positions to destroy the power and poison the water over all the major cities. They poisoned all the major hospitals and sent volunteer children infected with a genetically engineered disease into all the schools!"

Scraback was an offspring, so he shook to hear how they made their children volunteer to kill themselves. "What was this disease that could kill so many?"

"They took a gene from a very deadly strain of Ebola virus, one where they bleed through their eyes and ears and their organs turn to mush. They took that gene that made Ebola so deadly and spliced it into a common cold virus, but made it so that the deadly gene wouldn't activate until after about ten days, which meant many people caught the deadly cold before they were even aware of how deadly it was. By then it was too late. It even took them a while to figure out it was genetic recombination, as they kept looking for Ebola and ignored the cold virus!"

Scraback was angry. "But why use *children?*"

Master GrrraGagag could see how very much this offspring valued his Alpha life. "Because apparently, there was no better way to spread disease. A single infected child in each school could quickly cause most of the other children to become sick.

Then the children go home and infect their parents, and their parents go to work and infect their coworkers. The terrorists simply took advantage of the two most common vehicles: children and the common cold."

GrrraGagag then proudly explained to his rapt underling about the country the High Council appointed him to tend. Actually, they allowed him his pick because of his excellent work. It used to be the northern half of the United States. Now there were all new countries after the effects of the Great Religious Wars split the old ones because of religions.

In the nameless country over which Master GrrraGagag has charge, it had long been decreed that all children had to be in public school. All children had to be present and accounted for so that they could be properly taught, until they found work as adults. Children had become the most destructive weapons in the Great Religious Wars by being falsely indoctrinated. GrrraGagag would have no more idly dangerous children running around in *his* country. He saw to it that Biological Evolution was the cornerstone of the curriculum, and all learning theory proceeded from this. The former religions were all but stamped out in his country due to his wonderful educational system. He kept their new religion around for fun and to make sure there would be no other.

In Master GrrraGagag's country, the people never could decide on a creative name for their new country and then it became *obvious* that the whole concept of naming a whole country with a singular name was ridiculous. It was a country of *new revelation* and Master GrrraGagag was proud of his creation. Soon, the whole world would learn of it. Soon, its borders would be expanded and with that, his domain. One day, the whole world would become his one nameless country.

GrrraGagag's Eye beamed a smile as he tasted within himself all the souls he had consumed and thought about how he'd use them to create his own children when the Earth was finally purged of all *glow,* allowing every Alpha the right to reproduce. It was a fundamental right to life. He could feel all those souls delightfully writhing within his ethereality, just waiting to be used to produce his own offspring.

"Brilliant, Master, absolutely brilliant!" Scraback was roused to nothing short of patriotism when he heard of his Master's plan for world domination.

Now their shimmering and rippling seemed to be synchronized as when fish swim in schools. They hovered together over the orb, watching Karen and smiling, as they peered into the dirty blueness, discussing matters.

"Master GrrraGagag, is it true that the Father might personally visit us?"

"Where did you hear that? You just never mind, and if he does . . ."

"Master, please don't lower your Eye on me again."

"If he does visit, you are to be perfectly *quiet*, do understand me? My patience is at an end with you." Master GrrraGagag wondered if this underling would be foolish enough to try to speak to the Father. He was beginning to get the sense Scraback was too stupid to bait into anything. He'll probably just listen to my order simply because I gave it to him.

"Yes, Master GrrraGagag."

His Master floated close and wrapped his tail around him. "Fortunately, your plan is excellent, worthy of praise."

Waves of uncontrolled ripples rocked through Scraback. "Master, I thought you forgot!"

"No, not at all, but I'm going to change it just a little bit, right here," he pointed with his tail into the blue orb, "because I can sense the Father is beginning to take interest in us. It's best that doesn't happen. So, we need to be even more ruthless."

If Scraback does tell of the plan, Master GrrraGagag laughed to himself. *The High Council will probably think me foolish like the last time. But when the Father sees how well it works . . . hmmmm, maybe He'll also make me a High Councilor . . . but that means there would be four, and there's never been four.*

"But you said there are dangers in that ruthlessness."

He tapped his tail on Scraback's back to reassure him. "But I know how to get around them. Listen, the way we avoid them is to first let them carry out *their* plan."

Scraback couldn't get used to nothing going as he would expect. He twisted his Eye. "Master?"

"They want to kill that misfit Gary, so let them, and we'll even help them!"

"But Master GrrraGagag, what about your investment in him."

"I have others. He doesn't matter, as he's too *stupid,* and he doesn't *think.*"

"But how will letting them kill him . . . ?"

"Because it'll make it easier for us to balance the score without being noticed. You see, I think I've learned a thing or two about how this *glow* operates, how it *thinks.*"

Scraback turned to his Master, his Great Eye had question written all over it. "It *thinks,* Master?"

"I don't know, all I *do* know is that it seems to respond, infrequently, yes, but it seems to respond to certain things. I think it looks for an odd kind of balance, so if we let them kill Gary, then . . ."

"Great Master, we kill one of them!"

GrrraGagag let his tail drop down. "*No, you idiot,* that would *not* be balance to the *glow,* that would be disastrous to us. We can't work directly at all in this . . . but, but, if an accident . . ."

Scraback excitingly burst in, finally understanding the way things should go. "We could kill one of them, both of them accidentally . . ."

Master GrrraGagag's Eye began to look strained. *I haven't yelled at him lately.* He growled then raising his ethereal voice exclaimed, "*NO!* That would be too obvious to the *glow,* but if we kill someone else . . ."

Drawing him very close, the Master continued. "Scraback, I don't know if the Father will approve of this because it's still meddling, and dangerous, so we have to be secretive about this, and hide what we're doing, as I don't see that we have any other choice. If we don't succeed, the Father's Eye will take us both. Now, come into this room here while I whisper it to you . . ."

Master GrrraGagag had somehow constructed a secret ethereal room in the corner of his general room, that from the outside looked no larger than a tall dark gray box, but once inside it seemed quite large. Mysteriously the walls on the inside were the blackest of black. Scraback asked no questions, sensing that even knowing this room existed put his existence in jeopardy. After a while his Master waved his tail and a doorway appeared and they left.

"Oh yes, Master, it's an excellent plan, well thought out, and there's no escape from it. The closer those two get, the more they love each other, and the more it will hurt, hence the more our success is ensured. It's wonderful, but Master, why are we concentrating so much on these two? Surely there . . ." *It would be best if Master didn't watch them quite so close so it's easier for me to try to develop the girl.*

"Scraback, out of all in our Forest now, from when they first showed up, their *glows* were the brightest! To corrupt these two, or even just to destroy them, means that the few others left haven't a prayer. Our victory in *this* very generation of humankind is at hand. Those human women down there," he waved his arm through the orb and many of the trees turned to women, "they could be the bearers of our first generation of human Alphas. Now, let's examine their trees."

"But Master, is such a thing really possible?"

Master GrrraGagag leaned close and whispered, "It is said, that there are secret files concerning this time right here." He pointed his tail and the trees zipped forward until the oldest trees were in sight, almost to the very first row, just past an enormous gap. "Just before the Great Flood mysteriously destroyed almost every human, there were Alpha-human hybrids!"

Scraback quivered. *What would that be like? The girl would make an* excellent *bearer. I wonder if Master has considered it.* "Master, you have excited me beyond description."

"Yes, well, if we're to succeed we must attend to *those* two.

Bring them back up into the orb, Scraback."

Scraback jerked back from the sight. Both trees had somehow moved to be next to each other. He didn't know trees could move, but worse.

"What in Grayness has happened? Surely the Father . . ."

"Shhhhh, the Father has patience you don't even know about, and he'll let us be for a while. See how their roots connect, now? Their hearts are joining, so this is good for our plan, as their lives begin to depend upon each other."

But Scraback's rippling was greatly disturbed, completely out of rhythm. He had never heard of so much *glow* let alone actually seen it. But was this good for his plan? It could be, because he figured it would certainly take a lot. "Master, so many new, glowing chaotic branches on each tree. The scars are healing over, surrounded by new *glow* life on *all* sides, it's terrible. His roots are now in the earth, and I can see the *glow* even under the ground." At each word he spoke, he seemed to coil up closer and closer to the ethereal floor as if he were shrinking.

"Yes, he's rooted in her heart, and that's even better. Learn this lesson well, Scraback. The more a human is able to love, the more pain they are able to feel. That's why most of them won't really do it, because they're afraid, and they sense this. But for those that do love, they can be destroyed gloriously."

Scraback was extremely disappointed and he sulked. "Master, her beautiful tree has become so ugly. I can't even see the broken branches behind all that new growth."

"You wouldn't see them, even if you took away that growth!"

Scraback was quite low now to the ethereal floor. "Master?"

GrrraGagag reached down with his arm and jerked him back upright, shaking his bulbous head. "Underling, he pruned the dead branches!"

Scraback flopped his tail over the top of his head in total frustration, and it hung down to one side. "He did? How?"

His Master sighed at him. "Don't you understand yet how this all works? The trees are people. They represent actions, ways, thoughts and feelings. He pruned them with his words, with his love, so now the glorious dead branches are *gone*. But, think how much more beautiful it will be when that new growth, after we let it grow a while, all dies."

Excitement returned to the underling and he coiled his tail back up in its normal position. "Yes, yes, Master, yes, I can't wait." But what really excited Scraback was to see where his Master's focus was at, and that GrrraGagag didn't seem to have a clue. Now the only trick was putting all the pieces into the right places. Scraback hadn't figured out how to do that, yet. *But all plans start with pieces, and the true Master is the one who can sculpt them to fit his purposes.*

Master GrrraGagag wrapped his tail around his underling, as he sensed his underling's impatience. "But we must wait. In patience we possess their souls. The trees are still ours. They are still in our forest."

Yes, that's the key, patience.

CHAPTER 9

Quick Love, Quick Loss

Clearly disturbed, Yanach approached the King while on his throne. "Father, I fear for Yana's safety. Our enemy seeks her affection."

Mafferan rubbed his chin. "He's free to seek, and your sister is free to reject."

Yanach shook his head. "I don't see him accepting no for an answer."

Mafferan nodded then asked, "Is he a madman?"

The son slowly shook his head. "I do not sense that in him at all, and I believe he truly loves her."

"Then it's not his pursuit that upsets you, but your sister's willingness to allow it. It's why he won't take no for an answer. If it's quick love, it'll also be a quick loss. If it's something more . . ."

"Yes, Father?"

The King said no more. The truce explicitly forbade Mafferan's people from *mingling*.

Vaughn and Stephanie silently strolled arm in arm up a grassy hillside which had become their favorite place. She wanted to try again to take him to her shelter, but began to worry he would make fun of her. In light of all that was happening, it suddenly seemed childish. *It's just some sticks and torn up raincoats, besides, what if we run into another of those creepy things?* She leaned into his side to feel more of his presence, and he squeezed her. *This feeling now is different from running away. I don't know if I'll visit my shelter any more.* Part of her saddened at the thought, but Vaughn squeezed her again. *No, my secret shelter will always be a part of me, inside. I found my heart there, again, but I've found my soul with Vaughn, what it is to be a whole person, a woman person.* He squeezed her again.

The whole walk from the edge of town where they met had been in silence, though when their eyes met, thoughts passed between them. For the past week they had done nothing but talk and cry together. Well, she did more of the crying. Stephanie still couldn't believe she could share so much meaning with a man, and that he respected, even valued what she felt and thought. *What about killing Gary? Is it really right? How much was I responsible for the way he acted? And what about that evil gray arm thing? Maybe he couldn't help himself. Should I tell Vaughn?*

Stephanie's worry about killing Gary had not stopped nagging at his thoughts. Though she'd not spoken of it since that first night, he could see whenever it crossed her mind. But every time he considered any alternative, he heard Gary's voice from that night, *'I'm gonna kill them and dump their bodies. No one will miss them.'* Every time he heard that voice he felt a darkness anger him. He wished they could go to the Keepers with it, but that would just draw their attention to Stephanie, and he didn't like that one bit. They were known to take advantage of vulnerable people. He had heard too many stories. Besides, the Keepers operated according to what benefited *them*, not the people.

Stephanie knew when he thought about Gary, because she saw a darkness creep into his eyes. She squeezed him, and he looked into her eyes. Every time he did so, it was as if he awakened from something. *I so love her eyes. No, if it was just me, just my life to worry about, I think I would take my chances and not do anything. But I couldn't bear for them to harm her any more.*

At the top of the hill a lone oak tree sat charge. A fat bushy brown squirrel disturbed by their approach darted up the nearest tree. They could see rolling wooded hills of oak, maple and beech with interspersed pine trees. Hawks soared on the updrafts over most of the hills in the late morning summer sky, and below, the rodents were plentiful. The smoke from the town seemed confined to its small intersecting valleys. Nature from all around energized them.

Stephanie wanted to sit out in the sun, but Vaughn preferred the cool shade of the oak tree. As they sat, she admitted enjoying the coolness falling from on high and so he explained it. "Trees bring the cool water up from the Earth and then breathe it out their leaves, they're nature's air conditioners."

Vaughn promised to sit out in the sun together, too. He'd already turned dark tan, but Stephanie had turned deep gold. "It's because you're a *treasure,*" he said with his broad smile. The trapped squirrel began barking intermittent protests. Vaughn moved the leather pack beside them so he could set their lunch out but Stephanie wasn't interested. She couldn't stand the pressure any longer, his plan was . . . so complicated.

"Vaughn, you've been preparing for a week. Are you ready?"

He paused, then explained. "I think so. Do you understand why it's important that we don't kill him directly?"

"Yes, I think so . . . even though you know Life has given you the OK, and even though you're just defending us from the inevitable, it's far *more* in the way of Love to give him an opportunity to save himself, yet not endanger us. But if he chooses not to save himself, he must choose to kill himself, though he won't realize it."

"Yes, that's it exactly. This way, he's judged himself by his very actions, condemned himself directly, which is better than if I justly killed him."

Stephanie had enough of planning, as her head was hurting from the utter depth of it. The squirrel kept shifting position above them to find a safe escape. Every now and then it accidentally knocked an immature acorn down upon them. Stephanie rolled out in laughter as one hit Vaughn square on top of the head, and he stared at her flatly, which only made her laugh harder. The squirrel seemed upset by her noise and started barking louder . . . or perhaps it was also laughing.

Vaughn finally shook his head. "We have to accept life." He looked up and shouted, "In ALL forms!"

Stephanie had been planning, hoping to be able to share something special. "Vaughn, I want to share something beautiful with you." She took both his broad shoulders in her hands and turned him to face her, leveling her eyes into his.

"What, Stephanie?" The tender love in his eyes was quite obvious.

Her rich brown eyes seemed to vibrate with the very essence of life itself. "When I was very young, I used to have the greatest feelings of joy. You can't imagine, just appreciating being alive. You've brought them back to me, Vaughn."

He looked down with a small frown and paused, then up again. "Stephanie, I don't have that power. You saw for yourself what life really is."

"Yes, but I saw it through *your* eyes first. If I hadn't had that doorway, I could never have walked into that beautiful house."

He took her hand in his. "You've done the same thing for me. Do you have any idea how much more knowledge of Life, and Truth I've gained this last week because of you?"

Stephanie wondered how that could be as she glanced away. "I don't see how . . ."

"Because, dear Stephie, your eyes are the same for me as mine are for you. Your eyes are like the sunshine a tree needs to grow many branches. I understand and feel so many new things and, and . . . it's like all these new things are talking together to both my new, and to my old things, explaining, teaching, making the trunk of the tree much stronger, the roots deeper, and the branches much broader.

"Do you have any idea how much deeper in Truth I've gotten just being able to tell you my meditations? The fact that you understand, agree, and love them, and ask me questions that make me think even further, not to mention *your* unique insight, well, Stephanie, we've only known each other a short while, but I tell you, and we have to remember, we have to grow up yet to truly be a man and a woman, but, but . . . I love you. And I just don't mean it only like words, but, what I see, feel, and think in the depths of your eyes.

"The way you figured out for yourself to stop taking that drug, the way you wanted to help Tracy and those others to stop too, how you restored your feelings for Life and examined your feelings so deeply. And you were already doing *all* that before we even met. All I did was just reinforce it for you, just like you do for me.

"Stephanie, you are a thinking woman, and I LOVE THAT. *A thinking woman!* And, you are a *good*, loving person. And besides being a good person, your particular goodness is everything to me. I love the way you challenge me to believe in myself, to trust my thoughts and feelings. If we can't do that, then we can never hope to find or honor any truth at all.

"Your mediations at your shelter are correct, you're right when you say, 'If when we discover something is true, and we don't hold our heads up with it, then we are worse than if we had never known.' I hold my head up now, in front of everyone, even though I know how they think of me. I hold my head up, because *you* have helped me understand and appreciate better what I am. From the very first when you asked me how I could not know there was beauty in me, and didn't I make sense to myself, to the way you look at me right now, I can't even imagine anyone I could love more, as I could live in your eyes my entire life . . . forever."

She took hold of his hands that were holding her other hand, as she'd never heard anything so beautiful. "Vaughn, I love you too, and in the exact same way, in the exact same words. I couldn't have said it more truly. Look, I want to show you the beauty I see." She waved her hand outward across the landscape. "You see how we sit atop this peaceful green hill? Look out into the distance, to the forest and nature all around the town. Can you feel it? Not just individual trees, but life as a whole. Life Vaughn, that has expressed itself in so many beautiful and meaningful ways. It all seems to be in balance, in peace as a whole, so I think everything of life has a deeper meaning, and those meanings combine to form a whole, because each came from the very qualities, depth of thought, of heart, of Life, of Love. The trees have deep meaning, the birds, the squirrels, and even the very earth . . . all has deep meaning. Hah, for that matter, everything of the physical world, color, sound! And Vaughn, I love it so, but what I love most is the sense that all these meanings somehow make a meaningful whole. It's so beautiful to sense, to *see,* can you see it, Vaughn?"

Her eyes eagerly searched his for signs he actually saw it, as she would recognize if he truly did. Even the squirrel seemed to have found a comfortable perch from where to watch and listen.

"I can see it in your eyes, Stephanie, *through* your eyes and it's so exciting to see, both through your eyes and through mine. It feels like we have forever to always learn more and more goodness about life and never get tired, and to somehow become part of this whole, this greater meaning."

She squeezed his hands as she bounced up and down a bit, her utter joy sending tears gently rolling down her cheeks. She saw what she hoped to see in him. "YES, Vaughn. *That's* what I wanted to share with you." This was *it*, this was her greatest, deepest, most precious treasure she knew she had. There was nothing she knew inside of her of greater value, and now she saw she truly shared it with him, and He received it, appreciated it, and made it his.

"You have tears, Stephanie?" He cupped his right hand against her left cheek and his thumb brushed away some of them.

"Yes, tears of joy . . . because, do you have any idea how absolutely special it is to share these insights? How rare it is, I think, that people do? And I feel pain for missing the feeling of these things for so many years."

Sympathy inundated his expression as he well knew the feelings. "I don't want you to have pain."

"I know . . . Vaughn?" She hung her head and Vaughn could feel her worry.

"What is it, Stephie? What are you thinking that wrinkles your brow so?" He touched her eyebrows to try to smooth them but with no affect. The sweet, warm summer morning breeze tickled across them with sweet smells interspersed by city odors drifting up from the valley below.

She looked up at him with determination to say something difficult. "We don't know what's ahead of us. I don't know, it's just a feeling, but . . . I can understand now how important I am to you because I can see the value, finally, in myself. I feel your love. I saw my value first through your eyes, my love, but I can see it through mine now, too, and it feels so absolutely wonderful. Like I'm a new person . . . or, like I just became a person, but . . ." She hung her head again.

He took his forefinger and gently lifted her chin. "What are you trying to say?"

It looked as if her heart were suddenly breaking. "I don't know. I feel my value now, as a woman person . . . but there are still times when it just seems to vanish. It doesn't when I'm around you. I'm afraid I mean too much to you!"

Vaughn shook his head immediately. "That's foolish. Value is what value is. To call it by a different value is a lie, so we *have to* live up to what value *is*, to be true, to be alive. And, Stephanie, no value is a value if there isn't also that which has supreme value. When people don't know Life and Love are supreme, everything becomes a gray mess in their mind and heart.

"Likewise, when people have no idea what makes a human being truly valuable, then almost any woman or man is about as good a mate as another for them. But I know both, and you are *everything* I am looking for in a woman. That supreme value, by virtue of what it is and how it relates to everything else, determines everything else's value. So my dear," he put his face close to hers and proclaimed loudly, "IT IS IMPOSSIBLE that I love you TOO MUCH." His loud expression sent the squirrel into a fit of barking, or cheering, depending on one's perspective.

Then Vaughn gently touched her cheek with his fingertips as if he were touching something hallowed and spoke softly but passionately. "It is the value that it is and I *have* to honor it." He spoke with the conviction of taking an Holy oath.

She saw his conviction but that only seemed to worry her more. "I'm afraid if anything would happen to me that . . . you would be too hurt."

But he leveled his eyes into hers, giving a question in answer. "And you think I'd be better off not to love you at all, or you me?"

Her eyes widened with instant understanding from the question, but nevertheless, the feeling remained. "I see your point."

He sat up straighter and looked her in the eye to explain further. "Faith, that's the deciding factor in facing this, faith in knowing what Love really is. No matter if we don't see a way in the future, we know what Love is, that it blesses goodness."

His words were so full of truth and goodness that she desperately wanted him. "Vaughn, will you make love to me, right here in this beautiful place?" *It would feel so right out here amongst nature.*

He hung his head and was silent. *Oh God! No, please don't tempt me.*

She bent over to look up into his face. "Vaughn? All I ever knew . . . and now I am *so* ashamed, because of . . . I want to use my body to express truth and love."

He well understood her reasons and her desire. "No, Stephanie!" he replied calmly.

She recoiled instantly as pain seared her, feeling like she was falling down a dark hole. She knew how he felt about women like her, and realized even asking made her dirty. She shouldn't have hoped that he would really be for her and wanted to crawl away, but then she realized he'd be leaving her anyway. *After the business with Gary is over he'll leave me.* Her voice trembled. "I'm sorry, I know I'm too filthy. I . . . shouldn't have thought . . ."

Vaughn saw where she was going and grabbed her arms.

"NO, Stephanie, it's not that. Love cleanses if you let it. It never holds true life back. Love forgives because love is life. I don't see you as filthy." He lovingly caressed her arms. "Your prayers . . . Love has restored you to life and put the filth to death. I love you with all that I am, and I am *proud* of you, *not ashamed.* You're a wonderful person full of kindness and goodness."

She was confused. Life resurged within her when she looked into his fiery eyes. *He's telling the truth, but why is it so hard to believe him?* She loved him even more for hearing his words, wanted him now even more, but he wouldn't have her. *Why? But why won't he make love to me?* She began to sink again. The squirrel began a cautious step by step descent down the tree trunk, keeping a close eye on them. Vaughn let her go and pulled a cloth from his pack, unwrapped a large piece of bread, and gave a piece to Stephanie. He broke a corner off and threw it in front of the squirrel.

"Then why, Vaughn? Why won't you make love to me?"

He leveled his eyes into hers with a powerful seriousness she had not seen from him before. "Because, I love you!"

She shook her head, as she kept her eyes in his and began eating the bread. It was sourdough, not her favorite, but she went on eating. The squirrel sat not more than six feet away, slowly chewing on its grainy morsel, watching and listening. She swallowed then spoke. "I don't understand."

"First of all, making love together shouldn't be in reaction to what either of us have done in our pasts, but what we are to each other in the present."

She stopped shaking her head to make the point. "Well?"

"I know, we love each other, and wouldn't be using each other for just our bodies, for empty, meaningless pleasure."

She urged the point more insistently. "Well?"

He winced a bit. "But in a way we would be!"

She began shaking her head again. "Huh?"

"Because, Stephanie, we're not grown up yet."

"Who says so? *Vaughn*, who says so?" The squirrel stopped eating and stared at her, noting the severity of her tone.

For the first time, Vaughn saw a deep blackness in her eyes instead of fire, so he eased back just a bit, wondering. She continued her argument. "We already know so much more about life than most *stupid* adults we know. Just because *they* say we're too young?"

Stephanie grew more heated so Vaughn leaned back just a bit more, waiting, and she continued. "We desire just as strongly, probably stronger than those moldy old people, so why should they cheat us out of our joy, our *meaningful* pleasure?"

Vaughn was very, very calm. He took a deep breath and let it out slowly. "It's not about them, but if it was, you'd be right. It's just about us, and what we're able to do for each other, *now*. It's about facing reality. If we don't act upon reality, just upon what we want, then we'll only end up harming each other. What love is there in that?"

She paused, remembering. *Oh God, that's just what I did with Gary and his group. I thought I belonged because I* wanted *it to be so, but it wasn't true. I just didn't face reality. Is it so now? But sex is a part of nature. It's not bad when two people are right for each other. There has to be more to his refusal.* Her sinking feeling rushed back upon her.

He could see the terrible pain in her eyes and desperately wanted to relieve it. But this was a pain he knew he must *not* sooth if he was to be true to both her and himself. *She has to face this,* he thought. The squirrel had finished its piece of bread and took a tentative step towards them. Watching them both, it froze with one paw in the air.

"Vaughn, I know you're wise, in fact, I think you're the wisest person I know, even amongst all the adults I know, and you're only fifteen. I'll listen to you, so teach me, I want you so much," she pleaded. *How can he turn me down? He believes his reasons, but maybe he doesn't realize how he* really *feels about me. I know I disgust him. Or maybe he doesn't want to hurt my feelings by telling me I'm really not the kind of woman he . . .* "I want you so much it hurts."

He took her face in his hands. His thumbs caressed her cheeks. He wanted her every bit as much. *God, I can't give in to my desire, I just can't. But I do love her. So maybe . . . NO! There's more to what she's saying than just mating, she wants me to* prove *I love her, but I know that's not the way to go about it.*

His eyes reached out and took firm hold of her. The squirrel saw they were deeply focused on each other and slowly crept toward the piece of bread that Vaughn had set down for himself on the grass.

"We teach each other, Stephie! We teach each other, remember that. We're equal, and if we forget that, then when one needs help from the other, they may be too arrogant to hear it."

She'd finished her bread then reached up to hold his hands. She could feel his love in them, which made her confused, and that confusion was giving her a headache. "OK. Vaughn, but it's your turn to teach me. *Please*, I'm listening." They placed their hands on their laps and concentrated on each other.

"Say we make love, fine! Then what? Am I able to take care of you? Support you?"

She had an answer to that. "That doesn't matter. It's not our fault that adults don't have real work for us besides some *stupid* little summer jobs. And then they want us to SACRIFICE!" Her frustration was mounting but he gently pressed the point.

"You didn't answer the question, answer to reality, please."

"OK, so, we can't support each other with money, but money is *crap.* It's not life."

"Stephie, you know no one knows *that* better than me, but being able to take fundamental responsibility for our lives is not *crap.*" Vaughn suddenly stood up. He almost felt like he was taking his mother's side! *But what I'm saying is different from her fears about money, I'm talking simple responsibilities, I'm not like her!* His mother's screaming about money played in his ears as if he were really hearing it.

His abruptness startled Stephanie. Deep blackness covered him at the same time, and she'd never seen such an angry look on him before. He paced. She was afraid to say anything.

Words started pushing out from him. "*Look,* I've been thinking really deeply about this stuff, and I want sex just as badly as anyone else. *I hurt too,* Stephanie." He paused and glared at her to make sure she got the point. She could see he knew she had tried to test him by telling him how much she hurt to have sex, so she hung her head.

He came and stood over her but waited for her to look up before resuming. "If our *persons* are for the sake of our *bodies* then hell, we could be like dogs or rabbits, and the person wouldn't mean *anything.* But our bodies are for the sake of *being a person,* and that means we have a choice as to what *meaning* we assign to our actions. You and I are both ashamed of the sex we had with others because it had the wrong meaning. In fact, it was pretty awfully meaningless. No, worse, *loving* the body but not the person inside, that's throwing the person away. That's *harmful.*

"A person is only included when true love is there. It's a choice, Stephanie, to either be worse than animals because we throw our persons away for *fun*, or to sacrifice pleasure and suffer patiently until we can sanctify our deepest love with the one and only physical action that is meant to go along with joining our persons into one!"

That one word set her off. "*Sacrifice,* I *hate* that word. It's just an excuse to coerce someone into whatever action the other wants."

"No, only when used falsely. Forgoing something for the greater good is the true meaning of sacrifice, and it can't be imposed." He could see she felt horrible.

She looked deeply into his eyes. "Don't you love me?"

His anger intensified. "How many times do I have to tell . . ."

Now it was her turn to bite back. "Actions speak louder than words, and I haven't heard *any* good reason why you wouldn't *ACT!*"

He yelled back. "Let's LOOK at what MEANING should go with what actions." He paused. *I don't want to be yelling at her, not her, of all people. God, what am I doing?* He tried to calm himself. "You and I both know we don't want to mate, notice how much more the word 'mate' says than the words 'have sex,' with anyone else but each other. Why?"

She got sarcastic. "Because we love each other?"

"You have to ask? Who are you doubting, me or you?" He didn't want an answer, because the question was just meant to make the point. He waved her answer off and continued, "The point is, that ideally every action should have a single true meaning that corresponds with it. If we whored around on each other and then made '*love*', would it have the same meaning as when we were true to each other?"

"Of course not."

"Precisely, because there is a sanctity in the relationship between true meaning and its corresponding action, particularly involving mating. When you break that sanctity you rob yourself of being able to express the true meaning by its *corresponding action!*" He didn't mean his words to bite so hard, even if they were true.

"But Vaughn, we do love each other." Tears filled her eyes. "If our past is truly past, then . . . ?" She felt as if she were breaking apart.

"Thank you, I'm glad you finally believe it! But let's not take that word 'love' too lightly, otherwise we risk destroying true love from ourselves. Kids have sex today worse than rabbits or dogs. Animals go into heat and are compelled, so they have no choice. Kids today think sex is a toy, but while they're playing around with themselves, what special actions are they saving exclusively for true love? If love is special, then it desires a special expression. Stephanie, I could take you right now and have sex with you and I'm sure we would enjoy the pleasure of it, but that's all it could mean, nothing more, because the *whole* meaning that true love requires isn't there yet!"

He paused, taking note of her facial contortions. "I see you don't understand. Love is more than just idea. Love is more than just emotion. It's even more than just those two combined. It's emotion, understanding, and *responsible actions* all combined. Love without justice is a *lie*, and I won't be unjust to you, Stephanie, because I love you too much for that."

He's got a strange way of showing it. "But how would . . ."

"Because, the action of making love is a whole lot different than just having sex. Making love accepts the *person* on all levels. Every touch is not just a touch of the body, but of the person. Think about what mating truly is. Our physical life here on earth is joined into one, and that's sacred, as we become one life together. Don't you think that meaning requires we be able to be fully responsible for each other, to commit to a future together? If our very lives are combined into one, but *someone else* still has to feed and clothe us, we don't have the power to commit to taking care of each other . . . *hell*, they might as well wipe our bottoms too!" Her mouth dropped open and her head jerked back.

"That's right. That's what it's really like to have sex before we can truly take responsibility for each other. It would be like getting our parents to wipe our bottoms! That's embarrassing! So is claiming to love someone, having sex with them, joining their lives into one, but having your parents still be responsible for you and having to answer to them. It's really not making love at all, because *responsible action* is not there in the meaning. So, my love, while I can truly say I love you now, if we had sex now, I couldn't say it because I would be just using you to feel good! That's all it would amount to until we can take full responsibility for each other." He got sarcastic. "But if you'd rather be like all these horny little bastards and whores out there who don't give a hoot about being real people . . . there's no gray area to this."

"To hell you!" she sprang up and walked away, *beyond* tears! She couldn't run from the tearing pain of his words, so the pain overran her. If he had just left out that last sarcastic part, he might have gotten through. But when she heard *that,* it completely wiped out all other meaning.

Worthlessness ate away at her insides as she reacted to, not the mental plan he had in mind, but the self-loathsome feelings he invoked in her, seeing herself as one of those *sluts*. He thought he was challenging her mind to be better, but her heart felt worse, beyond shame, because she had so quickly fallen from the top of the Life mountain where she had been feeling only moments before. She was used to him always saying everything in just the right way, but now her negative feelings used this to crush her further. '*You're nothing*', they screamed to her in her heart, '*and he has made you so!*' Yet, in some distant place, she couldn't tell where, she heard a single, peaceful word: '*listen*'.

But he was still heated and followed her. Part of him, in some distant place, was telling him his approach was wrong. He heard a single word calling to him: '*see*'. Part of him wondered what was pushing him forward, but he decided not to let her tears sway him. The squirrel was nowhere in sight. "Hold on there." She turned and crossed her arms over her chest. "I've been studying on this too. I think you *women* have lost a crucial piece of knowledge from yourselves." He patronized her. "Oh, it's not your fault now because I think this was thrown away *generations* ago."

Now added to her anger and frustration was insult. "Oh please enlighten me. If it's been lost for so long, and you're a man, then how the *hell* would you know?"

Vaughn smiled, as she walked right into it. "Because Life itself is a preserver of truth and knowledge . . . all you got to do, dear, is just *look!* Where should a person get their value from, their body or the person inside?"

"It's obvious."

"Right, which is why I think the knowledge was lost!"

Her eyebrows shot up, and then bore down. "Are you saying it's just our *bodies* that give us value? You're not making sense."

He loved it when she demonstrated the exact point he was making. "See, your reaction is *precisely* what I think lost the knowledge!" She shook her head and waited. "You set up the dichotomy, since all true value can *only* come from the person, then *none* can come from the body. That's a lie!"

She couldn't restrain herself any longer. "Vaughn, what the *hell* are you talking about? How can it be a lie?"

"You said it yourself earlier, 'Everything in life has a deeper meaning.' That means even our bodies! Meaning is the value of something, but it's just that the meaning, the value of the body, isn't an *active* contributor to our value as a person."

She shook her head. "Active contributor?"

"Yes, a *person's* meaning is a direct result of their active will to maintain and seek more goodness. But the body requires no such participation of will to be what it is, it's passive, but it *also* has great meaning, great value! You're *missing* the meaning of your *body*!"

What's he accusing me of with that tone? He backed up a step, because the blackness that was in her eyes began shrouding her while his was fading, because most all his points about responsibility were made.

Vaughn tried to tone down his speech. "Dear, women are the vessels of life, *babies* live in there." He pointed to her tummy. "That's sacred in and of itself, as sacred as you are to yourself. That sacred meaning requires a whole set of special actions, feelings, and thoughts, even when you're not pregnant, otherwise you dishonor the meaning of your body. Your *person* has a responsibility to that meaning, so when you break the meaning of your body, you also *fail* the person inside!"

He paused and was getting an uneasy feeling. But he needed to finish his point and was almost there. "Women today automatically disdain such meaning, both out of ignorance and because that's what they were taught to do."

He backed up a bit more. "*But* also out of *arrogance* because they *hate* being chained to a responsibility that is *SACRED.* Because the baby grows inside her body, it also grows inside the woman's soul, her person, as well. That gives women a special responsibility between body and soul that men don't have, because *women* are the vessels of life. Therefore, treating their bodies as mere toys degrades their persons in ways that a man can *never* be degraded, and because they degrade themselves, they force babies to have to grow up in that *mess* of a body and soul! We clean our dishes, wipe our bottoms before we leave the bathroom, but women don't have enough sense to keep themselves with integrity so their precious children don't have to choke on their *filth*! I hate to say it, but today, women are really STUPID*!*"

Stephanie smiled, and with deliberate patience, walked up to him and slapped him so fast he never saw it coming. It was so hard that he was knocked onto his backside. She leaned over him with her hands on her hips and began by speaking calmly. "Maybe, if men weren't such *jerks,* always messing with our heads and hearts, WE WOULDN'T BE SO *STUPID*!" She stormed off down the hill and left him.

Vaughn rubbed his cheek. *Now why did I have to go and say all that? I never thought she would* hit *me! Am I a jerk? Wow, what a woman!* But he hadn't realized how Stephanie was taking all this. He couldn't conceive of the backwards feelings she was having, when he so obviously loved her and was trying to uplift her.

He went to collect his things and while gathering his pack, he blindly reached for his piece of bread. But it was gone because the squirrel had stolen it. *OK. So what does* that *mean?* A twinge of pain shot through him, but he shrugged it off.

A boy in the gang tried to grab Gary's binoculars, complaining, "Let me *see!*"

Gary snickered as he described the unfolding scene. "Fanie can really hit! She just knocked the mighty Vaughn to the ground!"

"They're fighting?" Another boy asked.

Gary nodded. "Which one should we go after, Fanie or the runt?"

While Karen filed her nails, she sweetly interjected. "Why don't you catch Vaughn when you can. Stephanie is much easier to find and trap. Besides, I think her happiness is short-lived!"

The gang stared at her, expecting some explanation but she simply tuned them all out as she often did with her sophisticated charm. It always left each one wondering if he was being insulted but never could quite make up his mind about it.

Gary leapt to his feet, interrupting everyone's thoughts. "Let's go catch him where the path crosses through those trees."

And as Vaughn rounded the bend into his favorite part of this walk, while his mind deeply considered how badly he screwed things up with Stephanie, only his instinct caused him to flinch at the last second, as a heavy walking stick swung past his head, brushing through his hair.

Immediately he dove for the ground, somersaulted twice, came to his feet and whirled around with a roundhouse kick followed by a forward sweep kick with his other foot, purely a defensive move. In practice, it left him standing with his shoulder pointing to his enemy, one of several defensive fighting stances. However, both kicks connected, knocking two boys immediately to the ground.

Both sides were surprised, and it provided the moment of pause Vaughn needed to make a decision. *I bet, just maybe, I could even beat them all out here. I don't have Stephanie to worry about. But if I kill them here, then my plans won't ever see the light of day and I'll probably be sent away.* With that in mind, Vaughn smiled at Gary. "Hey you fat tub of lard! Try and catch me!" And with that said, he broke out in a run but it wasn't long before his pursuers were left far behind, doubled over and panting.

Vaughn called back, taunting them, "You're the most *sorry* excuse for a gang I could ever imagine. Must be your *leader*!" Immediately after that poke at Gary, Vaughn shook his head at himself, wondering, *Now why the hell did I say* that! *It's not wise to provoke them even more. What is* wrong *with me? First I speak stupidly to Stephanie and now this! I'm gonna get myself killed if I don't stop being so cocky.*

CHAPTER 10

Round and Round She Goes But . . .

"Tell me again why we should not be too concerned, even if the humans taint with glow understanding?"

Instructor Claynomore patiently explained, "Their history proves it. How many of their best humans, knowing what they think is right, still follow our life instead? That just proves our life is superior. But why is it superior?"

"Master, I don't know how to put that into words. On every account, Alpha life is superior."

Claynomore rippled in agreement. "But mainly because our life is forceful, it's strong, not weak. The glow life is easily shoved aside by ours. I've seen many a tree with glowing branches of understanding, and yet others with both glow understanding and action. But then, in a short time, those branches wither and die. Do you know why?"

"Because our life pushes the glow away."

"Not exactly. When a branch starts to glow, many times it is stimulated by only the briefest of glow encounters. In order for the branches to keep glowing, they must pull more glow from the center. But glow is unnatural. Humans just weren't made for it. They are far better suited to our purpose. We have no real concern until roots on at least two sides, and branches on at least three sides glow in a sickening sort of synchrony. If glow understanding, action, and a warped sense of responsibility sprout branches, then we have infectious trouble, but that almost never happens. Without that, the lone glowing branches of their mind don't seem to be able to maintain a strong enough pull. In other words, they stop glowing simply because the glow is weak. Thank Hell that so few humans are so aberrant as to be able to maintain it, and that all the rest are food. "

"What about the glowing roots?"

"Human emotions are powerful indeed, but never underestimate our ability to use them, and the ease in keeping their mind separated from their heart. Without the roots and branches connecting effectively, they both die."

Stephanie sat at the pool hall she used to go to when she was mad at her former boyfriend. *There's no chance Gary will come here unless he wants to fight with his rivals.* She laughed to herself. *I'd like to see that. He deserves to get whooped really well.*

She looked around the shabby hall, confirming that all the young men were Ralph's associates. Two of the boys who chided her on the last day of school in the playground were there as well. *Maybe this wasn't such a good idea. But I can't believe Vaughn said that to me. Now I have to come* here! *He hates me. I think he hates women just like my father. I can't believe he called me* stupid. *How can he say he loves me if he won't make love to me? I'm too filthy for him, he said so. He was* really *angry, but that doesn't make sense. Well, I guess his reasoning makes sense in a way, but I make sense too. Oh God, I hit him* really *hard. I thought we were meant to be together. I shared my most precious thoughts with him, but then maybe again, I just wanted something to be real, but I wasn't seeing what was really there. What is love anyway? Maybe just a fairytale. I wonder if he'll still help.*

Ralph pulled his chair up close to hers to sit beside her at a small table. "Hey, Stephanie! Sorry to hear what that jerk did, I mean tried to do to you."

"Jerk? Which jerk?"

Ralph laughed hard. "That's really funny. That's good you can have a sense of humor about something like that. But if I were you, I'd want to kill the bastard and *all* his gang."

God. What was I thinking? Of course he's talking about Gary.

"Yeah, right."

"Hey, that kid Vaughn, you think you could send him to me? Anyone has guts enough to go up against Gary, I'd like to talk to."

"I don't think he'd be interested. He's kinda . . . well, a loner."

"Hey, maybe he'd make a good new boyfriend for you."

"I don't know. I think maybe I need a break from that."

Well, I guess the rumors are true. He is *weird. I can tell he hasn't gotten into her pants yet.* "Oh yeah, right, it's good to take a break sometimes. Hey, let's go for a walk, and you can tell me first-hand all about what happened. Maybe I can, ahh, arrange something, with your help, to put Gary in his place."

Vaughn probably won't help me now, so I guess I've got nothing better.

"OK."

He put his arm lightly around her waist, barely touching her. It was courteous, and Stephanie gave him a perfunctory smile. *He is cute.*

I can see she's attracted to me. She didn't make me move my arm. I'll add just a tiny bit more squeeze to it, but not enough for her to object. They walked out the back door and down a small side street. "Hey, Stephanie! I have to stop up at my place for a minute, so just wait down here and I'll be right back."

Stephanie looked at the dingy back street and saw no one around. *This doesn't look like a very good place to hang.* "These are apartments, do you live here?"

"Oh yeah, my business allows me the luxury. I live with my parents of course, but I worked this out on the sly for myself. Wait here, I'll be . . ."

"Don't you want to show me your place?"

Good, it worked. She's hot, and I've always wanted Gary's whore.

"If you insist."

Up narrow warped and worn stairs to a dingy, stained hallway they went, then Ralph pulled out a key, flipped a light switch, and closed and locked the door behind Stephanie. She turned to him. "What did you have in mind about Gary?"

They sat down on an old couch with a dingy brown cover over it. His knee gently leaned against hers. "I was thinkin' if you could lure him to a special place, some of my associates and I could teach him a lesson." His gray eyes began to burn as he stared into her. He placed his hand on her knee.

That might work, but could I do that knowing they . . . "What would you do to him?"

His hand moved up very slightly. "I'd teach him a lesson, just for you. Make him hurt for a while." *I'd kill the fool and anyone with him. Hell, maybe I could set it up to look like Vaughn did it. That would be believable.* His hand moved up a bit more.

Oh God, his hand is moving up my leg. It's making me hot. But . . . but, it doesn't feel right. But Vaughn *doesn't want me.*

He leaned over and kissed her lips lightly, and Stephanie didn't resist, but she didn't contribute either. She heard his breathing quicken, she heard hers, too. His hand's pressure increased as it crept further up the inside of her leg. *This feels so different from when Vaughn just holds me.* She heard his words echo in her mind, 'Love cleanses if you let it. You're a wonderful person full of goodness.' *Love. His hand doesn't feel like love touching me. Oh God!*

She grabbed his hand with precious little room left to travel. "Ralph, it's a bit too soon for that."

He burned for her. *I could have her right now. Hell, why don't I?*

He pressed her down on the couch kissing her hard.

Oh God, he feels disgusting. "What's more important to you, getting Gary or trying to force me? Choose now!" *I know he wants Gary out of his way.*

Damn, that's a good question, but I can feel she wants me. Hell, if I'm just a little patient I can have both. "I'm sorry. I guess I got a little confused. Misread your signals. Let's figure out how to teach your old boyfriend a lesson he'll never forget."

Stephanie was glad to be finally out of there. Hurrying down the dilapidated stairs she could barely stand to look inside herself. *Oh God, what was I thinking? What was I* doing*? I can't let myself be touched like that if, oh my God, if a man doesn't truly love me, it just feels* sick. *I feel him just* using *me without any concern at all. My body might not know better but my heart does. It's just that I wanted Vaughn so badly. But when Vaughn touches me it never feels* dirty. *Oh God, what have I done? How could I tell Vaughn after all that he's done for me? He loves me. He'd be so ashamed of me. I'm ashamed of myself. This almost got me raped,* again! *How could I be so* stupid*?*

Stephanie began to weep. When she got home, she quickly avoided her mother and went to the bathroom and threw up, and then spent the rest of the day in bed. Her mother tended to her, but every time she saw her mother's change of attitude, it made her think of Vaughn and she got sicker.

A whole week went by, and she avoided every place she knew Gary, Ralph or Vaughn would go, which didn't leave many options at all, as the town was small. Actually, it really only left one place, and even though the monster had been in the woods, Stephanie went to her shelter every day.

At first she thought, *If another monster comes, I'll just do what I did to protect Vaughn,* but that only made her realize how much she loved him, which made her feel even worse. But then she began not to even care if a monster came, until one day she heard sounds in the woods, and a terrible growl. The first word she uttered was 'Vaughn.' She also realized she had no control over whatever power she might have because she didn't understand how it worked. *But I think it has something to do with love. Oh God, what have I done to myself?*

His mother burst into his room screaming. "Vaughn! *What is the matter with you*? You've locked yourself in your room all week!"

He had the sudden urge to screech, like he did a long time ago, but instead he yelled back, "LEAVE ME ALONE!"

"It's that *slut* isn't it?" Rage boiled in him at her words, but he did his best to hold it down. "Girls like her are a dime a dozen." She paused, and then fear struck. "You didn't get her *pregnant* did you? Oh God, abortions cost money."

Jumping up onto his bed, and turning red, he shouted, "To hell with your FILTHY MONEY! GET OUT! Get out of my room!" He saw fear in his mother's eyes as she backed away in shock, and ran down the stairs without a word.

I can't stand it! She always knows EXACTLY the WRONG thing to say. I hate *my life.* He picked up the nearest thing to him, Book Six from the *Art of Fighting,* and hurled it across the room, sending pages flying everywhere.

He ran down the stairs to get out of the house, but the sound of a voice stopped him, and he couldn't help from turning his head. It was the TV and this Jargon fellow was speaking.

Vaughn froze. It was the first time he actually saw him. *His eyes! They're the same strange color!* He checked his memory several times just to be sure. *They're that same rich brown Stephanie has!*

Jargon's words were warm, comforting and yet with hidden force. "Our country is based upon the finest of understandings, our science and reasoning has made our destiny clear. We have suffered too long from the irrationality of countries and people ruled by distorted religions. Look how we have suffered because of it! How long should decent and reasonable people tolerate irrational people to rule and consume the world and to box us in unfairly? Our glorious government has long ago discovered the true religion, and the purpose for true religion. Our FOOT . . . OURS is supposed to be on top of the world.

"We are a reasonable and peaceful people, peaceful because of our reason. But if we let the irrational others destroy us, what good is our vanishing peace? Reason demands of us that we fight to preserve a clear way for the sake of the whole world, but we must be careful. There are those who have already infiltrated us, who still hold the old foolish religious ways we thought we had purged. *Be wary,* be reasonable, STAND TOGETHER WITH THE *FOOT*."

Images of the gray foot on top of the world flashed upon the T.V. from various angles. Then the foot grew larger and larger, as the sounds of a crowd's cheering intensified. This speech was rebroadcast many times. Church attendance, which had been nil, began to increase.

It was an odd mix of experiences that converged upon Vaughn. Seeing Jargon's eyes made him feel Stephanie's presence so deeply that he hurt all the more to be with her. The irony of his mother's corrosive words, *'You didn't get her pregnant did you?'* inflamed his memories of the fight that split Stephanie and him up. In tears, he headed for the countryside. But a little ways on his journey someone called his name, so he wiped his eyes before turning around.

"Hey, Vaughn! Haven't seen you around lately?" Tracy's brown eyes were large, expectant, and soft. He didn't feel like saying anything so she continued, "I haven't seen Stephanie around, either. I guess you two aren't together anymore." She took his arm in her hands.

He wanted to walk away but she held him with more than her hands. "I guess not."

"Well, these things happen all the time. I heard some woman on a talk show say the best way to get over someone is to squeeze someone else." She smiled and squeezed his arm, leaning against him.

She meant well, he could see that, even though those words were exactly what he didn't want to hear, but he knew she meant well. "Tracy, thanks, but I just don't feel like talking right now. Excuse me." He pried himself from her grip and hurried away before his arousal got the better of him. He desperately wanted someone, any woman to hold, to mate with. *But I've been down that road already . . . I* hate *my life.*

Finally, out in the countryside, he headed deep into the woods. He didn't care anything about any monsters, there was a bigger battle he had to fight within.

I'm sure my reasoning is all correct but maybe . . . there's more to life than reason. Maybe emotionally she's right, we both love each other. I guess loved *is more accurate. NO, I love her still! We can't help but desire each other that much more. It's not right for me to make her suffer by not fulfilling it. Oh God. But that contradicts my reasoning. What difference does it make now? She's been avoiding me. It's too late.*

Suddenly Vaughn began grabbing bushes, grass, even woods thistle in his hands and tearing them from the ground. He whipped them away from him roaring like a lion. He even uprooted whole raspberry bushes, whose roots were tangled in the earth. He didn't care about the thorns or the thistle toxin.

He screamed in anger, but it was anger at himself, at his loss, not at the woman he loved because all he could see was her wonderful goodness as it danced before his eyes no matter which way he turned. And the more he saw it, the more he loved her, and the angrier he got.

After exhausting himself, he fell to the ground. "Oh God, I miss you Stephanie, I can't imagine anyone else for me! My life is nothing without you, because you help me so much. Forgive me. I'm sorry for being such a jerk. Give me another chance and I'll do better, I'll make love to you." But then the voice from his vision came into his hearing, or was it just a remembering, *Save the child, save the world,* and the unnamed feelings associated with that flowed against him, seeming to require something from him. *What? What should I do? What do you want from me?* Vaughn sobbed. "What do you want from me?"

Falling, falling, falling . . . "Mommy, MOMMY!"

The little black haired child screamed. Fred remembered being here before, many times. Part of his awareness knew this was a dream, yet part of him was still thinking about just returning from Stephanie's town, wanting to speak to his daughter, but not letting her know or see him. Part of him frantically clawed to wake up, but he never wakes from this dream 'til the end.

A bitter voice split the blackness. "Let your father take care of you."

Falling . . . "I want Mommy!"

"George, take care of him!" she commanded.

Falling, falling . . . He heard his father's puny answer. "I have to work. Besides, he wants his mother."

Falling, falling . . . "Mommy, mommy, I want MOMMY!"

The mother laughed. "You *expect* me to be some slave at home?"

"Mommy, I'm falling! Help me!"

The venom in her voice was unmistakable as she defended herself. "Listen you. I'm nobody's slave. You hear me?"

His father's arm reached through the blackness, and the little boy grabbed at it, but the arm had no substance and the boy's hands passed right through. "*MOMMY*!" he screamed with all his heart, "SAVE ME!"

She began her tirade again, a script that played over and over. "This is totally unfair! Why should I be the one to have to save *him? I have my OWN life!* You think just because I have breasts and a womb *I'm* supposed to take care of the kids? Are you *crazy*?"

Just then a magical cord appeared around her waist, and it glowed.

"Wife, throw the magical cord, it's our only hope to save our son!"

But her bitterness intensified. "Why should I have to throw the cord? It's mine to do with what I want to!"

Falling, falling . . .

Fred woke up in a cold sweat, burning with anger. He glared over at his wife sleeping peacefully at his side, and stormed out of bed. He raced to the mirror in the bathroom to see himself, but jumped back a step because he looked like the child in the dream! He couldn't breathe, his heart pounded, and he threw his hands to his face, trying to rub the image away. When he looked up again, it was gone.

He had been having this dream so many times since he was child, but he couldn't remember which parts were a dream and which were reality. He recalled never seeing his mother that much, but when he did, she was a tyrant, always yelling, screaming, ruling, but his dad did nothing. She even smacked him whenever she felt like it, and still he did nothing. His mother would leave the house, but he never knew when, or if, she was coming back. "Those times I remember for sure." He heard himself say bitterly.

Besides falling, he remembered another feeling. 'Mommy, mommy, I want mommy!' He just wanted to climb into her lap, nestle into her breasts, and feel her warmth. Feel her gentle, soft touch as she patted him. He remembered once, or was it a dream, that she held him that way.

All of the sudden he felt his face redden, and he saw the image of a burly man in the mirror, his image, the chief of the factory and head of the new Home Guard. But it began to fade, and aside it was the image of the child crying for his mother's breast. He was that child, too! It seemed to become sharper and sharper, and blackness burst inside of him. When he looked up again, the mirror was shattered.

His wife heard the terrible crash and was at his side without even awareness of leaving bed. Worried, she spoke caringly, "Dear, what did you do? You're bleeding." She reached for his hand to tend the wound, but he jerked away, sneering. *She's a woman.* He stormed out of the house, bleeding and still in his nightclothes. Being used to his outbursts, she went to check on Lana, her daughter from a previous marriage.

I can't go on like this. How can I go on like this? She was everything to me, but now all I feel is emptiness. A sudden urge to twist his arm till it hurt racked him, but he maintained himself.

Truth, we saw truth together. But truth always remains truth. I should live by it even now. Oh God, why can't I feel it now? Truth has to be the most important thing, even above anyone, even above myself, no matter how I feel. Then why don't I feel anything?

I can't go on like this. No! NO, I won't kill myself. Why? I do *want to live. Sacrifice. At least I would do some good. What is life without Stephanie? That's a good question. I guess I should be honest and try to see.*

His original insights and feelings for Life began to return to him as he sighed, but as soon as they did, his first thought was that he wanted to share them with her. But that only increased the emptiness he felt at the loss of Stephanie. *No one to share them with! OH GOD, it hurts! Why does it hurt so badly? The more I feel the love, the more it hurts . . . and I can't stop it. Oh God, because I still love her . . . I always will. How do I deal with all this pain?*

He tried meditating, but the head bumping fell flat . . . *Oh No! It's not working. Through all I've been through, I've always been able to meditate when things got tough. Help me, Oh Life, I'd give anything to have us be right together.*

She knelt in her shelter and prayed: *Oh God, you have made the trees, the forest, all nature by Love, by Life. You are Goodness, I know, and I've been such an* idiot. *But . . . I don't understand myself. How can I love him one minute and doubt him the next? He's still the same person. He's more consistent and understanding than anyone I've ever known. What is* wrong *with me? How can I ever really enjoy Your life that You give me if I am to always be ashamed? I know Vaughn says love cleanses all, and I believe it, but . . . why do I still always feel so dirty?*

Alright, I don't always feel dirty, because I felt so good telling Vaughn about the beauty of Your Creation. But then everything got all messed up . . .

ALL messed up. Why did it have to get messed up? I wanted it to just stay good . . . forever!

Because I felt ashamed when he called me a slut…but…he didn't really call me that…he…he only asked me if that's what I'd rather be. Then why did I hear it differently? It sounded like he was implying that was what I was. He was so sarcastic. *But . . . I could have just said, NO! I really don't want to be that, I'm not* that *any more.*

But why didn't I say that? WHY DIDN'T I FEEL THAT? Oh God, I almost became that again with Ralph. I was so close to failing. Oh God, please, PLEASE help me. I'd give anything to be really true to You, to be free from all my shame, and then I think I could really love Vaughn the way he deserves to be loved. Then I think I wouldn't hear things backwards.

Unable to meditate, Vaughn burst out of his house without thinking any further. His parents glimpsed him as he left and couldn't help but be concerned. His wavy hair appeared not to have been brushed nor washed for days and had become much curlier than they'd ever seen. In fact, there was a brief moment of consideration as to whether the boy leaving was actually their son.

Quite unlike him and more than unwise, given the insults he'd hurled at Gary just a week ago, Vaughn ran into the countryside not caring about his life, totally unaware that they'd posted a watcher at his house.

Hurrying out into the countryside, all he wanted to do was destroy. All his feelings raged. Once again, he tore up the forest he loved. Not just the understory of bushes, he grabbed low hanging tree branches and wrenched them till they snapped, then taking them, he beat the trees from where he stole them.

Gary whispered to the others, "He's funny. Fanie dumped his ass and he's such a pussy he can't take it. Wait till he exhausts himself more, then we'll kill him. I like to watch him suffer like this."

Now on all fours upon the ground, panting from exhaustion and unquenchable rage, the image of the half-man half-demon came to Vaughn's mind. *Oh God, I feel like I'm him!* He remembered the monster's words, *I'm you!* That memory sent shivers through Vaughn as sudden fear made him wonder if at this very moment the blackness from his vision might return to claim him. *Could I fight that off now, by myself? In this condition?*

Then again, the memory of his vision of the little girl crying to be saved filled his heart. Shame and defeat flooded him and the strength of his rage fled. How could he ever be good enough, strong enough to save her?

Gary made eye contact with everyone, still whispering. "It's almost time. Wait till he stands up to get a better shot." And as his message passed from one to the other, they all nodded in agreement to show Gary they knew their instructions. They had surrounded their prey.

When Vaughn finally stood up, he suddenly had a sense of danger and jerked himself sideways. It was enough to evade the first brick that hurtled by. But this time his enemies knew better than to start with a single attack. Bricks and large rocks soared at him from all directions. One caught him in the head and dropped him immediately. He now knew what it meant to see stars. After that, he became aware of being beaten by heavy sticks and assaulted by kicks everywhere. He remembered the last time he'd curled up in a ball like this. *I think I would have died if . . .*

"This time you *bastard,* you're *not* getting away. We're gonna bury you right here!" And a certain craze consumed the gang as the more they beat Vaughn, the more bloodlust they felt, and the more powerful they felt. It felt exquisitely joyous to them.

Vaughn could see the little girl in his vision reaching for him. *Help me, save me!* He whispered, "I can't."

Gary heard him and thought he was talking to them. "Of course, you can't. Die now. DIE!" And in the ethereal, those same words were also urged, "Yessss, die now, DIE NOW! I can't kill you but *they* can!"

Strange sounds had been coming from above that in their revelry the gang had ignored. It wasn't quite barking, but it was definitely angry. Suddenly one of the boys screamed, causing everyone to turn their attention. A brown squirrel had leapt down from the tree and was clinging to the screaming boy's back. With an ear already bloody from bites, the boy frantically pleaded, "Get him off. Get him OFF!"

But when the others came near, the squirrel jumped and crawled onto *another* boy's back! The creature was too quick to grab, and seemed to be foaming at the mouth. "What the *hell?"* Was a cry repeated by the boys. "What the hell? What the HELL?"

His beating having stopped, Vaughn was able to view this unfolding scene and summoned one word: "Rabies!"

"Rabies? RABIES!" They all cried in unison as the squirrel jumped off his last victim and sat on the ground still barking at them all. Every few seconds, he ran at a boy who responded by running away, further from Vaughn.

Gary had a bright idea. "Hey, let's just ease back slowly. Let the squirrel eat Vaughn or bite him. He'll get rabies! I hear that's a miserable death!"

But then two of the boys who'd been bitten, earnestly shouted, "HEY, don't we have to get shots or something?"

Fearful and with their bloodlust gone, they quickly departed from this dangerous situation. The two boys went straight to the doctor where they found out they had to get fourteen shots in their stomachs if they wanted to live.

When Vaughn finally sat up, the squirrel posed peacefully at his side, watching him. There was no longer any white foam coming from the little animal's mouth and in fact, the creature seemed to be begging! Vaughn searched his pockets to see what he had and finding a candy bar with nuts in it, he broke off a piece and offered it. The squirrel slowly ambled forward and took it from Vaughn's fingers. Squinting at the animal, Vaughn spoke softly, "I know you, don't I?"

Having finished the piece of nutty candy, the squirrel sat begging again and Vaughn could swear it answered *yes* to his question!

HrorrarrAggrang, a very ancient demon, sighed. "Almost had you and GrrraGagag. Yes, they most certainly would have blamed him for upsetting the balance if the boy had met his untimely death!"

ᘓ

The last place she would have ever expected to find herself again was here, but . . . *Where else can I go, considering I feel like* this? And there were those same conflicting feelings again but at least she wore a long pink dress with flowers. *This time the* priest *won't have anything to stare at. This church* does *feel special though, but . . . I don't see anything special here. Could these feelings be left over from some time maybe long ago? How old is this church anyway?*

Stephanie began examining the architecture. The pews appeared extremely old, worn, and badly in need of good wood polish. *But there've hardly been any people in here in my whole lifetime, I don't think.* But it was then she noticed that there were indeed quite a few people here today, even several young people! *Hmm, Jargon* is *really having an effect on folks.*

Gazing past the altar, Stephanie tried to examine the logical places for icons and the like, to try to get an idea of the church's age and history, but that same tapestry with the gray foot still hung there blocking any useful information. She was vaguely aware of herself standing, sitting, and repeating prayers and verses with the rest of the congregation, but the only definite observance she noticed was her joining in a final *Amen!*

Yet, something still held her presence there while one after another worshipper filed past her end row seat. After the church was empty and even the *priest* had disappeared, Stephanie followed another of her mysterious urges and walked up to the carved wooden tree on the wall. The plaque was about five feet wide and seven feet tall but some of the dense branches, which were many, came down low. Gently, she ran her fingertips over the highly polished surface. *This must be why I thought it was glowing. It's the polish reflecting the light.*

As she inspected it further, she noticed many fine details carved into its trunk and branches which gave the impression of a very old, if not ancient tree. But not only that, she realized the whole piece had been carved from somewhere else and as a block of wood, it had been set into the church wall. She inspected along its edges. *Maybe I'll find a clue where this was made, or by who, a signature or something.* In the very corner, in ornate letters it said APEN ART. And as soon as she read it, she began to tingle all over. *This is so strange. Why do I feel this way?*

Then she noticed there was a tiny gold emblem at the very bottom and Stephanie bent over a bit and squinted. In finely etched letters, it said, The Tree of Life. Then the tree began to glow again and Stephanie jumped back.

This time, Stephanie strained to see from where its glow came, but every time she focused her eyes upon it, the glow disappeared. Yet every time she decided it was gone, it reappeared. She tried shading it from any light but it made no difference. But when she heard, in that same odd voice but stronger than before, the words: "FIND ME!" she jumped back again, knowing that this time, it was definitely not her imagination.

"Excuse me Missss, can I help you?"

And this time there was no mistaking the priest's hand that had come to gently rest upon Stephanie's backside and now squeezed ever so slightly. Whirling around, Stephanie had no idea how deeply red her eyes blazed, nor the power that had grown in her voice, even though she spoke it as calmly as possible. "I think *not!*" And some invisible force seemed to hit the priest and he fell backwards.

Startled, Stephanie didn't know what to do. *Oh God, should I help him up? What if he thinks I did that?* "Oh God, are you alright?"

But as she knelt down to offer assistance, he began to crawl away from her in fright. "No, no . . . I'm alright. Don't *touch* me. I mean . . . Go in peace my child. Don't forget to say your prayers!" And having issued his holy advice, he stood, brushed himself off, and walked away as if nothing had happened!

∽

The next day she left her shelter early with no direction in mind, but she found herself heading back to the last place she'd seen Vaughn. It was the first time she couldn't find peace at her shelter.

Heading back to the tree where they had their fight brought back vivid memories. She willed her legs to move forward through the slow and arduous climb up the hill. Sitting down with her back against the big oak tree, she looked down at the smoky valley below, weeping out loud in bitterness and disgust, "Oh God, I've been such an *idiot.* Vaughn was right, I see that now, he doesn't want to be like those rotten men. He's not at all like them. I can't believe I even let Ralph touch me. Oh God, forgive me, I know it was only a touch, and he didn't even get there, but I feel so *dirty.* 'Love cleanses.' Please Love, cleanse me. Oh Vaughn forgive me, please don't let it be too late."

A voice! "I forgive you." Vaughn's voice! She looked up half in fright, half in hope, but no one was around. But the voice spoke again. "You are a good and kind person, we all make mistakes. I love you. It would be a terrible mistake for me to deny what is real."

The voice . . . it's coming from around the other side of the tree. On all fours she crawled around the big trunk and peered, but as soon as she saw Vaughn, she recoiled in shame and wept. But he reached out and pulled her onto his lap, holding her, cherishing her. His heart pounded with the second chance. It felt so very good to hold her, and this time he wouldn't restrain his passion for her. But all she could do was to keep repeating: "Oh God, I'm sorry, I'm so sorry."

He spoke softly, "In those weeks we were apart I became many things I didn't like. I was so angry. At first at you, but then the anger quickly changed *only* to myself. You *are* the one I love more than anyone. Without you I felt like nothing. My old habits pressed in upon me, and I had to fight so hard to keep them away. I felt ashamed of myself for being so weak. I'm sorry I spoke so hard to you, and even though what I said made sense, I didn't consider your needs. I don't know!

Maybe . . maybe we should make love, 'cause I don't want you to suffer."

He kissed her deeply, passionately, which ignited her as she grabbed the back of his neck, squeezing his thick, wavy hair between her fingers. She wanted his kiss to burn away her encounter with Ralph.

She felt all of Vaughn's love and meaning in his kisses. *Now,* this *feels right.* But after a few minutes, she pulled herself away and looked up into his eyes. *Oh God, he would do this just to please me, but I know he would never really believe he was doing the right thing. I think it would take his love away just like he said. He* did *make sense.*

She put her fingers up against his lips to stop him. "No Vaughn, I think you were right originally. Thank you for being willing to change your mind for me, but please, when you're right, don't change. I don't want to be fighting with you, but if it means sticking to what's right . . . well then I guess we'll just have to fight!"

"But Stephie!" He had made up his mind to please her. *I know I would enjoy her, too.*

Oh God, please don't let him press me on this, I don't think I can resist if he does. I want him so badly. She began to grow angry, even encouraged herself to be so. "Vaughn, do you want to fight again?"

He stared at her while all in a muddle. *Women are so* confusing*! First they want you to do one thing, then, when you finally agree, they change their minds! I wonder if she'll hit me again, but this time for* wanting *to make love!*

The look in his eyes made her remember hitting him. *Oh, I couldn't do that again, but Oh God, at the time it did feel good . . . but it also didn't feel good. He was trying to* protect *our love. I'm an* idiot. *I thought he was trying to get* away *from it.*

Stephanie turned red, and she sighed. *The picture is so strikingly clear now, how could I not see it before? I knew everything has meaning. My body has* meaning! *His description of reality was correct, and just because I wanted to be able to make love now, doesn't make it real now. I'd better change directions.*

"So what's the meaning of the man's body?" She asked timidly.

The change in direction worked, as he got a far-away look as he considered her question . . . then he smiled, slapped his cheek where she had slapped, and put on a stupid, confused look. She couldn't hold back her laughter, asking, "The meaning of the man's body is to take abuse from the woman?"

He nodded. "In part, I think . . . for goodness sake, but not the other way around because as I said, the woman's body is the sacred vessel of all future life." He paused for a bit. *I never really considered what the meaning of the man's body is. Why? I guess because I wanted to make sure I respected women, to treat them right. But what's the meaning of my body? Seed, the man produces much seed. But only one seed out of all the seeds he produces bears a child, although all the seeds help the cause. The woman takes one seed from the man and nurtures an entire new human being, one seed out of so many...*

She watched him intently. *Oh God, I love that faraway look he gets when he's thinking so deeply.* She waited in his lap as still as she could be so as not to disturb his concentration. *I wonder what he'll say!*

"I think that a man has much to offer in life, but he lacks a certain fineness. It's like he holds basic principles, but a woman refines them, deepens them, and brings out their life more fully, just like she takes one single sperm from the man and makes a whole child. I think the meaning of a man's body is to stand strong upon the basic necessities of life, being sure to provide a wide range of good offerings, while the woman chooses amongst them.

"Men are made with a certain strength and offering, but by themselves, they can't attain fullness of life without the woman to cradle, nurture and focus them. At least that's what I feel you do to me. I feel so much stronger because of you, and so much weaker without you. I think I need to meditate further to fully answer, and I think there's more to this, but I keep thinking that you have to start with the basics before they can be refined.

"When men fail . . . they have failed the very basic of life's principles." His last saying brought back the power of all his previous arguments for waiting to make love. *The woman's choice to receive seed can only be made AFTER the man offers. The responsibility is* first *mine! So the guilt of offering wrongly is mine even before the woman decides to accept or reject.*

They stared into each other's eyes as Vaughn told her what happened right after she had left, "Remember the bread I had? After you left, as I collected my things, I hungrily reached for it without looking. When I couldn't find it, I looked to see it was gone. I thought to myself, this is what just having sex is like, people reach blindly for what they think is great, but afterwards when they look for greatness, it's gone! They never really laid hands on it, as their souls are empty, just like my stomach was! I remember it well!" He leveled his eyes into hers, "If we start being that kind of character now, it would, I believe, even change our love for each other. It would destroy it! But even though I know this, I am still willing to consider any other perspective you have."

Thank God, he's back to being Vaughn again. "Oh Vaughn, I would never want our love to change." She breathed heavily with more tears, as her burning desire for him now wrestled with the more powerful truth of his words. *He really does love me even though he doesn't want to make love. I'm such an idiot. I almost caused him to go against his understanding. His* true *understanding.*

She yielded to the feeling of truly being loved, of feeling one together, which caused the picture of his last words about character to bloom in her understanding. *Character, it's a whole. It's either one, or split into fighting parts.* She hesitated, waiting for the full understanding to crystallize. The contrast of almost losing each other made the picture even sharper. *I want to see clearly this time before I speak . . . or hit him.*

Stephanie looked into his eyes with determination. "You're right. Our love is based on true meaning which comes from a true nature, and if we ignore our full responsibility to love, even ignore the smallest part of it, that's the same as being against it. Then our hearts' nature would change, and our love would die because it only lives through purity."

She grabbed him by the shoulders with intensity. "But Vaughn, this applies to all our actions, not just the ones between us, but between everyone else as well." She looked to see if he understood the far reaches of this point, she'd know if he did. She finally continued anyway. "I didn't know things could be so hard, as all reality is connected! We can't say we love each other truly over here, and be untrue over there to someone else. If we are truly true, we must be true everywhere. And if we are false anywhere, it will make us false everywhere, because that would be the nature of our hearts."

She did it to him again. While he held her preciously, he sat transfixed by the clear picture her words painted. Even though it started with his idea and intuition, she filled it out with much more than he had seen. She seemed gifted at seeing things as part of the whole.

"Stephie, you've painted a much better picture than I could explain, and something I hadn't put into words, but felt in the back of my mind, all reality is connected!"

"In more ways than you realize, my love, because you've been true *everywhere,* you have caused my Mom to change!" She stared at him, wanting to subtly emphasize her next point. "It's important you stay true *everywhere.* Did I tell you how deeply my Mom and I have been talking? Did I tell you she even said she thought you must be pretty good after all!?"

Her words made him tingle all over, as he knew the feeling of things having greater meaning. "Really? No, Stephie, you didn't tell me."

Stephanie scooted out of his lap and sat up straight. "Yep, I can't believe it. Apparently, that question you asked her when you first met really hit her hard, and she began asking about you. I told her some of the things you said, and some of the things I saw, and . . . I think she's changing for the better! She's even starting to really smile. I think I feel love in her again!"

Vaughn knew how much this meant to Stephanie's life, but it also had personal meaning to him. He had *finally* made a difference in people's lives, a *good* difference! He began to think of goodness like a tree, that once it drops seeds, they sprout and grow, and in turn, they keep on dropping seeds, until there's a whole forest of goodness. He began to feel that he and Stephanie had the potential to help bring about that forest of goodness if they just remained true to Life and Love.

"Oh Stephie, I am so thrilled to hear that. That's great news, I'm so happy for you and your Mom."

"You don't know how it makes me feel, Vaughn. In some ways, I feel like I'm three years old again when I'm around her, and I'm *loving* it." As she spoke it, Vaughn noticed she now looked three, felt three, and he smiled. He wished they could have known each other sooner, as he was sure they would have been friends. Maybe he could have prevented her from whoring herself. He wished he could have.

"I understand, Stephie." He patted her knee through her long, thin, pink summer dress.

"I believe you do." She squared herself and rubbed the tears from her cheeks, and as she did, a more sober look took over. Now she seemed older than her years, and she loved him even more. She took hold of his hands, "Vaughn, you know, we are *really* beautiful together."

The depth and maturity of her expression brought to life in him a clear vision of that forest of goodness, and he desired her even more. "I *know*, Stephanie, I know. I can hardly believe it, and you know, more than anything I want to make love to you. But for it to be true, and to have everlasting meaning, we must wait 'til we can take full responsibility for each other."

His words were like an explosion in her, and her eyes seemed to burst forth with sparks. "Really, Vaughn, *REALLY*?"

"Yes, we have to wait," he said resolutely.

"No, I mean you really want to make love to me?"

"From the time you climbed onto my back, when I heard your prayer, I felt you Stephie, I felt you so deep, like I never felt anyone else. And every day I feel you more, I want to make that much more love to you."

His words did something to her inside, like something that had been broken just mended itself, and then she remembered how it made her feel to rebuild her shelter, and this was something similar, except in a different place inside. There was a place in her heart she could now feel, and because she could, she realized she had lost that feeling previously, that is, if she ever even had it. Vaughn looked into her eyes and saw this new sensitivity burst alive in her, and it comforted him.

"For now, Vaughn, we'll just have to settle on holding each other, as I do love that so." She turned her back to him and leaned against his chest as he wrapped his arms around her and kissed her head.

"Me, too"

Then she twisted, looked deeply into his eyes, and spoke his name seductively, "*Vaughn*?" She purred as she snuggled up tighter and grabbed him tightly with her arms.

He cocked his head back and narrowed his eyes. "Oh, oh, what's that mischievous look in your eyes and that sneaky smile? Don't be giving me those *eyes*."

"Hee, hee! *Vaughn,* do I sound romantic?" Her little girl voice asked.

"YES, VERY, you both sound and look," he said while tensing more.

"Vaughn, if I tried to seduce you, what would you do?"

His eyes almost popped out of his head, because he couldn't get away in this position without completely dumping the woman he loved on the ground. Worse, he wasn't at all sure he wanted to get away. "STEPHANIE, I . . . I would probably fail and give in!"

She smiled a little girl smile and chirped out her response. "OK. I just wanted to know, that's all. You know, a girl's got to know what a girl's got to know."

Vaughn's head was spinning and his heart pounding and she could feel it through her hand on his chest.

"Oh my God, what is a woman?" He sighed.

Her smile was gleeful. "It will take you a lifetime to know that."

"That's fine by me, as long as it's with you," he said as he wrapped her more tightly in his arms and cradled her across his lap.

Now her expression shifted with the subject of her thoughts, and she started picking lint off his dark brown shirt. It generated a special sense of caring. "Vaughn, so what do you want to do to earn a living?" She changed his whole demeanor, which caused him to sit up straighter, and he even cradled her with a different feeling, it was protective.

"I think I'm strong, so I could work with my hands. But I'm smart, too, so I could work with my mind. I love living things, but people don't like me very much, so maybe I could become an animal doctor, 'cause then I could work with both my hands and mind, and care for life at the same time."

Stephanie beamed to hear it, and she pinched his taut stomach. "Vaughn, I think that is an *excellent* idea, and we have a college right here for that."

"I know, I've already been working helping out some farmers with their animals on weekends and through the summers, so I'm already learning a lot about animals. You know, the farmers like me, and they're very smart people, too, not at all dumb like the city people think."

"I didn't know that." She became like a student intently waiting to learn more.

"They are, and one of them has that abandoned barn I told you about."

"Oh Vaughn, are you still continuing with your plan? I thought . . ."

He looked at her to reassure her. "Yes, I'd decided no matter what you did, I had to continue, as it's the right thing to do if they don't change from their meanness. It's an old run down barn, so no one will suspect anything if the upper floor gives way. I've pulled up a lot of nails, and loosened the remaining ones on the floorboards, and made ragged cuts in the support beams. Then I rubbed dirt into the cuts so they would appear old and weathered, just in case anyone might check. But they won't, because first, city people aren't so smart about those things, second, they won't care, and third, the obvious impression is that an old floor gave way."

"How high up is it?"

"It's the third floor, so it's pretty high. The second floor is gone from using the wood elsewhere, but farmers keep their property up pretty well, mostly because when you're a farmer, you pretty much have to know how to do *everything.*" Vaughn spread his arms wide to stress the point, "They not only raise things, but build and fix everything themselves. But the city people have no idea at all about any of this stuff."

"Vaughn, it's probably a pretty dumb question, but I really don't know what a barn is for?"

"Well, the first floor is to store equipment, tools, and board animals. The second floor used to be for specialty stuff, part workstation to make things, and part for crops needing special kinds of storage. They load hay and stack sacks of grain way up on the top floor through big doors that swing open in the front, or by this kinda elevator type thing that you pull up with your hands. They keep the hay and grain way up there to try to keep it out of the way of mice and things. Then, when they need some, they climb the ladder outside or the stairs inside, and drop what they need down to the ground outside the barn through the same doors, or lower some on the rope elevator."

"That's pretty clever."

"I think so. The pulleys are a very, very old device, but they don't break down because they're so simple. Have you ever smelled fresh hay? It's beautiful."

"No, but I guess I will soon. It's just that I wish it was going to be under better circumstances." Stephanie knew her expression changed, but she couldn't help it. *Why does this crap have to get in our way?*

He looked deeply at her with question. "OK, so you know what you have to do?"

She couldn't help that her tone wasn't enthusiastic. "Yes, Vaughn, I know, I know just who to let it slip to. She thinks I don't know that she hates me, but it's so obvious in her eyes. She'll tell Karen, and she'll tell Gary, and Gary is too *stupid*, too *arrogant*, too *hateful* to even suspect a trap. Besides, it's believable to their always horny minds. And because he'll think we've gone up there to make love, he'll really want to be there to do harm."

"Good."

"But how are you going to keep them from backing away if only one of them falls through the floor before the others get there?"

He gave a wise smile. "I've thought of that, too. I've rigged the floor behind them so they'll be able to cross halfway over to us, but not cross back, because I have a rope hidden under some hay that I scattered on the floor. And when I pull that rope, it'll pull out a hidden peg that supports a cross beam holding the whole back part of the floor."

Stephanie wrinkled her brow. "Well, Vaughn, it sounds good, but . . ."

"I know there are always unforeseen things. But the mechanics aren't the part I'm worried about. We can have safe passage as long as we walk close up against either wall, because the supports there are wide since these floors were meant to hold a lot of weight close to the walls. They used to stack things up against them, so I know they'll hold us." Vaughn's brow wrinkled which caused Stephanie's eyebrows to go up in question then he finished his thought. "But to get them to make the choice, and not me, well . . . I have to play that by ear."

She shook her head. "Huh? *What's that mean*?" Stephanie's brow re-wrinkled as her eyes bore into his worry. She held his back tighter with one hand and pressed his chest with the other. He looked down at her in his lap, smoothing and re-smoothing her hair. The sun was rising higher and getting hotter, but the cool shade of the oak tree sheltered them.

"When a true musician hears music for the first time and he doesn't have the script before him, he just plays it as he heard it from memory."

"Vaughn, that's sounds awfully hard."

"It is for anyone except for those who have the talent. The problem is, I don't know if I have the talent. All of this, trying to do exactly the right thing and let life take its natural course, which I believe is the only way that they'll be guided to make their own choice without my direct interference, well, I've never thought or understood that kind of life before."

Stephanie's voice sharpened. "Wait a minute, you mean, you really don't know how to keep from killing them directly yourself? And I thought we were originally only after Gary?"

"Stephanie, they were all going to rape you and then kill us. Shouldn't the followers justly pay for following their leader with the same judgment as their leader gets?"

She paused, then persisted. "I believe they should, but it's just harder somehow. But you haven't answered my other question."

"I don't know, I really don't know how to keep from killing them directly. All I know is that I'm being led by the understanding from Life that it must work out the way I said. I know that this is faith, or at least that this is the way I must go about it for me, for it to be truly right. That's all I've got to go on here, Stephie, the faith I told you about. If I just wait on Life, they won't die by my hand, but they'll have a choice to make for their own life, a choice that I can't influence toward death if I don't want their blood, as guilty as they are, on my hands."

Stephanie considered Vaughn's thinking. "I suppose that if you just tell them when they reach the top floor that they shouldn't come any closer, and to stop trying to harm us, and that they should all go home and be good boys. Hmmm, I suppose that when they come forward to hurt us and then fall through the floor then that would be their own choice. Their being evil would in essence kill them by their own choice.

"Vaughn, if anyone else in the whole world were to tell me this must be done like this, I know I would think they were crazy. But I understand you, and I know that same faith led you to save *me*, and in more ways than just from them. I believe in you! Anyway, you still have the back part of the floor rigged so they can't escape. I sure hope we don't have to do it ourselves!"

"Believe for yourself in the Life I told you about, because that's even better than believing in me. I may miss something, but if you're open through that faith, you may pick up on what I missed."

"I feel it, too, Vaughn." She looked deeply into his eyes. "I understand this faith in Life. I'm ashamed I didn't keep it like you have."

He put his hand to her mouth to hush her. "Stephie, I haven't told you a lot about my childhood . . . I was a mess. My faith isn't very old, it really only began a couple of years ago, and slowly." He went back to smoothing her long, rich hair, he loved it so very much.

After a while his thoughts wandered, and she could tell he was somewhere else. When she saw blackness shimmer around him again, she jerked out of his arms and rolled off his lap. It had startled her to be so close to it, or perhaps it was just the quick contrast in feelings.

"What Stephie?"

Should I tell him of my ability to see things? But it's so odd to explain, and I don't want him to think I'm crazy. Besides, what is it I'm seeing? I can't tell him before I even understand it myself. She leveled her eyes into his. "Vaughn, I just sensed you were thinking very hard about something . . . so different."

Vaughn nodded and when he began thinking of it again the blackness came back sharper, as deep as before, maybe even deeper. Stephanie fidgeted with her dress, trying to hide her reaction as she sat in front of him, but even more so she was trying to figure out exactly what she was seeing. It didn't feel evil.

"Stephanie, there's something really wrong with humanity. When I compare what I know Life and Love to be to what and how humanity is, well they don't match up very well."

Stephanie nodded. "Yet, when you look at nature, the feeling in nature is all life."

Vaughn agreed. "Yes, but to love, Stephie, is strictly for humanity. You know how I figured this out?"

"Please tell me, Vaughn?"

The blackness vanished and now she saw light in his eyes. "Because we can choose, and the most distinguishing characteristic of this is that love is not love if it's forced. So, only humanity can love, because we're free to choose, free to appreciate. Humanity deals with the very fabric of thought and emotions and can transform itself across that vast continuum but nature has access only to its finite forms—a dog will always act within its nature, likewise a cat, a fish, a bird, all according to finite capacities. They are *finite* expressions of Life. But we're more than just expressions of Life.

We're *beings*. The wellspring of the Creation itself lives inside of us with all that capacity! Love is something offered freely that cherishes what it loves, but mere nature can't do that, because nature doesn't have the capability to choose. Nature can't appreciate, although there's caring in nature, but not love, not freedom of thought." The darkness returned again, but this time more deeply.

"What is it, Vaughn?"

"Love can neither be forced, nor force another if it's true love. If it forces, it's not appreciating the thing of its focus, but trying to bend it to its will, trying to *take away* freedom. And it's freedom that gives love life, so freedom must always be preserved. Stephanie, I find this understanding wholly lacking in humanity! Everyone seems to be out to take what they can from each other!" He looked like he had much more to say.

"Please Vaughn, continue. What you're saying is more than interesting and I love nature and want to understand it more deeply."

His gaze probed her to see if she would accept the next thing he would say. He thought he knew the reason for the malformed man that exploded in the woods. It was the natural result of a loveless society. He wanted to tell her about his vision from his trance, that for some unknown reason, it was given to him and that made him responsible to stop the evil blackness that was blowing people up from inside their hearts, and that's why the vision was a giant heart. "Stephanie, I think I'm supposed to do something in life, given to me by Life!" He wondered if she would think he was crazy, but he knew this was what he was becoming, and he couldn't be ashamed of it and be true to himself.

Stephanie's eyebrows went up. "Like what, Vaughn?"

"I don't know, but when I look at humanity, I get angry." He darkened even more. "But it's anger because what I see doesn't match up to the Goodness that Life and Love have taught me. Just look at this crap religion!"

As soon as he said it, a fire ignited in Stephanie and she broke in. "God, I know, it's disgusting. Stealing the name 'God', and then slapping it on whatever they made up, and taking people's *money* for it!"

Whenever he saw that fire in her eyes it captivated him. "Yes, but that's only part of it, because it takes human dishonesty, both to others and to themselves, to allow such things." Vaughn stood up and Stephanie noted that he darkened even more, that there began to be something foreboding in his demeanor. Yet, she had no fear of it as he leveled his eyes into hers. "Stephanie, if no one speaks up for the knowledge of Life, then how does anything have an opportunity to change?" His question was partly a plea and partly a statement.

Now she saw a strange mix of both darkness and light. *How am I to figure out what these things are,* she wondered to herself. She considered again telling Vaughn what she saw.

"Vaughn, the only thing is, you know the government, if you start saying *anything* that sounds wrong to them, you'll disappear!" Now, she was searching him deeply, earnestly. *Oh God, I never knew it was possible to love this much. Oh God, I just can't tell him about the gov man at my door, not now when he's so fired up.*

Vaughn nodded. "I know the government frowns on any thoughts different from theirs, and they don't even have to carry out their threats, because just the fear of them keeps everyone in check. Nevertheless, I've been holding my mouth closed, and you're the only one I've told. But sometimes, the words push pretty hard to come out, and I have to *struggle* to hold them in." He stared at her accusingly. *Maybe she'll think about what she said in class.*

Stephanie blushed as he looked. *Oh God, he's talking about me, not himself!* As Vaughn smiled knowingly, she picked up an acorn and threw it at him. She knew he knew what she'd said. "Yes, Vaughn, sometimes I say things before I can even think to stop them. How'd you know?"

"Dear, I think the wiser question is how anybody could *not* know, because those kinds of things spread like wild fire. Questioning what right the government has to build the cities?" he looked at her, "Right in *school?*"

"What? I didn't say that, I just asked why, *why* was it right to build the cities and ignore where we live?" Vaughn just stared at her, waiting for her to think. When she saw that stare, her eyes shifted around until she looked inward. "OK, so maybe it's pretty close to asking what you just said, but I just wanted an explanation." He kept staring at her until she looked around again, and then . . . "OK, well, if the explanation wasn't good, then I suppose my question does kinda sound like the way you put it."

Vaughn nodded emphatically. "*Precisely,* but that just shows you how everyone knows the truth! Because that's the only way they heard your question, because they knew the gov has no good answer!"

"God, you're right. But then why do we all put up with it?"

Vaughn narrowed his eyes. "Dishonesty, lack of character, *fear*...for many not so virtuous reasons. This is what I'm talking about Stephanie, if people don't base their character on truth and decency!" He shook his head in disgust. "Then we have what we have today! Everyone knows the truth and won't do *anything* to defend it."

Stephanie shook her head. There was a feeling surrounding them, vibrating between them, that was greater than them. She was trying to understand it when one of her many thoughts pushed its way out. "It seems to me, that people should be presented with the kind of knowledge you're talking about so they can at least choose. Goodness has all kinds of knowledge worth teaching. God, they should teach *that* in school. " She paused, thinking more deeply then resumed. "Yes, goodness is not religion, so they shouldn't have a problem with that, because goodness just makes good sense."

Vaughn relished her words, and feeling her speak so much truth, intensified his passion for her and for their discussion. "Stephanie, if someone would have just explained to us why it wouldn't be good to do the things we're now ashamed of doing, I believe we wouldn't have done 'em."

But Stephanie shook her head. "I don't know, Vaughn. I think there's more to it than that. Home life has a lot to do with it."

"Well then, someone needs to stand up and explain the goodness about a lot of things, so people won't screw their kids up! Someone needs to tell people the truth about right and wrong." Somehow, he thought if this could be done it would also put an end to the heart-monster from his vision. Maybe too, the little girl crying over her mother's blown up body was symbolic of all the people on Earth.

"Vaughn, I don't think there's a single virgin in our whole school!" She hung her head.

His heart paining, he sat down beside her and put his arm around her shoulders. "Stephanie, it's the same for the guys. But now that we do know what's right, because we know *why* it's *right*, we can be true to it."

She turned towards him and they couldn't help kissing. As their inner lips touched together, they could feel a personalness they hadn't known before. They became acutely aware of each other's physical life, but also of their inner purpose. Their arms reached to hold each other more tightly, and they fell over locked in a tight embrace, feeling like one life together, and neither of them wanted to let the other go.

Stephanie finally eased out of Vaughn's arms. "*Wow*, that was the best kiss I ever had." But then she changed the subject. "Hey, that bread you had given me was good, but you said the squirrel stole your piece? Serves you right for feeding that little thief!" She chuckled, thinking, *We'd better be careful what else we feed,* she thought as she recovered her bearings after their kiss, *I don't want anything else to come up to steal our love away.*

Vaughn pondered aloud. "While our life was taking its course, the squirrel was taking my bread."

Staring at him, when he looked as if he would pass by his thoughts without sharing them, her finger poked him in his side with a look, almost a demand that he tell her. "Stephanie, since you say everything has meaning, *even the squirrels,* what's it mean that he stole my bread?"

She thought it was funny because he was half teasing her, but she also couldn't turn the challenge down, so she decided to take his question seriously. *Everything* does *have meaning.* She sat up straight, crossed her legs, folded her hands on her lap and cleared her mind. Then she brought the question into focus and held it up to the picture of Life she had as a whole. Vaughn was intrigued, as he hadn't expected her to do that. But suddenly she turned pale, and her eyes got wet as she looked away and shook her head.

He touched her arm lightly. "Stephie, what is it?"

She shook her head. "Nothing, I was just trying something but it didn't work."

"Stephie, please tell me what's upset you." He took her hand and held it, but looked away, because he didn't want to press her, but wanted her to know he was concerned. If he had done it any other way, she could have resisted him and not told him. But since he left it open without pressing, she felt compelled.

"Vaughn, I ate the bread and you didn't! It was one piece, our piece, and I ate, even the squirrel ate but you didn't. I think Life is going to split us apart! I think that's what it means!"

Vaughn couldn't seem to resist her words, but he was unprepared to hear such a thing, and see the seriousness with which she said it. A dead stillness hit him when he heard it, but he shook it away. "Ehh, well, I think it means that even though we've been so deeply involved in each other, like there was no other life but just ours, Life was just showing us it's still much greater than us . . . even through a simple squirrel."

It was her turn to stare at him, and he looked away, and looked around, but he looked no further. His reaction reminded her of something hard she felt *she* had to face.

It was difficult for her to ask it, and she had to force it out of herself, but she couldn't let Vaughn go ahead with his plan without hearing all of it. Besides, she knew the meaning of the squirrel, now. Maybe she could change the squirrel's meaning if she changed his mind. "Vaughn, what if I was responsible for what Gary did?"

"That's *ridiculous.*"

She turned red, and couldn't look him in the eye, but she couldn't help from speaking, yet her words came out strained and hoarse. "You don't know what I did, how slutty I acted."

He paused for a bit. "Stephanie, I remember seeing you once behind the school. I don't think it was much different from what I saw!"

She listened to the way he said it, she listened closely this time so she wouldn't misunderstand. She *knew* he had disgust for her, and now it was plain as day. *But he has a right to feel that way. Will I ever be rid of this terrible shame? Am I to always hang my head?* Memories of all her lewdness danced before her, and she bowed her head as she whispered with tears, "*I'm sorry.*" Then she was sorry for imposing her tears on him. "I'm sorry I'm crying."

He squeezed her hand. "Never be sorry for true tears, I told you that before. I *still love you,* and I won't hold your past against you."

Now she had to try even harder, because she couldn't let such a noble man become a murderer for her awful behavior. *Oh God, but I think my past is holding itself against* me. "Vaughn, I *really* enticed them, and I didn't even think I was doing anything wrong or out of the ordinary, but now I see what I really did."

Vaughn had heard enough of this foolishness, and his eyes darkened, and his voice rose. "Stephanie, if human beings were mere animals in heat, then what you're saying would be true, but *any* person who still *is* a person would know it's *wrong* to RAPE!" He didn't mean to yell at her, but something about her defending the utterly wrong thing . . .

Oh no, this isn't going to work because he's right. "But Vaughn, what if, well, what if some evil were controlling them and that . . . well, they weren't responsible for their . . ."

His look was never sterner, and his words were sharp. "Stephanie, I grew up in a home where *everything* was contrary to truth. *Everything!* Yet, I still *chose* to become the person I am now. I do *not* believe evil, in *any* form, can truly force us to do *anything!* Sure, maybe it can make us feel pretty miserable, but we can still choose against it and there's *no excuse* when we follow it, *especially* if we follow it to harm others.

Consequences must be suffered." He got up and walked away a bit. *Besides, Gary already tried* twice *to kill me and he almost succeeded. Ha, if it wasn't for that squirrel! But is this influencing me now? No, I would do this for Stephanie regardless, but if it was just me in danger . . . I don't know . . . maybe. I mean, don't I have a right to protect my own life, too? Should I tell Stephanie how they tried to kill me?* He shook his head firmly. *Absolutely not. I don't want this to be about me.*

"Scraback, I have a funny feeling about the way that boy talks. I want you to do an extensive orb research and tell me where he comes from."

Scraback hid his displeasure, as it was the girl he was interested in, not the boy. "Master?" He poked his tail into the orb and waved his arm, for he had learned quickly. "He comes from that town right . . ."

Master GrrraGagag reminded himself he really wasn't temperamental, and that it was all just an act for better reasons. He put on anger. "*Idiot. Slow, stupid underling!* How long shall I suffer you? *Research his family tree!*"

Scraback laughed to himself, as he knew, *This one should really make his Great Eye pop.* Scraback put on his most innocent Eye. "*Master,* there are trees for whole families, too?" He started searching in the dirty blue orb. "What does a family tree look like? All that I see are just for single individuals."

Master GrrraGagag floated in stillness not believing his Eye, as *no* Alpha had a right to be this *stupid.* He sensed he truly was angered, and thought: *No wonder even Scraback's sire is ashamed of him. No wonder Scraback is the tail of all jokes around the ethereal hall.* He whispered to his hopeless underling. "I want to know what his lineage is, the people he comes from. You'll have to trace it back to ancient times, so start with his tree then go to his past, and as soon as you reach the point just before he was born, the orb will jump you to his mother."

"What about his father?"

"They're not as important in this matter. Besides, *they usually live together, don't they?* So, keep track of the father's side, too, just in case nothing interesting shows up on the mother's side."

"Interesting, Master?"

"Just do it, Scraback."

"Yes Master! Right away Master, for *I* am your faithful underling."

CHAPTER 11
The Roots of Fate

"What is a human's greatest weakness?" asked first class underling Scraback to his first instructor.

"The glow causes them to hunger, therefore they can be starved."

The underling followed up with another question. "But do we not also hunger?"

"We desire, that is our choice, but they have none. The glow has made them to hunger."

Master GrrraGagag needed time away from his ethereal room, as he felt closed in there, so he didn't return until the next earth day. Scraback did very little of what his Master had requested as it was boring and unimportant to him. Instead, he studied the girl, probed at her, and watched her response. He tried to see what would make the *glow* jump out, like he'd seen when his Master thrust him into the orb.

Dreams were best for such experiments because he could access her without her conscious resistance, manipulate different factors, and hold others constant. On closer inspection of her life, he stumbled upon another of her gifts. It was too weak for his purposes, but it was interesting nonetheless. He'd seen a diffuse *glow* fire surround her and drive away the Black Essence.

Discovering this was only an accident when he accessed his Master's secret orb files. *I wonder why Master hid that particular file.* He was surprised to see the Black Essence on Earth. *Come to think of it, I haven't heard mention of this by any Alpha at all!* But he couldn't ask, because then his Master would know he'd snuck in.

He began to investigate further, particularly why his Master hid the missing time from her life. Only an orb expert, as Scraback had become, would pick up on his Master's subtle alterations, as it was far easier to hide something than to do the actual detecting of the hidden.

Scraback didn't know of any Alphas that were interested in orb technology as much as he was. *Stupid Alphas, they take technology for granted! They have no idea about orb potentials. Hmm, so now we're* both *hiding parts of her life. I'll give my file priority over his, and hmm . . . with a little adjustment I'll be able to have his secret files send copy to me.*

Quickly, he flipped back to Vaughn's lineage, sensing his Master slinking up on him, and he snuck his tail-tip into the orb to reset the timer on his Master's self-monitoring spy-wear. He laughed to himself as he did this, as he could imagine the frustration and confusion his Master would go through when he found all the wrong times recorded.

"How's the orb search coming, Scraback?"

His Master appeared right behind him, and Scraback drooped, blearing his Great Eye. "It's . . . proceeding."

His Master patted him on the back. "Well, today's the day your plan gets put in motion. I must say, I can hardly believe you gave me the idea for it! But with my adjustments, it should prove beneficial in the extreme, even amusing."

Scraback was scratching his bulbous head with his arm. "Well, what do you think, Master? Will we have to interfere?"

"I think we may *not* have to interfere at all, and that's for the best, as it makes it that much easier for us to meddle safely later. I have to say, that kid, if he could only be made to understand our true reality . . . well, he has the stuff to rule the world. It's a small chance, but we should keep our Eye open for the opportunity. Let's check Gary's tree."

"Master, would that all the trees were as glorious as his."

"Yes, but unfortunately, his is about to take a back row. I don't see how the boy can avoid killing him outright, because Gary isn't *that* stupid to just *fall* into their plan. Surely he would sense not to just walk right over, especially if they do as the little whore said, 'Oh, you'd better not come up here. Be good, boys!' Surely Gary would see right through that, and if he's *that stupid,* I'll warn him. Vaughn will *have* to kill him and the others *directly,* not that it's going to make that much difference. Murder is still murder, even if you dress it up. It's just that I don't want any gray areas when it comes to dealing with balancing the *glow.*"

Scraback considered his Master's words. *Gray areas . . . hmm, it seems there's greater meaning in this than meets the Eye.*

We're gray . . . hmm, before we're black. "Or maybe, Master, they'll kill him and the girl without our interference. That would be even better."

His Master crossed his tail into his arm thinking. "Hmm that would be acceptable, too. I hadn't thought that the humans would do the best thing possible for us without even coaxing them."

Gary ecstatically jumped up and down on his back porch and the whole thing shook and creaked, making the new white metal porch table and chairs jump and bang. He remembered when he had trapped Vaughn there with a dirty magazine more than a year ago, how he riddled Vaughn with lust, and how he humiliated him. *It was so easy to lure the outcast and set him up. He was so happy that* someone *finally invited him over.*

But Gary also remembered Vaughn knocking him out, so he'd decided way back then he wanted to kill him. Glen's order made it imperative, but he also knew he couldn't risk Glen's father investigating him and discovering that Gary was using some of the drug for himself instead of selling them. *Killing Vaughn will make me look good, too. Glen is right about all of it. Now that the little bastard invaded my house, he* certainly *has to die, otherwise, what's to stop even Ralph from doing the same thing? That bitch has to die too. The nerve! I can't have women thinking they can get away from me.*

Gary announced his joy to his gang. "We've got him, and he hasn't even jabbed her yet, oh that's great, I just *knew* he was a faggot! Well, let's get there early so I can be sure to interrupt them at the right time. This way he can watch me have her before I kill him. Wait, I'll have her, then make him watch me kill her, and *then* I'll kill him. It'll be easy, because we can just throw them off the floor of that barn. What an *idiot,* he thought he could hide from me."

A boy from his gang questioned, "But if we get there early? He might see us there, or we might run into him while he's on his way."

But Gary was tasting revenge already. *She had no right to try and leave me. Karen was right, Fanie slept over my house all the time, I even fed her. That bitch, at the party I could see it in her eyes that she was leaving me.* "No, this is too good an opportunity to pass up. If we fail this time, he'll still die, but this is a chance to *really* hurt him before he dies. Pack up, and let's go." *Vaughn dies because I want him to, and because he has to, because I need to send that message. But* she dies *for my pleasure.*

Master GrrraGagag's frustrated sigh told how tired he was of things always seeming to get messed up. "*Idiot,* he'll spoil everything!" And the Master closed the orb in disgust.

"But Master, if he kills them, then that'll solve all our problems. Remember?"

"That's true, but it's a big risk, because killing either one of them now might provoke a very strong *glow* reaction, something I don't want to be held accountable for. Yet, if Gary fails, but Vaughn *doesn't* kill him, then it'll be much harder to get away with what we planned. We need Vaughn to succeed so what we do to the girl balances with Vaughn's liberties. He gains but she loses, see?"

"Well, you have control of Gary's thoughts, so Master, why not just guide him to do what you want?" The underling was testing out a theory, so he watched his Master closely.

"Yes, bring up his tree."

Scraback felt more and more important as he was allowed to do more and more things for his Master. He expertly focused and waved his arm, bringing up Gary's tree.

"There, Master."

"Watch how easy it is as I lower my Eyeee over his tree." His big, black, glistening Great Eye twisted, and twitched, strained, and then bulged, and . . .

"No! *No*, NO*!* . . . *NO*, you *idiot!*"

"Master?"

"These things aren't *sure* things, as they're too often built on tiny subtleties. He won't listen to my thoughts when he's so single-minded in his hate, so we'll just have to watch it play out. *Men*, Scraback, still have the ability to act on their *own*. When we separate them completely from *glow*, I intend to *make* them understand that they must act in accordance with *our* desires."

Scraback nodded. *Just as I thought, he doesn't pay attention to the extra details, all those things he tells me that aren't important about humans. All reality is connected, and he doesn't even know how to use the little things to control them. In fact, he doesn't really know how to control them at all.*

∽

One boy still had a cast on his arm, and the black and blueness was fading on the other's throat. Another's face was still purple, yet another walked daintily, as the doctor had told him it would be a while before his ribs healed, and that he should be careful.

One of the healthy boys who knew the area pointed up at the barn. "Up there, top of the hill, do you think they're there yet, Gary?"

Their leader sweated like a stuffed pig from the exertion in the hot day while gnats lit and relit on him to bite and sting. "It's way too early, it's only noon. They're probably just getting up for the day, so they'll have to meet up and travel out here. No, they're not there yet."

"What should we do?" another boy asked him.

"We'll sneak up on the barn. We have time."

They wound around the edge of the line of oak trees to the nearest point of the rectangular, faded red barn, creeping through the tall aging grass, keeping low, and only peeked above it every so often. It all increased the anticipation of what was to come, as they had decided to complete their interrupted plans for Stephanie. The excitement of that night had never really left their imaginations, and every one of them moved awkwardly as they eased silently up the stairs to the third floor.

Gary whispered, "OK, they're not here yet."

"How do you know?" one of his cronies asked.

"Because, *idiot*, we would hear them. STOP!" he shouted at a boy about to step onto the third floor from the steps.

"What?" he complained.

"Don't walk across the center! Don't you see how the hay is so evenly scattered? If you walk across the center, they'll see your footprints or something. We'll walk along the edges and hide among the old bales of hay in the back."

ᔓ

Tap, tap, tap went his tail on the ethereal floor and then it swished from side to side in delight. "You know, Scraback, they just might pull this off. I didn't give Gary enough credit."

"Master, shouldn't we open up the orb focus a little more to see more of the surroundings? Wouldn't that be beneficial?"

"It's their thoughts and feelings that concern us, the rest doesn't matter."

I'm not so sure about that. There was much his Master took for granted. He longed to *consume* him, but meanwhile, Scraback focused and became totally engrossed. "This is like watching one of their thriller movies. I really don't know what's going to happen."

Master GrrraGagag eyed him. "And how would you know *that*?"

"Ahhh . . . when I began my orb research into Vaughn's family tree, one of them was watching a movie at the time, and I could see it."

Master GrrraGagag wrapped his tail tightly around Scraback's throat and drew him close, then whispered, "Our time is *far too precious* to spend on such trivial things as *Earth diversions*."

But Scraback found the movie quite useful, the monster in particular, because it stung its victims to make them feel so good they wouldn't run away, and then it began eating the humans from the feet up, which seemed positively delightful. He was doing everything he could to ensure his Master would feel so good he wouldn't run away. Did his Master know he was being eaten from the tail up? *Let's not get carried away,* Scraback warned himself.

The sun was sinking into the horizon, and the smell of the old hay was making some of the boys sneeze and their eyes water, so they began to be eager to leave. They were anxious to find some girls this evening, having been so thoroughly frustrated in waiting so long.

"It's getting late, Gary, and they're still not here, where are they?" complained one hungry boy.

"How should I know, maybe we got the day confused." Gary scratched his head.

Another spoke up, "How long should we wait? It'll be dark in another hour. How are we supposed to get home in the dark? They were supposed to be here hours ago."

Gary answered in disgust, "Damn, I could almost taste sweet victory. I wonder if there's some way to lure them here, maybe have Karen tell something to her friend who could tell something to Stephanie. Hmmmm, then we could turn this barn into a trap, 'cause this is an *old* barn. We could make this floor collapse to make it look like an accident. That would be more believable than if we just throw them off, and tried to make it look like they've killed themselves. After all, too many people know I want him dead. Still, if I could have trapped them like I planned, I would have risked it, but we have to face reality, they're not coming. OK, Let's go!"

All six boys and Gary came out of hiding from among the bales of hay, five of whom walked ahead of their leader. Suddenly, there were terrible screams followed almost instantaneously by a thunderous crash.

Gary shouted to whoever was left, "*Stop!*

"What happened, Gary?" The last boy whimpered in fright beside him. Gary crept slowly to the edge and peered down in the dimming light.

"Well, I'll be damned! We didn't have to rig the floor. This old barn is ready to collapse without our help!"

"Gary, what are we gonna do? They could die." The boy whined, crying, because he could here moans and cries from down below.

"Too bad they never showed up, it would have been them down there. Oh well, c'mon, we'll just walk along the edges. You'll be fine, as that's the way we came."

"I, I . . . don't know. It's dark in here and I can't see too well." His eyes were swollen from the hay dust and from repeatedly sneezing.

Gary stared at him incredulously. He had half a mind to toss him over with the rest. "Fine, then stay here! I don't care. Bye!" He turned his back as he waved and hurried across the edge of the floor.

The boy pleaded, "Gary, don't leave me here in the dark!"

"Look, I'm here at the other side now, and I'm safe."

"Do you think the other half of the floor is safe? Maybe I just have to walk around the hole? I don't like pressing up against the wall in the dark. There . . . there are spiders!"

"Oh hell, what a baby, I don't know. Look, I'll toss some of these bales of hay across to the other side, and we can see if they hold. Two or three should weigh as much as you."

The boy was delighted. "OK. That's a *great* idea!"

Gary took bales from near the stairs and tossed them one by one onto the part of the floor that was still standing. He felt the exhilaration, the power of throwing them, and thought it might be fun to work on a farm. "There, that's five, so it should hold *you*."

"I don't know. Can you get the bales off the floor? Maybe my added weight will be too much!"

But Gary was too smart to do a stupid thing like that. "Hell, then mine will be, too." He looked around. "Wait, I can reach across with that pitch fork and spear a couple then I'll go get the rest."

He took the pitchfork off the wall where it hung, and he speared one after the other. *Hey, stabbing things is even more fun than throwing!* He could reach all but the last one.

"Thanks, Gary, you're a real friend!"

"I don't know what's come over me. There, that's four! I'm goin' over to get the last one. C'mon, because I'm leaving after I move this." Gary decided he would come back to the farm again and practice spearing bales of hay as he found it relaxing. He wondered what it would be like if the pitchfork went through a person. He got up close to the last bale and drove the pitchfork as hard as he could through it, trying to imagine. The other boy felt his foot kick something. Kneeling down, he felt around with his hands, poking through the hay.

"Hey, I found a rope, maybe we can use this!"

A light bulb came on in Gary's imagination. "Oh yeah, that's a great idea! I don't know why I didn't think of rope before! Heck, if we get them, we can tie them up for as long as we want, and then play with them for as long as we want! Heck, we could even keep them here in this old abandoned place for weeks if we want! I knew there had to be a reason why I didn't leave your sorry ass behind!"

"It's stuck, Gary."

"Well, *idiot,* give it a yank and see if it comes loose!

"OK." Grunting with effort the boy fell on his rump as something suddenly did come loose. But as he fell, he thought he heard Gary scream. A moment later, he heard another crash like before. Trembling as he got up, he crept slowly against the wall, imagining spiders all around. He found that another large section of floor had given way. He then crept along the edge, anxious to get out of that barn. Once he got to the stairs, he peered down, and in the dim light he thought he saw . . .

"Gary? *Gary*? GARY, oh God!"

Master GrrraGagag had heard long ago about a human custom of throwing salt over their left shoulder to ward off bad luck. He began to wonder if perhaps something like that might work for him. "I can't believe this!"

"What shall we do, Master?" Scraback wrapped his tail around his master's back.

"We'll still have to proceed. Remember I told you only if it was necessary? Well, it's necessary."

᪥

They sat next to each other on the cut-up remains of a huge evergreen tree. The piece of trunk that now lay on its side was so thick that their feet didn't touch the ground. Stephanie still wore her pink flowery dress and Vaughn had *another* brown shirt on to match his pants.

"Vaughn, we missed the time for our plan!"

But he looked into her eyes with sympathy. "We couldn't have left that farmer pinned under that huge tree. What would have happened if you hadn't gone for help when you did? All of us together barely got him out in time. I know how you feel, but I'm sorry, I just couldn't keep from helping him. We can try again." Vaughn wrapped his arm across her shoulders and squeezed.

Stephanie sighed. *I have to tell him.* "I have a confession to make. I didn't let it slip we would be at the barn!" *Maybe he'll just chalk it up to me being a woman. We're supposed to do unexpected things!*

She was trying to hide her smile and thought it was kind of impish to do what she did. "I hope you're not mad at me, but I just couldn't see you becoming a murderer for me."

Vaughn didn't look at her. "I figured you couldn't! No, I could never be mad at you for holding true to a principle you really believe to be true."

Sudden worry flooded Stephanie. *That was too easy! I deserve at least a scolding.* "Vaughn, what are we going to do now?" Even while asking it, she somehow knew his answer, and a tear already fell from her eye.

"I knew the boyfriend of the girl you were going to tell, so I let it slip to him!"

Stephanie's heart pounded while visions flooded her mind, although she tried to deny them. "What if they went up to the barn floor and discovered the trap?"

Vaughn shook his head strongly. "There would be no reason for them to go up, because if they didn't hear us, they would know we weren't there and would just leave. They might go up to take a peek, but why would they walk all the way across an empty barn floor for nothing? They'd risk disturbing it, and they'd know that would give us warning."

"Yeah, I guess you're right. And you told the farmer the floor wasn't safe?"

"I did. I told him I went up there to think and found it unsafe. There's no way anyone could get hurt because of us."

By the next day, the whole town had heard the escaped boy's story. After Vaughn came back from farm work, he met Stephanie that evening at the ice-cream parlor as usual, but she wasn't hungry, and before he even sat down, she silently got up and walked out past Vaughn, so he followed her.

She couldn't look at him. He hadn't considered her reaction to this at all, just that it had to be done to protect her. He hadn't considered this outcome. A sinking feeling grew steadily as his gut began to turn over. "Stephanie, why are you being so cold to me?"

She opened her mouth, but no words came out. She tried to look at him, but couldn't. It was murder. And it was all for . . . *nothing! Of all people, why does it have to be YOU? You don't deserve to be a murderer. You shouldn't have to suffer because of me or the others.*

If only I wouldn't have been so slutty. *Oh God, what have I done to you? What have you done to yourself?*

He knew she didn't want to be around him. He'd failed her, and could feel her quickly moving away from him inside herself. The more he sensed it, the sicker he got. *But even if Gary is still alive and it didn't work out like I thought, it was all true what I did, ALL OF IT. No one ever accepts me because of the truth I live by. She should appreciate me for that, regardless of the outcome.*

Anger erupted inside of him, and Stephanie could sense it, but this wasn't a good anger. When she looked up, she saw the gray arm over Vaughn's head. There were two distinct types of darkness swirling over him as if at war, never mixing but fighting for position. Without thinking, she took his arm. "Vaughn, what are you thinking?"

He didn't want to say. *What's the point? She'll just reject me like everyone else. She already has.* He pulled his arm from her and walked away. The gray arm's rippling intensified.

Stephanie began to cry with fear as she chased after him. "Leave me alone," he said gruffly and quickened his pace.

She softly said, "Please, wait! Let's talk!" But her voice wasn't enthusiastic at all. In fact, her heart wasn't in it at all.

He threw his arms down in disgust as he crossed the street, and she almost had to run to keep up. She was still a pace behind him when he spoke without turning to her. "What's there to talk about? You can't stand even the sight of me anymore, all because I did my very best to help you and treat you with *respect*. You're just like all the rest!" He stopped and whirled on her. "And I didn't do anything wrong, I'm *not* a murderer. I'm just sorry that bastard didn't die, too! Life took over just like I said, and I didn't influence them one *single* bit."

He grabbed her arms too tightly. "It was *their* choice to go up." She couldn't help flinching and he noticed it. "What? You're even scared of *me* now?" She regretted flinching, didn't really know why she did, but he let her go in disgust.

"I can't believe you! You *honestly* think I would *hurt you*? You know what? I'll tell you about hurt. I took off summer work early and found that little twerp, and I made him tell me everything that happened! Don't *ask* me how or *why*, but I did! Do you know they were planning to tie us up and PLAY with us for some time before they murdered us? Gary even thought about building the same trap for us, but that was *before* that little idiot found the rope which gave Gary the idea to tie us up and *play* with us . . . *for weeks!*"

Stephanie covered her mouth with her hand, while her other went to her stomach, as the memories of her being trapped that hideous night played in her mind. She could feel Gary's hand still on her throat. She couldn't imagine going through it for weeks. And Gary wasn't dead . . . *Gary isn't dead!* And Vaughn could see her thoughts.

"Ahh, I'm the murderer, but you *still* want him dead!"

His words stabbed her heart but she couldn't help her anger. "Of course I do, you *idiot!* If you'd have gone through what I did . . ." She cut herself off as she looked into his eyes, realizing what she was saying, what she was feeling. *I'm as guilty as he is. Vaughn loves me. He knew all along I really wanted Gary dead, even though I also felt otherwise. There was no way he could have pleased me. Of course he would protect me. How can I fault him?* "I'm sorry, Vaughn. I didn't mean . . ."

He glared at her. "Sure you did, but for which am I an *idiot*? For being a murderer? Or, for not murdering Gary, too?"

She felt ashamed of her thoughts towards Vaughn. He had saved her from that night and was doing his best to protect her, and she hadn't even told him the whole truth, because she just couldn't. "It's just that I feel responsible . . . and . . . I can see things other people can't!" *Oh God! Why did I just say that?*

His look intensified. "What are you talking about?"

She didn't mean to tell him, but the stupid words just pushed themselves out. But now she had to tell him the rest, even though she was sure he would abandon her. In fact, he already was, just like her Father and his anger did because she's so strange.

He spoke with even more anger, knowing she faulted him even more deeply. He could see she was ashamed of him, because she had shame written all over her face. *That's why she's hesitating.* "I see, you had some *special* knowledge that it was wrong for me to do what I did, so you're even *more* convinced I'm a murderer and you can't stand me." He gestured in disgust and walked quickly away from her. *What's the point?*

As he rushed off, she felt faint, frozen in place. Something had changed in him. He was already mocking her special abilities. She knew he was leaving her for good. With her hand to her aching head, she sobbed and she gasped as her worst fears were coming true. All that they had was dying. She could see the rippling gray arm over his head shimmer ever more vibrantly, but suddenly, she felt cheated, laughed at, by whatever that *thing* is.

Anger ignited in her, and fire flared in her eyes as she yelled after him. "Wait a minute! What kind of *love* did you say you had for me if you're just going to . . . *abandon* me?" It was hard for her to say the word 'abandon', as pains shot through her heart when she spoke it. She immediately broke down weeping, as she held herself against a streetlight remembering. *Is that all I am, just a bunch of bad experiences all piled up? Now it feels like it. That's all my life was ever meant to be.* She wept pitifully, as one who had given up on life, barely able to stand, and hardly caring if she did.

Something about the power in her words stopped him in his tracks. H turned, saw her pain, her longing, her desolation . . . She noticed the gray arm dulled and struggled. But her words didn't make sense to him. *If she can't stand me, then why is she chiding me about what kind of love I have for her as if she doesn't want me to leave? But what difference does it make, nothing's changed! I'm still a murderer, right?* He turned away from her.

But she picked herself up, ran, and caught up with him, grabbing his arm and whirling him around, just as he had turned into a narrow alley. But when he looked at her, she wasn't looking at him, but above him. He never saw her eyes blaze so brightly. She squinted. Vaughn felt a kind of invisible fire spread around him, but it wasn't harmful or uncomfortable. It was that same fire that had surrounded him after the man-beast blew up. "*Leave him ALONE,*" she ordered. The gray arm vanished!

Vaughn instantly felt a pressure leave him, and he stared at her. She still had his arm in a steel grip, and he waited for her to explain.

She looked into his eyes. "I can see things other people can't. I don't know what I'm looking at most of the time, but I see evil sometimes manifest itself. There was a gray arm thing above your head, and I think it was controlling you . . . or at least trying to."

He was notably calmer but still resolute. "I've told you before, evil can't control anyone except when they let it."

"Well, it doesn't change what I saw." For the first time *ever,* she stood up for her special abilities.

"And that's what you were looking at and telling to leave?"

She saw his skeptical look, but she stood firm. "Yes."

Vaughn began to nod as goose bumps crept from his head downward. She knew he was trying to figure out just how crazy she was. But understanding seemed to be falling on him from above. "Is that what you saw that night above Gary's head? Is that why you were talking about evil controlling people?"

She just sheepishly nodded, as now it was suddenly embarrassing to tell him how strange she was. *But I just have to tell him the truth. I owe him that much, no matter what.* "I saw the same thing. It wasn't his fault, Vaughn."

"What happened to the gray arm above me?" He knew it vanished.

"It left as soon as I commanded it."

"Why?"

It was an odd question, but this ability was distinctly Vaughn. She had no idea where he was going, "Because I commanded it?" But she wasn't totally sure.

"Perhaps, but somehow I think that if I'd truly wanted it to be over me, you could've commanded it all day long and it still would've been there!"

She was beginning to see where he was going but still not sure.

"Look, if a tree doesn't have a good root, the wind blows it down, but if rooted well, the wind can't uproot it. I just have a feeling that both good and evil relate to us that way, whichever is rooted the deepest holds on. I'm sure you desperately wanted the gray arm to vanish from Gary."

"But I didn't command it to leave, because I didn't even know I could do such a thing until just then."

"Which makes my point even stronger, 'cause this knowledge comes from Life. If it would've made a difference, I believe Life would've brought it to you then, but he wanted the evil with him, so you wouldn't have been able to command this evil to leave. Nothing short of *killing* Gary would stop him, and it's the same for the others, too. Like I've said, they chose to die, so I'm no murderer." He stepped back from her to leave.

She saw him look at her strangely, and she knew it, she knew he was just humoring her by accepting her words. *His leaving proves it.* She knew he was going to leave her now that he was sure she was crazy. She was defeated but she just had to ask. "Are you going to leave me because you think I'm strange for seeing things?"

Vaughn tried to shake the confusion from his head, as she was worried about him leaving her when he was sure she had already left him. "You're not going to turn your back on me because I'm a murderer, or because I didn't get Gary, too?"

They both just looked at each other realizing that neither wanted to leave the other. In fact, neither had ever intended to leave the other and they now knew it. Their eyes widened together, and they began shaking their heads at what happened. Stephanie shot him a glance. "I'm hungry."

He raised his eyebrows and peered into her face, but she looked away. Nothing had really changed. The boys were dead, but Gary still lived. He took her cheek in his hand and turned her towards him. His touch felt strange to her, and he knew it. "I'm sorry if I have offended you by what I've done, but I can't undo it, and I won't ask you to change your opinion of it, because you are *You.* But can you accept me for what I am now and still love me?"

His words seemed to make time stop, and she hovered inside an eternity seeking the answer to his question. 'I can't undo it … you are You.' *I am me . . . I am ME! He's accepted ME! ALL of me and he doesn't think I'm crazy. He thinks . . . it's real! I'm real just the way I am . . . I'm me.* She fell against him, squeezing him tightly, burying her head between his neck and shoulder.

"You could be right, Vaughn, about not being a murderer, you could be. But I know what I love about you . . . it's *YOU.* I'm so sorry I didn't live a decent life, because more than *anything,* I wish I could have been a decent woman for you. I'm so sorry my filthiness has brought you to do what you did." She wept uncontrollably. *If I had only known the consequences of my actions, that I would bring so much harm to the only man I could ever love. Oh God, hear my prayer!*

He held her up in his arms as tears ran down his cheeks. "I know, and I'm sorry if sometimes I show disgust at it. But now that you understand, you are even more disgusted at it than me. I told you, I will *never* hold your past against you. If I am disgusted, it's only a natural reaction, the same that even you yourself are now having. It's *not* a rejection of you, Stephanie, because *I truly love you,* and the fact that you've turned away from evil, makes me love you even *more.*" He threw his arm around her shoulders and they headed back to the ice-cream shop.

She rubbed her tears away. "Vaughn, what just happened between us? We almost split up when neither of us wanted to."

Vaughn thought a bit. "I think our parents have screwed us up more than we realize. It seems like we're almost bent on making our worst fears come true! We're going to have to figure this stuff out Stephanie, because I don't think it's gone away."

"But we're fine now."

"I don't know, I'll know it's gone when we understand it fully, and when we do *know,* we'll finally be free of it. Just assuming it's gone is just a trap for the next time, I think. When we can explain why we almost split up when neither of us wanted to, and feel free of the causes, then I think we can relax about it."

"What about Gary?"

"There must be some reason why he lived. Remember the squirrel? Life is so much larger than us, and most of the time we just have to wait to understand the little bit that we're able to, but I won't let him hurt you."

She stopped walking, as impressions of what Gary was at this very moment planning flashed in her mind. She didn't know how she knew . . . only that she did know with a peculiar certainty. She shivered then grabbed Vaughn's shirt at his chest. "Vaughn, what if he realizes we set the trap. He's got to."

"No, I don't think so, at least not from what that punk, Harold, told me. He said Gary thought the floor was just old. Anyway, it doesn't matter whether he knows or not, as he's still going to be just as bad."

Her grip tightened, and his shirt dug into the back of his neck as she pulled. She could feel Gary's perverseness suffocating her, and Vaughn could see the terrible fear in her eyes. She leaned in close to him, her voice hard and desperate. "Vaughn, you've got to kill him. This time you've got to make sure!" They stared into each other's eyes, as she heard herself say it, but she couldn't believe she did.

Vaughn didn't mean to, but he backed away from her, just a bit, and she felt it through her grip on his shirt. They stared into each other's eyes, both thinking about what just happened. He gently placed his hands upon hers, and through his gentleness her hands relaxed and he straightened. He squeezed both her hands in his.

"Life has always given me the OK to kill him, that hasn't changed, but to be right, I must do it as Life guides me to, otherwise, I'll be just as evil as he is."

Stephanie felt instant guilt, and she hung her head and covered her face with her hands, speaking through them. "I still think it's wrong."

Vaughn was tender. "I know, part of me does, too, but we have to remember, *no* part of Gary is even considering that."

They resumed walking. He paused in his speech and she kept silent, because she could feel something inside him wanting to push itself out. It had been there a long time and she patiently waited. They entered the ice-cream shop and Vaughn bought her a chocolate sundae which they took to their private booth away from everyone. He kept his voice low. "Stephanie, I need to tell you about a vision I had while meditating. It's how I knew what that *creature man* was in the woods."

She listened silently to his vivid description, then to his explanations as to what he thought it meant. He could see how astounded she was, and something in him told him that she was embarrassed by him, and that was why she looked so astounded. But he now knew that was all a lie, because that's how his parents treated him, but not Stephanie. He tried to look past the fear to see what she was really thinking and feeling, but it was hard.

"Vaughn, now I want to tell you about all the things I've seen. I think you'll be surprised at how much goes along with your vision!"

She started by telling him about the blackness that came out from the creature and came for him. Then she told him about the other gray arm things she'd seen in her life, about feelings of monsters and evils lurking around corners, and about how she felt evil often watched her. The whole time she had to force herself to tell him more. The only things she didn't tell him were about the blackness she saw appear in him sometimes and about the glowing tree carving calling to her. *I still think telling him those things would still be a little over the top, yet. Besides, I don't understand it at all.* She remembered again when she was little, she used to talk openly of such things, but her father and mother scolded her and punished her severely for it. But Vaughn wasn't them.

Vaughn looked skeptical. "Stephanie, what you've told me changes things a bit. Not a lot, but a bit."

Her heart went into her throat. *He* does *think I'm crazy.* But again, a distant voice within her spoke, almost too soft to hear, *Listen.*

"I'd been thinking all this was just a case of good versus evil within a human heart, and that the blackness in my vision was symbolic. Even when you told me you saw a gray arm above my head, my first thought was that your mind was creating an interpretation of what you saw inside me.

But now, I *do* believe evil is also a spirit, and that what you're seeing is real!

"I felt a fire come from you when you tackled me in the woods, and again tonight, when you commanded the gray arm to leave me. I have to tell you, I *did* feel the difference it made in me when you said that gray arm left. That fire is a gift from Life, it has purpose, I'm sure it!

"I believe your special sight is also a gift, and that they obviously work together, and that means even to me, even though I can't see what you can see, I believe what you see must be true! My vision was even truer than I realized, as this blackness *is* an *evil spirit.* That all goes along with other feelings I've been having lately, but have been ignoring, because I thought it was my wild imagination." He didn't tell her about the voice that had told him to *sacrifice.*

She had a hard time accepting his new faith in her, perhaps because it seemed too good to be true, since both her parents vehemently rejected her oddness from early on, and the gov would certainly make sure she disappeared if they found out, so she had to ask, "You *really* believe me? And, you don't think I'm odd . . . at all?"

Vaughn saw that her expression looked like that of a three-year old child and her voice sounded three, as well. She sat so still, so timid all of the sudden. As he studied her, he began to understand. *Oh God, when she was little she must have spoken of all these things to her parents . . . no wonder she looks like a little child now! They must have traumatized the hell out of her as soon as she began to show her abilities.*

He took her gently but firmly by her arms, but this time she didn't flinch. He looked deeply into her large, rich brown eyes. "Stephanie, not only do I believe you, I have faith in you. Besides, our consciousness doesn't come from being a body, as Life itself is a Spirit. So, if we can be evil, why not spirits, too?"

She took hold of his hands, quietly weeping on them the stored up tears of her whole life, as many past feelings merged into the present, as his confirmation sank ever deeper into her. As the tears flowed, she felt lighter and lighter, almost as though she were floating. After a while, *Thankfulness, that's thankfulness . . . Oh God, sweet thankfulness. He knows me, he understands, he believes me...He has FAITH in me!*

She looked up into his sharp dark brown eyes and made an oath, or was it a prophecy. "I love you so much, and I accept you, not only for what you've done, but what you are now and will always be." He just nodded because he didn't want to cry, too. But he also knew it wasn't that easy. "Vaughn, but since evil is a spirit, doesn't this change things a lot?"

"Only a bit, because it really doesn't change how good and evil work in us, only that we now know it has its own collective consciousness and can move around, and apply pressures that I hadn't understood before. Not only must we fight the evil within us, but whatever attacks us from the outside. I think that's what your fire is for, to fight the evil outside of us, as words with *true* meaning fight the evil within us." He paused, and once again, she knew he wanted to say more.

This time she prompted him. "What, Vaughn?"

"I think we're meant to stop the evil that blew the man up!"

Shaking her head because of the weight she felt, she protested. "Why do you say that? We're just kids."

"Ahh, besides the fact that our knowledge now makes us responsible to act against the evil, do you know anyone else who has visions of evil hearts and can see evil spirits?"

She wanted to deny it but couldn't and so sighed heavily. *Oh No! Well, if* that's *the case . . .* "There's something else I haven't told you, but I don't know what good it would be."

Vaughn just sat waiting until she began again, and he listened as she described in vivid detail her two experiences at the government church and how some carving of a tree seemed to glow and call to her. The more she revealed, the more unreal it all seemed.

Stephanie was hoping for some kind of immediate reassurance, but Vaughn just sat very silently. His absolute stillness was beginning to irk her but she'd never seen such a look of concentration so she forced herself to wait longer for his response. As she drummed her fingers on the table, finally, she couldn't stand it and kicked him sharply, making him jump.

"Oh, sorry. Look, Stephanie, maybe since evil manifests itself in so many ways like we just described . . . maybe, maybe God might too? Or maybe, just like there seems to be several kinds of evils manifesting themselves in various ways, maybe Goodness does too?"

"But what does that have to do with some dumb carving glowing and saying 'FIND ME!' " And she tried to make her voice echo with the quote. It was almost funny to her.

But Vaughn wasn't amused and looked at her sharply. Seeing his expression, Stephanie echoed the joke a little more to lighten him up, but he won that exchange. She sank back in the booth and looked away. After Vaughn's usual thorough questioning, he announced: "I think we should both go back to the church!"

"Oh no. NO! I swore I'd never look at that *priest* ever again. Besides, what do you want me to do? Go up to that priest and say 'Hey, God called to me, not you, right here from this glowing piece of wood?' Vaughn, the church and the government both would probably fight over who got to torture and kill me first!"

But he looked at her frankly and said, "Stephanie, I was called directly through my vision. You were called directly, too. I can't help but believe that, somehow, Goodness is calling us both. Stephanie, the God we know as Life and Love is calling us both and putting us together to fight all this evil. I'm sure of it."

"But Vaughn, at least your vision has . . . possibilities. I mean, you can kinda interpret it. But what the hell does a glowing tree-carving in a corrupt church calling FIND ME have to do with anything?"

Vaughn leaned back. "Well, isn't that a good question? I think you're meant to find out." And he paused for a moment as he had some greater feeling send increasingly familiar goose bumps all over him.

"What, Vaughn?"

"Do you think you were called so you *wouldn't* find out why?

Begrudgingly, she conceded. "Good point, but what can we do? When that black stuff came for you, I was barely able to protect you. I didn't even know what I was doing."

"I don't know. My vision hasn't been completed, yet, either, but I don't think it was given to me in vain. That evil blackness you saw is gonna find someone . . . who'll become a very evil creature. I'd like to stop it before that could happen, otherwise when the creature comes about . . . I think we're meant to destroy it . . . *no matter what* Stephanie. "He looked sharply at her to emphasize something she couldn't quite understand, as he reiterated. "*No matter what,* that *is* our first responsibility.

"All I know is that we're very strong together, and we're growing stronger. I think the more deeply we understand and live by Goodness, the stronger we'll become. I think we need to concentrate on that, then the rest will just take care of itself in due time. But I'm *sure* you need to find the meaning behind your glowing tree. You need to do that for both of us, Stephanie. I'll do my part. You have to do yours, too, or . . . I think we'll both fail! Thanks for saving me from that evil spirit, because based on my vision, I wouldn't have wanted to fight it by myself."

"I saved you," she said distantly as if pondering the words, and he nodded.

CHAPTER 12

Do All Good Things Have to Come to an . . .

His Queen took his hand while they sat together on their bed. "I know you were proud of the truce you fashioned, but perhaps it was not meant to be."

"Your prophecy is unclear. It seems to speak of times far into the future, while also speaking of today. Also, equally unclear concerning Yana's relationship with the young man, for even though she's young, she could not possibly live as long as indicated. Wouldn't it be ironic if I, through fear, destroyed the truce I love so much when it needn't have been?"

Queen Yinauqua nodded, but accepting the end of their good times. "The Tree of Life has been good to us my dear husband, so what shall we say about baring a daughter who will bring an end to peace? The Tree of Life shall call to another."

King Mafferan repeated. "Your prophecy is unclear, and also unclear is whether a truce of any kind equals peace!"

Many weeks passed since Vaughn and Stephanie heard how Gary lived and the others had died. School would start up again, soon, and they kept on hearing about more people being blown up from the inside out, as the evil blackness was spreading all around the country. More people than usual were getting angrier at the strangers and the foreigners that were squatting near the borders, and for the first time, there was regular national news covering these events across the whole nation. Jargon said he was close to finding the answer, and Vaughn wondered if he, too, had the vision, but somehow, that didn't feel quite right to him. It didn't make sense to show two different people the same thing. *Unless, they were meant to work together*, he thought. In the meantime, Vaughn and Stephanie concentrated on home.

During Gary and his gang's absence, the neighborhood changed, and it was awesome to see just how many troubles simply disappeared. Life and death take their natural courses, but much of it they planned. Or did they? It was humbling being part of something much greater than they could comprehend, and they wondered whether it was their plan at all, or if they were just part of Life's plan all along. The surviving boy told the town they all went up to the barn to play and the old floor gave way, and no one heard what Gary had to say.

Life around the schoolyard, the hangouts, and the neighborhood in general, seemed to improve immensely for everyone. There were more smiles, more laughter, and children felt safer. Little girls no longer felt the need to stay close to their door, and little boys left their toys in the yard. One would hardly imagine that missing only six boys could make such a difference in a whole community. The whole thing turned out to be a public service. Vaughn had no idea how he would maintain this when Gary came back, but he knew he had to try.

He began to study Ralph, too, since he would try to replace Gary's gang, now given the opportunity. *There's no sense getting rid of one devil just to let another take his place! But can I go after him when he hasn't done anything to me? I don't like what he did to Stephanie, but he didn't really do anything that warrants what I really want to do. Am I wrong for wanting to get rid of him, too? The bastard's a drug pusher. How can I be wrong? But can I kill him for it? If I did, would that deter others? Oh Hell, these kinds of people are like cockroaches! They look innocent enough when you catch a glimpse of them . . . until they multiply so much they take over your house! That's why they always say, if you see* one, *KILL IT!*

Stephanie and Vaughn sat across from each other in what came to be known by them as *their booth,* a little cove corner in the ice cream parlor offset from the end of the counter. That was the only booth in the cove as it was only big enough for the one. Yet from its vantage point, they could see many patrons' reflections in the mirrored wall behind the counter.

They always waited for that particular booth to be empty, as it was the most private. All summer long they had a date, every evening, to meet after Vaughn was done working for various local farmers. He worked very hard and learned much.

Stephanie didn't find work, the word '*sacrifice*' burned hotly in the back of her mind.

Stephanie's dark blue, flowery, long cotton dress sported short sleeves which was the extent to which she was now willing to uncover herself. She found she was now so appalled by her own past behavior, that she made Vaughn make a fire in the country to where she carried out a huge bag of sluttish clothes and burned them. Some of them he thought weren't that bad, but she just gave him the eye and said, quote, "Yeah, I suppose so to your male eye" unquote. He threw out his hands in submission and gave her that broad smile, bowing his head slightly. He was hers to command and he loved it, but what he loved even more, was that she made him think.

Every day she brought some unique insight to him, some beautiful feeling. The descriptions of what she saw with her special sight also strengthened him, because they went so well with the understanding he was developing about good and evil. That's also how he knew she saw truly, because what she saw made sense. *That's why it's so hard to change, sometimes, because as soon as I get rid of evil within, it comes from the outside to attack and to force itself back into me.* Even though she never said much about the evil she saw around him, he was developing a good guess based on what she saw around others.

As he sat across from her, he was painfully aware of just how deeply he loved everything about her, and that love just seemed to grow more intense every hour. She just seemed to keep growing more beautiful, like a tree gains greater glory with age. The warmth and intelligence in her eyes grew hotter and sharper, even her cheeks seemed to gain a deeper golden glow.

Her eye color now seemed richer somehow, her touch more tender, and she appeared so much more feminine.

He had grown accustomed to instantly feeling her heart through her hand whenever she placed it upon him, but he also noticed that even when he saw her at a distance, it seemed as though he could feel it. At first he told himself it was just wishful thinking, imagination, but when he'd ask her how she was feeling, she confirmed his insight. To go from being so lonely, so alienated, so deprived of natural human affection and contact, to this depth and quality . . . was heaven for him. The experience was so powerful, that it became like an unquestioned mountain upon which a great fortress was built. The fortress was strong, but the mountain made it unassailable.

"Vaughn, I so love meeting here every day with you," she said as she held his hands atop the shiny, dark brown table while sipping on her chocolate ice cream soda, which he had proudly bought for her. Every time he bought anything for her, he exuded a special pride as he handed over the money. More than once it brought a tear to the corners of her eyes, not knowing how to deal with being thought of so highly.

Vaughn smiled a smile that through the long summer Stephanie had become affectionately familiar with, as it was a smile of complete peace and satisfaction with her. Every time he did it, and he did it often, she felt as if she were being elevated to the top of a mountain. *Such feelings,* she often said to herself, as she reflected on how much she had learned from him.

She never thought it was possible that a man could be so meaningful to a woman's understanding. More than that, she never thought it possible that she could *ever* be meaningful to his. But she saw the powerful affect she had on him, how he thought so deeply on her questions about his thoughts and feelings, but she also saw how deeply he considered her feelings as well. She began to notice little parts of herself appearing within him, subtle changes in his expression, in his feelings, that she knew were distinctly hers but now naturally part of his as well. Then she looked at herself, after that observation, and saw there were pieces of Vaughn in her the same way, so she smiled, and thought, *How wonderful this is! Oh God, all that we've suffered can't compare to the beauty YOU have now given us!*

Yes. She said to herself as she peered intently into his eyes, and saw how much he had changed. In every way he seemed to have become even smarter, quicker, calmer and stronger than when they first met. Every day, she observed some further development of beauty in his character, his expression, and in his emotions.

"Well, for the summer anyway, I'm able to make consistent money helping farmers, and what better enjoyment can I get than to watch you sumptuously consume various ice-cream sundaes and sodas?"

She wrinkled her nose at him. "You're going to make me fat!" she scolded him, trying to maintain a serious look.

He matched her seriousness with innocence. "I haven't noticed any extra cushion."

Stephanie blushed and began scolding him in earnest, "Vaughn, not so loud, people will hear you!" And then she realized. "You've been paying attention?"

He leveled his eyes into hers. "Stephie, I pay attention to everything about you." His intense stare sent her blood to rushing and her mind to . . .

"I can't imagine having to wait years before we can . . ."

But he cut her off, as he already thought out his answer, an answer he had given to himself when having the same imagination. "Stephie, I can't imagine having met you, that's what I think about every day. Every day, whether in a barn or out in a field working, I'm thinking that each step I take, each bale of hay I bundle, load, or carry, each new thing I learn, will help me grow into the man I will need to be to care for you responsibly."

She sat up straighter, suddenly looking very much like a mature woman, then her shoulders drooped a bit. "Vaughn, you're kidding!"

"Look into my eyes!"

Moments went by, until she acknowledged. "You're telling the truth." *He did it again to me, he overwhelmed me with his love, a new devotion I never knew he had. Oh God, I love him so. Oh God, I love looking into his eyes.*

Vaughn took her hands. "Every evening we meet here and I watch you eat, I watch how your eyes shine, how your thick, long red hair drapes your shoulders, how your cheeks *blush*, and I think of how I would like to kiss your lips. "

"People will hear you, Vaughn!" she said blushing brightly through her golden skin, and grabbing his folded hands in hers more tightly than he had held hers. She peeked out from the booth to see if anyone was paying attention.

"I *love* your modesty."

"Hmm, modesty? Modesty. I suppose you're right, I hadn't thought about that, considering the way I was for so long."

Vaughn leaned back and sharpness entered his expression. She knew this look too. He was going to teach her something profound. "To our young minds, a year seems long. That's what a farmer told me. But he showed me how he planned out all that his farm is now, thirty years ago! He said wise people need to be wise when they're young because great things take a long time to build, and can only be gotten when started young and pursued with patience and understanding. Then he told me that line I just told you, because it's the reason why most young people today are not wise. They live for the moment and think even a week is too long to wait or plan for something. Stephie, I am planning for you."

Tears flooded her eyes as she felt the depths of his heart pour over her and gently sink into her. "Vaughn, you're always making me cry, I'm going to stop wearing any makeup at all." She grabbed some napkins and began dabbing.

"Good, 'cause you really don't need that crap! Don't you know natural beauty is better than any imitation we can put over it? Do you have any idea just how much more beautiful you are since you got rid of those rings in your body and toned down your makeup?"

"You think I would look prettier without *any*?"

"*Yes!* I think everyone would look prettier being real and not *fake*. The young put on makeup to look older, and the older put on makeup to look younger. It makes no sense! No one wants to be what they are. Heck, that's probably what makes people look so ugly a lot of times, always hating what you are can't make you look beautiful. Ha, in a way, maybe it's a cruel self-fulfilling prophecy. The more they hate what they are, the uglier they get, the more makeup they put on, the more they show self-hatred, the uglier they get! That's probably why the oldest ones wear the most!

"But the old ladies in the country, they're wrinkled but they're so beautiful. In fact, I could look at their beautiful faces all day for what they express, and they don't wear *any* of that crap! That is, at least not when they're on the farm where I see them, and they look so very happy with themselves, too!"

With expressions of mock fright, Vaughn hinted to Stephanie the people in the parlor who fit his *ugly* description. Stephanie had to duck down in the booth across the long cushion, trying to hide her uncontrolled laughter, and even though the booth was partly hidden away, she was sure her laughter would draw everyone's attention. But every time she sat up, he would make those mocking expressions again, which sent her ducking even further back down.

Vaughn's explanation sounded plausible and she couldn't believe she actually considered it, but why else would she be laughing. She finally sat back up again, but when she turned her gaze to a new old lady sitting on a stool at the counter who was covered in makeup, Stephanie laid back down again, bursting at the seams. Then she sat back up once again, gaining control, but Vaughn nodded at a teenage girl a couple of stools away whose makeup colors looked sort of birdlike, and this sent her again into uncontrollable fits, and she ducked under the table yet again.

Finally, she resolved what to do, as it had to be the *only* way to resolve the situation. She took a napkin and dipped it in her water glass and wiped off the rest of the makeup she was wearing, which made Vaughn smiled broadly.

"Beautiful," he said.

She finally was able to contribute to their conversation. "Did you know I lay awake at night imagining how to be the best wife to you I could possibly be?"

Vaughn sat back in amazement. Her words were like a giant, wonderful hand that picked him up and set him in the sky. She always made him feel truly special, but this? *The best wife she could possibly be to me? Wow!* "What are you giggling about?"

"Oh, Vaughn, you don't know but I have a wild imagination, as I often day dream about all kinds of trouble we might face, and what we have to do to overcome it. I often imagine what advice you'll need me to give you during terrible times, or what question you'd need me to ask you, or how sometimes I'll be too weak and you would protect me and make me stronger. You know, I actually learn a lot from my imagination. It seems to have a life all its own."

He saw that familiar special look of revelation and discovery in her smiling eyes. But he now had that keen look again. "Well, if it's guided by the goodness of life, goodness itself *does have* a life of its own, and your imagination becomes like a door you allow yourself to be taught through."

"I never thought about it like that, but that really feels right. Wow!"

Then he spoke loud enough for everyone to hear. "I can't believe how much stronger I feel since I've met you, Stephanie. Every bale of hay I lift, I lift it with more strength, not just because I'm physically stronger, but because my very *person* is stronger. It makes me see just how terribly *defeating* and *destructive* my family is."

"Vaughn, we're like a light to each other. *You* are worth waiting and planning for and just think of all the life we'll have shared together before we marry. VAUGHN, you can't kiss me in . . . !" But she didn't push him away as he took her cheek in his right hand and drew them together.

"We're in a booth, I looked, and no one was looking."

They sat quietly for a while just looking into each other's eyes. It was good to forget about evil hearts, exploding people, and gray arm things.

Tracy sat while speaking softly to Karen, trying to keep the conversation private. "Karen, are you sure about that?" Tracy's eyes had tears in them.

Karen's eyes were sabers ripping some offender to shreds, and her voice was not soft. "Oh yeah, I'm sure, that *bitch* is going to have to leave because there's no one to take care of her now, and you know where she'll have to go?"

Tracy whispered, "Where?"

"To the one person I heard she hates most, her *father*, who lives *all the way* on the *other side* of the country."

Tracy's mouth dropped open, as she knew how horrible that would be. "No!"

"Oh YES! The State doesn't allow unguardianed children and requires parents to support them, or they put them on a work farm and those places are hell holes."

Tracy took a napkin and dabbed her eyes. "I feel so bad for her."

"I don't. She got what she deserved! I'm sure they killed the boys and put Gary in the hospital somehow. I don't care what that babbling idiot said about it being an accident, because he's probably too scared to tell the truth."

Tracy urged her to be quieter. "Karen, your anger is going to melt your ice-cream. Did they find out who ran her mother over?"

"No. She always went to work early while it was dark, took the same street crossing every day. Because she left so early, there was no one about to see what happened. Stephanie's mother is dead and I'M GLAD!" Karen proclaimed.

Somehow, Karen and Tracy were sitting in the booth just around the corner from Vaughn and Stephanie, so they overheard the whole conversation. Stephanie leapt up and was on her before Vaughn even had time to rise. He couldn't believe anyone could move that quickly. Karen had her back to them and was the closest. She didn't see her coming when

Stephanie grabbed her beautiful blond hair and violently wrenched her head back.

"You're a lying *dog*," Stephanie yelled, but it was the fire in her eyes that scared Vaughn, as he had never seen so much of it. He could feel something strange emanating from her that he never knew before, and that scared him even more.

"Stephanie! I didn't know you were here," Karen said with her head bent way back exposing her white throat.

"Stephie, let go of her hair!" Vaughn gently urged her as he put his hand lightly on her back. Tracy's mouth was agape.

Karen oozed sympathy. "Oh, I'm so sorry about what happened."

"That's not what you were just saying a minute ago! You're *lying!*"

Vaughn saw streams of blackness swirl through and around Stephanie while her fire gained intensity, and he wondered if anyone else could see it.

"Stephie, let's go find out." He moved his hands to her upper arms, but dared not apply any pressure, as he knew Stephanie very much had a mind of her own, and would let go when she wanted to. He couldn't believe Karen was that big of an idiot to say what he heard her say next, even if it was in that sweet tone.

"You know, they'll never find out who killed your bitch mother!"

Vaughn *had* to try and restrain her now, as he was sure Stephanie would kill her on the spot!

"Let me *go*," she screamed at him, but he felt it better him than letting her kill Karen. He had his arms wrapped around her from behind, and she couldn't get her arms from under his. She had to let go of Karen's hair, and when she did, Vaughn backed Stephanie away from her, although she desperately tried to free herself.

Vaughn spoke softly into her ear, "What's important here? Look at me Stephie! What's important here?"

She turned her head as far around as possible, leaning over so she could see him. He was cut in two by the look on her face, but he had to hold her in his stare so that she could see as eyes are like a two way street. She couldn't keep herself from looking into them and finally admitting what she saw: "Truth." She relaxed and with his hand on her back, they went to the Keeper's Station.

Karen straightened herself out, took a brush from her purse and smoothed her hair, checked her face in her pocket mirror, and then in very proper fashion, replaced the napkin on her lap to finish her ice cream sundae.

Tracy felt like throwing up. She stared at Karen. *No, it couldn't be.* She pushed her ice cream away and then got up and walked out. As she walked down the street to go home, tears ran down her cheeks, and a voice was echoing in her memories, '*We can do this, Tracy.*' It was Stephanie telling her she could quit doing drugs. Tracy's heart pounded, seeing Stephanie's rich brown eyes staring into her. She ran the rest of the way home, not wanting to hear or see any more. *'It's not just a choice not to feel pain, it's a choice not to feel anything real.'* "Stop it!" She cried out, "Oh God, stop it! *I don't want to feel anything real!*" She cried as she held her head with her hands, ran into her house and locked herself in her room.

ꝏ

The crumbling stone foundation of the ancient Keeper's Station could not hide the function all such places have performed from the very beginning. They sat outside the door to the main office, on a hard stone bench in a dim hallway. Stephanie didn't feel strong enough to walk outside yet.

"Just hold me, Vaughn."

"I'm sorry, Stephanie, I don't know what to say. I know you two were growing so close."

She spoke as if in a daze. "Vaughn, she was really beginning to change, to understand herself and me."

Vaughn wished he could take back what he said next, even before he had completed saying it. "Oh, God, why?"

She whirled on him in accusation. "*That's what I'd like to know. Why? Why would God do something like this when she was just beginning to understand Life?*"

Vaughn eased back a bit. *Oh* idiot*! Why'd I say that?* Now, he didn't know what to do, and he had to play it by ear.

"Stephie, I know what Life is; it's pure, it's Love. *That* God didn't do this, *couldn't* have done this!"

She was bitter, and questioned, "*Then what good is He?* What good is He Vaughn if He can't prevent evil from happening?" They both waited in silence. He wanted the guilt of her question to sink into her, but she wanted a quick answer, bearing down upon him with her eyes.

When he saw that his condemning silence was growing unbearable for her, he clarified, "Did it make you feel better to ask such a thing?" Vaughn listened to her reply with a strange calm.

Almost involuntarily she looked inside herself. "No." She bent over weeping into her hands.

He didn't respond to it, didn't hold her, didn't look at her, but kept facing straight ahead. "Why didn't it make you feel better?"

Eventually, she squeezed an answer out. "Because I feel dead inside, beyond pain now. She paused. "It's all so terrible."

She didn't answer the question, only how it made her feel to ask it. Let's try again. I think her life depends upon her answer, and that's all that matters now. "Answer the *question*, then, Stephie!"

"What *question*?" she snapped.

I must have her face this now, before evil turns her further down an even darker path. He pressed the point. "Your own question then! What good is the God *we have come to know*? Not the god other people play around with in their phony religion, but the One we have found to be what, Stephie?" He bent over to stare at her, and she could feel his eyes upon her, even though she looked away.

The outside world disappeared. *My question?* She wanted to fight him, but he was no longer asking her to answer his question, but her own. She was alone with herself in a world made up of just her. *What good is the God we know?* She heard that question pounding in her solitary world, but at some instants, the question sounded mocking, but at others, sincere. True meaning sent her pictures she was fighting not to see. She wanted to run away, to go hide in her shelter in the woods, and she almost got up to run there, but Vaughn was here with her. She found her heart back at her shelter, but she found her soul with Vaughn. *But the God we have found to be* what, *Stephie?* This now pounded in her world. Vaughn was in her world. Love and true value were in her world. Meaning was yet alive in her heart. Unwillingly, her dead feelings were compared to her live feelings of true meaning, and her anger grudgingly gave way to goodness.

Something in her broke when she heard her answer, "Life and Love." She could feel Vaughn's presence surrounding her, holding her up while pains racked her. The contrast made both the pain and love even more sharply defined. She reached for the love, or perhaps love reached for her. "Even this terribleness can't take away the meaning of goodness. It can't change what we've found together . . . or even the reason why my Mother and I were getting closer in the first place. *I still feel our love. It's real life.* How could I ever even hope to have a true relationship, if I fault Goodness? Then from where would I get mine? Goodness is worth dying for. God forgive me, I spoke wrongly. Life is still worth living for no matter what happens, as long as you don't give up! As long as you still keep loving . . . being true. "

He still sat silently while staring at her.

"All right, as long as *I* don't give up." He finally reached out and put his hand on her shoulder, and they straightened up together, never taking their eyes off each other. "I still feel sick inside though, and abandoned. And I still don't understand why God didn't spare her."

Vaughn sighed. "Some of your childhood needs from your Mom were finally being met, needs that are still present with you, Stephie."

"*Vaughn!*" She buried herself on his shoulder.

Truth often hurts. He hugged her tightly. But it was better to make the picture clear than to allow it to bury itself and become distorted in later life.

"I know it hurts, but to run from it will harm you just as you ran away from yourself before. If you're going to be a true person, Stephanie, you have to accept the true pain that true love and true need brings."

"How?" she sobbed.

"You wouldn't hurt that way if you didn't truly love. The pain is partly a *result* of love. *But* pain is *secondary*. But if you try to kill the pain, you risk killing your love, your capacity to feel *anything*."

This was familiar to her. *That's my very reason for quitting drugs, so I* could *feel.* "Yes, I see this."

"Because pain comes second to love, love has more power than the second, because the first has living purpose. The pain is just telling you that part of that purpose was hurt, like a tree having a branch ripped off by the wind. The tree responds by slowly growing more branches. Eventually the scar heals and shows contrast to the new life, and that contrast makes the new branches be even that much more beautiful!"

Stephanie shook her head at him, but he knew it wasn't rejection. "How do you know such things?"

"Because, every day when I walk through the woods, I see it, Stephanie, as there are many trees just like that, in all stages of life."

Her face scrunched up. "But, I'm not a tree."

He countered her expression with his profound challenging look. "Are you sure? Maybe we're more a tree than a tree is! Maybe the meaning of 'tree' is to help us understand what *we* truly are. A tree has the capacity to live forever if disaster or disease doesn't kill it, and it's hard to kill a tree as long as it possesses a good root, because it can come back to life, just like keeping a good heart no matter what."

"What about the need, Vaughn? What about the *need*? I needed her so much."

Vaughn hated to have to answer it. Unfulfilled needs are not like the pains of love. He took hold of her hands and kissed them, held them tightly. "Stephie, God made us with needs and specific fulfillments for those needs that are extremely hard to substitute. But Stephie, what about those children who never had a mother? What about those who never had a mother turn back toward goodness as yours did? I think the answer is, in part, a greater humility and thankfulness for what you *did* have, and then determination to supply to others all the goodness you have come to be.

"There is an old song I heard a farmer woman sing to her little granddaughter. It had such a beautiful tune, it brought tears to my eyes. The part I remember most comes right after singing about terrible hardships, losing crops, losing your only child, having a hard life of tears. 'We can't have all things to please us, no matter how hard we try.' Then it says 'til we meet God in the end. The song is implying that even in terrible hardships, there is always greater goodness to appreciate, because we know God is real. I think the hidden meaning of the song is that there's something so fundamentally beautiful about being a human being regardless of all the suffering we undergo!

That something is what allows us to appreciate goodness *in spite* of all the suffering we endure, that's what the line 'We can't have all things to please us demonstrates." Then Vaughn did his best to sing the song to her, and the tune brought her different tears.

"Oh, Vaughn! Who wrote such a beautiful song?"

"She said she heard it was written by a country woman named Gillian Welch, who was from a country called Wales, but that country doesn't exist any longer. It's a very old song. Stephie, no matter how it hurts, let love be love, because Love will keep you, if you keep it."

Her eyes pleaded with him. "Vaughn, come home with me?"

"Alright. Stephie, I'll come."

When they got to Stephanie's house, Vaughn made her wash up and even brush her teeth. It was important to maintain self-respect, especially now, as he knew if she let it slip now, it could fall very low. Then Vaughn went in to the bathroom, did the same thing, and returned to her bedroom.

She laid down in bed in her cotton nightclothes. Vaughn remembered how she had dragged him home and labored to put him in her bed the night they met, and he remembered how wonderful the touch of her hand felt that night.

"Vaughn, will you lay down next to me, just until I fall asleep?"

He couldn't resist her eyes, but he already knew this was going to happen.

"Yes, my love." He lay down behind her, and she immediately curled up into a ball, hugging a pillow. He wrapped his strong arms around her, bringing his legs up to press behind hers. When they woke in the morning, they were still in the same position.

That day was the last day she'd look upon the peeling plywood walls, the last chance to get a splinter from the rough wooden floor. But it had always been her private room since she was old enough to remember.

Early in the morning, a solid rapping on the door startled them. Stephanie quickly threw a brown long dress over her pajamas and answered the door to a tall shadow falling upon her. "Excuse me, sir, but who are you?"

The thin man in a black uniform that she didn't recognize spoke in an official tone. "Are you Stephanie?"

"Yes."

"Your mother's funeral will be paid by the state because she had no savings. Your father has been notified and will be here by plane at nine tomorrow. The funeral will be later that day at three, and you will go to live with your father."

The words struck her as if a giant meteor had slammed to the Earth.

"But . . . but . . ."

The man rudely and coldly interrupted. "If you do not wish to live with your father, arrangements can be made but, you are a beautiful young girl, so I would not suggest such arrangements. I am sorry for your loss. What is your decision?"

Why do I have to live in this world? How can I go to live with him*? We can't have all things to please us . . . but what if we have* no *things to please us?*

Vaughn stepped beside her and answered for her. "She'll go with her father."

The officer raised a single eyebrow but otherwise remained emotionless. "Who are you?"

"Her best friend, and we've talked so she'll go with her father."

The officer turned back to Stephanie. "Is this so? I need *more* than just a *head nod*, young lady."

She felt like she died inside when she answered. "Yes sir, I will go with my father." She felt and sounded hollow. The officer gave a slight nod and stiffly left. Stephanie closed the door and leaned her back against it.

"Vaughn, I feel dead inside, again."

But Vaughn felt the same way. "I know, Stephie, I know, but it's the pain of . . . loss." His heart was pounding so hard he thought he might throw up, so he leaned against the wall as well. Too many feelings all at once . . . *meant to be together . . .*

makes no sense. How can we stop the evil if we're not together? How will she . . . survive her father? *What's life without her? Why is* everything *being destroyed?*

Stephanie turned to Vaughn and saw him crying, shaking! *That* sight jolted her. Till now he had been like the rock she so desperately needed. She then realized that she hadn't looked inside him since . . . she did now. *Oh God, I at least I had my mother for a short time, but he only ever had me his whole* entire *life*. She took hold of his sobbing shoulders and squeezed, "Don't you cry too, Vaughn. You're my hope!"

He didn't want to, was angry at himself for being so *weak*, but he had to explain. "I cry not only because it's my loss, *our* loss, but because I understand how *terribly* this hurts you. On top of all your loss, our loss, you have to go live with *him*. And I know that is about the worst possible combination of things I can imagine for you . . . and I'm . . . I'm . . ." He sobbed again.

She grabbed and held him tight, then they went and sat on the brownish couch in her living room. *Oh God, I've got to help him, somehow.*

". . . scared for you, Stephanie, as I don't think I would have the strength to endure what you must." *Why did I just say that? I'm a* fool. *How's that going to help* anything*? I'm such a jerk.*

Stephanie was in a void, as if lost in the unknown. She looked inside herself to see what else she could see. She realized she still possessed feelings that were so much richer now, in spite of everything. Her attention to them made them burst forth inside her, as she recognized this as the light that Vaughn had first said he saw in her eyes. *I am me, and I'm more than just a bunch of experiences.* She felt that light still shining, still loving, still appreciating life even greater than ever. She looked into that light and listened, and then words came from her mouth, and she listened to them as they came out. "Vaughn, after a tree suffers loss, does it *know* . . . *feel* the life it will yet come to be?"

Vaughn picked up his head that had been hanging down and looked over at her, as he understood why she inflected it the way she did. "I know what you mean. No, it starts where it must, with what life, what strength it has available."

She grabbed and squeezed his shoulders and turned him to face her. She knew she had to do this for him. "Then *that* is how I will somehow make it through what I must. I *promise* you, Vaughn, I will *not* let you . . . I will not let *myself* down . . . I will not let *you* down. But I have something more than a tree." She had to convince him, but she had to convince herself, also.

"What's that, Stephanie?" Vaughn couldn't think at that moment but could only listen.

"I can *appreciate* life. Before I met you, it was buried so deep inside me, but when you came into my life, it was all the sunshine my life needed to begin sprouting all over the place. Now I have hope, and we *still* have each other."

Vaughn hung his head back down. "Stephie, it's very expensive to communicate long distances, and you know how the government put a stop to all that. If we try to communicate too much, we'll be breaking their doctrine, and they'll think we're trying to bring the Old back. Fear, Stephie, does terrible things, especially when in the hands of the powerful."

From somewhere she couldn't explain, because it made no sense given the situation at hand, she felt determined. She remembered lifting him up when he was unconscious the night he fought for her. Love always blesses goodness, that's what Vaughn had said before, but she knew he'd forgotten about that now, so she fought to honor what he'd taught her. She grabbed his cheeks and turned his head up to look at her with fire in her eyes that half pleaded, half scolded. "Then, we'll talk through our prayers to one another . . . have faith that we hear each other's heart and mind. What we have is greater than *distance!*"

But his mind was on the practical. "Stephie, I want you to listen to me, even travel is restricted, so we have to face reality. I will never give up on our love. *Never!* But you cannot cut yourself off from finding truth where you'll be going, *especially* when you'll have to deal with your father! You just can't!"

Her hands dropped because she didn't like what he was implying, and she hoped it wasn't what she thought. "What are you saying, Vaughn?" Stephanie's eyes were growing wide.

"I'm not saying you should look for someone else, but if Life brings others to you, don't go against the flow of life, that's all."

Then it occurred to her how hard it was going to be for him. "But what about you? You told me yourself how much stronger you felt because of me. What will you do? What will happen to you when I'm gone?" The painful picture cut her like lightning across the sky and she had a sharp pain in her heart. Her head suddenly ached terribly. The full realization of how terrible this would be for him now fell on her and was at least equal in pain to all the rest. She felt nauseous.

"I don't know, but truth is truth, and reality is reality."

Then she had a great thought and asked, "Why don't we run away together, Vaughn?"

But he immediately shot it down. "You know those things are no longer possible, it would be a death sentence." He turned his head away and hung it down heavily, and the sight of that stabbed her through the heart, it seemed all her bones ached.

But the fire in her kept burning, urging her to speak. "Vaughn, look at me. *Look* at me!" She scolded him to look, and grabbed his arms tightly and shook him 'til he picked his head up, then she cupped her hands tenderly on his cheeks.

"My dear Vaughn, I hold in my hands the face I saw in the window that dreadful night, and there will never . . . never be a more precious sight to me! But the meaning of this face tells me I *must* take your advice, and you must take your *own* advice as well!"

She dazed him, not only with the meaning of her words, but with the power she put into them. He tried to escape back into his being lost. "Stephie, you make friends easily and I don't."

"Friends . . . friends? *What* friends?"

"I remember seeing you with lots of people."

"Vaughn, they were all like that *evil woman* at the ice-cream shop, except for maybe Tracy. But they were a long way from understanding anything much about me that would allow me to call them my friends." Then the idea burst upon her, like the birth of a star. "Vaughn, do you think you could maybe help Tracy, like you helped me?" Her request dazed him even further.

"Oh, I don't know, Stephanie, she was part of . . ."

"Not really, Vaughn, not really. She's very weak, and lost, and they're using her just like they used me. Now someone else will just take over, and when Gary comes back, *he'll* start all over. Vaughn, don't let that happen, *Pleas*e don't let that happen to her." She begged him in earnest.

"I'll think about it. Stephie, I'll think about it."

She pressed the point. "Vaughn, I want you to *promise* me you'll seriously think about it."

He became suspicious. "Why?"

Confidence lit in her face. "Because I know you, and I know if you do, you won't be able to keep from helping her."

He saw that Stephanie had outsmarted him; he sighed slowly and lolled his head.

"I'll take that for a yes," she said of a surety. He sighed again.

The rest of the day centered upon two very important tasks: Stephanie packed up what little she had, and then she straightened the house. There really wasn't much, but Stephanie kept shifting things around the broken down hamlet.

Suddenly there was meaning to every little thing, to every position of every little thing. How should one leave behind the sole representation of one's entire life? The people coming after her would be the only ones to see it, and it was important to her that everything make the proper statement. And then, it would be gone because they'd change it.

For his part, Vaughn simply followed her around wherever she went, answering the repeated question, "What do you think?" concerning the slightest movement of a picture, a knick knack. The next day when they left, in truth, one could hardly notice any difference to the dilapidated place. The meaning would simply be lost to a stranger.

Her newly rebuilt shelter flashed in her mind, and sorrow washed immediately behind, as she hadn't even shared it with Vaughn, and now there was no time. *One day I WILL revisit you,* she spoke within as if her shelter could hear, *And I'll show you to Vaughn.*

There was left over beef stew her mother cooked from the night before. When Stephanie saw it in the refrigerator, Vaughn saw her stare at it. "Stephie, she wouldn't want you to waste it. It was her care for you."

Stephanie wept as they ate together. Food prepared out of love tastes so much better. It was the best meal her Mother had ever prepared. Their new relationship had kindled a level of care Stephanie had not known before and every bite, every savory flavor sharpened Stephanie's new picture of her Mother as a loving, caring person, as if she could feel every tender touch of her soul. When she finished, she pushed her plate aside, put her hands upon the little table, her head upon her hands, and she wailed. Vaughn let her grieve, and then he cleaned up the dishes, and when he finished, he sat down quietly beside her.

When he sensed she was beginning to doze, he took her by the arm and led her to the bathroom to wash and change for the night. She didn't want to, but she looked up into Vaughn's eyes and saw he wasn't considering any other possibility so she complied. *Self-respect, Stephanie, self-respect,* he willed it into her.

They slept arm in arm that night as the night before, except this night, they faced each other. The pleasant aroma of her hair, of her skin, became distinctly noticeable to him like never before, increasing his desire to taste another kiss from her, but he knew that would only make the suffering worse. Each beat of his heart sickened more with pain as he realized she was a part of him in many ways like his very own internal organs were a part of his body. *You can't live without your liver, without your heart,* the pain kept telling him with every beat. Now, the exact point of every beat cried that she was more than just in his heart, or even also in his mind, she was everywhere within his being and she was being ripped away from him.

After wondrously overcoming the evil of the town gang, the future had widened unlimitedly. But reality is what it is, and having her so close in bed only allowed the torment to replay over and over. He left early in the next morning while she still slept, so he could pick up his father's car.

Vaughn drove up in his father's black, boxlike sedan. It was the standard government model since the auto industry collapsed a hundred years ago. It made for a fitting symbol of the whole country, Vaughn thought as he exited the car, being careful not to slam the door. As he walked up to Stephanie's shabby house, it struck him that no one had come to pay their respects to her for her mother's loss. *"Not even Tracy,"* he mumbled to himself.

He entered without knocking, but a strange thought occurred to him as he did so, *This is what it would be like if Stephanie and I were married. I'd enter without knocking.* In the next instant he saw the single bag of old luggage standing in the middle of the living room containing all of Stephanie's possessions that she deemed worthy to bring with her to her new life. Vaughn still couldn't figure out why the order in which she packed her clothes was important, but Stephanie had insisted that it was, and proceeded to repack them four times yesterday morning.

She nodded to him silently, and when he picked it up, he was surprised at how light it was.

She held the door open for him, then shut it, locked it, and dropped the keys in the mailbox that still hung on a loose board by one nail. Halfway down the walk, she stopped, and turned around to stare at the weatherworn little house, and thought. *I think at one time, this house used to be painted white!* Certain lighter blotchy areas on the dry-rotting wood siding hinted at it. She sighed once then resolutely turned to the car. Standing erect, with her head held high in a way Vaughn had never seen before, she seemed regal as she waited on Vaughn, and he held the passenger door open for his queen, as the sun peeked over the tops of buildings and trees. She lifted her black dress slightly as she sat in the car and Vaughn was sure it had belonged to her mother, but he didn't ask.

"Thank you for coming with me to pick up my Father, it was nice of your parents to let you use their car," she said to him once they were on their way.

He frowned. "It wasn't exactly like that."

"What do you mean?"

"We had a big fight. Apparently they see no future for me with you, so they thought it would be a waste of time to help."

She looked at him as he pulled out onto the two-lane street. "You're kidding!"

"No, I couldn't even imagine something so sickening."

"Then how did you get the car?"

"I took all the money I saved up from work and smacked it down on the table in front of them, and said, 'Fine, I'll rent the car for as long as Stephanie is here! C'mon Mom, you can't pass up money!'"

Stephanie practically hit her head on the ceiling of the car, because she jerked up so hard. "*You're kidding!* You're not kidding?"

"My Mom told my Dad to let me use it."

"I can't *believe* that!"

Vaughn flatly looked over at her as he drove. "Reality is what it is."

She just kept shaking her head from side to side, mumbling. "Vaughn, were we born into the right world, on the right planet?"

"Ha! You know of another one?"

Very upset wouldn't even describe her feelings, because she knew how hard he had worked. *How can he possibly make it without me?* She thought so hard as she stared at him. *Oh God, help us.* "But you need your money."

"For what? School starts back up next week, and I'll have no one to buy ice-cream for."

"Vaughn . . ." She began to weep, frightened at what this loss truly means, his words crystallizing how valuable they are to each other, bringing back the memories of all their wonderful meetings at the ice-cream shop all summer long, the deep discussions, the delicious treats, his kindness, wisdom, challenges to always think deeper, how he treasured her in his gaze.

He realized what an *idiot* he was for saying it. *How could I be so selfish?* The last thing he wanted was for her to hurt even more, and he couldn't imagine what had gotten into him. He felt truly ashamed.

"I'm sorry." Vaughn apologized, angry at himself for being so weak.

She took out a napkin from her purse that she had gotten from the ice-cream parlor, and wiped her eyes and then looked up. He glanced over and noticed there was no makeup running, in fact, there was no makeup at all. Stephanie saw he understood and smiled through her tears. *Now would be the perfect time,* she thought.

"Don't be sorry, but remember your promise, to think seriously about Tracy?"

He couldn't resist now, especially not after how *stupidly* he was acting. "I give you my word."

She knew he would be true to it, but there were different levels of true, and she wanted his whole heart to be in it. "And you're a man of your word, and that's one of many reasons I love you so. You always search the deepest meaning of things and act accordingly, because it's the only way to be true."

In her last words he could tell not only had she learned from him, but she had surpassed him. "I give you my word according to your standard."

"Is it only mine, Vaughn?"

He couldn't help smiling, because he had phrased it that way on purpose. He began to feel hope, at least for her. Then they arrived at the airport, parked the car, and stood waiting at the main gate. *Her father must be a very important man,* as there were precious few airplanes, and only the wealthy, connected people flew them. Wealthy and connected always seemed to appear together.

"Oh God, there he is, and he hasn't changed!" She waved, smiled, and called out, "Hello Papa!" She remembered everything Vaughn had taught her, and also much she had discovered on her own. But she didn't yet know that none of it would work with his kind.

He was a burly man, balding on top with straight, black, medium length hair helplessly conforming to a round head and dark eyes that were possessed with something uncomfortably unnamable. His broad shoulders and thick arms made his belly appear not to stick out as far as it really did. He was dressed for the funeral in a black suit and white shirt. His first communication to the daughter he hadn't seen in seven years was a hand gesture of spinning his finger as if stirring something. It was obvious that he expected her to, not only understand on the spot what he meant, but quickly reply, too. Yet, he was condescending enough to add words to his command moments later, as he continued the gesture more emphatically. "Well, let me look at you. Turn, turn, turn, hmmmm, you're coming to be a woman. I hope your mother at least taught you what you needed to know!"

Stephanie blushed and turned round and round, as Vaughn detected a soft, controlled sigh from her, which made him burn inside. If the feeling he had about Gary was terrible, what he had now was a nightmare. The man spoke as if his daughter had less value than Vaughn couldn't tell what. It was worse than what he remembered about her mother the first time they met.

Stephie smiled and held out her hand toward Vaughn. "Daddy, this is my best friend, Vaughn."

Vaughn smiled and held out his hand. "Pleased to meet you, Sir."

But the man barely acknowledged his presence and ignored his hand. "Yes, yes, well Stephanie . . ."

"Daddy, Vaughn rented a car for me and you while we're here."

That pricked his attention and he actually looked over at the boy for an instant, "Hmmm, you rented a car?" Then he raised one eyebrow in suspicion.

"Yes, Sir, I worked hard and saved up enough money."

He quickly returned his attention to his daughter. "Why would he do that, Stephanie? I have money." He didn't look at Vaughn as he spoke to him, but kept his eyes riveted on *his* daughter. "I don't need your car. Why don't you go play or something?"

Vaughn and Stephanie looked at each other in amazement. "Stephanie, will you wait down at the bottom of the stairs over there. I want to talk to your father for a minute." Vaughn was burning up inside. Although he knew this was a full-grown man, a powerful man by the way he carried himself, and an evil man, Vaughn just didn't seem to be in full control at that moment.

Stephanie looked at him very doubtfully. "Vaughn?" There was a note of caution in her voice, almost warning.

But he seemed to already be prepared for her reaction. "Faith, dear."

There was a feeling that showered over Vaughn. He remembered how he felt in his life and death struggles to be free of the terror within him, that terror imposed upon him from his own parents warping and distorting his internal world. Somehow this man represented this terror. He knew Stephanie was too good a woman to have to put up with the likes of *him.* He was a boy standing in the shadow of a grown man that had presence about him. But the feelings overwhelming Vaughn had a presence of its own, and it seemed that Vaughn was bound to yield to its direction.

Vaughn's request of Stephanie and her obedience to it drew a scornful look from her father towards Vaughn.

He stood up straight to the towering man who was a head and shoulders over him, and Vaughn looked him dead in the eyes. "Sir, there is nothing more important to me than your daughter. *Nothing!* She is my best friend, and of such high character that I respect no one more. Now I realize, compared to you, we are nothing but children, but I would like you to remember something very *clearly.* Children grow up and become adults, while adults grow old and often become weak like children. I don't know what you have planned while here in my home town, but I know what I'm going to do. I am going to drive your daughter wherever she wants to go, and you can rent, buy, or do whatever you like with whatever you like, except her! I worked hard for my money and I spent it all to make Stephanie's last days here bearable."

He burst out with a belly laugh. "You're smitten with her. She's a looker, isn't she?"

Vaughn didn't mean to yell, but he just couldn't help it. "I'm not talking about her looks, I'm talking about her character, the *person* she is." Vaughn paused a moment, not sure where all his words were coming from, only that he knew he was going to say them. "One day, Sir, I'm going to *marry* your daughter! This isn't *puppy* love. Look into my eyes! When that day comes and we meet again, if I don't find Stephanie better off than she is now, you will once again look into my eyes, and mine into yours. Do you understand me, Sir?"

It tickled her father that a pipsqueak boy actually threatened him. In the back of his mind he wondered if he should lower himself to look into his eyes, but that would be giving in to his demand, and he couldn't have that. He couldn't be pushed around by this pipsqueak boy. *But I should show how gracious I am. How much better I am than her boyfriend. I AM A MAN.* He had heard about Vaughn from his contacts here. He lowered his eyes expecting to see trash. But when their stares locked, Fred asked, "She means a lot to you, huh boy?"

"I won't be a *boy* for much longer, Sir, remember that."

Her father broke the grip Vaughn's eyes had on him and looked away. He had more important things to think about than this inconsequential thing. Vaughn wouldn't be able to come between him and *his* daughter anymore. "Yes, yes, alright. You may be our chauffer, no sense wasting my money. *Fate* is a strange thing, my boy, I never thought I would have to raise that girl. As pretty as she is, I know I'm gonna have trouble."

But somehow, Vaughn managed to relock the burly man into his stare, pausing just long enough to make sure Fred knew that he couldn't get away this time. "Fate is in the heart, Sir. If you don't understand it, it will do you in before your time!" *What am I saying?* The only way Vaughn could understand what he had just said was as some kind of message dropped down from above, or he was just losing control of himself.

The man squinted down at Vaughn, his eyes telling a story Vaughn could not understand, but had the sickening feeling that he needed to comprehend. "Yes, yes, quite true my boy, *quite true.*" There was nothing to be made of the ambiguousness of his words or tone, but the hairs on the back of Vaughn's neck told him he was in danger.

Vaughn recognized the feeling he had. It was the sense of fright one gets in a monster movie just before actually seeing the monster for the first time. But Vaughn remembered how he confronted raw fear and beat it before. In fact, he wouldn't be standing here right now if he had lost that battle. He narrowed his eyes back at him. "And if you do understand it, you have the opportunity to have a beautiful life with all those who understand it with you."

Fred looked past Vaughn to Stephanie waiting at the bottom of the stairs and called down to her. "Hey, Stephanie! It seems you've caught yourself a wise king." He laughed deeply at his own joke.

She called back up. "Father, you're very perceptive!"

The funeral lasted all of ten minutes, with only Vaughn, Stephanie, her father and the machine driver in attendance. There were no words spoken over Stephanie's mother's grave. A nod of acknowledgement from the machine operator signaled he recognized their presence, and then he drove forward, pushing a large mound of dirt into the hole. That was it.

Stephanie stared numbly. *That's it? Her whole life, our whole life, reduced to one cold push of dirt by a machine and a man who never even knew us?* She shook her head in disbelief. She had wanted to say some words, had prepared her heart to say them, to tell how close they had gotten before. But there wasn't even acknowledgement she ever lived except that they buried her body.

There was a blackness enshrouding Vaughn, as *nothing* felt right here. He wished he could put words to the feeling that beckoned him to listen. He hardly knew the deceased, but even he felt that there should be more. He still remembered the feeling he had of this woman's worth when he helped Stephanie carry her to her bedroom on the night they met. He could still feel his arm wrapped around her.

While gazing at Fred, a sense of looking into the future befell him. One knew oak trees grew from acorns. Somehow, death seemed connected to this man. Something in the way he moved, in the almost imperceptible tone behind the sound of his voice. He saw her father slip something into the grave tender's hand, then just as efficiently, he motioned to them he was leaving.

Vaughn and Stephanie followed him back to Vaughn's car. Fred had scheduled the return trip only two hours from now, and he was treating Vaughn exactly like a hired chauffer. "To the airport," he simply said.

Stephanie was taken by an air of dignity in Vaughn's manner as he deflected her father's continual insult. Looking deeply into Vaughn, she saw that his sense of purpose made him answerable only to a higher calling. Vaughn was definitely the stronger of the two. He stood very erect while holding the front door open for Stephanie, and she got the sense of the great man he would one day be. His slight deferential bow as she passed by him made her feel like a queen.

As she rode, she thought about how their last hour together would be. Stephanie had planned out their last moments together after Vaughn left to pick up the car early that morning. She had prayed very hard that their last moments would be very special or at least as good as possible under the circumstances. She'd never prayed harder in her life, and by the end of the prayer she had been flooded with so much, that she couldn't keep track of all that was swirling around inside her, only that she knew it would be released in their last hour. As she sat riding, she remembered the day she had hurried from her shelter into the government church and prayed their prayer. *Prayer?* She muttered to herself. *They don't know the meaning of the word.*

She requested of her father that he wait at the airport while she and Vaughn walked into some nearby woods. Actually, it was more like informing him than requesting, and this was the only defiance she would ever do, she told herself. Her tone had just enough hint of question to soften it. Since he knew she had no choice about returning, he decided not to make an issue of it. When they got home, *then* he would try to make her what she was *supposed* to be.

They could feel the comforting softness of the forest floor even through their leather shoes. Their path had been traveled more by deer and other animals than any human. Everywhere were the rich smells of life. The first fall wildflowers showed off their glory in pinks, purples, and whites. Vaughn recognized asters, morning glories, and forget-me-nots. Bees were collecting their store for the coming winter. The decay of newly fallen leaves added to the rich smell of the forest as fall seemed to be coming early. Squirrels digging for nuts left tufts in the thick rotting leaf litter that had built up over many years.

Woodpeckers knocked out sporadic rhythm, trying to earn their living. Vaughn laughed to himself through his misery, thinking about earning a living like a woodpecker. *Your whole life spent banging your head into something hard just to pull out a grubby meal.* He laughed again. *God made the woodpecker to enjoy it!* He thought about how Stephanie had said all things in life have meaning. Stephanie watched him musing and gave him a nudge.

"Oh!" He smiled, realizing it must seem like a private joke as he waved his hand around. "I was just thinking about how beautiful life is all around, and how you said everything has meaning."

Then they reached a spot that Stephanie seemed to be searching for. It was about a twelve foot round opening in the wild raspberry and other forest undergrowth that seemed to weave its way in broad swaths amidst patches of shorter trees. A huge tree had long ago fallen and its rotting corpse stretched past where they could see. The root stump was all but decayed, but in its wake it left the soft remains of dry rotted wood scattered about. There was another, newer, younger tree fallen across the opening providing the perfect spot to sit. When the sun reached noon, it would pour straight down into the little opening.

"Have you been here before, Stephanie?"

"No, but I just had this feeling about the kind of place I was looking for. This is it."

They turned to each other with tears in their eyes. Vaughn could hardly speak. "Well, Stephie . . ."

"Just hold me." They squeezed tightly together and couldn't help but feel one together and to embrace it while all around them life abounded.

Vaughn drew back for a moment to reach into his pants pocket. "I have something for you. Something I would like you to do for me." He pulled a piece of paper from his pants pocket and she was taken with delight and surprise.

"What, my love?"

"This is a list of all the references on an ancient King Metran that Waverly told me about. Our library is so small, I couldn't find anything except these references. But, where you're going, they have very large libraries within the huge universities so I figured inside those places they even have computers that you're allowed to use. At least, that's what I hear. Will you try to locate anything and everything on the book this King is supposed to have written?"

She looked quizzically at him. "You mean the King of that fairytale Waverly spoke of?"

"Yes."

"Alright, Vaughn, I give you my word I will seriously do this for you." She knew her words would also remind him of her request for him to help Tracy.

"I have something else for you, but I don't want you to look at it until you've settled into your new residence!" He dug into his other pocket and pulled out a sealed envelope which he handed her. He never looked her more seriously in the eye. "It contains the secret to all my strength, and the reason why I was even able to help you, and the reason I will *always* love you."

She took the envelope and held it as if it were a sacred object, in fact, it had to be because of its meaning. There was no question that she would do as he requested. She opened her purse and carefully tucked it against the inside so it wouldn't wrinkle.

Vaughn eased back from her and stood up straight, holding her by her upper arms. "Let us have a secret code so that any message that comes from me or you must have these words, or we know it's false!"

Surprise added to surprise. "Vaughn, why?"

"I don't know, but you never know what the future will bring. We'll be separated, but there is nothing more sacred to us than that our communication be true and trusted."

"All right, what should it be?"

"Something that won't appear as code, so that if anyone else finds our communication, they won't think to duplicate it because it'll appear ordinary, but it'll be something special to us that no one will know the meaning of but just you and me."

They paused, pondering, looking each other in the eye, and then Vaughn softly said, "Through our prayers . . ." He had remembered those passionate words she spoke from the night before, and though he didn't acknowledge them then, he wanted her to know they had not gone unnoticed, and that they were dear to him.

"Yes, that's *very* good, Vaughn!" Stephanie smiled with understanding. She felt his suggestion connect to whatever it was she would shortly be doing, and it excited her. Tears of love wet her eyes as Vaughn continued his instructions.

"Those words must appear naturally in the flow of our communications somewhere, and always in different spots each time, or we know we can't trust what we have." He leveled his eyes again into hers, eyes that for an instant seemed to turn into the eyes of a grown man, as he took firm hold of her arms in his strong hands. "We *will* grow up Stephanie, and we don't know what fate will put on our hearts. We have no idea what Life will require of us because we live by it, but let the world only be able to say of us that we live by the God of Truth."

"Alright Vaughn, it'll be *our* secret. Vaughn?"

"Yes, my love." He came closer and kissed her cheek and eased back again to see her face.

"Will you let me say a prayer for you?"

Vaughn froze, because praying in one's heart was one thing. "A prayer?" He felt timid and was transported to a different place. It was such a strange request to him, because no one had ever prayed for him or even indicated such thoughts. He never even saw it done, not really. His former religious training did not have personal prayer for another that the other would be present for.

Stephanie had felt a forewarning of his reaction and already had answer. "Yes, ever since that night when I prayed and you were sent to me, well . . . different prayers have been coming to me, and it just felt right to pray them."

He felt awkward. "I don't know much about praying, Stephanie."

She looked at him with that same challenging look that she gave him their first night together. She had asked him how he didn't know he was beautiful when he was speaking such beautiful words, and how he wasn't sure he made sense when he did. "Vaughn, your whole life has practically been one big prayer. What do you think you do when you meditate?"

And like before, his eyes opened wide with understanding about himself. "Please do, Stephanie, it's just that . . . I don't know exactly what to do."

"I asked father to let us stop here in these woods just for this, because I knew this is where you would feel the most peace. Sit here on this log with me, while I pray for us, for everything."

"I shall do as you wish," he seriously spoke it as if he were speaking to a queen . . . *Well, because she feels like a queen to me.*

Stephanie gathered her long black dress up as she knelt on the soft forest floor, leaning her side against Vaughn's leg as he sat on the trunk of the fallen young tree. She propped herself with her arms on the trunk, folding her hands and bowing her head. This was not customary to do so, but she had invented it for herself.

"Dear Holy God, our Life, our Love, our Light. We do not know what we have to face, but we know we need so much of Your help and strength. Dear Love, who has brought us together to love, this love can only be Your will, so it must be Your will that will somehow bring us together again in peace. Keep us True to You, dear God, in every way, everywhere . . .

She continued for some time as the words poured out sounding as pleasant in spirit as a gentle spring running over rocks. When finished, Vaughn helped her up to sit beside him, but she remained standing, instead. Vaughn was in awe, permeated by a peace he had never felt before, and he hardly wanted to speak for fear of disturbing it. He looked up into her soft, rich brown eyes. "It was beautiful, Stephanie. Never did I know prayer is like that." His eyes were wet with cherishing her.

"Vaughn, remember that tree you told me about that the storm tore up, and then I asked you if it could feel the life it would one day become?"

"Yes, I remember."

"Well, there is something else we can do more than a tree."

He was all hers, as he waited for her instruction. "Yes, Stephie?"

"Through true prayer, we can feel the life waiting on us!"

Vaughn recognized what she said. "In a way, like we were already living it?"

"In a way. Vaughn," she hesitated, holding him in her loving spirit, then continued, "I don't want you to leave here with me! I want you to sit here while I go back to my father!"

He didn't like it, and protest came out in the guise of reason, "But Stephanie, I have to walk you back through the woods."

But she answered in peace. "I know the way. I want this time, *here,* that we just had, to be the last thing we remember of being together." Her tone didn't insist. Tears welled up in both of their eyes, and Vaughn began to stand, but Stephanie put a hand on his shoulder to prevent it. She took both his cheeks in her hands and raised his face up. "This is the face I shall always remember that helped to bring me back to life." She knelt down and kissed the top of his head, then turned and walked softly away.

"Through our prayers," Vaughn called to her back.

"Through our prayers," she called back without turning around. She felt as if she were walking away from her very self, but she knew too, that if she turned, she would not have the strength to leave. Every fiber of her being screamed in wounded agony as she forced herself to step further and further away, knowing it was futile to deny reality.

He sat there in that spot in silence for the rest of the day until it was almost dark, and then he hung his head and prayed. It was the first time that he could remember doing something that he actually could call a formal prayer.

"Oh God, my life has changed. You took me from being a mess, a misfit, a terror to myself, and You caused me to love and understand some of Your Life, Your Truth. I do not understand why we have been parted. Every fiber that is my being is in agony. But You have taught me that it is better to love and bear the pain than not to love and be dead inside. You brought me so much strength through that woman, oh God. And now, she's gone . . . gone to a place of great destruction. I am in agony for her. If I could drain every last bit of blood in me to keep her from harm, to keep her in your Truth, I would sacrifice it gladly. But it is not for mere mortal men to make such sacrifices. I beg You, Oh Light, which is Light because You are Love and Life, make a peaceful way for her through the storm so that she is not swallowed up. As for me, help me to continue on, for my strength has left me this day."

CHAPTER 13

Divide and Conquer

Instructor Claynomore on the Hierarchy of the Food Chain: "Why should it surprise the humans that they are not at the top of the food chain? A mouse doesn't see the cat until it's too late, yet the cat often plays with its food. How much more so should we enjoy ours?

"Why do they call us evil? Is the cat evil? Behold, they have them as pets!"

"Has any Alpha ever had a human pet?" Advanced first class underling Scraback inquired.

"The difference between Alpha and human is far greater than between human and cat. It would be insulting!"

They shimmered and rippled as one. When one floated this way, the other floated this way, and when one floated that way, the other floated that way as they continued to watch the unfolding scene through the dirty blue orb.

"Are you sure this will work, Master?"

"Oh, yes, quite sure. You have to look at the whole picture.

They only had a brief time together, a short season, it was hardly enough time to really even think. Look at us, *we* have always been, and we are *still* perfecting our thoughts, our reality. The girl is of no consequence now, as her father will bring her back to *our* reality. She'll be sticking those rings in her body in more places than just her nose. In no time at all, the damage that wretched boy did to her will be erased, *forgotten,* and all those new branches will be gloriously dead, even much more so than before.

Fortunately, she's not a *thinker,* like Vaughn." Swish went his tail, and swish went his underling's tail.

"So, Master GrrraGagag, so . . . so how shall we divide our time between them?" Scraback was doing his best not to be obvious, because he sensed something about the girl that worried him. Besides, he needed an excuse to keep tabs on her, as he still couldn't figure out how to make the pieces of the puzzle work for him.

Master GrrraGagag growled again, and he didn't even notice that his underling didn't care. "I told you, the slut is of no consequence, forget about her. She's weak. You saw what she was before. It's the boy who's the threat. If you like, after we've destroyed him, we'll send her word of it." He laughed disdainfully. "I'm sure if there's any spark left in her by then, that will definitely put the finishing squash on it. These pitiful humans . . . the *glow* makes them so weak because it confuses them with *love,* which makes them vulnerable to such severe pain that it destroys them. Ha! Thank our grayness and blackness that no such weakness exists in us, Scraback."

"Yes, Master, all the time I think about it. Master, why are we to destroy the boy? Why waste him? Why not bring him back to reality?"

"I've told you before. It's the *glow* that will destroy him. All we have to do is just set up the right circumstances. Besides, I've seen this before, his kind is too stubborn. We have to accept the fact that they're lost to us and simply have them destroyed."

Scraback coiled up tighter in anticipation. "How shall we proceed, Master?"

"Stretch out your arm over his tree and focus on the time when our troubles began with the boy, around when he was thirteen."

"Master, we already covered that ground, so why relive it?"

"Details, *detailsssss* . . . if we want to have him destroyed perfectly, we must study the details of his thoughts and feelings, so that we're able to frustrate him at every point."

Scraback brought up Vaughn's past on the orb.

Vaughn's head rose up and down, softly banging upon the back of his hand. Lying on his bed with a pillow stuffed under his stomach, and hands under his forehead, the outside world disappeared from Vaughn's senses. The bed gently creaked, and its sound worked its way through the house like a mysterious odor. It could be heard all through the well-kept, two-story yellow brick house as Vaughn dove deep within himself in meditation.

"Master, why's he banging his head? We'd never . . ."

"He obviously doesn't like what's inside it. Scraback be quiet and study."

"Why am I here?" Vaughn screeched sharply as he questioned himself. "What am I?" He screeched again in more distress but continued speaking out his thoughts. "Need to stop this . . . it won't solve the problem. Why do I do this? It's in my feelings. I am what I feel and think . . . I'm terrible, I'm nothing. That *can't* be true! . . ."

"Master, if he was like *that,* how did you ever let him . . ."

Master GrrraGagag's eye bore down upon his underling with more force than he intended. "The humans have a saying: 'Silence is shining blackness.' "

Scraback seemed to become small as he went back to studying the vision. *I never heard such a saying. But it still doesn't hide Master's failure.*

"It's really not the body, because the body is irrelevant compared to thinking and feelings. I am a *person*. But, but . . . what AM I? What *is* a person? I'm different than a rock, my bed, non-living things, because I am alive. But . . . But what is my life? Hmmm, that's odd. I'm alive, but I don't know what life is?

How can I not know this, being alive? It's not just experience after experience. It certainly isn't anger, it's not worrying, not fear, not hate, it's not hurting people, making fun of them, putting them down, because that's *destruction of life*. So that can't be life. This feels the opposite. So what *is* life that makes me different from dead things? I'm conscious, dead things aren't. But, but . . . what are these feelings inside me? They feel like they're tearing me apart, twisting, torturing me . . . It's emptiness. That's *not life!*"

Scraback couldn't help himself. "*Yes*, that's right! Just get rid of that *glow* and you'll feel better." He found himself rooting for Vaughn almost like he rooted for the monsters in the Earth movies.

"*Idiot,* this is his past. Besides, he's not calling Alpha life, Life, he's calling it emptiness."

"Huh?"

"That can't be life, because, because if these feelings would have complete control over me, they'd destroy me. They're death, a conscious death . . . but life . . . life would be. . . Alive, growing. It doesn't make sense that life would have these feelings of self-destruction, tearing apart inside, wanting to tear *everything* apart. How would that make me alive, if all I'm doing is destroying? What's the purpose of being alive?"

Vaughn paused because he had no answer, then he increased bumping his head until his thoughts flowed and could be articulated again. "To be happy, is that the purpose, but why? Because happiness makes sense? If things didn't truly make sense they would be . . . destructive, chaotic, like I feel now! Oh no, no, just because these feelings are in me, in my consciousness, they aren't necessarily part of Life. They're part of what I experience *while I am alive*, but the essence of life, that which makes me alive and *not* dead, those terrible feelings and thoughts can't truly be part of life because . . . because they don't contain each other. The feelings of life and feelings of conscious death are so different in purpose, in quality that they are really different and distinct."

"Yes!" Scraback whipped his tail around in cheer, accidentally stinging his Master. But then he instantly cowered, and went back to the orb.

Master GrrraGagag was incensed. "You worthless *worm*, you've still got it backwards!"

Vaughn persisted in his Socratic self-questioning. "Why do I feel so? Hmm, *idiot!* What else would I feel if I wasn't in touch with life? I'm obviously blinded to life or else I could immediately answer my own question: what is life? The feeling of life I get from the trees, the animals and nature is . . . growing, fitting together, somehow peaceful, balanced, working and helping together. that's what I want to do with my life. Help people! But why?

"Master, I think I'm going to be sick. I thought . . ."

"No, Scraback, I don't think you do."

"It makes me feel good. Why? Because, there's life in helping. It's promoting life, goodness, appreciating what is good for life and achieving it, adding strength to those who are weak, giving understanding to those who are ignorant, appreciation to those who are love-lost. Life feels open. But many people think *things* are life, like money, cars, sex!

"But if those things were truly life, then anyone who had them would be happy. But many have them and aren't happy. So those aren't life. Besides, the things achieved for life must be *inside* things, like . . . understanding. If I understand something, I can appreciate it, I can love it. Also, like truth, because I'll always act rightly and not deceive myself or others so *that* has to be life because life must be based on reality. And there's no understanding without truth."

"Master, how many truths does he think there are? If he helps others with each one having his own truth . . . well no wonder he's all screwed up! He can't serve *Truth*, because he'd be split into as many parts as there are people!"

Master GrrraGagag met his question and observation with silence.

"But also doing good, but what *is* good? That which promotes life, but *what is life*?"

Vaughn suddenly screeched so hard it hurt his throat. "This is all very frustrating." He began another screech but cut it off. "I can't give up! Oh God. *Help me*!"

He repeatedly bumped his head quite hard but it never hurt, even then. "Who am I asking to help me? But I must look *inside* to find where God is. I must think and see. Start again: What is life? . . . Life is . . . has to be . . . what's the feeling? Why can't I feel it? Pressure, pushing, emptiness . . . but I *am alive*, so I *should be able to feel life!* Something's growing, something . . . rejoicing, feeling, reaching out, appreciating, understanding, applying understanding, and building on it, yes, making sense, cherishing, *loving!* I couldn't have been born with all these *dead* feelings I have. How did I get them? From my parents, mostly, I think. But these feelings are lies. Why? Because they fight *against* what life is, they are *not* the true reality."

"Do you see, underling, right there is where we lost him."

Scraback seriously nodded his bulbous head even as he thought the opposite. *Master's the* idiot*! How could he have* *let him have these thoughts? I could have done a better job than he did!*

"They are the destruction of it. These empty, torturing thoughts and feelings say they have a right to exist *but they shouldn't.* Why should self-destruction exist? That's why they're lies. I *hate it.* I hate that I can say so much more about what life is *not*, but not see clearly as to what life *is*. Even when I say the few words describing what life is, I only see them at a great distance.

How can I see more clearly . . . see *Truth*. I, I . . . babies don't come into the world like *this*, feeling dead. All they would feel is being alive . . . life . . . happy, in wonder, giving, appreciating, growing, seeking understanding. How can I feel like this again? If I . . . can I . . . can I push away, forget, let go of all these *dead* feelings, *everything* that was forced into me until I feel just like when I first came into the world? I have to try. Let me see . . ."

After several minutes of thumping his head, Vaughn's frustration moved him even more vigorously. "Oh my God, there is all this, this *crap* in the way. What is this? Fear. OK. It's a lie. Fear is . . . bowing to death! Making my heart, my mind cringe at the threat of death or destruction or . . . pain . . . and that cringing is stopping me from being alive! Yes, it's the claws of death sunk into my being. Death is in control by fear making me into a *conscious death*. Oh, I feel it, so *terrible*. It sure isn't life. *Deny it*, forget it! OK! . . . Tightness, what is this tightness in my heart? As if I was being threatened. Oh, *life* wouldn't threaten me. That doesn't make sense because *life* . . . has to be *good*, Otherwise, if it was both good and bad it would contradict its own self, self-destructive! It wouldn't even feel like *life* if it had both good and bad together. To feel like real life, *life* has to be . . . *pure goodness!*"

Although everything in the ethereal was different shades of gray, Master GrrraGagag distinctly thought he saw his underling turn green. He patted him with his tail, and asked, "You see how important it is that we eradicate such perversions of existence? We must purify reality for us to be *happy*."

"Yes, I recognize this somehow. Otherwise, all is hopeless. There would be no reason to even try for anything if the true essence of *life* was self-destructive. Love wouldn't be real. Kindness, helping, none of that could really be love if they came from a primary essence that was self-contradictory . . . No, that self-destruction doesn't look right . . . to think we cannot truly love.

Hmmmm, in fact, I couldn't even be having this conversation with myself if only self-destruction were true! *Why*? Haha, because there wouldn't even be a way to conceive of a pure goodness! No way to *feel* it, either. I couldn't see it, or think it. That reality, that feeling, that understanding would be completely excluded from conception if a self-destructive, self-contradictory essence were the true essence of reality because it would always be inputting its let down. I couldn't separate the good from the bad because there would be no good to separate out. True *Goodness* is not overpowered by evil. True goodness doesn't *fail*."

"Master! *He's right!*" Scraback jumped up and down, while whipping his tail back and forth like an Earth puppy. As his

Master's Eye grew larger by the microsecond, Scraback waited until GrrraGagag was on the verge of tirade, and then said, "I mean, in one way he sees so clearly just like us! There is *no* goodness." The underling paused again, scratching his head with his tail. "Hmmm, but he's saying *our* life doesn't make sense . . . but we know his *glow* doesn't make sense. It's almost as if we can use the same logic he's using, but to prove our life is the *real* life. There's no way for us to see or feel or think by that *glow*, so it *must* be unreal!"

GrrraGagag folded his tail in his arm. *How can he be so brilliant and* stupid *at the same time?*

"Anyway, it doesn't even make any sense to live like that, to just be a self-destruction. Ahhhhh, *Yes*. This is *Understanding*, Life is *pure Goodness*. Oh, my *first understanding*. Real Understanding. What is this feeling in me? I feel . . . tingly, goose bumps all over . . . awed. Oh, I want more! "

Master GrrraGagag grumbled. "I want to throw up, and Alphas never want to throw up."

"Just because I feel both good and bad doesn't mean they are both part of life. Hmmmm, they're a part of my experience, yes, but the bad can't be coming from that which is Good. Then where does it come from? Oh, yeah, because if I'm turned away from Life, then I would have to feel . . . *dead! Then it's a choice!* I mean, I think I can choose *not* to be dead! In the way I react to anything, I don't have to feel in any given way, do I? I don't have to be turned *away* from Life. "

The demons both shook their bulbous heads in unison, and uttered the same word together, "*Trouble!*"

"Let me try again. Back, back, back . . . no fear, no tightness, no threat. But I feel put down. No, Life wouldn't do that to me, forget about it. I have to *feel*, to *see* what true life is. Back . . . back . . . can't be distracted! "

"Sex. Ahhh, it feels good, but not to a true heart and mind. Why does it feel good? Well, it feels *good* to the body, but that's not enough to cause people to chase it so much. Hmm, what's really in the feeling? "

Vaughn drew upon his own experience. "For a short time it makes a person forget everything else, it makes people feel . . . Alive! When the body experiences its full potential the person temporarily forgets their conscious death. But this isn't real life of the heart. It's a trick, because using people isn't real life. It's a total giving of the body but nothing else. "

"You see, Underling? We can catch him with sex. See how weak he is to it? He talks like he's trying to convince himself its wrong. If he really wasn't mastered by it, he wouldn't have to convince himself!"

"Oh, got sidetracked again. Real Life is . . . back, back, let go . . . how would a baby feel? No fear, just experience.

Life . . . *There it was!* Oh no, where did it go? What did I do?

I saw it, but then it was gone. Why? Ahhh, my mind, my heart is so used to death inside, stubborn, must try again, how did I get there?

Life. Gone again. Try again . . . *there!* This feeling, oh, it makes sense.

It's just total giving! *Oh No, gone again.* Back, back . . . *there.* Hold on this time, remember. Life . . . appreciating, reaching out, *free*, feeling of energy, it's what real power is, unlimited, giving . . . heart is also accepting . . . moment by moment these feelings and thoughts take in what is inside and out and somehow are ordered into goodness.

I can feel myself appreciating, in motion as if in a preordered pattern."

"Right here, Underling, flip to his tree. You see how the *glow* began its infection?"

"Yes, *Life* is the first essence, pure, of reality. It has *Being*. Life is Goodness in heart and mind. At every moment, every instant, there is something of meaning to appreciate relating to life, yes, there has to be since Life has to be continuous. Oh, this life in me isn't just in me, but in others, it's really the same life for everyone, the same unbounded qualities of pure goodness. It defines itself, we don't define it. It created us. Life had to be our Creator. It's giving. It teaches and predetermines its qualities, but we don't. Life is not just individual people! My life comes from *Life!* I *feel* it! Surrounding me, so sweet, so beautiful . . . because, because . . . so beautiful because it's one way for life and Life, but life didn't place itself, but life always relates to its, its . . . *Greater Self* . . . Life! But Life made us free! Freedom . . . *freedom!*

But, how can I be free if I don't live by this true life? Death will destroy me. . . ." *Pain . . . pain!*

"Master, is that your ARM reaching in to touch his . . ."

Master GrrraGagag shoved his underling out of the way.

"Arm? What arm?"

Scraback finally squeezed back in between his Master and the orb and replayed the last sequence. "But, I'm *sure* I saw *your* arm . . ."

"What feeling is this coming to me now? Love, I feel Love pouring in and over me, trying to tell me something. I don't want to die, but . . . but Life doesn't want me to die. I feel its feelings added to my own life's feelings and they combine. My life's love calling out, loving, and Life's Love *wrapping me up*, so *great!* Oh! . . . Life *is* Love . . . and . . . Love *is* Life. I feel it . . . I understand it! Oh, what new wonderful feelings! Oh my tears, tears I've never had before! . . . Life has to be love because . . . anything short of that would not be Life, it would be holding back the best, holding back giving life. That doesn't make sense for Life to do! And . . . and love doesn't make sense if it did anything other than what is truly life promoting. If it did, then it wouldn't be true Love. How could it be? Love always seeks Goodness."

Vaughn stopped thumping and flopped onto his back with a new feeling. He reached both open hands all the way up. "Oh, I know how to beat all this death killing me. My life has meaning . . . *Meaning!* I don't care what others say about me, feel about me. I see the *meaning* inside me. No one can take that from me because . . . it's *truth*, even truth for all those who fight against it, but they live a lie . . . Lies! But that doesn't change what truth is."

I know how to beat this death in me. "All I have to do is . . . why don't I ask? Ask Life, Love to help me. Oh Life, Love, if anything deserves to be called God, you do, what else has all power and deserves to be truly worshipped, truly served but Life, Love . . . and . . . serving you isn't slavery, it's freedom. How beautiful Your ways are! Oh Life, Oh Love, help me, because I don't even know how to help myself. I feel even now, death squeezing me . . . to death! Help me, help me . . . HELP ME!

"Oh dear God, dear sweet God, I take one day at a time waiting on how You lead me moment to moment. I know this death will drag me back, but please, come for me, because I can't help myself, chase me...I love you, but my love isn't strong. I'll continue to seek Your feeling and to understand and to change my ways from death to life, ignorance to understanding. Even now You are adding more understanding to what I just had. A tree . . . a tree doesn't have to die. It can keep adding roots, branches . . . just like . . . Oh Lord, *everlasting* life?"

"Could this be true? I'll find out. Too much for me now, one step at a time. I have to beat this death in me. Those things I do, screeching and other things tearing me apart. When they come to me I'll ask and give myself over to Life. I'll put my life on the line each time. I'll get help, feelings of life and meaning in place of being torn apart."

Jolting, harsh yells pulled Vaughn away from his contemplation of Life and Love. His father was angrily calling him. "What's that kid doing up there? VAUGHN, DINNER IS READY! Who do you think you are to make us wait? We don't live for you, you know. If you don't come down now, don't come down at all!"

"Coming, Father!"

Each demon folded their tails in their arms and was briefly silent, meditative.

"That's it, Scraback, details. See how that *glow* deluded him? Now, we have to dissect that self-discovery. *Tear it apart.* He thinks life is love. We'll show him life with no love. He thinks love is life. We'll show him love with no life. He thinks there's goodness. *We'll show him none.* We'll make him *hate* his life, but that *glow* won't give up. He *will* be torn apart. Torn apart by that *glow* because he's so stubborn and refuses to be like most people who accept their life for what it really is: THERE IS NO MEANING TO THEIR SO-CALLED LIFE. At least not the way they think. Their meaning is to allow us to purify reality. *That is the only reason they exist,* to give us that opportunity! OH Scraback, can you feel it? Feel the POWER . . . the power and importance of that meaning! OH, HOW I LOVE THESE HUMAN BEINGS! There is such great meaning in bringing our reality to them. That is why we are so patient and will accomplish our greatest desires."

Scraback was overwhelmed by his Master's oratory, even though he was planning on eating him. "Yes, Master GrrraGagag, I can feel it, too, but don't you think . . . ?"

"Ha! Of course I do, underling. You just watch and learn. Let's begin his torments, shall we?"

Education must be presented correctly. That was the government's first directive a hundred years ago. It wasn't hard for Master GrrraGagag to accomplish it. One thought leads to another which can be connected to another. *As long as a human has some evil in them, there is a place to start freeing the whole beautiful tree of death, death to that* glow. But in the case of government officials, school administrators, and the educational system as a whole, well, there was plenty of fertile ground to work with. Besides, Master GrrraGagag wasn't called Master for nothing.

Every school looked exactly the same. It was the one place the government did invest money into every small town. One policy covered everyone. Every room was exactly the same square size with the same sparkling white walls throughout. The hallways were also the same color. All floors were shiny black. If there was a single mark on the walls the perpetrator had to be found or no one was allowed to leave school. Then the *criminal* was required to repaint the whole wall after school, thus did they deal with *any* assault on the educational system. The walls had remained spotless for a hundred years and so it went for all furniture, books, and everything else.

No student dare implicate another falsely because of the *rule of implication*. Specifically, anyone could implicate anyone else and the accused was assumed guilty. Therefore, false implication didn't work, because the accused would turn around and accuse the accuser. Mischief had to be planned much more artfully than that.

Each class had exactly one hundred students, except for the remainder class. There was no misbehavior, simply because of the zero tolerance rule which meant that any slight misbehavior was immediately brought before the principal and parents. If it happened again, the student was thrown out. But the government then required the expelled student to either be placed in an expensive private school that most couldn't afford, or sent to a State Work Farm until employment age. However, only when they could find *gainful* employment would they be permitted to leave.

But of course there's a catch. The State had to approve the job before their release. In other words, bad kids ended up being slaves to the State until they said otherwise but there was no reason to let them go because they profited off them.

These rejected students ate when they were told to eat, worked when they were told to work, rose up and went to bed accordingly, and even urinated when they were told to do so. Everything about their lives was controlled by the State, or rather, by those cruel people they placed in charge. The government put together documentaries of life on their State work farms so that everyone would know what it was like. Even so, there was a small, steady flow into them, one here, another there.

Thus, it was a well-known fact by all children that they didn't want to go to the State Farm. The only students that ended up there were either very *stupid* by being overly rebellious, or they were mentally ill, or for some reason got on the bad side of the teacher or staff. All adults were addressed by title, and students were only permitted to speak when spoken to. Any infraction was punished as above. Hidden noises and other such pranks didn't work either because of *the law of communal guilt* combined with the *rule of implication*. The system worked so well, the government was thinking of increasing class size.

There were only three grades given: A, B, and C. Nothing else was acceptable to maintain enrollment. Those who were intellectually challenged were sent to special factory jobs to meaningfully contribute to the State for the rest of their lives. It was a fair treatment for those mentally challenged, ensuring they had gainful employment, thus contributing rather than burdening the taxpayer.

Vaughn started his eleventh year. He would turn sixteen within a few months. Mr. Reed was Vaughn's teacher in eleventh grade math which is where he spent the first two hours in school. The other six hours were divided between reading and writing, history and science. There was only one teaching method: *Do whatever the teacher said, when he said to do it.* State tests were administered twice a year, and a teacher's job depended on the results.

Mr. Reed was a no-nonsense teacher with a clear idea of how a student should learn and act. He had studied every student's file, all one hundred for each class before school began, and he knew every student's face and name.

"*You*, what is your name?"

"Vaughn, Sir."

"And do you think that is a wise way to begin your first week of school?"

"Sir?"

"Making all those noises?"

Vaughn turned red. It was the teacher accusing him and the rule of implication wouldn't help him. "Sir, I didn't . . ."

"Don't lie to me! Everyone knows what you do." Mr. Reed was no fool. He was ready for the only time students thought they could get away with *anything*, that time before the new teacher knew who they were, but he *knew*. He was ready to make an example.

"Sir? That wasn't . . ."

Mr. Reed jumped out of his seat behind his white metal desk and his chair flew backwards and crashed to the floor.

Everyone's eyes widened. He placed his hands flat on his desk and leaned over. Every student was dead silent. "*Are you arguing with me?*"

Vaughn swallowed. "Sir, please, I haven't made…noises since about two years . . ."

Many in the class began to giggle softly or hide it behind their hands.

"And I suppose that is why the whole class is laughing now?

Apologize!"

Vaughn's heart was in his throat. "Sir?"

"You have to learn manners. Be disciplined. If you can't, then you don't belong in school."

"But sir, where would I go?"

Mr. Reed came out from behind his desk. When they saw their teacher coming close, all the student's straightened and folded their hands on top of their desks. They stared straight ahead, and at this point were even afraid to be caught peeking.

"That is not my problem. There are private schools."

"But sir, I, I...that costs a lot of money."

Mr. Reed came and stood over Vaughn who was seated first in the most middle row. "You know the law. All children must be somewhere, in school or at a State Work Farm. *Well?*"

Vaughn was near tears. This was so far from anything he could even imagine. His mind went blank. Yet, he started to speak, and speaking got him to thinking.

"I'm sorry." *Truth, I can't violate truth, not for* any *reason.*

Mr. Reed placed his hands on Vaughn's desk and leaned over. Some students gasped. "Apologize to the whole class."

Vaughn had tears in his eyes as he stared up at his teacher. His voice croaked. "Class . . ."

Mr. Reed slammed his hand down on Vaughn's desk. "LOUDER!"

An instant of time seemed to lengthen in Vaughn's mind. It was as if he were in a meditation. When meditating, time often distorted for him so that he had no sense of it. Sometimes an incredible amount of thought occurred in almost no time at all. Other times, hours went by unnoticed with him seemingly unaware of any accomplishment. In this instant his mind sped up. He came back to himself, remembering the awesome experience of Life, and how death-defeating it is, and how he had promised not to give in to death anymore.

I will stand up straight and face this class. They know the truth. I will look them all straight in the eye . . . and I will NOT lie.

"Sir, May I get up and face the class?"

Mr. Reed backed up, a little surprised. "You may, young man, for that is the way a real man would do it."

"Yes sir, you are correct, and thank you." Vaughn got up slowly. He felt a presence swoop down upon him and spread out through him and through the whole class. The class rustled in their chairs. It was the presence of Meaning. He stepped away from his desk, turned around, and squared his shoulders.

"Class, I am . . ." *Look them straight in the eye. Yes. Their laughter dies because I look at them with truth, the truth of their wretched selves. I know it.*

Mr. Reed shot the class an angry look.

"Sir, please, I am sorry if I should cause my class such a thing. Class, I am very sorry for the noises I made. I understand them, now. It's no longer me. *Now*, you *all* know that, *right?*"

"Yes, Vaughn!" The whole class bellowed, then Vaughn sat down.

The teacher went and picked up a pile of papers, handed some to each in the front row to pass back, and class began.

After school, Waverly ran up to his friend as soon as he saw him step out the front door of the building. "Hey, Vaughn! I was so glad to see how you handled that," he said as they walked away from the crowd.

Vaughn shook his head with the memory of the mystery. "I don't know, Waverly. I just let Life bring me how to live . . . then wise things come to me. But I really wasn't sure there for a second. I thought maybe I was going to be in serious trouble."

They walked away from the white school building and carefully stepped across the crumbling schoolyard.

Waverly shook his head. "God, that sure was weird. There was this strange feeling in the class when you stood up, kinda scary, almost. Hey, I'm really sorry about Stephanie. I know you meant a lot to each other. Sorry!"

Vaughn gave him a serious look. "It's not over, Waverly, true love does not die."

"You're just fifteen, Vaughn! You can't . . ."

"I can be true to what *is*, Waverly, it's better than being a lie. No matter my age, no matter the situation, this love I have has good reason. Not lust, not want, not even just need, but I love her because of what she is. How can I fight that or deny it?"

"Hmmmm, I guess when you put it like that . . . but let yourself enjoy others, too."

"I'll not fight off life. I promised Stephanie I wouldn't."

"Hey, here comes Tracy. You know, I heard she *likes* you, *and she really puts out*."

"Thanks." Vaughn said dryly as Tracy sauntered up close. "Hi, Vaughn, how are you? That was *terrible* what that teacher did to you. I *hate* him."

"Thanks, Tracy. Who made the noise?"

"I don't know for sure, but you want me to find out?" She was eager to please him.

"No, just forget about it."

"Really, it's no trouble. I think it was Glen, the new kid from out West. He's Gary's cousin. Just what we need, a sequel. He's bad news, I can feel it. He was asking about you. And I don't like the way he looks at me. He really reminds me of Gary, only *worse*."

Waverly was studying Vaughn to see his reaction. Her words troubled Vaughn, but he felt it best not to give away his feeling. He changed the subject. "Want to get some ice cream, Tracy?"

"Oh yeah, I would love that."

"C'mon, then, I made a little money after Stephanie left, so I'll spend it on you and Waverly."

Waverly patted his friend on the back and gave him a secret wink. "That's kind, but I have plans. You and Tracy go alone."

At the ice cream shop, Vaughn kept glimpsing her in the mirror behind the counter, but she was intently watching him the whole time. Yet, he couldn't bring himself to speak, because being there with another woman felt like a violation of his heart. After they were done, Tracy broke the silence.

She put her hand tenderly on his arm. "Vaughn, thank you so much for the ice-cream, it was very sweet of you. I'm sorry about Stephanie, I know you loved her."

Vaughn corrected. "Love, not loved, present tense." She nodded and pressed her lips tight. "I'm sorry Vaughn, of course. I just enjoy you. I think that was so brave how you stood up against Gary. Did you really kill his friends? Glen is spreading the rumor."

Vaughn stared into his empty ice-cream dish. "No, Tracy, it was all because of their choices. I did *not* want to have to kill them, but you know he wanted to kill me, but they ended up killing themselves."

She stared at him while he spoke, and she could feel his arm tense just a bit. *Something in the way he said it.* "Somehow, I don't think it was as simple as that." She bent over to try to see his expression, but he turned to face her.

"Tracy, look into my eyes and tell me what you see?"

"Ahh, I usually don't do that. I . . . OK. Oh, I don't know . . . it's hard to . . . I think you're telling the truth, but there's so much I don't understand when I do that."

He rubbed his chin between his forefinger and thumb as he assessed her, remembering Stephanie's plea for him to help her. Eyes were a two-way street, so Vaughn gazed into her mind, her heart, and her soul. He looked back at his ice-cream dish to hide his grimace. To prevent him from sighing, he began licking his spoon. The sigh came anyway, and then he looked back and grabbed her eyes with his.

"Because you first have to understand yourself, Tracy, then you'll begin to understand others."

"Oh, Vaughn, I don't think I can really do that, I'm not a good thinker."

He shook his head and resumed his hold on her eyes, trying to draw her mind into his so she could feel his meaning. "It's a choice, Tracy, just a choice."

"What is?"

"To think."

She changed the subject. "Do you like to walk out in the country?"

"I love it," he said more seriously than he intended to share.

"The leaves will be turning so beautifully now, would you go for a walk with me? It's a beautiful evening."

"All right, Tracy, let's go." They left their empty dishes and Vaughn paid the bill. Somehow it didn't have the same feeling as when he used to pay for Stephanie. A lot of the pride he had felt seemed to have vanished.

They walked up the main street. Once on the circular path surrounding the town, they veered up a smaller path out into the tall, dry grass where sparse oak and maple trees gradually became more numerous. The sun was a huge, glowing, red ball as it headed toward setting off to their right. Vaughn knew this was a peaceful time of day, but he just didn't feel it.

Tracy had her own idea of this wonderful autumn evening. *This is so romantic.* She grabbed his hand.

Thoughts jolted Vaughn as he became aware of her appearance. Her long, straight dark brown hair, her full breasts moving in her skintight tiger-striped top, and the sway of her hips in her tight tiger slacks. *Oh, she's grabbed my hand, what should I do? I don't really want to hold her hand. She's pretty, attractive, sexy, but she's not Stephanie. But I don't want her to feel bad. What if Stephanie found out? Hmmmm, I won't be untrue to her. All right, I'll hold her hand, but with the meaning I choose, and if Stephie would find out, I'll tell her the truth. Uh, uh, now she's holding my waist.*

"Isn't it beautiful out here? The trees are so beautiful. Let's sit under this one. We're all alone out here. You're very handsome, you know." Her fingers began to rub him where she held his waist.

"Tracy, give me your hands."

"Alright Vaughn, here, you can hold *both* my hands."

Vaughn leveled his eyes into hers for a second try. The coolness after the peculiarly hot fall day was invigorating. "Tracy, what are you?"

Her head jolted back as if she were hit. "Huh?"

"These hands, feel me squeeze them. Are you just a body?"

"I don't know what you mean."

Vaughn sighed. "Tracy, it's better for you to think for yourself than for me to tell you what I'm thinking. Just take a minute, while I hold your hands. Use your imagination. For instance, you seem like you like me a lot, but imagine what you would truly want from me."

She already had the answer, and smiled with pleasure. Vaughn knew the right answer could not come that quickly but her smile widened even more.

"Well, Vaughn, you're holding my hands. Actually, the way I feel now, I would like you to have all of me."

Maybe I can use this to her advantage. "Why?"

Tracy was dumbfounded by the question. "Huh?"

"Why?" he asked, still trying to pull her mind into his so she could look around inside it.

"Why what?"

"Why would you like me to have all of you?"

She took her hands and wrapped them around his waist, moving close in on him and purred. "Because that's the way I feel. I'm *very* attracted to you and that's just the way it works. You're silly!" She smiled, looking up into his eyes, trying to pull him into hers so he could feel her desire. But Vaughn's thoughts had already moved beyond her plans. *Perhaps if I can't draw her into* my *mind, perhaps I can enter* hers *through the door she's opened.* Vaughn allowed himself to look with some desire into her eyes

And she connected immediately, drawing closer, but he held their eye contact.

"And after we go together, then what Tracy?"

Another light bulb of understanding flashed in her eyes. "Oh, you want to have more than just one time. I can understand that. All the boys I know can't get enough."

Vaughn sighed again. "Tracy, how does it make you feel after you've gone with a boy, and then he leaves you?"

She looked away, then back up. "Oh, I don't know. I guess it depends on if I got some too, or if it was just him having all the fun."

"Tracy . . . and the next day, if he passes you in school and acts like he doesn't even know you, even want to see you, even if you did get *some*?"

"Oh, that's just the way boys are."

Vaughn calculated his next tone. It had to be done just right, without emotion, analytical, flat. "OK, so you feel great when someone you've been that close to just tosses you aside like you were nothing. I guess I can understand that." His tone was almost cold. *It was perfect.* He watched her reaction, maintaining a blank expression that matched his tone.

She paused. Something didn't feel right. "Actually, I don't like that."

He entered her doorway. "Why?"

"Because . . . I just don't. I don't feel like a person when I get treated like that, I feel terrible. He could at least say, Hi. That's *all* I really want." *I don't feel like a person. Those words seem familiar somehow, but where have I heard them before?*

"Why do you want the extra treatment?"

"Because, it would at least make me feel like I mattered a little."

"And that's all you want, just to matter, *a little?*" He could see frustration beginning to build in her.

"You know, I never really thought about it like this before, I guess because boys are just boys, and I accept that, and . . . but now that you make me think . . ."

"I can't *make* you think, no matter how many questions I ask you. Thinking is *your* choice."

"Yeah, well, I suppose it would be much better to matter a whole lot."

"Why?"

She put her hands upon her hips and straightened. "Is that your favorite word?"

"One of them." He wouldn't let her escape that easy. His face held the question in his expression to her.

"OK, well, because the more you . ."

"I? Me? Are you talking about me?"

"You know, you're too *tough*." She tried to break him down with her whining stare, but he wouldn't allow it. She squeezed his waist, but he ignored it, still silently posing the question. "OK then, me. The more *I* matter, well, the more I matter."

He pressed the point. "What is it Tracy, that is *mattering*? "Well, I think the sex when it's really good, so they think about me much more."

Vaughn shook his head and sighed even more deeply. *Stephanie, what did you get me to promise?* "OK, so they go over and over in their mind about your body."

"Mmmmm, Vaughn, you're making me . . ." She pressed against him, thinking she saw her chance.

But he gently took her shoulders and eased her away. "Just pay attention."

"I *am.*" Her eyes were now heated as she ached for his closeness and arched her back a bit.

"So they go over and over about your body and then after sex what if you started talking about something that interested you and they then just ignored you and didn't even want to hold you."

"Ha, that's the way it always is. Boys are just like that."

"C'mere, Tracy!" Vaughn grabbed hold of her and held her right cheek in his left hand and her shoulder with his other. As he held her, he poured meaning into the way he held her, cherishing her as a person. *Maybe she can feel it, that she's a person.*

"Mmmmm, Vaughn . . ." She breathed heavily. "No sex, Tracy. I just want to hold you."

She was again dumbfounded. "Huh? But, but, I want to . . ."

"I know, maybe later. For now . . ."

Frustration mixed with confusion and passion and she whined. "You sure are strange. How can you *turn me down*?"

She called me strange . . . and it doesn't matter to me! Vaughn was awed by it, but he pushed it into his memory so he could attend to Tracy.

It was a losing battle and he needed to change direction. He sighed, but from more than his original frustration. This was getting harder and harder. "Tracy, you know I really appreciated how you left that party and didn't participate in what they were going to do to Stephanie."

Her eyes looked distant, "Yeah, it was wrong. Although, Stephanie was so *irritating,* always putting on a show, throwing her sex around. You know, she made a lot of girls hate her."

"It was an act!"

Tracy backed away from him this time. "Huh?"

"It wasn't the real her. She felt so low about herself, that was the only way she could think to feel important. The lower she felt, the more she threw her sex around!"

"But she enjoyed it, *I could tell.*"

"Of course she did. Everyone has to take enjoyment in *something*, even if it's only the lowest thing possible, otherwise they'll go crazy. But in truth, she felt terrible. And then, when she realized what was going to happen to her . . ."

"I can see that. That really was too much, even for a girl like her. It would be like dying."

"Why? What would die?" He saw her trying to think.

"Hmmm, I don't know, it just feels like it."

"Don't run from this, Tracy, *think*. Putting your feelings into words is a precious doorway into understanding yourself and then others. It will allow you to grow, too. But if you can't put your feelings into words, it's easy to lose the treasure your feelings possess."

Tracy stared into Vaughn's eyes. There was something she thought she saw. She looked inward. "Because she would just be a nothing, her body just being passed around like that, not being special to anyone, not even while having sex . . .I mean, at least when two people do it, for the time, at least, you can feel special, you know? But being passed around . . . oh, God!"

"So, it's important to be special?" He felt her enter into the question in her mind.

"It is, Vaughn. You know, I see your point."

"It's your point, Tracy, *your* point."

"Yes, I suppose it is. It *is* important to be special. For a man to . . . hmmm, what?" She looked like a small kid asking him to reveal the mystery of life. Parents were rarely home and many children didn't know what it felt like to be special, to be focused upon in a meaningful way.

Vaughn pressed her to dig deeper. "You tell me."

"Well, I guess to want his woman to be for him and not for anyone else, because she's too precious to him to want someone else to have her. And then, since he only wants her to be for him, that makes her special to him. Or actually, that would make him special to her because she's only going with him, so, actually, he should only go with her, and then she would be special to him because he only gets pleasure from her. Then they're special to each other."

"You make a lot of sense Tracy. How much of her should be special to him?"

"Huh?"

"Her legs?"

"I guess."

"Well, what if he just likes her legs?"

She frowned, beginning to understand her feelings. "That's not much of being special. What I mean is, there'll be things you don't like in a person, sure, but there's more."

"In a what?" He kept his analytical tone.

"*In a person.* You know, maybe you like her breasts and legs but not her hair."

"Is that what makes a person?"

"Well, I guess how they laugh, talk. . . "

"What about how they feel about things? Would you want a man who has sex with you to not care about your feelings, like wanting to be special?"

It was like she was on a teeter-totter, and the fun was beginning to wear on her. "Oh Vaughn, you know, I never really thought about it like that before . . . maybe we should just go."

"How does it feel, me just holding you, appreciating our conversation?"

"I don't know . . . different . . . kind of uncomfortable, really. But the way you hold me and speak to me is so . . . dear. Oh Vaughn, *you make me feel special!*"

He let the Spirit of Love fill his eyes then and asked for that to speak through him with its meaning. "You are, Tracy, you are. There is no one else in the world like you. And the more you think, the more important you'll become, because your body is probably just about as beautiful as it will ever get, but the person you are can grow more and more beautiful every day by adding important thoughts like how to be a good person that helps people. Think about it. Who would you rather be with? A person who would *not* value you, the person inside of you? Or, would you want someone to love your body *and* think that your feelings are most important?"

Her eyes widened. "I think the second is better."

"Good, Tracy, it's a start."

She pressed against him again, but it was different this time. It carried with it her new appreciation for him, and he felt it. It was truly warm, her femininity calling even deeper. "When do you want to have sex?" she asked softly. She moved and snuggled up tight against his side and ran her hand across his lower stomach. "You've really got me now, you know." She purred more deeply.

Vaughn was stoic but his tone was soft. "Maybe when you really understand what it is to be a whole person."

She stared into his eyes with all her desire and the love she felt developing for him. "Why wait, Vaughn?" She pressed her pelvis into him, hugging him with her hands on his stomach and back, moaning deeply.

"Because, sex is best when you can do it with the whole person, not just their body, because then you can look each other in the eye and enjoy the whole thing."

She pulled back again, truly amazed, her mind sent into a whirl. "Hmmmm, I always have my eyes closed. Is that how you and Stephanie did it? Eyes open?"

"That's how people who truly love each other do it, because they are so special to each other, they want to know all of each other's thoughts and feelings and help in all ways."

Her grip on him slackened noticeably. Her eyes widened again, and she spoke more forcefully. "I never really thought that knowing these things was so important, but I can see it should be."

A sound of grass rustling for some time had played in the back of Vaughn's mind, but now the hairs on the back of his neck began to stand up. The sound didn't feel right. When he heard the voice he knew why.

"Hey, Tracy, what ya doin' with the runt? C'mere to a *man.*" He threw his arms out boisterously wide.

Tracy looked down and then around. They were all alone in the country.

"Oh! Hi, Glen! Vaughn and I were just talking." She eased off Vaughn further.

"I bet so, I'm sure of it. Just thought you might like to know, Gary should be back in a few weeks. Well, *come here,* I don't want to *talk.*"

Vaughn had the keen feeling Glen had been watching for some time.

Tracy was frozen in place for the moment. "I . . ."

Vaughn had heard enough but could also hear Stephanie's plea ringing in his ears, 'Vaughn don't let that happen to her, *Please don't let that happen.'*

He focused on Glen. "I think a decent man would allow a lady to decide what she wants to do. Why don't you take your hand off her arm and stop pulling on her until she makes up her mind."

Tracy was scared, not only for herself but for Vaughn. She realized she really didn't want him to get hurt, especially over her. Glen was quite a bit larger than Vaughn. "I don't want any trouble, Vaughn!"

Tracy began to ease toward Glen and away from Vaughn, so Vaughn responded to that by asking her pointedly, "How do you feel, right now?"

"I . . . I . . ."

As she stammered, Vaughn noticed a tear in the corner of her eye so he turned and leveled his dark eyes into Glen's ugly gray eyes, commanding him, "Take your hand away, NOW!"

Glen was strikingly similar in features and size to Gary, except more muscular, with less fat, and his hair was curly black. Vaughn already knew where his blow would land and felt strength pour into him from all sides. It didn't matter that this boy was a giant compared to him, because he could see him going down. Glen forcefully threw Tracy on the ground like a piece of scrap and squared his shoulders.

Tracy screamed in panic as she crumpled to the right of Vaughn.

Vaughn spoke with deadly calm. "So, this is how a man treats a woman? Throws her down like that?"

Glen swung his fist out toward Vaughn's head but Vaughn ducked and spun under it, away from Tracy. Glen followed him.

"Your thoughts are *so* elevated." Vaughn taunted him, wanting anger to cloud his enemy's mind.

Tracy fearfully cried from the ground. "*Please* Vaughn, don't . . ."

"No, I've decided you're mine. I don't want this *oaf* to have you."

That sent Glen over the edge so he ran straight at Vaughn with both arms extended outward as Tracy screamed. Vaughn reacted instantly, just as he had imagined and practiced over and over in his bedroom, on the farms, and out in the woods. He had followed each old book in the series with loving care for the last two years. *The Art of Fighting for Beginners, For Novices, For Average Fighters, For Good Fighters, For Very Good Fighters.* He had just completed *The Art of Fighting For Advanced Fighters.* There was only one left in the series, *Advanced Future*, that he had just bought yesterday.

Glen barreled down upon him. "*You little . . .*"

In one fluid motion with lightning speed, Vaughn spun backwards, his head dropped way down, and his foot snapped up from behind him, catching Glen square under the chin. It was less of a roundhouse and more of an upward thrust because Vaughn wanted most of the force snapping his head back instead of to the side. Indeed, his head snapped violently back, but his feet kept going forward as he fell hard onto his back.

"ARGGRr." was the last sort of word Glen uttered.

Tracy's eyes popped, watching Glen fall onto his back, motionless. She leapt up and ran to Vaughn, grabbing his arm, jumping up and down. Her scream had quickly changed to celebration.

"Vaughn, you . . . you knocked him out!" She had a fit of laughter as she ran over to Glen. "You big *oaf*."

He watched her as she attacked Glen and he wanted to laugh but his books expressly forbid such displays, or even the attitude. It degraded the fighting ability of the righteous. The blessing was to be appreciated, not flaunted.

Vaughn spoke dispassionately. "Tracy, he's unconscious. He can't feel you kicking him."

"Yeah, well, he'll feel it when he wakes up." She kicked him repeatedly in his side and head until Vaughn reluctantly pulled her away. "You're really strong, Vaughn. OK, I'm *yours*. Oh, this is so *good!*" She threw herself around him and began to kiss him, and Vaughn lingered with it for a moment. He didn't want to cut off her gratitude. Then, almost reluctantly, he eased her back an inch and looked lovingly into her eyes.

"Now, since you're mine, that is, if you want to be mine."

"*I do!*"

"Then to please me, you have to do what I told you to do."

Eagerness erupted from her lips. "OK, *anything*," she panted.

"What I told you to do," he calmly said as he held her gaze in his.

She began to sense he wasn't talking about the same thing she was thinking about. "What *now?*" Doubt and a bit of irritation inflected her question.

"When you can explain to me what it truly means to be a whole person, then we'll see what this sex thing is all about." He gently reached around her and patted her on the bottom. She squinted in passion and scrunched up her nose at the same time because she realized he'd outsmarted her.

"Hmm, Vaughn, I think you're trying to trick me somehow."

He flashed a broad, friendly smile. "Oh you do, do you?"

She poked him sharply in his side with her finger and made him flinch, "Don't try to con me with your sweet, sexy smile."

"OK, then, look into my eyes and tell me what you see?" She looked. He had her, and he knew it. "I see . . . truth?"

He kissed her on the cheek, squeezed her arms and walked away thinking, *Gee, she really is . . . HOT, sigh!*

Several days later, a girl in long, curly blond hair, tight halter-top and a low cut, short skirt sidled up to Vaughn's side after school. He was on his way to the woods to meditate.

Her extended greeting was meant to allure. "Hi, Vaughn." Her deep blue eyes caged him on contact. "Can we talk about being a person?" She ran her forefinger across his cheek and under his chin as her soft breast grazed his arm.

Thoughts instantly assaulted him, *Oh good grief, what a look and smile . . . Hot!* "Arianne, what are you talking about?"

She smiled seductively as she rubbed her hand on his muscular chest. "Well, I heard how you're trying to make persons out of all of us, and how *hot* you are when you do it."

The Art of Fighting ninth rule: A quick retreat often saves a miserable defeat. "BYE, Arianne, I'm *busy* right now." He tried to turn away, but she grabbed his arm and held him fast to her breast. He couldn't resist looking into her burning blue eyes.

"Busy thinking when you could be *living*?" Staring at him as she let him go, she rubbed her tight, bare tummy. "Mmmm."

Pulling himself out of her hot-eyed, iron grip, Vaughn followed the rule to the letter and quickly headed home thinking. *So hot . . . what's happening to me? Stephanie, I miss you so.* He thought it so strongly it seemed the whole world should be able to hear.

School settled down. Vaughn was making top grades as usual. *One more year after this and I apply to college out West. I'm getting out of this hellhole.* However, lately he seemed to be misplacing his homework. Several times he found himself redoing it just in time. But this time, distractions kept him from checking his locker early enough. Unfortunately, it was always Mr. Reed's class.

Of all Vaughn's teachers, Reed was the newest, most dedicated, most near sighted, pompous, fair replacement for a donkey's posterior as one could possibly imagine. Frankly, he had no insight into what makes a human being a human being, not that understanding such things was at all on the list of requirements to be a teacher, as it had long since been dropped from the important list.

However, the administration *loved* Mr. Reed and gave him rewards. Not because he was a good teacher, but because he had the best behaved class. Any time inspectors came in, every student's hands were in the proper place, their feet flat on the floor, and they appeared to be studying. The fact that he ran surprise drills to practice it with severe consequences if anyone was found in noncompliance went unnoticed. Once again, he loomed over Vaughn's desk in pre-emptive strike mode, applying his rulebook to the letter.

"Mr. Vaughn, and why don't you have your work today?"

"Sir, it was in my locker. But, now it's gone . . . again!" Leaning into Vaughn's face, his voice gathered intensity.

"You must be responsible. Do this again and *you* will be gone. Do you understand?"

Vaughn hung his head down, "Yes, sir." Though he wasn't told what to do, it was understood what he now had to do. The school rulebook explained it all.

"*Look at me when you address me, young man.*"

"Yes, Sir."

The harsh penalty for missing an assignment effectively deterred misbehavior. Reed's glee at using Vaughn for an example only strengthened everyone's desire to comply with the rules. No student wanted to give him the satisfaction. He would have four times his normal work tonight.

That afternoon he didn't go to the woods to meditate like he normally did after school, he just didn't feel like it. Instead, going straight home to do school work seemed more important. However, as he opened the front door and one foot entered the house his mother's shrill voice greeted him.

"*Vaughn, why did you attack that boy?* The keepers came to the house, and his parents are *very* upset. He was in the hospital for *two weeks*. I don't know what's gotten into you. Ever since you met that trollop, *Stephananie* . . ."

"Stephanie, Mom."

"*I don't care what her name was,* Thank God she's *gone*! But whatever she did to you, it's got to stop. Glen is well enough to go to court now, and we're to appear in court tomorrow. The first thing you're going to do is *apologize* to Glen, or the keepers will put you in a work farm without even a hearing. You know they don't tolerate mischief out of boys, and they don't care what happens to the bad ones. Even if you have a hearing, they may *still* send you away." She shifted her eyes around nervously, "Vaughn, I hear Glen has . . . connections."

Vaughn brought his other foot into the house. He didn't like the sound of the word 'connections'. He probed her to see if she knew their nature, "What do you mean?"

"He has relatives or something in the government or in the keepers. We can't risk our family being watched by them . . . They're thieves. *They'll want our money,* and all because of *you!*"

Vaughn winced as the full force of his Mother's fear and anger tore through him, "I'll do what I can, Mother." He went to his room to finish all his schoolwork.

Tightness began to work its way inward, and he remembered the feelings he had purged some two years back. By the time he finished all his schoolwork, it was dark.

Vaughn sighed and walked out into the cool night. The full fall weather carried special scents of both fruit and decay. The coolness of the air brought a longing to hold Stephanie close. He remembered the scent of her hair and skin from the last night they had spent together. He needed to meditate, to pray. He needed to talk with Stephanie.

"*Through our prayers*", he whispered to himself as tears came into his eyes. A sense of failure was creeping closer and closer to him, but what really scared him was failing Stephanie.

CHAPTER 14
Sacrifice

All of their children gathered together at the throne. All were weeping, including the Queen. Yanach, the oldest at thirty-five, couldn't help his angry tone towards his father. "I told you this would happen. Where are your wise sayings now, Father?"

Queen Yinauqua lifted her head in disbelief, in dread. Seeing her expression, Yanach instantly froze.

The King, his father, leveled his eyes into his eldest son. "I love each and every one of you as if you were my only child." Yanach hung his head and after a long pause, the King swallowed hard and continued. "Yana is gone from us and the man also is gone from his people. All of us are in the most painful place that ever exists, the unknown."

"Father, forgive me."

"Thank you, my dear son, for making my heart known to me again."

The courthouse was attached to the same building as the Keeper's station, which made for efficient administration of justice. It had the same large, crumbling, light-gray stones. The only distinction between the two buildings was that one had a worn carving above the main entrance saying 'YOUR KEEPERS', while the other had 'YOUR JUDGES'.

The buildings were built seam to seam with the same number of continuous crumbling steps. In one day, it was possible to be arrested, judged, sentenced to death, executed in the basement, and cremated in the back, that is, if the crime warranted the punishment, of course. Perhaps this sounds harsher than it really is, but not to fear, the country had long ago passed a law that it would not enforce personal morality, only national legality.

Inside the courthouse, the same continuous black halls as the Keeper's station held black, windowless doors, behind which no one dared ask the purpose. Vaughn entered one such door into a barren courtroom. There was nothing but a high wooden judge's bench joined at both ends to the far black wall. Crossing the empty black floor, watching the judge's bench grow larger, and standing before it, made anyone else small and inconsequential. A black-robed, white-haired judge's head and shoulders jutted from above the dark mahogany as if his body grew straight out of the bench top. Vaughn couldn't see any way possible for the man to have assumed his perch. It was as if he had always been there. His white head seemed to float in the blackness of the walls and bench.

Glen's parents had flown in all the way from the west coast and were red-faced. Their mouths sprayed with their tirade. His mother spoke first. "This, *this* Vaughn brutally attacked my dear son when he was out for a peaceful walk in the woods."

The father filled in the details. "That bastard, that *freak* knew where my son walked after school and hid in the tall grass and snuck up behind him and hit him in the head with a board. We sent him here to make friends. That *boy* made fun of our son in school from the first day he arrived. It's because he's a *freak*. Ask anyone. I've investigated him myself since the incident. He killed a bunch of boys before we got here . . ."

The judge slammed his gavel down. There was instant silence. But breaking him off in mid-sentence was like trying to dam up a stream after a heavy rain. Glen's father lurched forward when the gavel rang out as if the force of his suddenly dammed up words propelled him. He turned purple with the effort of withholding the torrent. It was clear from his black suit that he was someone *important,* and he wasn't used to being cut off. Both parents put a comforting hand upon their son's shoulders. The judge groaned secretly to himself.

Everyone's own kid is always an angel and everyone else's is a devil. Yeah, yeah, heard it all before and before and . . .

Glen stood stiffly with his neck in a brace, his face black and blue from where Tracy had kicked him. The very sight of this very large, young man forced Vaughn to hold back his snicker just as he had when Tracy punished him. Vaughn put himself into the only safe place he knew. Meditation.

The judge bore down on Vaughn with a raspy, sharp voice, shaking the written account Vaughn had given him. "And you *admit* hitting this man first? Do you know what that means?

What is going to happen to you?" The judge's forehead drew together, lowering his heavy gray eyebrows on Vaughn. They were so thick he couldn't see the judge's eyes.

Glen chided Vaughn. "I told you, you would get what's coming to you."

Vaughn stood up straight, ignoring Glen as if he didn't exist. Whatever happened, he decided to go to his grave being true. He spoke clearly and proudly. "Yes, your honor, I admit I hit him first," and then he suddenly switched direction, "because the *fool* missed me."

The word *'fool'* instantly dug into Glen, even more than being ignored. He knew this was already a done deal. Glen instantly took the bait. "You little runt, you're lucky I did, or . . ."

The judge slammed his gavel even sharper, jolting everyone in the room. His eyebrows now lowered upon Glen. "What's this? So you swung at *him* first?" Then the eyebrows raised all the way up to obscure his forehead. His wide-open, blue eyes looked almost fearful.

Glen stammered. "Huh? Ahh, only ahh, after he . . . he swung at me."

Vaughn didn't allow for any more time to think. When gaining a slight advantage over a superior force, quickness is your best ally. Rule Ten. "I did because he was trying to pull a girl away against her will."

The judge turned red, and his eyes somehow got wider. He almost looked like a trapped animal, except that he also had a presence that Vaughn liked for some reason. "And can you produce this girl?" The judge inquired, as if holding his breath.

Vaughn quickly smiled with confidence as he pointed. "Oh yes, she's right outside."

The austere judge's head leaned so far forward toward Glen that Vaughn wondered if he would float off the bench and hover over their heads. "Young man, do you realize that if this girl confirms his story, it will not be Vaughn that goes to the work farm, but *you!*" One eyebrow was up and the other down, driving the question into Glen like a lance into an enemy's heart.

Glen babbled incoherently as he tried to answer but the judge quickly cut off his stammering with a question. Vaughn wondered if he had read the same fighting books. "Do you have something to *say*? Would you like to withdraw the charges?"

"Yes, your honor," his father answered. Glen couldn't hang his head down because of the neck brace. He was forced to hold his head up in shame, as if suddenly caught naked in a crowd. If he lowered his eyes his shame was obvious. But he couldn't look anyone in the eyes either. His parents felt the overpowering humiliation. They would be the laughing stock of the town. Never had three sets of eyes looked upon a solitary soul with such malevolence.

The gavel rang so loud it popped everyone's ears. "Case dismissed."

Everyone shuffled away to make room for the next case. Vaughn sighed in relief. His parents were dumbfounded. They were ready to admit the shame of their son and give him up.

Outside the courtroom door, Tracy got up from the stone bench and grabbed Vaughn's arm, her heart in her throat,

"Vaughn, what happened? I hope you're all right. I'm sorry, but I just couldn't go before the judge and tell him *anything*. You can't protect me all day."

Glen's family heard it as they came out the door behind Vaughn and they all stopped still and glared.

Vaughn acted as if they never existed and took Tracy by the arm. "It's OK, Tracy. It all worked out fine, anyway. The case was dropped, and I didn't need your help." Vaughn's parents looked even more dumbfounded. Their mouths dropped open.

Tracy scowled at them as she grabbed Vaughn's arm and pulled him further down the hall away from his embarrassing parents. "Oh, thank God." She paused to look deeply into Vaughn's eyes. She wanted him more than ever. Maybe she loved him. "I've been thinking *really hard* on your question, but, well, I haven't made much progress, I'm afraid. Can't we just make love anyway?"

Vaughn turned red. Under such current circumstances Vaughn was sure the mere thought of it could be heard to the ends of the world. "*Tracy,* people will hear you." The halls had an echo.

"I whispered." She defended herself urgently.

"Then that was a pretty loud *whisper! No*, Tracy, I gave my word how it had to be. Would you want to be my friend if I was a liar and didn't keep my word?"

She began to think again, "No, I guess not, but . . ."

He kissed her cheek to cut her off and spoke tenderly, "Then there can be no buts about this. Got to go, Tracy, see you later. Thanks so much for coming and helping me out."

Pressure built in Vaughn as thoughts pushed upon him. *Hot, hot, hot . . . maybe . . . yeah . . . I could help her even more that way. I* am *beginning to like her and she me. Then what would I do afterward? Like is not love. How would I feel? I would lose my heart, my strength. I would be heading back to self-destruction, contradiction. I can't live like that.* Vaughn's long sigh carried with it the pent up frustration from all his previous sighs. He noted to himself how his desire tried to bend his reasoning. *Amazing, how devious this stuff gets.*

Vaughn's parents left him at the courthouse when they saw Tracy pull him aside, so he headed off down the street to walk home, get lunch, and return to school. As he strode home, he thanked God for delivering him from his enemy, yet again. He was beginning to laugh at the futility of evil trying to trap him.

"Thank you, Life, for giving me the courage, wisdom and understanding to face my enemy. I was helpless, caught in their trap. I didn't know what words to speak. I opened my mouth and You were there. You have given me an ear so that I can play well. Now, I *remember* the tune."

Days later, Glen sat next to Vaughn in advanced biology class. Every time they met, Glen counted down the days to when Gary would return. His recovery was said to be taking longer than expected. Vaughn didn't believe it, but hadn't a clue as to what was happening.

Glen wasn't like Gary in some important ways. He was smarter and wasn't afraid of Vaughn, even though Vaughn had knocked him out. And, he had more control over his feelings. Vaughn knew he wouldn't be able to bate him again like he did in the fight or the courthouse. Glen was simply dangerous in a way Gary never thought to be. What made things worse was that Glen knew Vaughn knew it and did very subtle things to reinforce it, a special form of communication that had developed just between them.

Vaughn figured they were behind his missing homework, but couldn't figure out how. It wouldn't do any good to accuse them. They would simply accuse him of something and they'd all end up together in some punishment. Besides, Vaughn loathed the idea of accusing people of anything unless he was absolutely sure they were guilty. Vaughn knew Gary was guilty of grievous offenses and had no problem now with killing him outright. Stephanie's terrible fear of him took away his last squeamishness. He would have to kill him if he started in on Tracy. But this made it easy for them to set Vaughn up as they could predict what he would do. Gary alone wouldn't be so thoughtful, but Glen complicated matters.

Vaughn was sure Glen was worse so killing Gary wouldn't solve the problem. But Vaughn couldn't justify killing Glen who simply hadn't done anything to warrant death. At least not that Vaughn knew about, but the Spirit of Life Vaughn had come to know so well revolted every time he brought Glen up to it in meditation. But that still didn't allow Vaughn to feel justified in killing Glen, too.

Now that Vaughn was alone and didn't have to worry about protecting Stephanie, he decided to just let everything drop wherever it would fall. There just didn't seem to be very much purpose in his life any more. He wasn't paying any attention at all in biology class when suddenly the hairs all over his body stood up. A second later, a terrible scream curdled everyone's' blood. Vaughn jumped out of his seat and whirled around. The rest of the students were fleeing from the middle of the classroom.

On the floor, Tracy writhed in agony. Her body seemed to be quivering, twisting. She growled then her real voice wailed. "Oh God, help me!" Her arms began to lengthen as claws began to appear on them. Helpless, she felt herself disappearing inside. A strange grayness began to cover her.

The panicked students fled out the door with the teacher close behind. Glen stood his ground behind Vaughn, who knew this but didn't care, because Vaughn's eyes had gone deep black. Glen would die on the spot if he tried to touch Vaughn. Instead, Glen came up beside Vaughn and studied him.

Vaughn knew he had to try and help Tracy. He was the only one who knew what was happening. He had to get to her while she still possessed a part of herself so he moved forward, throwing desks out of the way. Glen moved forward with him, helping to clear a path. Vaughn put out his arm to stop him, looked into Glen's eyes and shook his head. Glen saw the deep blackness and somehow understood. "Leave Glen," Vaughn told him in a husky voice.

Glen eased away from Vaughn. He stared at him then over to the transforming Tracy. Back and forth, Glen's wide eyes traveled as he slowly eased out of the room.

Alone, Vaughn knew what he had to do. But then he heard the same voice that spoke to him from the cloud. It boomed in his head, making him dizzy. "SACRIFICE!" *Sacrifice. Oh God . . .* Vaughn knew what he had to do. He had meditated a long time on this very possibility. He looked up and spoke out loud. *"I'll gladly sacrifice myself."* He waited a bit to let it sink in. *"But not in the way* you *want me to!"* Vaughn turned towards Tracy. "OK *demon,* You want me? Come on, let's *fight!"* Rule twenty of *The Art of Fighting*, 'If the cause is just, better to sacrifice oneself in battle than in surrender'.

Ignoring the growling, Vaughn jumped onto the writhing, transforming Tracy, hugging her tightly, trying to feel everything about her as she bucked. He searched for her person, but feeling the demon's angry presence, he focused his mind and heart into one to try to bring love into her consciousness. *I have to feel it, so I can send her that feeling, that spirit.*

He knew love was the answer. His diving onto Tracy made him remember how Stephanie had tackled him to save him from this very thing. Still feeling her fiery love, still awed by it, *I love you Stephanie,* he thought with all his being. And he felt that love touch the greater Love. Surrendering to that, he focused that overflowing feeling straight into Tracy, heart to heart. And then the evil left her and entered him.

Vaughn roared as he was tossed across the floor, rolling over and over. Tracy sobbed as she weakly turned over to watch. She knew what he had done. She felt his love touch her. *I understand! Oh God, I understand!*

Vaughn's arms flailed. Every time they did, a desk went flying. Some of them shattered against the wall. He was losing, and felt his body struggling to keep from transforming. He needed to change the direction of the battle or all was lost. Love worked in banishing it from Tracy, but he couldn't find that same love for himself.

He remembered his vision of the little girl. "Help me. Help me," she cried as the blackness came to take the innocent child. *She doesn't deserve this.* Vaughn heard himself think as he began to weep. *I have to save her.* Anger erupted all through him. *"SHE DOESN'T DESERVE THIS,"* he roared.

Anger covered him in the deepest blackness. *Better to die fighting being what you are than lose the battle from within,* Rule one, *The Art of Fighting. I know what I am! I KNOW!* He shouted in his heart. He shouted in his mind. His voice thundered through the halls. "I WON'T BE YOU!" It howled. He howled. The fleeing students running down the halls could hear it.

The evil threw him against the wall trying to knock him out so it could take him while unconscious but Vaughn focused all his anger at the evil blackness inside him and crashing into the wall had no effect! "SHE DOESN'T DESERVE THIS. *DIE!*," he shouted.

Vaughn was thrown across the room into the other wall. The evil left while he was still in mid-flight and Vaughn slid down the wall and landed limply, barely conscious.

Tracy crawled all the way over to him and wept upon him. "Vaughn! Oh Vaughn, don't die. *Please* don't die."

Tracy's tears seemed to give him strength. He smiled then weakly put his arm around her. "It'll take more than that to kill me! I'm hard to kill."

I have to figure out how to destroy this evil. Oh God, Stephanie. We need to be together. He stared deeply at Tracy. *No, she's not the girl from my vision either.*

School was closed the next day as a government official was flown in to question everyone. It was Glen's father. He never questioned Vaughn. When school resumed, no one spoke anything about what happened. Everyone acted as if *nothing* happened. Silence always followed government visits. Glen told his father they might be able to use Vaughn, that somehow he had some power against this evil. But his father told him Jargon was far more powerful, and it had already been determined what was to happen to Vaughn by someone even higher up in the government than he was. Strangely, Glen felt sad for him. When he saw how Vaughn pushed him back, away from the evil to protect him, he felt a strange bond with him. Perhaps it was the old saying about common enemies. He felt that they should be fighting this evil together. After it was beaten, that was a different story.

The rest of the week finished as usual. Vaughn still had to redo his homework several times. He couldn't believe these things still kept happening. What's more, they didn't make sense. Glen seemed almost sad when he saw him. His comments and hints had ceased. He detected no hostility from him at all. Then who was behind his homework disappearing? *Gary could be doing it. Maybe, but I doubt he would be divided from his cousin.* Vaughn kept spinning it around all the way home.

When he opened the front door and had one foot in his house, his father's angry voiced crushed him. "*Vaughn*, we got a call from the principal. Some students claim you broke into a teacher's desk and *stole* the answers to a test. They found them in your locker. Your teacher said you haven't been doing your homework!" His angry tone squeezed Vaughn like a tightening vice.

Tears welled up on Vaughn's face as he had a strange feeling of breaking inside. The sense of impending failure was no longer impending. It had fallen upon him and somehow he knew he wouldn't escape it, not this time. He stretched out his palms from his sides pleading, his right foot still holding the door open. "*Dad*, you see me doing my work every night!" Fear swarmed around him like hornets around a disturbed nest. Vaughn was trying desperately not to get stung when his father cut him off.

"I don't know what you were writing. Probably love letters to that girl you lost your mind to or that nasty little slut at the courthouse. But this is serious. We all have a meeting with the principal tomorrow. It doesn't look good."

"But . . ."

"THERE are no BUTS to this." His father's screaming tipped the balance.

Vaughn lost control and bawled. "But Dad, you know me. I'm not that kind of person."

"I know you? I don't know you. All I know is you've brought shame to our whole house. First you act crazy and make us laughing stocks with all those noises and faces you make and banging your head!"

Still bawling, Vaughn pleaded. "Dad, I don't do those things any more, not for years, *please!*"

"You *still* bang your head. You're CRAZY!" He screamed back, shocking his son.

Vaughn shook his head at himself, ashamed at his weakness. *I can't act like this. I can't be* this. *This is not life.* He calmed himself, picked his head up straight. "*Dad*, it's a form of thinking deeply. I tune out the world that way to think, to meditate. It doesn't hurt. I bump softly until all is . . ."

His dad looked even more ashamed to hear his gibberish. "I don't know where you get your craziness from. Your mother and I have decided you're a great risk to us. She is finally pregnant again and we can't risk our new child's future."

"Dad, I'm your child, too! Mom's pregnant?"

"Don't you worry. I don't think you'll be here to see it."

"But . . ."

"There are no *buts*."

Vaughn withdrew his foot from the doorway and ran out into the woods. At a private place far from people, he fell on the soft forest floor, scooped the decaying leaf litter up under his stomach for support, folded his hands under his forehead, then thumped his head gently. "Oh God, help me. I don't understand what's happening to me. Why is everything going wrong?" *What have I done?*

Vaughn thought deeply, prayed earnestly. "I've truly kept all You have shown me so far, except for just back then when I got afraid. I know I have kept Your ways. What am I going to do? If they put me in a work farm, how will I become an animal doctor? How will I come to take care of Stephanie? How will I survive in a place like that? What am I going to do?"

Vaughn fell asleep in the cool forest. His dreams were of blackness until he woke at evening time. Sneaking in the back door, he went inside his room.

The next day, Vaughn listened as the whole case was laid out in the principal's office. His desk was cluttered with papers haphazardly stacked in falling, blending piles. The windows were badly in need of washing. The sun shining on them only accentuated their filth. But the walls were immaculately shiny white, and the floor immaculately shiny black. His dark, long mustache was waxed at the corners and his black bowtie upon his white shirt fit his personality. He was pure administrator.

There were no witnesses! The principal had the evidence in his hand. It was found in his locker and no one had access. There was no opportunity for Vaughn to speak a wise word or even ask a question. The fact that he was a top student and didn't need to cheat didn't matter. The rules were clear. An example had to be made. They needed an example because there hadn't been one in a very long time. Vaughn couldn't figure out how anyone got into his locker. Only the administration had the combination. The principal ignored Vaughn and spoke sympathetically to his parents.

"I'm sorry Sir, but Vaughn must be expelled."

His father answered quickly. Had *he* been reading Vaughn's books? "That's fine by us. My wife is expecting another child. We have devoted our whole lives truly to *this* child, but all he has brought us is shame."

"Then he will be taken from here and sent to the work farm at Grinova." The principal definitely seemed to be hiding a smile. "At the work farm, he'll have plenty of time to think about being a *person.*"

Vaughn felt the principal's snide remark had some extra meaning but wondered, *What it could be?*

His mother winced. "Uhh, Alex. That's the really bad . . ."

His father looked at her and raised his brow in question, but he spoke a flat statement. "We can send him to a private school."

"*We* don't have that kind of money, Alex. Vaughn, you did this to us. Do you *see* what you have done to us?"

It all reeked of staged formality. Vaughn, past listening, got lost in thought, trying to hold on to whatever it was he had left. *No. I* won't. No, *I won't screech or do any of those things. Please!* Please, *Oh GOD HELP ME, I can't bear it! But if I give in to this emptiness, I'll be choosing death. That's even* worse *than all I'm suffering now. I* was born to live. *I will* not *let pain and destruction define what I am. The only treasure I have is the one* inside of me. Life *has proven it's meaning to me.*

In my imaginations, I asked myself, what if this, what if that, all kind of things to test whether I really loved Life. *What if I was told I had to lie or my life would be in danger? If I lied, I would be dead already because* Truth *is* Life *and* Life *is* Truth.

Sex without true love. Then I'm dead already and it's worse suffering than mere terribly lusting. What if I was offered power, only I had to hurt someone to get it? Then that's not real power because Life, Goodness, *is the only real power. Being able to threaten, to destroy, is not the true power, because after all is destroyed there's no power in that to build . . . and if Life really didn't want something destroyed it would just give strength against the destroyer . . . but what about now?*

What's happening to me? Maybe this is just what I have to face. No matter how terrible it is, I have to be true to Life. *OH GOD, Help me! All my dreams, my hopes have been destroyed!*

He could hear his father shouting at him as if from a distance. "Vaughn, can you hear me? Your mother and I are leaving. We'll try to visit you in a few months."

Alex tried to console his wife. "Stop crying. *Stop crying.* You know that boy will never measure up."

The parents turned their backs without any acknowledgement from Vaughn.

Vaughn's focus was somewhere deep within. *Faith, it's not real if it's not kept, no matter what,* no matter what. *If Life isn't important above all things, I have never been true. I said I wanted truth, but I lied.* No, *Truth is all I have left."*

Their rippling and shimmering seemed to crescendo.

Never before had Scraback witnessed so many beautiful shades of gray upon himself or anyone else. To see Vaughn's tree actually wilt before his very Eye astonished him. It was exactly as his Master told him. Still, he couldn't get over the feeling that this was somehow only a small part of his Master's plan. But his Master's plan was beginning to take shape with innumerable possibilities. The key for Scraback was to be adaptable and to be able to take quick advantage of any opportunity. He had to admit though, that the ruthlessness his Master added was perfect.

His Master spoke as they continued to monitor Vaughn through the dirty blue orb. "You see Scraback, what did I tell you? I thought for a moment he would completely lose it right there. I could have just touched him a little, and he *would have* lost it. But it's so much fun to watch them do it to themselves without our encouragement. But now it's time to help him do it to himself because he thinks he has nothing left. We'll show him otherwise. Remember this lesson: *There is always a lower low.*"

It was an hour ride south into the country to Grinova State Work Farm. Vaughn was the only passenger in the black police car. A large, black, metal electronic gate squealed open to allow the car to enter. The officer pulled to his destination, opened the door and stepped out. He let Vaughn out and then got back in his patrol car and was gone. Vaughn was left standing alone at the foot of the steps. He was dropped off in front of a building that resembled the Keeper's Station and

Court House, except it said Grinova State Work Farm above the door. He hadn't eaten in a whole day, but he didn't care. He sat down on the concrete steps.

About an hour later an elder came down the steps, tapped him on the shoulder and motioned him to follow.

In a fog, Vaughn walked around to the other side of the station and down a gravel path to a long, low, gray metallic barracks building. There were no trees in sight. He was given a key to a locker number nine, and told to do what the others did. That was it.

He walked into the barracks through the middle door in the middle of the long building as the sun was beginning to set on the other side of it. Hungry, tired, and drained, he hoped it was dinnertime.

Row upon row of beds lined the far wall. Opposite them, rows of lockers butted right up to the door Vaughn had entered. *They must eat in a different building.* There were no officers in sight. Vaughn began to notice that there were many more grown men sitting on the beds than schoolchildren. He realized that to run such a massive facility, unless they had a certain number of occupants, they would have to shut it down. A farm is labor intensive. He had seen from the car as he was driving through the farm that it was quite large. Even with modern machinery, they would still need many people. The sinking feeling hit him that he would never leave this place, that for the rest of his life he would be a slave *here.*

Then one of the young men called out to him. He was muscular, looked about twenty-three, and had a long scar on his left arm. He was a whole head taller than Vaughn, but Vaughn knew his confidence to be misplaced.

"Hey, pretty boy, *yum*, c'mere!"

The tone of his voice turned Vaughn's stomach as another realization hit him. *For the rest of our lives, we'll never be with a woman.* Images of Stephanie and all the women that had chased after Vaughn flashed in his feelings. There was a moment of regret for not having sex, but then a stronger guilt against the thought.

Well, there was no need for pretense. It was obvious what needed to be done. Vaughn smiled at him, strolled up close, and put a left uppercut under his chin.

Because Vaughn was so much smaller and younger, the man never expected it, nor did anyone else expect to see the man fall backwards and not get up.

Vaughn turned to the rest of the people. "Which bunk is his?" He pointed at the unconscious man. Others pointed. Vaughn declared, "Not anymore." He tore off the bedding and threw the blanket and sheet on top of the man who was beginning to stir. Then he took the two drawers underneath that bunk and dumped them on top of him. Someone threw him some clean sheets. Vaughn paid it no mind.

Days faded into weeks, and weeks faded until Vaughn lost track of time. He no longer cared. He loved farm work, but this type of farm was highly mechanized, had long, boring fields of the same crops, and long, boring barns crowded too tightly with a particular livestock: one barn for cows, one for pigs, and one for chickens. It wasn't the type of beautiful farming he had done on the small farms back home. Worse, the newcomer got the worst jobs and these animals' manure stank particularly badly because of the chemicals and type of feed they were fed. Naturally fed animal manure wasn't that bad at all, but Vaughn was sure he had acquired a permanent stench in his body from shoveling this stuff.

Everyday seemed to empty him out a little more, a little more. He found out no one could remember the last time anyone was dismissed from this farm. The older men who ran the place now, were actually kids who had been sent here. People who escaped were hunted down and shot. *Still, that might be better for me than continuing on like this.* Except for one nagging, little thought, *Rule Two, The Art of Fighting: With time, there are always possibilities. Never throw it away. Never rush to battle when time is open. Is my time open?*

A young man came up to Vaughn and smiled. He looked familiar, but Vaughn couldn't place him. "I wasn't sure until I heard you knocked one of these guys out, but you must be Vaughn. I'm Ralph. We go . . . went to the same school."

Ralph studied Vaughn, then continued. "You're the guy who knocked Gary out. Because of *you*, I was able to make good business." He slapped Vaughn on the shoulder. Vaughn shook his head, not understanding. "You made him look so bad, a little strange pip squeak knocking him out like that. Don't get me wrong. I know you're not. After that, I was able to convince people to join my business and buy from me."

"Business," Vaughn stated flatly.

"Yes, and one not sanctioned by the *government.* Did you know that in the old country, people had *their own* businesses without government approval?"

"Really, I didn't know that. What kind of business? How were you able to get supplies without government approval?"

"What business?" Ralph laughed. "Connections. Money talks, talks loud enough to get people to break the rules. And I got the materials cheaper than the government ends up paying for them because I cut out all the middlemen. Then I mixed the stuff myself. It's not hard. My Angel Seed was ten times better than Gary's ever was."

"Drugs!" *I know what that stuff does. Stephanie told me how badly it messed her and others up. I could kill him right now. It would be easy, and wouldn't make any difference at all to my fate here. These lowlifes don't deserve to live.* "I understand now why you didn't have government approval!"

Ralph looked at him, surprised. "You really are naive, aren't you? Gary *has* government approval! It's just done secretly. They figured since kids were going to do the stuff anyway, why shouldn't the government get the profits instead of some criminals. But just like them, I figured why shouldn't I get the profits instead of the government."

Vaughn stared at him, but only blankly. *How could I be so blind? How else is all that crap able to prosper if the government didn't support it somehow? Killing him is inconsequential. Getting rid of the government would be a good place to start.* "I see that judging by the fact you're in here, while Gary's out . . ."

"Yeah, I guess you're not that dumb after all. Hey, you know we're stuck in here for life, you know that. And we're young. It's bad to be young in here. We should team up and watch each other's back."

Vaughn squirmed inside as he mulled, *Team up with this drug pusher who only a second ago I wanted to kill?* "I'll think about it."

Ralph saw Vaughn wasn't going to be as easy a mark as he thought. He needed someone to take his place this weekend, it was his turn. Theoretically, if they kept sending in new boys, he could make the same deal over and over and avoid it altogether. He put his arm around Vaughn. "Hey, I've already got other offers to team up. That's the way it's done here. I've got to give them an answer soon."

"Soon is not now. I don't like repeating myself and if you want to keep your arm attached to your body, remove it!" Vaughn didn't know his game, but he knew Ralph sickened him. Honor precluded him from teaming up with such a scoundrel. *But what does wisdom say? I'll think about it.*

The glow of the golden vision accentuated the folds of concern she tried to mask from her husband. Taking his hand gently, so as not to overly invade his concentration into the glowing golden orb, she leaned into his ear. "My dearest, is it supposed to be proceeding in this fashion?"

A rare heavenly sigh, almost imperceptible, escaped from his spirit. He knew, of late, that Yinauqua's subtle warnings were coming from something she didn't understand about her prophetic insight. He remembered long ago, when he, too, was faced with insurmountable challenge in a mortal frame ill equipped to handle even a tenth of all he endured. But why did that same feeling now stealth into him? "I like him, Yinauqua, I like him very much. But these things are out of our hands."

There was no subtle way to imply it, so she just came out with it. "The timeline seems all wrong. Weren't they supposed to grow up first and then come together? It's too soon."

He put his hand to his chin, as he sternly twisted his mouth at the golden vision. "That's not supposed to be on Earth."

She looked at the Black Essence possessing yet another body and blowing it up like all the rest. The little nudge in her voice said so much more. "They've broken the rules."

"Perhaps, but the way they did it is a very *gray* area, very clever, indeed. And the Lord hasn't given us anything but to proceed by the spirit we now have. We *can't* interfere." His not so little emphasis told her he knew her thoughts.

But she knew her husband. That rascal! She saw the utter depth of his concentration. "Then you would do well to remember those words for yourself!"

Another heavenly sigh escaped from the King. *I know I can't hide anything from her, I never could.*

She waved her hand. Stephanie came into focus, weeping upon her bed in the dark. "And she? How can she be prepared in such a short time?"

He waved his hand. A young woman with long black hair appeared, kneeling on her knees in the sacred room, before a tree that glowed. "Ask her!"

Yinauqua nodded slowly, while also studying the young lady. Arlupo was a mystery, even to her.

Just then a tall, jovial young man walked in. The tree's glow vanished moments before he entered. "Still praying before that sleeping tree, I see."

Arlupo raised her head but didn't turn around. "Jargono, it's nice to hear your voice again, it's been a long time. Have you come to rejoin us? We've missed you so."

Mafferan's countenance noticeably darkened as his jaw clenched. Yinauqua squeezed his hand tighter as a heavenly tear glistened in the corner of her eye.

* * *

www.TheFaithwalkerSeries.com

www.ingramcontent.com/pod-product-compliance
Lightning Source LLC
Chambersburg PA
CBHW020540120726
47903CB00001B/62
9780981846965